Amanda James has written since  asked her parents for a typewriter imagined her words would ever dream of becoming a writer came true when she had her first short story published.

Originally from Sheffield, Amanda now lives in Cornwall and is inspired every day by the wild and beautiful coastline. She can usually be found playing on the beach with her family, or walking the cliff paths planning her next book.

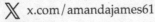 x.com/amandajames61
facebook.com/AmandaJamesAuthorPage

Also by Amanda James

THE GARDEN OF MEMORIES

AMANDA JAMES

One More Chapter
a division of HarperCollins*Publishers* Ltd
1 London Bridge Street
London SE1 9GF
www.harpercollins.co.uk
HarperCollins*Publishers*
Macken House, 39/40 Mayor Street Upper,
Dublin 1, D01 C9W8, Ireland

This paperback edition 2024
1
First published in Great Britain in ebook format
by HarperCollins*Publishers* 2024

A catalogue record of this book is available from the British Library

ISBN: 978-0-00-865778-9

This novel is entirely a work of fiction. The names, characters and incidents portrayed in it are the work of the author's imagination. Any resemblance to actual persons, living or dead, events or localities is entirely coincidental.

Printed and bound in the UK using 100% Renewable Electricity
by CPI Group (UK) Ltd

To the memory of my grandma Tacey. Though she never had a garden of her own, she adored flowers and plants and could tell me all their names.

Prologue

Apparently, forty years should seem longer. Before people speak about the passing of large measures of time, they shake their heads in bewilderment, click their tongue against the roof of their mouth and sigh. Shortly after that, they say things like, 'I can't believe it's been forty years!' Next, some repetition to emphasise their surprise, 'Forty. I mean, who would have thought it?' Well, Rose would. Because when she started nursing, her eyes were bright, her skin was line-free and she had enough energy to power a hospital ward. Now her batteries are flat, and the majority of creases around her eyes aren't made of laughter lines. They've mostly been created by exhaustion and burnout. Forty years of nursing will do that. Forty years of staying on past the end of your shift, caring, mending, lifting, guiding and healing. Forty years of carefully ironed uniforms, precisely tucked hospital corners, sensible shoes and quiet footsteps. A gentle smile, the touch of a hand, and a well-placed word.

The last shift. Forty years of a career that will end today. To Rose, this ending is much harder to believe than the passage of all that time. Since the age of twenty-two, she's known nothing else. Nursing is who she is. It defines her. Rose Lanyon, the nurse. After today, what will she be? Who will she be? The words, 'I used to be a nurse' will find their way into her conversation. She's not sure she's ready for that – a 'used to be'. She tells herself she needn't worry too much, because she'll only have to explain to those who don't know her. Most do know her in this little Cornish community of which she's part. For the past thirty years Rose has been a nurse in the local GP practice. A drawer of blood, a shoulder to cry on, a dresser of wounds. Before that, she walked the wards of The Royal Cornwall Hospital, until she swapped that for walking the bedroom, her baby daughter falling asleep on her shoulder, just as the dawn rose over the ocean.

Rose's uniform is hanging on the wardrobe door, ready. Unlike her. Though her long career has taken its toll, she's no regrets. None. She's loved being a nurse. Though not all of it, because some parts have broken her. Sometimes she lies awake at night, remembering the faces of those who passed before their time. Rose thinks about the kind words offered to her by grieving relatives. Little gifts on parting. *Thank you. You were there for my loved one. We will always remember you...* At the time, she watched them go, never imagining that she would also remember them, in the still quiet of the night. But she does.

The uniform waits. Under her fingers the material is cool, navy, no-nonsense. The uniform represents professionalism, inspires respect, garners trust and confidence. And sometimes she's been grateful for this uniform, this barrier between the personal and professional. Rose would hide behind it to protect herself, especially during the hard times, but much more often, there have been happy times. Joy, even. The maternity ward was full of it, new life spreading light, its echo in the ringing bells of the cancer clinic. The love of the job and the people she met carried her up, over and through – knitting a pattern, a pathway along a working life for her to follow.

Acknowledging all that happiness, Rose finds herself smiling as she slips the uniform free of the hanger. Acknowledging too, that she's grateful for such a long and happy career. It registers like a thump in her gut that this is the last time she'll wear this bit of cotton. This bit of cotton that's so much more. On the dressing table, from a photo taken on their local beach, her husband, Glen, smiles too. His grey curls ruffling in the wind, his eyes, blue chips, squinting in the sun. She has the fleeting impression that he's about to say something. *Probably get your uniform on, go to work and stop all this pondering, Rose.* Glen always said pondering on things too much was no good for you. He might have been right. She takes a breath, slips the uniform on, touches her fingertips to her lips and then to his. 'See you later, you old grump. Love you.'

The wheels of her little car rumble over the uneven surface of the staff car park at the surgery, and she thinks of all the times she's avoided potholes and cursed every bump and jolt. For too long, staff have been assured resurfacing will be done, but it never is. Funds are tight, and other more important issues are always way ahead in the queue. Well, at least this is the last time across the assault course. Rose sighs, pats the steering wheel and leans across to grab her bag from the passenger seat. The last shift waits, but the short distance from the car to the door suddenly appears too far away. A heaviness settles in her chest, and two potted palms at each side of the surgery entrance rattle their fronds in the breeze and go a bit blurry. Rose opens the glove compartment and pulls a single tissue from the packet, then on second thought, she grabs the whole packet and shoves it in her pocket.

In through the nose out through the mouth breathing, and staring straight ahead gets her from the car to the door. The early morning air capturing her breath in little white puffs – temporary exhibits of panic. The reason for the panic is unclear. It's not because of today, she decides. It's the rest of it. What comes after. The rest of her life. Glen would have said she should have a nice cuppa and try to relax, calm the nerves before the first patients arrive. Yes, that's what she'll do. Rose's stomach loses some of its heaviness and she smiles as she steps through the door.

Once inside the waiting room, the silence and dim lighting are unnerving. Very odd. The main light should be on and a few members of staff are normally around by now, especially her lovely friend Sally. Sometimes Rose wonders if she gets in early to avoid being at home. Reading between the lines of Sally's story, Rose has gleaned that her husband is not the nicest man in the world, which is such a shame, as she's such a kind and caring woman. Rose pops her head through the office door. Nope. No Sally on reception either...

'Surprise!' Sally leaps out of the darkness as the lights come on, and the waiting room erupts with a rush of workmates. Multicoloured balloons and banners festoon the walls and a cheer goes up on the count of three.

Gathering her senses and a weak smile, Rose says, 'My goodness. I wasn't expecting this ... and certainly not first thing!'

Sally's moon face looms at her, and she gets a noisy kiss on both cheeks. 'We did it first thing, because some of us will be off to the other practice later, and we didn't want to miss you. And yeah, we know you said you didn't want a fuss. Just wanted to slope off quietly into the sunset like the hero at the end of a western. There's no way we were allowing that, eh gang?' Hands raised, she turns to the assembled doctors and nurses.

'No!' They shout in unison.

Then the senior partner, Dr James Gregson, steps forward with a sparkly bag and a handful of cards. 'Just a little something to show our appreciation for such a wonderful member of staff and friend. There are no words adequate to describe the phenomenal contribution you have made to this practice, the hospital and the wider community over the past forty years, so I won't try. Suffice to say, we all thank you from the bottom of our hearts and quite frankly, dear Rose, we don't know what we'll do without you.'

Rose has known Dr James, as she calls him, for the entire time she's worked here. They are of a similar age, and she's watched his career advance. Seen the young junior doctor that he was, a little shy and unsure, become a gifted, confident and well-respected senior. Now as he looks at her glassy-eyed, she's glad she put the whole pack of tissues in her pocket.

Rose takes the sparkly bag, nods a few times, dabs her eyes with a tissue and allows a stretchy smile to speak for her. Perhaps she can get away with not actually saying anything, because there's a good chance she won't be able to. There's an overwhelming wave of emotion rising up inside, and if she opens her mouth, it will all come flooding out. But they're all looking at her with expectant faces. Sally's wiping her eyes and blowing her nose, then flapping the tissue in the air. Not a great idea in a surgery. A few other colleagues have damp eyes too, and Rose can't bear it. This is why she didn't want a fuss. Didn't want to do a speech.

There are too many memories to mention. To many people to acknowledge, some still here, some gone elsewhere, some no longer on this earth. Happy times, sad times, funny things that have happened. Little things, big things, things that have made all the years of walking through these doors worthwhile. The worry of missing out a person's name, or a time that was special to anyone in this room renders her mute. Rose suspected it would when she pondered on the 'to have a fuss or not' day. What does she do now? The big smile is making her lips ache and one or two people are beginning to look uncomfortable. Perhaps the best thing to do is just say:

'Thank you so much, everyone.' The wave swells in her chest, ready to crash onto the shore, and she has to take in a big breath and blow it out. 'I will miss you all very much.' Her voice sounds wobbly and weak – an assessment of her whole body – and she grabs the back of a waiting-room chair as the cheers go up again.

Sally shoves another chair under Rose's bottom, puts some music on her mobile phone, and Dr James magics a big yellow-and-pink cake with her name on it from somewhere. Everyone gathers round, wishing her luck and asking what she plans to do in the future. A future in which she 'used to be' a nurse. She finds another tissue, a bright smile and a carefree chuckle. Then she shrugs her shoulders and tells them, 'Oh, lots of things. I have *so* much I want to do. No idea where I'll find the time!' Luckily, they seem to believe her.

Chapter One

Rose looks through the kitchen window over the fields towards the thin blue smudge of the ocean. In one corner of the sky, a huddle of dark clouds is rolling towards centre-stage, which is a mixed blessing, as the pot plants could do with a watering. That had been Glen's job, in fact the whole garden tending thing had been his domain. In the two years since he's been gone, she's only done the bare minimum. Mowing the lawn when she remembered and snipping off anything dead. Her gran had taught her that in gardens you always had to make room for the living and new growth ('A bit like us old 'uns shuffling off this mortal coil,' she always added), as well the names of some plants that Rose still remembers. Grandma Ivy had been a good teacher. A shame she hadn't listened more attentively. She makes a mental note to get the garden sorted in the next few days. Sorted, in so far as watering and maybe a strim of the long grass was concerned at least. The rest could wait for proper spring weather.

One of the things Rose promised herself she'd do in the aftermath of not being a nurse, was to have a lie-in and a fry-up. These are two things she rarely has, apart from on 'high days and holidays', as her mum used to say. Rose never really knew what the 'high days' bit meant. Her mum had a plethora of sayings, part of which often made little sense. She'd had the lie-in, now time for the second promise.

The smell of bacon crisping under the grill lifts her spirits, then she notices the sparkly gift bag looking accusingly at her from the kitchen table. She hasn't opened it yet, or the cards. When she got back home a few days ago from the surgery, all she wanted to do was watch TV with a takeaway pizza and have a glass of wine or two. Wanted to push the memory of her last day away, sweep it under the carpet, pretend it hadn't happened. She has to say, over the weekend, she's been pretty successful in this pushing and sweeping. The wine helped, but once again in the middle of the night, more ponderings poked her awake. She does wish her brain would have a rest. It's time it had a high day, possibly a holiday. Leisure time, as they say.

A lady of leisure. Rose puts her plate and cup into the washing-up bowl and looks out of the window at the sky again. That's something else people say, isn't it? They say it tongue in cheek, with maybe a little smirk. They often add a sprinkling of 'ladies wot lunch' to the conversation too, like some hilarious in-joke. It invokes images of women around her age, retired, at a loose end, looking for something to do. It's okay to poke gentle fun at these women, because they're vaguely ridiculous, aren't they? Pushed to the margins of society. They aren't doers. They have outlived their usefulness – become afterthoughts on invitation lists, joined the ranks of 'used to bes'.

Rose reminds herself that some women might never have been 'anything' in the first place, according to some. So 'I used to be' won't even be a consolation prize for those who had been 'stay-at-home mums', or God forbid in her mum's generation, 'only housewives'. Maybe the worst of all fates was to 'end up a spinster'. That's a word you don't hear often nowadays – spinster. It was common when Rose was a child. Her mum, gossiping to a neighbour, would sometimes hide that word behind her hand like an embarrassing secret as she passed it over the garden fence. Sometimes it would be mouthed silently above Rose's head (though she missed nothing) in a café, along with a sly finger-point towards an unsuspecting woman sitting at another table. Rose asked her mum what it meant afterwards, and she said in the kind of hushed tones befitting a funeral parlour, 'An unmarried woman, sometimes living on her own.' Shock horror.

A flash of yellow amongst the green interrupts her thoughts, and she cranes her neck to see beyond the holly bush to the left of the wall. Daffodils! There seem to be many more than she remembers from last year, though she didn't plant more, did she? And especially not there. There were just a few at the front, around the gate. Odd. But oh, aren't they cheerful! Rose smiles at them. Little drops of sunlight to brighten her day. The sight of them galvanises her spirit somehow and lifts her mood no end. So much so that she decides to go for a walk along Port Gaverne beach, despite the iffy weather. It's only five minutes away, and shouldn't be too windy in the sheltered narrow cove nestling under the cliffs. Beach walking is something she hasn't done for … actually, she can't remember the last time. Silly, when you think about it, because she can see the ocean from the kitchen window. Then again, when has there been the time? There's lots of that now, so Rose should make it a mission to get out more in the fresh air. There. That's one thing she's found to do already. Perhaps she needs to think outside the box more.

Critically appraising her appearance in the bathroom mirror after a shower, she finds herself wanting, however. Wanting a new face, hair and body, if she's honest. Preferably a body that's twenty years or so younger, with a face to match. The chin-length blonde curls clinging damply to her cheeks seem to have given way to grey again. Maybe it's time she stopped dyeing her hair. Lots of women of her age surrender to the passing of time and 'embrace the grey'. Blonde hair is for younger women, isn't it? Another phrase of her mum's comes to mind. *Mutton dressed as lamb*. If she does carry on with the blonde, will that be Rose? Mutton?

In the bedroom, she pulls on jeans and a turquoise jumper. Glen always loved her in turquoise, said it matched her eyes. They seem greyer these days too. Maybe all her colours are draining away to leave a fading image in a sepia photograph. Once spring comes, like her garden she'll get more colour. Winter has dragged on so long this year. Meanwhile, she'll make do with a sweep of blusher over her cheeks. *Mutton*. Two defiant pink flashes across the sepia cheekbones add colour to her eyes. Rose puts the blusher brush down and nods at the mirror. Not quite turquoise eyes, but more blue than grey now. Who cares what people think? She won't conform to expectations. She's decided to think outside the box after all.

Rose pulls her still-damp hair into a ponytail. What the hell *is* the box, anyway? Do we put ourselves in them? Do we create them – fashioned by routine and day-to-day life, or are we put in them by society, friends and family? Maybe her box has a label on it – *Rose Lanyon, sixty-two, widow, mum, grandma – 'used to be' a nurse.* If people were interested enough to look inside the box, they might find this extra information – *not very adventurous, no ambitions for the future, mutton dressed as lamb.* This box feels claustrophobic – restrictive. Definitely a box to break out of.

About to put boots and coat on, Rose notices the sparkly bag again and looks away. Why the reluctance to open it? Pondering a moment, she acknowledges it might be that she's scared that all the sweeping and pushing away of the last day of being a nurse, could come undone. All the little threads of emotion that she'd so carefully tied together might be unravelled, leaving her exposed and vulnerable. *Dear God, it's just a bag of presents.* In two strides she's at the table and yanking it open.

There's an envelope, with *whip-round money* scrawled across it in Sally's handwriting. There's a voucher for a cream tea and spa day for two at a swanky local hotel, and lastly, from Dr James, there's a card with a picture of a galloping brown and white horse on it. Inside is a voucher for horse riding lessons. Horse riding lessons? Rose has to read the thing again to make sure she wasn't seeing things.

On the card is written – *About time you went for it, Rose. Must be at least twenty years since you told me you'd always wanted to learn. Lots of love, James. Xx*

Twenty years ago? Did she tell him that? She's no recollection of it, though it's true she always wanted to learn to ride ... just never got round to it. Rose shakes her head. Fancy him remembering. *Horse riding isn't normally a thing to be found in my box, is it?* She laughs to herself as she pulls her boots and coat on. *Perhaps it should be, Rose. Perhaps it should be.*

Chapter Two

Flora Granger looks up from her crossword just as that nurse from three houses up stomps down the hill. Scooting across the window seat to get closer to the living room window, she watches as the nurse stops and zips up her red anorak, her blonde curls whipping round her chin. Funny, she normally gets in her car and drives off of a morning. No uniform, either? Flora wonders where she's going. Maybe she's just having a day off, but on second thought, she's not had a Monday off before, as far as Flora remembers. Flora prides herself on her good memory. At seventy-seven, she'd bet she'd give a much younger person a run for their money in the memory stakes. She's sure this is all down to her teaching background, and the fact that her brain is kept active. Use it, or lose it, as they say nowadays. She uses it in the shape of crosswords, reading, taking a keen interest in current affairs, and in the local community.

Flora watches until the nurse turns the corner at the bottom of the hill, then takes her empty cup and saucer into the kitchen. It is her considered opinion that the nurse was going to the beach. She had that bouncy step and lightness of being about her that people often take with them when they go to the cove, along with their dogs, and sometimes picnics in more clement weather. Flora knows that she's always had good observation skills, along with powers of memory. Some might say that taking this level of interest in her local community could be seen as nosiness. She would disagree. Take the nurse, for example. If anything untoward were to befall the woman at the beach (God forbid), Flora would be able to inform the police about the date, time and what type of clothing she was wearing when last seen. That kind of evidence could be crucial in an inquiry.

She rinses the cup and saucer and puts them to drain, then wipes some crumbs from the kitchen table she missed earlier. Her memory is good, but her eyesight could be better. Now. What to do with the rest of the day? Library or coffee shop? As she ponders, she notices the calendar on the kitchen wall. It tells her she's been in this little cottage for a whole month. A month of adapting, adjusting and fitting in. Flora acknowledges that it hasn't been plain sailing, but at last she feels her little boat is heading to safe harbour. She isn't ready to drop anchor yet, but she will be. When she left Truro, lifelong friends told her she was mad to uproot and leave at her age. Flora knew otherwise though, and much as she regretted it, realised it was actually *because* of her age that she soon wouldn't be able to cope very well in the old house. Big, draughty and in need of repair, the house had to go – well, she had to leave it, to be precise. Though Flora was born in it and had lived there all her life, she couldn't afford to be sentimental. *Flora Granger was always a practical and forward thinker.* She joked to her friends they should write that on her headstone when they brought arguments for her staying put to her door, along with worried faces and downturned mouths.

In front of her bedroom mirror, she holds a multicoloured kaftan to her chest and does a few steps to the side and back, a quick one-two-three waltz. Perhaps she'll join the dance class she saw advertised on the church noticeboard last week. It was entitled *Strictly Fever* in shouty red letters, and had a variety of colourful cartoon people jiving, waltzing and doing the tango. Flora likes the idea of learning the tango, but who would partner her? Maybe they provide them as part of the class. She slips the kaftan on and re-applies the kohl pencil lines under her eyelashes, then adds a slash of crimson to her lips. Flora is satisfied with her appearance, though maybe the pink streak along one side of her long grey hair could be replaced by lilac. It's almost spring, so it would fit in nicely with the flowers in her garden. Then she remembers she no longer has a garden – just a tiny terrace with a few pots. Never mind, she's beside the sea and that's the main thing. Isn't it?

The library has won the toss-up between it and the coffee shop, but perhaps she'll have a coffee afterwards, if she doesn't spend too long reading in her usual spot next to the window. Flora smiles at this. 'Usual' is actually twice. But thinking of it as a spot she frequents makes her feel like she belongs here more. Makes her new life seem less alien. And after all, it is a very welcoming spot. Even on cloudy days, the sun tends to sneak through the pane and warm her face. She's quite at home there. And isn't there something in the back of her mind saying that there was an advert in the local paper for a part-time librarian? Now, that would be ideal. Although renown for taking an active part in her community ... that was then, she reminds herself. Once retired, the Flora in Truro had built up a whole raft of people who she saw on a regular basis. All from different walks of life, personalities gathered from the diverse interests and activities she's pursued. The Flora here, needs to be seen. She needs to be doing things. Become someone who people can depend on – learn from. Flora has always been someone's point of reference, but right now, she's a bit like a lighthouse without a light. She furrows her brows at that image, takes her yellow mac from the peg and shrugs it on. At the end of her path, she wrests her hair from the wind and looks towards the sea. No sign of that nurse. Flora hopes she's not been blown away.

Chapter Three

S ally Penwith takes off her shoes in the small courtyard at the back of the surgery and wiggles her toes. There's a painful blister on her little toe because she's not 'worn in' the new shoes enough before wearing them to work. Her daughter Pippa commented on her mum's choice of footwear that morning as she left the house. It was as though she was psychic. 'You know what you're like with new shoes, Mum, and no tights or socks with them either? Come lunchtime you'll be in agony.' Pippa's frown was so like her dad's, Sally had to look away. She had waved away the concern and gone ahead anyway. At almost fifty, she ought to know better than her twenty-year-old daughter, but the throbbing little toe tells her she doesn't.

The early afternoon sunshine pokes a few warm fingers through the thin cloud and Sally turns her face to their caress. She could do with going home after her lunch break and sitting in the garden in the spring sunshine, if she were honest, rather than sitting on reception. It isn't that she hates her job, it's just that it all feels a bit disjointed lately. Her life, not the job, though the job is part of it, of course. The last two weeks have been a bit of a rollercoaster. Normality has been turned upside down, inside out and stripped of all familiarity. Sally dribbles a bit of water from her glass onto her blistered toe and considers the order of things, or disorder, more like. First, Paul, her husband of twenty-five years, left her for another woman, a much younger one. And if that weren't totally devastating enough, both her children moved out of the family home too. Well, Pippa was moving in with her girlfriend this coming weekend, but Angus left to go travelling with his friends the day before his father walked out. Last she heard, they were in Thailand.

Thailand. Sally thinks about that. How exotic. Even the name sounds exotic; it's almost as if it exists on a different planet, not just across the world. The furthest she's ever been is Mallorca. Memories of white sandy beaches and lazy days flood her mind, and she smiles. The kids were little and she and Paul were happy … well, as happy as they could be, as he was never really satisfied. They must have gone about five or six times over the years, but then latterly, Paul said it cost too much money and he was getting busier at work. Newly promoted hotel managers couldn't be swanning off abroad at the drop of a hat, didn't she know? Sally wonders whether he was actually busy with other women at work, because that was where he found the new one, apparently.

A seagull's cry startles her out of her reminiscing, and a quick glance at her phone tells her she only has five minutes left of her break. Rose's laughing face looks at her from the screen saver – a photo from her 'surprise leaving do' a few weeks ago. This was another change in her life she could do without. Rose had been like a mooring buoy Sally could tether herself to when she felt like she was floating adrift. Rose had always been there with a kind word and a listening ear. She was one of those people who was ready to support people, no matter what. She always made time for a chat and seemed genuinely interested in Sally's life. Such as it was. Sally hadn't told Rose the whole story of her marriage (which had been struggling long before Paul walked out), but Rose knew enough to get the gist without Sally having to divulge the whole humiliating plotline. No spoilers, please. Now Rose, too, was gone. Maybe that was a bit dramatic, because she was on the end of a phone, if need be. But it was the end of a lovely era when Rose hung up her uniform for the last time.

Sally finds a sticking plaster in her bag and gingerly applies it to her toe, still thinking about Rose. The surgery seems to be lacking something, now she isn't in it. Exactly what, Sally can't say. That indefinable something that held them all together. Not to say that their little staff group is falling apart – Sally expects that's just her – but the whole is fragmented, more fragile. Cracking, like a much-loved vase that no longer holds water. Shaking off that thought, she decides that she will go over and see Rose in the next few days. Take her some flowers and chocolate, to show how much she's missed. Maybe Sally won't say that's what they're for, though, because it could be seen as being a bit needy. This is something Sally prides herself on – not being needy. She's an independent woman who's had to put up with years of shit from her husband and managed to do it without anyone knowing. It takes a strong woman to hide the scars of abuse. Not physical – no, that wasn't Paul's way. Cruel words and sneers were his fists, and the wounds ran deep.

Without intending to, she watches again the scene from two weeks ago playing out before her eyes like some grim TV drama. Her waking early to find Paul's side of the bed empty, going downstairs to find him talking in hushed tones on the phone in the kitchen, his back to her, a cup of coffee in hand. He sounds like a teenager, all breathy whispers, sighs and chuckles. He just said the word *babe*: 'Of course I do, babe.'

This is wrong. Very wrong. It's the kind of wrong that twists her stomach and clamps a hand over her mouth to stop herself speaking – she can't let him know she's listening. She needs to hear it, more than she's desperate to turn and leave. She can't leave. She's welded to the spot. Frozen. Drawn like a moth to a flame. Moths are oblivious to the danger, but Sally's not. She knows her wings are going to burn, but she's unable to prevent it.

Sally tries to blot out what comes next, but as on almost every occasion since he walked out, she fails. He turns and sees her, fleeting surprise in his eyes becoming contempt, then resignation. Paul ends the call and calmly answers her anguished question – 'Are you having an affair?' – as if she'd asked him if he was enjoying his coffee, with, 'Yes, I am.'

She slumps into a kitchen chair and listens slack-jawed

as he folds his arms and tells her in a flat monotone that he's leaving her. He's had enough, Sally doesn't excite him anymore, they were just going through the motions and he's not prepared to fritter away his life doing that. Paul sees her as an old friend now, really, and does have affection for her, but that's not enough. Not anymore. Not now the children have grown up and are flying the nest. This new woman is his soulmate, they didn't intend for it to happen but...

Sally's aware of pain in the palm of her hand as her fingernails dig into the flesh. She's been trying this method to shock herself out of constantly reliving these awful scenes the past few weeks, and it sometimes works. She tells herself she must stop it. He's gone. She's strong, she's independent, she's ... falling apart. A deep breath swells her chest and she holds it for five. Releasing it slowly, she tests the plaster on her toe again. It's still tender, like her heart, but it's time to go back into work. Sally winces as she squeezes her shoe back on, finds a welcoming smile from her ever-depleting reserves and goes inside.

Chapter Four

Rose hurries up the sandy incline from the beach, utterly energised and raring to go. It never fails to amaze her how a breezy walk on the beach next to a noisy, wild ocean, immersed in nature's elements, can send the spirits soaring up with the seagulls. Often people say it's because when they stare at the ocean, it makes them realise how insignificant they are. The ocean is so vast and ancient their lives seem irrelevant. Well, Rose doesn't really understand that. If you feel insignificant, why is it so uplifting? For her, it's the feeling that she's part of something bigger and she belongs to it. The ocean has always been here. It's timeless, ageless, and magnificent. All humanity – our lives, our spirits – are intertwined with nature, the elements. We are all part of the whole. Connected.

As she walks, Rose thinks about how the planets and the ocean were first formed, and her mind boggles. She remembers years ago asking a schoolteacher if he thought

God made everything. He said, if God made everything, who made God? This kind of question sends her mind scurrying for cover. She'd asked her dad what he thought. He said that if she thought too much about all that kind of thing, she'd go mad. If she accepted things as they were and didn't ask too many questions, she'd be much happier. Her dad believed in God and said that there was a bigger plan that we knew nothing about – we just had to have faith. One day we'd go to a 'better place'. Rose is still not sure what she thinks, but she has a sneaking suspicion that not asking too many questions isn't the way forward.

Rose is still pondering as she goes past the little cottage with the red door that used to belong to old Mr Jenkins. Mr Jenkins passed away last year aged ninety-nine – bet he was fuming he'd not reached the ton. He might know the answers to some of her questions by now, assuming he's arrived safely at the 'better place'. A shame Rose can't ask him. Through the window of the cottage, she glimpses a quick movement and a flash of colour, as though someone's doing a twirl or dancing. Rose looks away before she's seen gawping. It's probably Hippy Lady, as she calls her, in the absence of a name. She's been here a few weeks or so, but Rose hasn't had the time to introduce herself. She will, very soon.

As she reaches her gate, she sees a familiar figure in a yellow puffer jacket and black jeans walking down the hill towards her. 'Daisy!' Rose waves as her old school pal gets nearer. She had no idea she was coming today. Surely, she hasn't forgotten?

'Rose! I'm glad you're home. I thought about ringing

before I came, but it was a spur-of-the-moment thing.' Daisy's amber eyes hold a shadow of uncertainty, but Rose's big smile banishes it.

'So pleased to see you, matey.' Rose gives her a hug and leads the way up the path and inside. 'It must be about three months or so since we had lunch?'

'Yeah. That's one of the reasons I just had to come and see you today. I was walking past a gift shop in Port Isaac and there was a painting of a cottage near the sea which reminded me of this one,' Daisy flaps a hand at the kitchen wall, fluffs her auburn curls and pulls her spotty red-and-black polka-dot scarf off, all in one elegant movement, 'and I knew I had to see you. You've been on my mind for weeks, and I wanted to have a chat with you – you know, what with you leaving work and all? I knew you'd be having mixed feelings about everything. But then life takes over, and I'm so busy with the grandchildren, now Millie's working full-time...'

Daisy's machine-gun-fire words register with Rose and land in her consciousness, but they're in another room – an echo of now. Because she's far away in a schoolyard, on a hot summer's day, playing catch with a freckle-faced kid with unruly flame-red hair dragged into bunches, laughter bursting from her chest along with a stream of chatter delivered at a hundred miles an hour. She's not changed, thank God. Daisy always made her smile, raised her up if she fell, was there to lend an ear and a heart.

'You actually listening to me?' Daisy folds her arms, drops a hip and narrows her eyes. Now she's Daisy the savvy teenager. The one nobody ever got the better of.

Rose laughs. 'I am indeed. Just thinking of our schooldays and that you haven't changed at all. Where have all those years gone, eh?'

'God knows. I was only thinking the same thing the other day. And put the kettle on, for goodness' sake. I'm parched with all that walking.' Daisy fans her face, scrapes a kitchen chair from the table along the stone flags, and emits an 'oomph' as she sits down. 'My attitude might not have changed since school, but my poor knees tell a different story.'

Rose smiles in sympathy and sticks the kettle on.

Daisy jabs a finger at her. 'And thinking about school, do you remember old Mr Hawkins? How he used to call us "little flowers" because of our names?'

A picture of a smiley-faced man with thick curly grey hair comes to Rose. 'I do. And I'm not sure kids of today would take kindly to being called "little flowers". Different times then, of course, and he meant it kindly.'

'Yeah, and I called him "old man Hawkins". I bet he was our age, or younger!'

This thought pulls Rose up short. It doesn't seem possible. *I expect Mr Hawkins has gone to the better place too, after all this time.* Melancholy finds a home in her chest as she busies herself with the tea. What does she expect? People don't live forever, do they? And she hasn't thought of 'old man' Hawkins since junior school, so why has gloom pinned itself to his memory?

'Talking of school, which we were,' says Daisy, 'my Steve says he saw on Facebook that there's a leavers' reunion in the summer. It's forty-five years since we left secondary.'

'Forty-five years? That's an odd one. Why not wait until fifty?' Rose puts two mugs of tea on the table and opens a packet of bourbons.

'Hey, they can't hang about at our age.' Daisy dips a bourbon in her tea and stuffs the whole thing in her mouth just as it disintegrates to mush.

'True.' Rose wishes she'd stop talking about old age, poor knees and school reunions. Isn't life miserable enough? That thought comes out of nowhere. Ambushes her. A miserable life. Really? And Rose was the one who brought school into it in the first place, not Daisy. The good mood she'd brought back from the beach seems to have evaporated.

'So, do you fancy it?'

'Fancy what?'

'The reunion. Me and Steve are going – it's at The Slipway in Port Isaac. No idea what I'm going to wear...' Rose gets a faraway stare as Daisy's brain presumably sorts through the items in her wardrobe, then she snaps to attention. 'So, what do you think?'

'I won't be going.'

Daisy looks like her imaginary wardrobe is on fire. 'What! Why?'

Rose doesn't know why. Well, she doesn't know how to put it into words. She does know that she has an aversion to attending the reunion. She sees doors slamming on the whole idea, one after the other, each one bigger and stronger than the last, until she arrives at the biggest and strongest door with a series of iron bolts, each firing into place. Daisy's still expecting an answer, and luckily, from behind the last door comes:

'There'll be lots of sad old people there, trying to make out that they're having a great life and making stuff up about themselves to impress everyone. Then I'll have to listen to stories about their grandchildren and how wonderful it is to spend time with them. I'll have to appear interested and say *ohh* and *aw*, and God forbid, *bless*, in the right places. While all the time I'll be wishing I was sitting in front of the telly with a glass of wine, right here in my cosy cottage. Reunions. Dear God. It's all so bloody tragic.'

A piece of biscuit gets stuck in Rose's throat and she has to cough to dislodge it. Her face is on fire, and she appears to have tears in her eyes. Daisy's got her *what the fuck?* face on, and well she might. That was quite the speech and was as much a surprise to Rose as it was to Daisy.

'Bloody hell, Rose. That was a bit much. You okay, love?'

Rose considers this. She thought she was okay, but that little outburst and the melancholy that's growing in her chest like a cancer, say otherwise. 'Yeah, 'course. Just a bit fed up, I suppose.' She shrugs and hopes there's enough expression in it to save her from thinking of more words. The ones she has are jumbled and fragmented, like her thoughts.

Daisy looks at Rose, her face a portrait of sympathy, which does nothing to help the melancholy. 'Aw, Rose. I know what's wrong. It's because you don't see Bella and the grandkids much, now they've moved up country, isn't it?

Plus the fact you've just retired and must be feeling all at sixes and sevens.'

At sixes and sevens. Another old expression that has no straightforward meaning. Maybe Rose's mum would have known. Or perhaps not. Is Daisy right? She looks into her mug of tea, as though she'll find the answer floating on its surface. 'Maybe I am a bit. But I have lots to be getting on with. Gardening, for one thing, and horse riding for another.'

Rose enjoys the look of incredulity rolling up Daisy's face like a spring tide. 'Horse riding? Since when have *you* ever done horse riding?'

'Never, that's the point. I'll be doing lots of things I've never done before.' Rose laughs and throws a theatrical wide-armed stance. 'I'm stepping out of my box!'

Daisy laughs too. 'You sound completely out of your box already! Have you been on the wine?'

'No.' Rose laughs along with her, but is irked that she thinks horse riding is something outside her remit. Maybe Daisy's made her own box for her. She's not sure she'd like to look inside it. Rose takes the cups to the sink and thinks about the reunion and the kinds of boxes she'd made for some of her old school friends, and if they'd still fit into them.

'Well anyway,' Daisy says to Rose's back. 'You might like to know that Tristan Carthew is going to be there. He's a friend of my Steve's on Facebook and he's coming down from Wales for the reunion. Thought that might change your mind.'

This is the second time today that Rose has been brought

up with a jolt. Tristan Carthew, the boy she thought she'd marry. Through the kitchen window, by the emerging and strangely abundant daffodils, a tall dark-haired youth looks at her across the years. The bright-blue eyes hold a question, the lopsided self-conscious grin encourages an answer.

'You listening, woman?' Daisy asks.

'Yes.' Rose turns around and answers her smile. 'It doesn't change my mind. The Tristan I knew left here when he was sixteen. I want him to stay the boy he was. The boy in my memory. We'll have nothing in common now.'

'You might do. It would be nice to meet just as friends, obviously, catch up on old times.'

'No thanks. It's all too much of a cliché, Daisy … and faintly ridiculous. Older woman goes to school reunion and magically falls back in love with her first love.'

'That's not what I'm saying at all. It's just that you're not too old to start again. I don't mean with Tris, necessarily. As far as I know, he's still married, so it…'

'Daisy. Can we change the record? This one is old and scratched.'

Concern draws a few lines across Daisy's brow and she scrunches her nose up. Right now, she looks like a disgruntled fairy and very daisy-like. A tall willowy elegant daisy, trying to avoid Rose's scratchy thorns. 'I reckon this leaving work malarkey has hit you quite hard. I knew it would, it's only natural. I was saying to Steve the other day that you…'

A picking over the bones of Rose's lost career is not what she wants to hear, so she pats Daisy's hand, hoping a physical interruption will speak volumes. 'Hey, enough about me. Let's talk about you. What have *you* been up to?'

Another few worry lines sketch around Daisy's eyes, then a half-smile erases them, and Rose listens as Daisy holds forth about her family and the part-time job she has at the library. It never fails to amaze Rose how she keeps quiet enough to do a job like that. Daisy is the type of person that can't help herself peering over shoulders and asking about the story. She's done that with Rose's story today. Trouble is, Rose isn't exactly sure what's happening in it. She keeps re-reading the same sentence but it's not registering.

'Anyway, I'd best get gone.' Daisy scrapes the chair over the flags as she stands. 'Need to get lunch and then I promised our Millie I'd get some shoes for Lottie before collecting her from school.'

Lunchtime already? The clock confirms it – where has the time gone? This is the second time Rose has wondered that today. Must stop it. Remembering her manners, she says, 'You can stay and have a sandwich if you like? Ham, cheese and pickle suit you?'

After a moment's hesitation Daisy says, 'Thanks, but I ought to go, or it will be time to pick up Lottie before I've got the shoes. You know what we're like for gabbing on.'

Daisy has switched on her twinkly smile, but her eyes don't get the message. Rose realises she's been a proper old grump and Daisy can't wait to get away. Who can blame her? 'I've not done much gabbing today, have I? I'm sorry...' Rose's words dry up as she wonders exactly what she's sorry for. There seems to be a bit of a list.

'Don't apologise, you dafty. Look, you'll be your old self

in no time. It will just take a bit of time.' Daisy pulls her jacket on and wraps her scarf twice around her neck. As Rose is searching for an appropriate response, Daisy pulls her in for a hug and says in her ear, 'You know where I am, Rose. Just give me a call anytime, okay?'

Suddenly thrust at arm's length, Rose notices tears in Daisy's eyes, but she turns away, pulls on her boots and scoops up her handbag. When she looks back her eyes are dry, and as she makes her way to the front door, she's trailing a stream of chatter over her shoulder about the scandalous price of children's shoes and what she's cooking for dinner later. Rose is left in no doubt that this is an act. One of Daisy's tools she keeps in her bag of tricks for awkward situations. One that Rose made for her. The situation, not the bag. She opens the door for her and says, 'It's been wonderful to see you, Daze. We should have lunch in town soon – my treat.'

Rose is gratified to see a genuine smile on her friend's face as she gently pats her cheek. 'I'll hold you to that, Rose. See you!'

Rose waves her off and follows her progress until the yellow of her coat and the red of her hair blend to form an early sunset as she grows ever more distant. Dear Daisy, what would she do without her? She needs to have a long hard look at herself because it's not Daisy's fault that she's feeling at sixes and sevens. And if Rose has a non-horse-riding box, maybe she's to blame for furnishing it. As she's already decided, she'll be stepping out of it very soon. This thought brings with it a smile and dilutes the melancholy. Adjustment needn't be a trauma. Yet more yellow daffodils nod at her in agreement. Hmm. Maybe she'll do a bit more than strim the grass in the garden and water the pots. Maybe she'll buy a few new plants from the garden centre too. Attending a reunion will be one step too far, however. Once Daisy's disappeared over the brow of the hill, the wind whips Rose back inside and she's left with a bit of a hole. She needs to fill it with something uplifting before the melancholy sneaks back in.

Chapter Five

To apply or not to apply? Flora pokes a fingernail at the flyer sitting in front of her on the library table and sniffs. She's been staring at it for over half an hour, while occasionally reading the book she's grabbed from one of the shelves. If she's truthful, she's not really been reading, because the flyer advertising a part-time assistant here at the library keeps distracting her. Through the window, the sunlight is pouring over it like molten gold, as if giving her some ethereal direction. Flora acknowledges it would be a perfect way to get to know the local community, get involved, be useful. But what exactly do they mean by part-time? As a seventy-seven-year-old woman, she doesn't want to be tied to a few hours every day – that's too much of a commitment. There are other things she wants to pursue. *Like what, Flora? Sitting in the coffee shop, eating your body weight in cake?*

Mother's back again, then. Flora's not heard her dulcet tones nagging in her head for a few months. Perhaps her absence has been because she's been so busy moving house and getting used to a new way of life. The faint hope that Mother was left behind in Truro has come to nothing. What a surprise. *Shut up, Mother.*

You know I'm right. Make a decision, for goodness' sake.

Flora decides that not replying is the best way forward, and her eyes slide to the pages of her book and then the flyer again. As she's about to turn the page in the book, the name of which escapes her, and is largely irrelevant as she's not reading it, a tall, slim, auburn-haired woman breezes in, dragging the cold air behind her. It bites at Flora's shins, which are exposed, and not for the first time that day, she wonders about the logic of wearing knee-length culottes on a dull day in March – sparkly, or otherwise. The woman looks familiar and then it registers. She's a librarian here, but she's not here all the time. Perhaps she could be the person to ask about the job.

Before her mother can spout more vitriol, Flora gets up and goes over to the desk, where the woman who's just come in is shrugging off her coat and pinning a badge on her chest which reads... Flora doesn't know, because she's left her glasses on top of the reading book. Seeing a puzzle form in the woman's eyes and feeling a prize chump for standing there staring at her chest, she hurries to retrieve her glasses. Back at the desk, she sees the name badge says: *Daisy – Library Assistant.* Ah, good. Flora's memory never fails her.

Well, what else would she be, apart from a library assistant? She's standing behind the desk with a name badge pinned to her jumper, you ninny!

'Hello, can I help you?' Daisy asks, with a smile.

Flora notes that Daisy's cheeks are pink, having been pinched by the cold wind, no doubt. Her own legs are only just recovering from the assault. Unusual eyes – brown, with orange flecks. Nice open face, too. Then, aware that she's staring again, Flora replies, 'Yes, please. I was wondering about the part-time job you have here.' Did she detect a twitch in Daisy's lips? Is she trying not to laugh because of Flora's age, or is it the blue shins and the inappropriate culottes? Flora lifts her chin and sets her shoulders back. 'Is there an age limit, and how many hours is it?' Maybe a bit snippy, but she won't be patronised.

Daisy looks unfazed. 'No age limit, and it's one day a week. Thursdays. Are you enquiring for yourself?'

No, for the King of England.

Shut up, Mother.

One day a week is very do-able and Flora begins to think it might work. 'Yes, I am. Is there an interview process?' Flora's used to interviews on both sides of the desk because of her long teaching career. There won't be a problem at all.

'Not as such. Just an informal chat.' Daisy looks around the almost empty library. 'We're quiet right now, if you'd like to do it – oh, and please fill this form in. Anna, the head librarian, has just popped on a break but she'll be back soon.'

The form is basic, takes just a few minutes to fill in, and then a rotund woman in yellow, presumably Anna, appears. She asks if Flora has ever worked in a library before and Flora tells her no, but that she worked in a school for nearly forty years and feels over-qualified, if anything. Furthermore, she's extremely well read and invites Anna to quiz her on the classics. Anna seems to have caught the twitch in Daisy's lips, says that won't be necessary and takes the form to her office.

'We will let you know in the next few days, Ms Granger. May I call you Flora?' Daisy asks.

'You may. Are there many people waiting to hear?'

'One or two.' Daisy says, with a smile.

As Flora takes her leave, she can't help thinking that Daisy will be nice to work with. She also realises she would be disappointed if she didn't get the job. Considering she's dithered about it for so long, this comes as something of a surprise. Though it would help her to settle in, and that was the main thing.

After a pleasant hour spent at the coffee shop, reluctantly Flora decides it's time she was leaving. Her reluctance is because of the culottes. She's unsure how they will stand up to the howling gale and driving rain that has replaced the brisk wind of earlier. Flora zips her orange cagoule up to the neck and tightens the toggles under her chin before stepping out. In seconds, her green canvas shoes are soaked through and she wishes she had windscreen wipers on her glasses. Every few steps she has to stop and remove them to give them a quick rub over with a tissue. The tissue is in danger of disintegrating and so is Flora's patience. Why the heck did she not pay attention to the weather forecast?

Eventually, on the hill at the top of her road, she has to hang onto various shrubs and fences as she passes to keep upright. Should have brought that walking stick gathering dust in the hallway. *You're much too vain to accept that you might need it. That's your trouble.* Mother might have a point there. On her way past the nurse's house, she catches a glimpse of her at the front window. The nurse opens it and yells, 'My goodness, you're drenched!' *No shit, Sherlock.* 'Would you like to come in and have a cuppa?'

Flora might do on any other day, but her bladder is near to bursting, and all she wants to do is get in the house before it's too late. She raises a hand and quickens her pace. 'Too busy today!' Then a gust of wind tugs a strand of hair from under her hood and gags her with it. She was about to add that she'd like to do it another time, but the wind has other ideas.

———————

Rose watches Hippy Lady struggle on and closes the window. How rude! Not sure she'll be popping round to say hello anytime soon. But then maybe she's shy ... the sparkly culottes say otherwise, then Rose reminds herself that clothes don't tell the whole story. It would have been nice to have some company, though. The idea of driving over to the riding stables and having a chat with them about a few lessons has been shelved today, because of this weather, so what to do instead? Maybe she could look out the old painting set of Bella's that preoccupied her teenage years for about three days, and have a dabble. Glen had likened their daughter's concentration span to that of a gnat. Another saying that has little relevance. How do we measure a gnat's concentration against that of any other insect? Have there been experiments done? And if so, what kind of experiments? Rose's mind is in danger of packing up and shipping out to the planet Surreal, so she puts the kettle on and thinks about Daisy.

It's been three days since she visited and Rose has wanted to call her to apologise for being so gloomy and brusque with her. She remembers how hurt she looked as she left, as she'd only been concerned, but something has stopped Rose making the call. Wondering how to explain herself is probably the stumbling block, because she'd have to explain her behaviour to herself first. Sixes and sevens is as good an explanation as any.

With a cup of tea and a biscuit or two, Rose sits at the kitchen table and opens up her laptop. She intends to answer a few emails and then maybe call her daughter, Bella. There was a missed call from her the day she left her job (Rose's brain won't allow the word 'retired'), and a WhatsApp message the other day from her that she hasn't answered, apart from saying she'd call her soon and adding a few hearts. Bella'll be getting worried soon if Rose doesn't let her know how she is. Rose has told herself to stop wishing she still lived in the village, as it does no good, but she misses her so much. Instead of doing as she intended, she finds herself on social media, which tends to be a major distraction for her these days. Truth is, it allows her to drift through the stories of other people's lives, see what snippets they find noteworthy and discover the bits of themselves they like to share all over the place. This is fascinating to Rose, as she tends to keep her own bits private.

Facebook tells her, amongst other things, that Daisy might have found the perfect person for the part-time job at the library; Sally has taken up yoga; and Bella has dyed her hair blonde. It suits her, but Rose notes that her roots will be a bugger to keep at bay, as she has her dad's dark locks. Facebook also tells her she has a friend request from ... she squints at the little profile picture, oh my goodness ... Tristan Carthew. Though his hair is mostly grey now, Rose can still see the boy she knew gazing out. His smile is self-assured and he looks like the kind of man people would like to know. Is he the kind of man Rose would like to know? She finds herself casting the net of her memory back through the years and hauling it back with a full catch of smiles and a warm heart.

About to confirm his request, she has second thoughts. She's already told Daisy she'd like to remember Tristan as the boy she knew, keep him in the past where everything looks rosier and you can make bits up that don't fit, smooth off the rough edges until they do. Reality is less forgiving and so is the present, Rose has found. Everyone knows you should never go back. Besides, it's such a cliché, as she also mentioned to Daisy. Her finger hovers over the accept button and withdraws – she shoves her hands in her trouser pockets. No. No, Tristan Carthew, best to leave things as they were.

Once the emails are answered, as is the WhatsApp to Bella, she decides to go up into the loft and dig out the paints she was thinking about before. A part of her is unsure that they will still be up there – perhaps they were thrown away during some spring-cleaning junk-dumping exercise years ago. Only one way to find out.

———————————

The loft ladder creaks down like old bones, bringing with it a veil of cobwebs and a musty aroma of wood and forgotten things. Glen, as well as being responsible for the garden, always used to be the 'loft person', going up there to retrieve Christmas decorations and suitcases. Rose rarely ventured up. Since Glen died, she hasn't been on holiday, so there was no need for suitcases, and she couldn't face the old Christmas decorations because they would have reminded her of Christmases past. She bought a few new ones from the garden centre and a little fake tree to hang them on. The strength to cherish those happy old memories, to embrace them with a nostalgic smile, has so far evaded her. Maybe this year she'll be able to.

Old bones climbing old bones. Rose allows herself a wry smile as she hauls herself onto the boarded floor section at the top of the ladder. Another reason she was never the 'loft person' is because her dad scared her when she was little by saying it was dangerous being in a loft. You only had to miss your footing between a beam and the layers of fibreglass, and you'd be through the ceiling quicker than a knife through butter. Glen told her that Dad had probably just said that to make sure she was extra careful and that their own loft had boarded sections, but Rose still preferred to keep out.

A while later, after tracing her fingers across the terrains of numerous dusty containers, boxes and lids, she finds what she came up there for – a wooden box, mildewed with rusting hinges. Once opened, she sees a rainbow of oil paints in three rows. Remarkably, their smell still perfumes the stale loft air. A stroke of the box brings a memory of Bella around fourteen, sitting at an easel, her dark hair up in a high ponytail, a streak of red oil paint above her eyebrow. Rose came into her room to bring Bella a drink, and she tells her not to look at the canvas. She's at that awkward, unsure age with fluctuating self-esteem – not quite grown into her personality. Rose looks at the canvas anyway, because she can tell part of her daughter wants her mother to see that she's painted a gorgeous sunset over the ocean. Bella's face grows as red as that sunset when Rose tells her how beautiful she thinks it is, and in answer to her pouty question, no, Rose is not just saying it because she's her mum. Bella smiles at her then, and Rose's heart fills with an impossible amount of love.

Cradling the box to her chest, Rose marvels at how vivid and 'real' that memory was. She could have almost reached out and removed a stray hair from her daughter's forehead and given her a reassuring hug. Hugs with Bella these days are few and far between, reassuring or otherwise, now she's no longer living around the corner. Thank goodness for memories. Bittersweet they may be, but she wouldn't be without them. Maybe Rose will try to commit that memory to canvas later, if she can find one in a cobwebby box. A whisper of doubt argues there is no canvas up here, and she tends to agree. Never mind, she will have to go into town to buy one at some point. That will give her something else to do.

Before returning to the bone ladder, she casts an eye around to make extra sure there is nothing of any use. On an old card-table, she sees an old photo album that was hers in her mid-teens. Velvet green and covered in dust, she remembers it hides a wealth of polaroid images stuck in with glue. Is her fragile mood, her 'sixes and sevens' mentality, ready to see what lies between the pages? Does she want to be reminded of who she used to be before she was a nurse, a wife and a mother? Can she look into the eyes of her fifteen-year-old self without melancholy slipping back in? Without jealousy, because of all those years she has ahead of her?

While Rose is considering this, her fingers run a path through the dust and before she can stop them, they open the album. Her breath is snatched by a jump back in time and she takes in an image of her and Daisy laughing in the sea, their not-quite-a-woman bodies clad in skimpy bikinis. Their age is not certain, she's plumping for fourteen rather than fifteen, but they could be either. The memory of that photo, or who took it, isn't clear at all, but the joy of that day at the beach and that moment in time registers a faint echo somewhere. Most of them are of her and Daisy doing various crazy things. They're at the fair in one, faces obscured by sticks of candyfloss that look like Marge Simpson's hair. In another they're in a park dancing in tight black jeans and yellow T-shirts with David Bowie's face on them. Then there's some more, groups of them – friends from school on boats, or surfing.

As she looks through them all, she finds herself smiling and glad that she opened the album. There's no jealousy or melancholy, just acceptance and a sense of peace. What fun they had. Their whole lives in front of them and the sun always seemed to be shining. The photo on the last page catches Rose's breath again for different reasons, and she knows exactly how old she is in this one. It's her sixteenth birthday and she's in the woods with Daisy, Daisy's then boyfriend John, and Tristan Carthew. They'd gone there on a day trip. It was spring and the woods were so green and fresh. In the photo, Tristan and Rose are standing in a patch of wild garlic, arms about each other, laughing at the camera. Tristan has a guitar slung across his chest and they'd been singing together. He always said they'd join a band and be bigger than Fleetwood Mac one day.

Daisy took the photo and told them to say cheesy peasy. Afterwards, Rose remembers, she picked a white garlic flower and ate it. Immediately, the memory sends Rose back to the woods. The pungent, yet mild taste of garlic and dew on her tongue, the exhilarating feeling of turning sixteen in her chest, singing her heart out to the treetops swaying under a clear blue sky, the boy she loved by her side. They were going to take on the world, she and Tris – have the crowds falling at their feet. Releasing a breath, she closes the album and finds her cheeks wet.

Back in the kitchen, Rose wipes the box of paints free of dust with a cloth and wonders if the wild garlic still grows in the woods. There's an idea taking shape in her mind and she likes the look of it. Why not drive out to Cardinham Woods and see? She could take some sandwiches and make an afternoon of it. She might even take these paints and a pad of paper. Through the window, the rain has stopped and the sky is the same blue as on that long-ago day when she turned sixteen. It would be nice to get out in the spring sunshine, wouldn't it? The cheerful daffodils nod their encouragement, and before she can talk herself out of it, twenty minutes later Rose is out the door.

Chapter Six

As ideas go, this was one of Rose's best. She stops along the woodland path, tilts her face to the patch of blue sky peeping through the treetops above, closes her eyes and listens. There's a soft sigh as the gentle breeze dances amongst the new leaves unfurling on the branches and rustles the tall grasses in the meadow beyond. Birds sing their hearts out, up high and down low, and everywhere new life is bursting from grass, shrub and tree. Setting off again, Rose reflects on how good it is to be out in nature, loosed from schedule and routine. Only this morning she'd been fighting off melancholy and gloomy thoughts, but now something's lifted. Things feel lighter. *She* feels lighter. Upon arrival here, as soon as she got out of the car, she noticed the shift. The scent of fresh earth, wet grass and the essence of damp woodland bathed in dappled sunlight overwhelmed her senses.

Buoyed by this new lightness, Rose's pace quickens, and

soon, the woodland path begins to widen and dip until she's led in wonder to an open copse of mighty oak trees standing in a circle around a vibrant mass of bluebells which carpet every inch of the diameter. From the roots of the oaks is an answering mass of white flowers. Wild garlic. Its pungency flavours the air and she swallows an ache in her throat. It's the exact spot in the photo she was looking at, the spring she turned sixteen. No ifs or buts, or question marks – this is it. Bending to pick a stem, giddiness overtakes her and she places a hand against the rough, damp bark of the tree trunk. The delicate white flower quivers under her touch and she pops it into her mouth, reliving and savouring the memory of that day, devouring the intoxicating lifeblood of youth and joyful expectation.

Rose finds that she wants to laugh out loud and sing. She hasn't sung for many years, even though people tell her she should. Her voice had been left behind in the past, to keep company with the ambition and hope that she'd join a band. With the tree trunk supporting her and the heady mix of crushed garlic and woodland in her lungs, she closes her eyes and goes back to her sixteenth birthday. Wrapped in that memory, she watches a young woman and her boyfriend dance through the bluebells, singing together, earnest in their self-belief and their belief in each other, delighting in the sound of their voices spiralling up and up, as spring awakened and carried them with her.

Few people have crossed Rose's path today and upon opening her eyes, she finds herself quite alone. With the taste of wild garlic on her tongue, an overwhelming desire to sing won't be quashed, and she opens her mouth, takes a huge breath and launches into 'Dreams' by Fleetwood Mac, one that she and Tris had loved. Independent of her control, Rose's arms rise and stretch, and she's lost in the music, twirling and dancing through the bluebells and garlic, her head tilting from side to side, hair falling across her face. This is the first time she's sung aloud like this for years – with abandon, with heart – and it feels incredible. She feels incredible. Incredible and ridiculously happy, steeped in the power of nature and growing things.

Out of breath, Rose slides her back down a tree trunk until she's sitting at its roots. Legs bent, she rests her forehead on her knees and for the second time today, find her cheeks wet. That phrase – *the power of nature and growing things* – has found a turntable in her thoughts and plays on repeat. As a breeze finds a clump of garlic flowers next to her, like the daffodils in the garden earlier, they nod along with her thoughts, and the compulsion to dig up a few bulbs is overwhelming. No ... no, she can't, because stealing flowers is probably not very good woodland behaviour, even though there are thousands of them. A sturdy twig is Rose's trowel and soon she has six bulbs in her coat pocket, which is a surprise, as she'd not intended to do that. After a furtive glance around, she jumps up and hurries back along the path. There's an urgent need to get them in the damp earth of her garden.

In her head on the drive home, Rose pictures the garlic growing amongst the daffodils in her 'wrap-around' cottage garden. Glen tended it well, but in his logical and organised way. Rose never really had much to do with it – well, apart from sitting in it when she had the time. It's always been neat and ordered, mostly laid to lawn, unadventurous (a bit like herself). A few namesake rose bushes and one or two splashes of colour grace the perimeter, but it's never been a place of experiment, of wildness, of vibrancy. Until today, that is. Rose thinks about the photo and the woodland and the memory. Mostly the memory, and she concludes that in the future, whenever she looks at the garlic, she'll remember the Rose from then. The songbird Rose. The Rose full of hope for the future. The Rose she was before she had a box.

The heady feeling from the woods is still riding shotgun as she threads her way through the tiny Cornish lanes. Rose marvels at the colours in the hedgerows, fields and gardens... It's as if she's seeing everything with fresh eyes. A line of birds perched on the wires resemble musical notes on a score. The yellow rapeseed fields in the distance look as if the sun's crashed into them, the hills dressed in emerald and olive slide down to the cerulean ocean, and in people's gardens, daffodils, primroses and tulips herald the birth of the season – an awakening of new hope.

Primroses, wow. She smiles as another memory comes at her, vivid and clear, of Bella when she was about two years old. She's dressed in her Paddington Bear top and patchwork jeans, her dark hair in bunches, crouching on her haunches to smell the yellow, blue and pink primroses that grew in pots by the back door. Bella always loved those flowers. She called them 'prim-noses' for a while, which caused much hilarity between Rose and Glen, and they missed it when Bella mastered the correct pronunciation. The pots and primroses are long gone, but she resolves to buy some tomorrow.

Chapter Seven

F lora is pacing up and down her living room. Pacing. Pacing. It doesn't help her think, it just keeps her from sitting in a chair and screaming. She's wanted to scream since the early hours, when a cheerful robin decided it would perch outside her bedroom window and sing its little heart out. Maybe it imagined Flora would be thrilled, but its imagination was way off, because sleep had evaded her for most of the night. The mystery of who got the library job was driving her crazy. Why couldn't they ring her and put her out of her misery? If it was a no, then so be it. She can handle disappointment; it hasn't exactly been a stranger to her over the years. Sometimes it would burst in, rear up and sock her in the jaw, completely unexpected. Other times, it would slip in quietly under doors, and through cracks, creep up behind her, fill her heart with that familiar ache until she acknowledged its return. Mother often put it there as a matter of daily routine. It was on her 'to-do' list.

Mother is gearing up to invade her thoughts right now, offer a few ill-placed pointers, so Flora slams the door shut on her and eyes the kettle. No. No more coffee or she'll be bouncing off the walls. It's time she was dressed and out. If the library can't be bothered to call and let her know, she'll go in and speak to the Daisy woman face-to-face. It's been three days, after all.

You're too impatient by half, madam. I've always told you that you need to bide your time and…

'Oh do fuck off, Mother!' Flora knows she's being irrational, shouting out loud at a dead woman, but it's not as if anyone can hear her, is it? In her opinion there is too much of this bottling-things-up lark in society – well, for her generation, at least. It could be argued the younger generation over-share. Especially on social media, which can leave them vulnerable to betrayal and abuse. Stiff upper lips, squared shoulders and keeping calm and carrying on was her uniform growing up, and through most of her life, but when she turned sixty and retired, she burnt it, along with people's expectations of her.

Ten minutes later, Flora's dressed in yellow polka-dot baggy trousers, a purple polo neck and comfortable trainers. She twists her hair into a ponytail secured with a leopard-print chiffon scarf and applies her make-up, taking extra care to wing her eyeliner. Very 1960s, which she loves. That decade is often characterised by free love, psychedelic drugs and rock music, all of which Flora missed out on. Mother made sure of that. In the hallway, it takes a few seconds to decide on a coat, but the long zebra-striped mac wins over the scarlet-and-green cape, and slipping it on, Flora leaves the house.

Instead of going up the hill in the direction of the library, she turns left and walks down towards the beach, which is a bit of a surprise, to say the least, but she goes with it. Flora believes that sometimes, you just have to follow your instincts, because you never know what they might lead to. Often, it's into a cul-de-sac, but this fresh spring morning is scattered with sunbeams, the sky is cyan, and she can bet the aquamarine ocean deeps are sending frothy waves to gently lap the golden sand.

On the beach, Flora takes a deep breath and lets it out with a contented sigh. She's right. The scene is exactly how she imagined it. And a bonus – just one dog walker and a flock of seagulls means she's practically got the beach to herself. From a sun-warmed rock, she sits and watches the waves roll in and out. Flora thinks their gentle shushing is having a soporific effect, as once or twice she finds her head nodding, or her chin resting on her chest. Must be the lack of sleep wondering about the library job. Thoughts of the library led to a flyer she saw in there last week, next to one about learning to dance, the same kind that she'd seen at the church hall. The flyer was all about pebble art – creating pictures from pebbles. There are hundreds of them all around her feet and she thinks she might as well collect a handful or two because she never knows when she might need them. Maybe the class would be something she could pursue, even if the dancing isn't.

As Flora collects pebbles, she thinks about the art college

she left behind so many years ago at Mother's insistence. Those arty types were apparently having a bad influence on her attitude, and what kind of a job would she hope to get with an art qualification anyway? Besides, she'd only be in such a job, if indeed one existed, for a few years until she met a suitable man and settled down. She'd have a brood of children and art school would have been a waste of time. After Mother had worn her down, she'd left art college and studied English literature instead. Mother said a job in a school would tide her over until she met Mr Right. The memory of Mr Right surfaces in front of her eyes as she looks at the wet, shiny pebbles in the palm of her hand. Her eyes try to copy the pebbles, so she shakes the memory away and walks back up the beach.

Another beautiful spring day. Rose turns her face to the sun and relishes the warmth on her skin and the smell of damp earth and fresh mint in the air. This is the day of planting her gorgeous array of spring flowers she got from the garden centre yesterday, and she bought rosemary and mint too. Since the 'wild garlic experience', as her mind is referring to it, her spirits still feel light and the melancholy and box-pondering that has been hanging around since she hung up her uniform seem to have, if not gone completely, certainly faded to her edges. When Rose thinks of the future, she sees possibilities, not dead ends. She's not entirely sure what the possibilities might be, but it's nice that they're in her field of vision.

The 'prim-noses' first, she decides, and a smile finds her lips as she picks up the container of blue and pink flowers from a little wooden table she found in the shed. Bella will love them when she and the family come for a visit. She stoops to pick up a trowel and from the corner of her eye, in the distance down the hill, she watches the figure of Hippy Lady get ever closer as she stomps along. The smile falters. After their not-so-friendly encounter last week, she's not sure she wants to chat, but if the woman's walking past, Rose can hardly ignore her, can she? Maybe she'll go back inside until she's gone. But that thought doesn't sit well. Rose has never been an avoider of people and she doesn't plan to start now. She'll just go about her business and acknowledge the woman with a wave. If she speaks, then fine. If she doesn't, also fine.

By the time Hippy Lady arrives at the gate, Rose has made a little hole in the border near the fence with the trowel, and aware of her presence, she straightens her back and turns to see that she's staring at her, arms folded, a frown creasing her forehead. In her stripy coat, she looks like a disgruntled zebra. A disgruntled zebra wearing yellow polka-dot baggy trousers.

'You're not thinking of putting those primroses there, are you?'

Nice opener. 'Hello. Well, yes. I was kind of thinking I would.' Rose's intention is to set a happy medium between sarcasm and dry humour, and she thinks she's pulled it off.

'They won't last long if you do.' Hippy Lady's tone is authoritative. She twists one side of her mouth to emphasise her point and nods at the primroses. 'Too shady, see. They need some sunshine.'

Rose notes a twinkle in her eyes the colour of acorns and says, 'Don't we all?'

The twinkle in her eyes becomes a glimmer and lines crease at their corners. 'Ha! You are correct!' Hippy Lady sticks out a hand and says through a wide grin, 'Where are my manners? Flora Granger, nice to meet you.'

This new demeanour transforms her whole face and Rose has to smile in return. It's difficult to square Flora's initial pompous attitude of today and the dismissive short shrift Rose received when she'd hurried past the cottage in the rain, with the now smiling lady in colourful flowing clothes and silver-and-pink hair. This is Rose's preference. The cheerful smile brings the whole ensemble together. 'Rose Lanyon. Likewise.'

'You giving the garden a spruce up, then?' Flora leans her elbows on the wall and nods at the plants on the table.

'Kind of. I'm hoping for a bit of a transformation.'

The frown again. 'I would argue it is either a transformation, or it's not. You can't really have "a bit" of one – the word means a radical change. Unless you plan to have one part of your garden radically transformed, and the rest left alone? Is that what you meant?'

She reminds Rose of one particularly pedantic English teacher who made her feel a bit stupid. An easy smile on her lips, she replies, 'No. You're right, of course. I did mean a radical transformation of *all* of it.' She's about to leave it there, as Flora's mouth is already opening again, but out of Rose's comes: 'I want my garden and everything in it to mean something – every flower, shrub and herb will be important. I've seen how nature can lift a spirit. When I was a young nurse, there was a lady near the end of her life who was pushed in her bed out into the hospital garden. I remember it was early summer; the birds were singing and all the flowers were out – the air was saturated with their perfume. The old lady's face became animated and she pointed to various plants and shrubs, naming each one. For a short time, she was transformed. The garden had done that. Lifted her out of her deathbed and connected her to nature ... to life.'

Well, Rose wasn't expecting that. She's not thought about that old lady for years, but the memory of her in the garden, and of the many others she's nursed, has visited her from time to time in the still quiet of a sleepless night. It's as if this particular memory has been waiting on the threshold of her consciousness to become a visual aid for her words. Flora nods and her warm smile elicits an uncomfortable knot in Rose's throat. This woman is a stranger; she can't allow herself to get emotional.

'Flowers, plants, herbs – all growing things are so important,' Flora says and leans a hip against the gate. 'It's a well-known scientific fact that they raise spirits. That colours, scents and tastes can invoke happiness and lift a mood. Some doctors have advocated various gardening activities, or walks in nature for people who are depressed.' She sniffs and shifts her weight to the other hip. 'Makes sense, if you ask me.'

'Me too.' Rose notes that Flora obviously finds standing for a length of time uncomfortable. Should she ask her in, or will she be dismissed, like the other day? Before she can decide, Flora's off again.

'I used to have a wonderful garden in my old house.' Flora folds her arms and stares at the primroses. 'My mother planted it and I tended it after she'd gone. "What I don't know about plants isn't worth knowing," she used to say.' An eye roll. 'Mother used to say that about everything, opinionated old bitch.' Flora attempts to lighten this statement with a tinkle of laughter, but fails. It's brittle and humourless. There's a silence which is hovering on the cusp of awkwardness, until she forces a smile. Rose can tell it's forced because her mouth looks like an overstretched rubber band. 'I must say, those primroses are a *gorgeous* colour.'

Glad of the change of topic, Rose says, 'Yes. They were my daughter Bella's favourite flower when she was a child. I'm reminded of those days each time I see them.'

'Indeed!' The rubber band assumes a more natural shape and the twinkle in the acorns return. 'Flowers can invoke such wonderful memories.'

'They can.' Rose picks up the tray of flowers and holds their delicate blooms to her nose. 'Planting these will be like making sure my memories never fade, as they'll pop back up each year, connecting me to happy times. As long as I have new life growing, there will always be hope and new memories to make.'

'Oh ... oh, that's lovely.'

When Rose looks up, she sees Flora pulling a tissue from her stripy pocket and dabbing the corners of her eyes. That catches Rose off guard. She doesn't seem the type to let her emotions show in front of strangers. *Neither do you, Rose, but here we are.* She finds the flowers have gone a bit blurry and she has to blink a few times and clear her throat. 'If you're not too busy, Flora, would you like to stay and have a cup of tea?'

More dabbing and a wobbly rubber band. 'That would be most welcome. Thank you.'

They sit opposite each other on the wooden garden bench, a table in between them in the shade of the old honeysuckle. It's gone rampant, clambering up and over the trellis on the back fence, as if trying to escape its earthly roots. Rose has been meaning to chop it right back, but now that she's going for a natural look, a less regimented approach to the green space, chopping it doesn't seem the right course of action. Flora notices her looking at the blooms – little yellow and white fists not yet unclenched, and says, 'I bet the scent of that is heavenly on warm summer nights.'

Rose imagines it is, but rarely has she taken the time to sit outside. There has always been something more pressing, or more likely something on TV. She promises herself that will change this summer. Too sheepish to admit this to Flora, she replies, 'Yes, I have always loved the scent of honeysuckle.' Rose pushes a plate of biscuits towards her. 'Another?'

'I shouldn't really, but it's not as though I haven't had some exercise today – and I'll be walking into town soon – so, yes I will, thanks.' Rose offers more tea, but she gets a shake of the head, and Flora's cheeks form pink apples. 'Better not … and I owe you an apology and an explanation for the other day.'

Rose thinks she knows what she's referring to, but an apology isn't necessary. 'Um … don't worry—'

'Thing is, when you called out to ask if I wanted a cuppa the other day, I was hurrying back from the café, where I'd had too much coffee, and then I got caught in the blasted rain, so my mood wasn't the best.' Flora's words pour out machine-gun style to the table, the sky, or the lawn. Rose's face is never in the line of fire. Flora's eyes flit away from hers like nervous birds. 'But the main thing was, I was dying for the loo, and knew if I'd stopped, I would have disgraced myself. Not the kind of thing you want to do on first meeting.' She laughs and this time it's less awkward. 'Or any meeting, come to that.'

'Don't give it a second th—'

'It's my age, you see – can't hold the water like I could. I'm seventy-seven.' A pause, just long enough for Rose to protest her youthful looks. 'That's nice of you to say.' Flora's apples have returned to normal and she heaves a sigh. 'I wanted to be honest with you, because I like you, and wouldn't want you to think me ill mannered.'

Rose thinks how refreshing it is to have someone say they like you right off the top. And despite Flora's prickly edges, Rose realises the feeling is mutual. Ill mannered – what an old-fashioned turn of phrase. Very proper, and again Rose is reminded of one of her old teachers. 'Thanks for being so honest, Flora, and nice of you to say you like me.' She wants to say the simple words – *I like you too.* But for reasons that escape her, she says instead, 'Love your direct approach. You remind me a bit of one of my schoolteachers. In a nice way, of course.'

Flora laughs. 'That's probably because I used to be one for more years than I care to remember!'

She talks about her teaching days, and while she does, a reason for Rose's reticence regarding letting Flora know she likes her, prods Rose in the back. It's not what we do, we British, is it? We aren't the gushing, no-holds-barred types. We tend to reserve judgement for later, certainly until we know people better. Or maybe it's just Rose. Time to change that, plot a new course – like she has for the honeysuckle. Let herself ramble where she pleases. Escape her earthly roots. Something Flora says brings her back to full concentration.

'Library job, did you say?'

'Yes. I was on my way there when I saw you in the garden. I'd set off from home, intending to go straight to the library, but my feet took me to the beach instead.' Flora rolls her eyes and scrabbles about in her hessian sack of a bag. 'Got these while I was there – what do you think?'

Rose looks at the two handfuls of sand-dusted pebbles she's showing her. Some are charcoal with white stripes, others are grey, some are the colour of wet sand. What's she supposed to make of those? 'Um, yes. Some are quite striking,' she offers, unsure what the knowing look and half-smile on Flora's face are about.

'I can tell you're wondering what I'm doing with these in my bag, eh?' The twinkle's back.

'Yes, I suppose I am.'

'Well, sorry to disappoint if you think they are all part of my eccentricity – but they aren't.' She holds the flat of her hand up to halt anything Rose might have to say. Luckily, she has nothing. 'Yes, I know people think me eccentric, and I'm happy with that label. But these pebbles are actually for an art class I'm planning to take. Pebble art – making pictures from them, you know?'

Rose kind of does, but not really. 'That will be nice.'

'Yes. I'm good at art. Saw the flyer for it at the library ... no, the church hall, and thought I might have a crack.'

Mention of the library leads Rose back to, 'You were talking earlier about a job at the library?'

'Yes. I applied a few days ago – part-time, obviously. A woman called Daisy was going to let me know, but she hasn't so far.'

Oh dear. Rose wonders if Daisy's comment on Facebook about finding the perfect person for the job means Flora hasn't been successful. It's doubtful she would have described Flora as perfect ... she's certainly interesting, but some would say she's an acquired taste. Rose's mobile phone rings, vibrating itself across the table top.

'Oh, those things make me jump!' Flora puts a hand to her chest. 'They're like little unexploded bombs going off.'

As Rose picks up her phone, she toys with the idea of pedantically pointing out that if they go off, then they aren't unexploded. But that would be facetious. Talk of the devil, it's Daisy. 'Hi there. No, nothing in particular. Just having a cuppa with a neighbour, Flora. We were talking about the library.' Rose emphasises her name, hoping that Daisy will put two and two together. There can't be that many Floras around these parts.

'Flora with the pink streak in her silver hair?' Daisy asks.

'The very same.' She looks away from her neighbour's laser stare. She's obviously twigged she's talking about her.

'Wonderful!'

'It is?'

'Yeah. Look, I'm in my car on the way to see you anyway, and I'm sure she won't mind if I join you. Oh, and can you put her on the phone?'

'Flora?'

'No. The Queen of Sheba.'

Rose sighs and hands the phone to Flora. 'It's Daisy from the library. We've known each other since school … she wants to talk to you.' Rose crosses her fingers and makes a wish. Surely Daisy wouldn't break bad news over the phone right now, would she?

Flora eyes the phone as though it really is an unexploded bomb and gingerly takes it between finger and thumb. 'Yes, this is she,' she says to the sky, wrinkling her nose and holding the phone too far away from her face … and upside down. Has she really not got one of her own? Rose corrects her mistake, and she can hear Daisy talking faintly as Flora's face lights up and the rubber band returns, impossibly and beautifully stretched from one ear to the other. 'I have! Oh my goodness, I'm thrilled. Thank you! I'd given up hope.' After a few seconds of quiet laughter, she hands over the phone and takes a deep breath. 'Apparently Daisy has been ringing my home phone for ages today. But of course, I've been out.'

'Congratulations! Daisy's coming over for a cuppa, so you'll meet her properly in a few minutes.'

'I know – she said.' Flora's cheeks turn back into apples. 'I'm quite overwhelmed, if I'm honest.'

'Three flowers. Rose, Flora and Daisy. How appropriate, as we're in a garden,' Flora says, as the three of them sit around a fresh pot of tea and a chocolate cake that Daisy has brought. She's also brought flowers. Yellow roses, their powerful scent and colour filling the kitchen with sunshine.

'Oh yes. How lovely. Rose and I were called "little flowers" at school by one of our teachers, years ago.'

Flora sniffs. 'A bit patronising, wasn't it?'

Daisy shrugs. 'It wasn't meant to be, but I can see how some might think it was.'

There's a bit of a lull while they ponder on this, punctuated by the clink of forks on ceramic as they eat cake. Rose notices Flora's eyes on the roses, a wistful expression on her face. Or is it longing? 'You said you used to have a lovely garden, Flora. Don't you have one now?' she asks.

'No. I have a few pots on the patio – that's all the space allows. Your garden is heavenly, and will be an Eden once you've put your new plans into place.'

Daisy is interested to know about Rose's new plans, and so she finds herself telling them both about the 'wild garlic experience', but she skims around the edges. It's personal, and if she shares, it will lose something. She's not mentioning Tristan either, or Daisy will never let it drop. So far Daisy's not said a word about him, and she was the one taking the photo, so she mustn't remember that he was there. Rose sketches out just the essence of the experience, and she's happy it's put a smile on both their faces.

'Plants are new life, and new life is hope. We need more of that these days.' Flora has the wistful look again.

Rose imagines her tending that big old garden of the past and measuring its beauty against a few patio pots. To Rose she seems like a free spirit, despite her proper turn of phrase and pedantry. Flora explained that age had made her move house, draw in her horns, and Rose can tell her spirit has been tamed by the situation. Restricted. So has her garden – reduced to pots on a patio. It makes her heart ache. 'You know we were talking about gardens and memories, Flora?'

'Yes.' She nods then turns to Daisy and puts her teacher's head on. 'Daisy, I was telling Rose about how therapeutic plants, gardens and all things growing can be. There have been studies – in fact it's a well-known scientific fact that they raise spirits. That colours, scents, tastes, can invoke happiness and lift a mood, put a person in touch with nature…'

Rose can tell Flora is going to ramble on, and what Rose is compelled to say will be left behind, its impetus lost if she doesn't interject: 'That's right, Flora. And memories can be awakened, revisited by looking at a familiar flower, or smelling its scent. You are most welcome to use my garden, Flora. Come and plant your memories with mine.'

The tissue comes out of the sleeve again and Daisy's eyes reflect the shimmer in Flora's. She says, 'Such uplifting ideas. Especially your wild garlic day and sharing memories and everything. You've convinced me to do a bit of pottering in my overgrown jungle now. I might contribute a memory to yours too.'

Flora dabs at her eyes. 'Wonderful. I'd love to plant a memory or two – thank you, Rose.' Her acorns fix on Rose earnestly. 'Do you know, I feel I might be starting to feel at home round here, at last. Now I have the library job, and have made two new friends.' She bobs her head as if in deference. 'Sorry, I know we've only just met, so perhaps I'm jumping the gun in the friendship stakes.'

Daisy and Rose both wave that away and Daisy says, 'Not at all. And we picked you for the job because we could tell you're used to talking to people, you're well read, and you have bags of confidence. Exactly what we need from you.'

'I'm sure you'll love working there,' Rose tells her.

Daisy leans towards Rose, a smile on her lips, and says, 'There's something we need from you too. I've not heard you sing for forty-odd years. Please give us a few notes of "Dreams", exactly as you did in the wood.'

'Eh? No. I don't think so. It's one thing to sing to the wild garlic and bluebells, all alone in a wood, but quite another to sing to an audience.'

Flora laughs. 'Well, I love garlic and I'm a bit wild. Tell me, have you met my friend Bluebell, here?' She points to a laughing Daisy, who's holding her hand out to shake Rose's.

This is not something Rose planned for and the thought of it makes her feel nervous, yet not uncomfortable. Part of her might like the idea, if she's honest. What could it hurt? This is the kind of thing people who don't have boxes do, she expects. Or the kind of people who used to have a box, but it doesn't fit them anymore. Recently, going with her instincts has led to good things.

Rose swallows the last of her tea, stands up, and sings.

Chapter Eight

Flora can't believe how quickly her life has changed over the last six weeks. Not only has she a new satisfying job, she's been to three pebble-art classes too. However, the biggest and most welcome change as a result of all this has been the new people she's met. Some, like Rose and Daisy, have become proper friends. Well, they feel like proper friends, anyway. Time will tell. A new 'almost friend' is the elderly gentleman who runs the class. James is an interesting character, and three years younger than herself, though he seems older. She suspects it's because he's quite serious in his approach to things. James rarely smiles, but is pleasant and informative. The only time he's really animated is when he's talking about art. Flora has decided that his seriousness has kept him in the 'almost a friend' camp, because she considers laughter and a carefree attitude an essential part of life. However, she does concede that sometimes the essential things are the hardest to achieve.

On a little easel by the patio doors, is a half-finished pebble picture. It's only small, but immeasurably huge in depth of feeling. So much emotion has gone into it, releasing long-imprisoned creative juices flowing through her fingers onto the canvas, urgent and insistent as blood through veins. Lots of people in her art class opted for beach scenes with little pebble-people holding hands at the shoreline, or walking pebble-dogs into a sunset. Flora painted an Eden – a flower garden. A kaleidoscope of colours, moving, clashing, shouting at each other, yet blending. What should have been irreconcilable differences of style, somehow work, nestling side by side against a turquoise sky, finding peace together under the shade of a vast pebble oak tree.

Flora traces her fingers across the as yet unoccupied canvas space to the left of the garden. Will she allow pebble people to inhabit it, or encourage more of nature to bloom untended? Enjoying the cool smoothness of a pebble seeping into her fingertips, she closes her eyes and thinks about it. Through the vertical blinds at the open door, the sun winks in, the movement of the breeze painting alternate hot and cool stripes on her face. Memories of another garden come unbidden, though not unwelcome. Laughter, the smell of honeysuckle, sweet peas, lilac and heavenly mock orange – a bouquet of summer picked at dawn and brought to her with love and hope. A face still heartbreakingly familiar after all these years fills her mind's eye, a constant smile, the silk touch of warm fingers threaded through her own, and a love binding them together as strong as willow roots. Yet not strong enough, as it turned out.

Flora opens her eyes and stares at the canvas. She will leave any decision about completing the picture until her mind is clear of the past. The present beckons and it's Thursday, which means library day. Another thought tags along behind her as she shrugs her yellow mac on and leaves the house. She still hasn't got round to planting a memory in Rose's garden, mainly because she couldn't decide on the right one. Flora knows exactly what it will be now, though. A mock orange will be perfect if there's room, in a quiet corner. Today's memory was filled with its scent.

Daisy's sitting in the middle of a group of primary school children when Flora arrives at the library. She has their full attention as she tells them about the importance of reading and books. The children are asking questions and saying what their favourite books and authors are. The impossibly young teacher sits to the side, a look of boredom on her elfin features, and she keeps stealing a sly glance at her phone. Maybe she and Daisy should swap jobs.

Flora takes a seat behind the desk and looks around to see who else is here this morning. A couple of elderly gents whispering to each other by the section on World War II books, and a woman, mid-sixties at a guess, sitting by the window at the table Flora used to occupy before she became a member of staff. Dark short curls peppered with grey, neat buttoned-up blue blouse, pressed brown trousers and shiny black lace-up shoes. Very shiny shoes, actually. The kind of shine on a shoe you only get with plenty of elbow grease, polish, a cloth and a shoe brush. Flora knows about these things. She can still remember the turpentine smell of shoe polish as she knelt on the cold kitchen flags of a morning, shining her school shoes. Her dad would come up behind her and always say the same thing: 'More elbow grease, young lady. I want to see your face in them.' Then he'd chuckle and add, 'We'll make a soldier of you yet.' Flora had adored her dad. She was devastated when he was taken far too young.

You'd rather it had been me, you mean? Mother's indignant voice pipes up.

'If the cap fits, Mother.'

'Sorry?' One of the elderly gentlemen had appeared from round the side of the counter.

'Oh, don't mind me. Just muttering to old ghosts.' The man looks at her askance, as well he might, and hands over his books to be scanned. Once again, she has to acknowledge that Mother is butting in more often since Flora's moved from her old home, despite her hopes that she would stay in Truro. Mother obviously disapproves of her new life, which gladdens her heart. It doesn't help in the long run, though, does it? Will she ever be completely free of her?

Flora stamps the man's card, and after he leaves, her eyes drift back to the woman reading by the window. She's got this nervous habit of pushing her tortoiseshell glasses back along the bridge of her nose with a forefinger, then wiggling them from side to side as they need adjusting, or her eyes do. Flora suspects she's not really absorbed in her book at all, but lost in thought, as she keeps cocking her head to the window and the warm sunlight, just as Flora used to when she'd sat there. Perhaps the woman secretly wants to be outside, but is unsure what to do when she is. It could be that she likes the quiet security of the reading space, a space where she's unlikely to be bothered by anyone. Or even that she's escaped here from a bullying husband, or relative, who makes unreasonable demands on her, and this is the one place she's free of them. Her safe place – her sanctuary.

There is a chance that Flora is making up stories where none exist. More than a chance, if truth be known, because she tends to do this. People-watching – making up imaginary lives for strangers. The woman might just be here having a quiet read and deliriously happy with her lot. After a few minutes, Flora thinks she might as well give the books a tidy, as apart from the school group with Daisy, and the woman by the window, there's not much else to keep her occupied. Daisy has done the orders and processed the new stock, so tidying is on the cards. Or on the shelves, to be exact.

Why do people shove books back on shelves higgledy-piggledy? How hard can it be to make sure they are placed back in an upright position next to the others? On a shelf near the woman at the window, Flora finds six books that are masquerading as the leaning tower of Pisa, so she grabs them and makes sure they are put back in the right order. As she turns back to the room, she notices the woman's cheeks are wet and she's dabbing at her eyes with a tissue. It could just be that the book she's reading has moved her in some way, and Flora should mind her own and go back to her desk. Trouble is, Flora isn't a minding her own and going back to her desk kind of person. If someone is distressed, then she will try to help. Always.

The chair makes no sound on the carpet as Flora pulls it out and sits down opposite the woman. The tissue quickly disappears into a pocket and the woman floats her watery hazel eyes across at Flora and then back to her book. She shifts in her chair and looks at Flora again, and her name badge, obviously discomfited by the impromptu appearance and unsure how to receive her.

'I hope you don't mind me interrupting your reading, but I couldn't help but notice you seem upset.'

A nod, as if answering an internal question, a push of the glasses along the bridge of her nose, and in a wavering voice, she replies, 'Don't mind me, I'm trying to distract myself by reading this book about horticulture, but I keep reading the same line, over and over.'

Flora waits, but as there's nothing else, she says, 'I tend to do that when I've a lot on my mind. The words don't go in, do they?' She threads a soft chuckle through her words, because that's what people do when they try to set others at ease – chuckle. Flora's not a chuckler, but it's a socially accepted thing to do, she's found.

'No. I always find this day difficult.' The woman looks directly at Flora and this time doesn't glance away.

Once again, Flora waits, but eventually has to fill the space with, 'Oh dear. Sorry to hear that.' Not Shakespeare, but better than nothing.

'Yes, my husband died five years ago today. He'd had a long struggle with cancer and it was a blessing in the end, as he was in so much...' The woman pulls the tissue back out of her pocket and flaps it in front of her face. A face which has turned pink, collapsed in on itself, twisted with grief.

Maybe minding your own would have been preferable to this, eh, Flora? You've made the woman even more upset now with your clumsy poking and prodding into her life.

Shut up, Mother!

'I'm so sorry. Is there anything I can do?' Flora doesn't recognise the small, sheepish little voice she's dribbled out into the still, quiet space between them. She was never great with raw grief like this. A sniffle and a few tears from the students at school she could cope with, but this kind of emotion is wild, uncontrollable. Naked. She notices the woman's eyes, full of tears, trying to focus on her name badge, so she adds, 'Please call me Flora.'

After a few moments, the woman heaves a juddering sigh and takes another tissue from her bag. 'Thank you for your kindness, Flora. But there's nothing anyone can do. I'll just have to grit my teeth, stop all this weeping and try to get through it.' A wobbly smile. 'My name's Louise, by the way.'

Louise looks so vulnerable, unloved and alone. Here she is, in her very shiny shoes, revealing her broken heart to a stranger. Well, she needn't be a stranger much longer, Flora thinks. 'Listen, Louise. If you're not busy this lunchtime, would you like to meet me at the café across the street for a bite?'

Louise raises her eyebrows and stutters out, 'I … I … I think you're very kind. But I'm sure you must have other things to be doing.'

'Nope. Nothing. I like meeting new people, as I haven't been in the area very long. It would be nice to share our stories.' Flora laughs and waves a hand at the bookshelves all around them. 'This is a lending library, after all – lots of stories here to share too.' A twitch of the lips is all she gets from Louise. Unsurprising, as it wasn't that funny. Maybe the twitch means that Louise can think of nothing worse than sharing lunch with an unfunny librarian, and is frantically trying to think of an excuse. Flora's wondering how to put her out of her misery when she replies:

'Well, if you're sure, that would be lovely.'

It would? 'Great. That's a date, then.' Flora's stomach plummets almost as fast as Louise's smile disappears. What a stupid remark. 'Not a romantic date, of course.' She follows that with a high-pitched embarrassed giggle, which was supposed to be a chuckle. Louise seems unfazed, however, and takes up her book, bag and jacket.

'I'll be off, then, when I've got my book stamped. What time shall we say?' she says over her shoulder as she walks to the reception desk.

'About 1pm?' Flora smiles as she scans the book and stamps Louise's card. Things feel much more relaxed between them now.

'Okay. See you then, Flora.'

At the café, after Flora has shared her story – well, the introduction and a few background chapters – Louise reciprocates. She was born in Padstow to a cleaner and a fisherman, has two older brothers, and the family never ventured further than Plymouth to visit relatives. Matthew was her first and only love. They met at a village dance when they were sixteen and afterwards it was 'only ever us', as she described their childless marriage. They were incredibly happy together, nevertheless, and he left a huge hole in her life when he died. Flora can hardly bear to look into Louise's doleful eyes. Though her story was very different, there had been a similar-shaped hole in her life many years ago. A hole that she'd plastered over with endless years of dedicated teaching, busy weekend outings and a plethora of activities to fill her empty evenings.

Flora has never allowed anyone to see that hole, that empty space that still refuses to be filled on long dark nights, or sometimes, even in bright sunny gardens surrounded by the memory of a heavenly bouquet. The well-rehearsed lies trip off her tongue whenever required, as they did for Louise today, and if she tries very hard, Flora can pretend that it's all true. Almost. 'No, I never met the right one, and I was far too busy with my career. No, I'm never lonely – I love my own company.'

The lies are rarely met with pity and disbelief, though

there have been some who have responded that way. Normally, people say what a strong character she is, and how they envy her ability to do exactly as she pleases, without having to get agreement from a partner. It must be liberating to be her, and so forth. And they're right, mostly. She has friends, a job, a new home and a community to involve herself with – though she still feels a bit of an outsider at times, if she's honest. It was a big step to uproot and move, after so long living in one place, one house. Albeit a house that was never a home, until Mother had gone. But it's true that she has freedom and money to do as she wishes. There are times, though, when she peeps through the crumbling plaster around the hole at what might have been and longs for lost things.

'Do you want another cup of tea, Flora?' Louise has developed a deep frown line between her eyebrows and Flora realises she's been miles away.

'No thanks. I'll be running to the loo all afternoon if I do.' Louise looks a bit crestfallen, but Flora's lunch break will be over in just over ten minutes. 'Sorry, you were talking about not being able to have children.'

'Yes. As I said, the realisation of that was very painful in my youth, and it would have been nice to have the comfort of children, now Matthew's gone. But we can't have everything, can we?'

Flora thinks it might be best to change the subject, as Louise looks ready to cry again. 'I guess we can't. And you said you worked in a shoe shop?'

'Yes, nearly forty years.' Louise lifts her foot and examines the shiny black surface of her shoe. 'You can tell a lot about a person from their shoes, I find. And feet. I learned so much about someone's life as soon as they took off their shoes. The way they stand, the bunions, and some ladies wear no tights, so you can see the neglected toenails and dry, hard skin. Some people don't moisturise at all. If they don't make time to take care of their feet, it means they don't realise their value. Imagine where we'd be without them?' Louise stares at Flora intently and gives a slow blink.

My goodness, that's deep. Louise is earnestly serious too, and Flora wonders if maybe that's the reason why Louise doesn't have many friends. Perhaps Flora could teach her to be more upbeat, take life with more levity. Recently, Flora remembers that she missed being someone who people could depend on, learn from, being someone's point of reference, and that right now, she's a bit like a lighthouse without a light. Could she be Louise's light?

'Yes, we'd be hopeless without our feet, that's true.' Flora smiles. That's a sentence she didn't expect to be saying. 'What was your husband's job?' She hopes he wasn't a chiropodist, or she had nowhere to go.

Louise taps her fingers on the library book about horticulture. 'He was a gardener at a National Trust house. The flowers were a substitute for children, really. Matthew adored them – grew them from seed, tended them, protected them from weeds...' She sniffs and swallows the last mouthful of tea.

An idea was growing in Flora's mind and sending out shoots of possibility. 'Tell me, Louise. Do you have a garden of your own?'

'No. I have a few pots, but I sold our old house with the

garden a year after Matthew...' The tissue is out again. 'Couldn't bear to live in it without him – too painful. He was everywhere I looked. Must admit, I really miss the garden.'

Flora pats her hand. 'Well, I might just have the solution.'

Chapter Nine

S ally tries on three outfits, looks at her reflection in the mirror and then shoves them all back in the wardrobe. One doesn't even make it back onto the hanger. The bloody skirt is too tight. She bundles it into a ball and hurls it across the room in anger. Damn it all. She's only going to the pub with a friend, so what does it matter? It shouldn't matter. But it does. It matters, because each time she looks at herself in the mirror, she's filled with self-loathing. Self-loathing that comes from Paul's voice whispering in her ear when she notices her stomach stretching the fabric, or the bulges that appear between her underarm and the elastic strap of her bra.

'You've let yourself go.'

'You can't go out looking like that.'

'A strict diet for you, Sal.'

'Your hair could do with styling. And get some decent make-up, for God's sake. Your complexion looks so sallow.'

These are all things he had said to her in the past, and

worse. At the time, he argued that it was for her own self-esteem. He wanted her to feel good about herself, as she knew full well that would help build her confidence. Sally closes her eyes and sits on the bed, his fake concerned voice wheedling in her ears like the whine of a mosquito.

'You've always struggled with confidence, love, so looking like a sack of shit will make you feel worse. Remember how gorgeous you were when we met? You need to be that woman again. You can do it – I'll help you.' Then he would drop a patronising little kiss on her forehead and ask where his dinner was, or had she remembered to do his dry cleaning? Sometimes she had felt more like a servant than a wife. A Cinderella who never went to the ball.

Sally's on the edge of tears now, but she can't cry, because she'll ruin her mascara. Why did she let Paul bully her all those years? Why did she just take it? Try her best to please him, make him happy? She realises now (too late) that no matter what she did, she never made him happy. And what about her own happiness? Years of trying to accommodate him at great personal expense. Jumping through impossible hoops, practically starving herself to make sure she looked good enough for him. Humiliation and hot shame flood through her. Even though he's gone, he's still there behind her – the puppet-master pulling her strings. The evening out is ruined now, before it's even started. Why even bother?

Before the mirror again, in her underwear, Sally does her breathing exercises and grits her teeth. More than once over the past while, she's drawn strength from her old friend

Rose. Not that Sally's actually seen her since she left the surgery, even though she keeps meaning to call, but she often finds herself thinking, what would Rose say or do? How would Rose cope with this or that situation? Rose wore calm and compassion like another uniform, but she was totally oblivious to it and unaware how much help she's been to Sally over the years. Sometimes a wise word from her or a little praise had meant all the difference. Despair had been turned into determination. Because of Rose's actions, Sally realised she wasn't a waste of space or a complete failure. Trouble was, she didn't believe it for long, because Paul's will was stronger. Nevertheless, she reminds herself that she made it through somehow, and remembering Rose's kind words, she'll try her best to continue to do so.

The crumpled brightly coloured skirt sits on the carpet like a grounded butterfly. Sally used to be a butterfly years ago. Light, carefree, enjoying life. Before she met Paul. A lump of emotion builds in her throat and she asks – *What would Rose do?* Would she make an excuse and stay home, or go out and try to have fun? She knows the answer even before she asks it. She smiles at her reflection, despite her imperfections. The smile looks unsure – wobbly, but it's there. The round of her stomach under her hand isn't going to stop her meeting a friend, nor the dimples in her thighs. So what if she can't fit into her old clothes? Is there any wonder she's been comfort eating, with everything she's had to put up with? Sally pulls out jeans and a smartish T-shirt and blots a few smudges of mascara from under her eyes. The thought of going out and pretending that things are fine is the last thing she wants to do. But she'll go anyway. That's what Rose would do.

The honeysuckle is heavy with moisture from a recent shower. Rose gently shakes the raindrops from a lemon-and-white bloom and inhales its fragrance. Heaven. Barefoot in the grass, she turns in a circle, looking at the riot of colour exploding from every corner and crevice of her hitherto regimented garden. No matter how tired, fed up or indifferent she might be feeling, a few minutes in this space has joy powering through her like sap through a stem – reviving, rejuvenating and filling her with energy. Quite magical. At the end of the garden, she looks over the fence down the hill to where a tiny smudge of ocean peeps back from the steep cradle of the rocky headland. Across the rain-washed blue sky the rainbow fingers of twilight trace a sleepy path for an early star to follow and she takes a big gulp of salt air.

Flora and Daisy are coming over with their memory plants, and they'll have a glass of wine and nibbles to celebrate. She turns from the view, the cloth in her hand reminding her why she came out here in the first place. It was to make sure the wrought-iron garden table and chairs were completely dry. As she wipes, Rose thinks about Bella and the family and how excited she is that they will be here next week. Though she hadn't got round to putting brush to canvas since finding the old paint palette in the loft, she hopes her daughter will be thrilled to see it again. Maybe she could even be persuaded to dabble while she's here. The grandchildren would love it, she's sure. Flora might even help. She's always talking about the pebble-art classes she attends. It's incredible how quickly Rose has begun to see her as a friend. It's as though they have always known each other.

Just as she finishes, the garden gate clicks open and in Flora walks, a vision in a sparkly silver-and-denim jacket over a pink jumpsuit. And on her feet – leopard-spotted pumps. Immediately, Rose gives her a big smile. Like the garden, Flora always raises her spirits. Flora has in her arms a small shrub sporting lots of green leaves and delicate white flowers, most in bud, dotted around them like confetti. 'Evening!' she says and holds the shrub up to Rose's nose. 'Have a whiff of that. The scent will be stronger once it's established and bigger, but you can already tell how gorgeous it will be.'

'So, this is the memory plant you were telling me you'd chosen?' Rose sniffs an open flower and catches a faint scent similar to jasmine, but not as strong.

'Yes. Do you know what it is?'

She shakes her head. 'I only know certain plants by name. Wish I'd listened more carefully when my gran used to point them out to me. But I'm learning all the time.'

'It's a *Philadelphus* or mock orange, to give it its common name.' Flora looks wistful. 'When I've had a drink or two, I'll tell you why I picked it. I feel it's time to share.' She gives a theatrical shudder. 'Much as I hate all that bearing of souls malarkey, something is insisting I must.'

Rose is about to ask why when a car door slams behind

them and they turn to see Daisy waving goodbye to her husband, who's dropped her outside the gate. 'Hello, you two! It's Daisy with daisies! Ready to plant some memories?' She bends and picks up a beautiful tall willowy plant resplendent with huge daisy-type flowers.

'Oxeye daisy. How glorious,' Flora says. 'It's blooming early too.'

Daisy laughs and looks at her watch. 'You said get here for seven-ish, I'm not that early.'

Flora looks puzzled and then realises Daisy's made a joke. 'Ah, yes. Very funny.'

Daisy walks down the path and sets her daisies next to Flora's *Philadelphus*. 'Oh, I love those.' She crouches and sniffs at a flower. 'Such a lovely scent.'

Rose is beginning to realise she's bottom of the class where flower recognition is concerned. Never mind, the main thing is the development of her garden, being close to nature and enjoying the feeling that growing things gives us. The memories too. Thinking of which. 'We won't plant these tonight, obviously, but you can decide where you think they will be best suited. Then you can either plant them in the next few days, or I can do it for you.'

'Yeah, feel free to plant the daisies. My dad said I should be called Daisy after them. He said I was bright and beautiful, and I'd be tall. I reckon they'll be best by the gate, nodding at people as they pass, in remembrance of my dad, who loved a good old chat to folk.' Daisy smiles, and Rose notices her glance at Flora, as if seeking confirmation.

'What a lovely way to remember him. And a good spot, yes.' Flora taps her chin with her fingertips and scans the garden. 'Now … I think my Phil would like to live near the honeysuckle, but not too near. Maybe by the back wall?'

'Sounds good to me,' Rose says, as if she knows what she's talking about. 'Okay, who's for a glass of wine and a chin wag?'

The wagging of chins starts as they walk to the kitchen to collect the nibbles and glasses. Mostly it's Flora and Daisy talking about work, but as they gather around the table outside, Flora raises her glass and says, 'Here's to the garden of memories, good friends, and good wine.'

They clink glasses, and Daisy sighs. 'This is perfect.' She puts her hand on Rose's arm. 'I'm so pleased you're more like your old self again, Rose. In fact, better than your old self.'

Her old self? What exactly was that? The concept of fitting into boxes seems relevant now, so she answers, 'Yes. I have decided not to be my old self anymore. I'm my new self. Since I stepped out of the comfort of my nursing box recently, the world seemed a bit scary, a bit alien, if you like. Then I remembered my young self because of the wild garlic experience, and realised boxes are traps we fall into – or maybe we're wilfully put into them by others. Maybe they feel safer around you when you're in a socially accepted box.'

Flora and Daisy are wearing identical frowns, and Rose bites her lip to prevent a giggle escaping. 'What boxes?' Daisy asks.

'Well, you know the phrase – think outside the box?' Before she can continue, Flora jumps in.

'Yes, but that means thinking in an original way –

outside the norms, values and traditions of society. Problem-solving in a creative way, even.'

She's using her schoolteacher voice which, Rose has to admit, can get a bit wearing. 'I *know* what it means, Flora. But when I left my job, I began to think about my life and where I was going to go next. People expected certain things of me.' She sneaks a glance at Daisy. 'For instance, horse riding, amongst other things, was seen as something I certainly wouldn't be doing. I decided I needed to think outside the box. Then I realised we all have our own personal boxes.' If Daisy frowns any deeper, her eyes will disappear. 'Do we create them ourselves, or as I just said, are we put into them? Are they created by others – are we weighed, measured up for them because of how we look, how we act, what job we do, our age? Things like that.'

'Hell's bells, that's deep.' Daisy knocks back her wine and holds her glass out for more. 'I remember you were on about boxes when I came round the day after you left work, too.' Daisy shakes her head as though she thinks Rose has become a bit obsessed. Maybe she has.

Rose pours her another glass and looks at Flora, who's staring into space, a half-smile on her face. 'You know, Rose, you've just described what happened to me when I was about your age. I completely dumped my box. I ripped it up and started again. But it wasn't really until now that I knew that I had – so thanks for that.' Flora finishes her wine and Rose refills her glass. 'Thing is, I have a new box. You're right, people put you in them very soon after meeting you. Or even before – maybe on first sight. I'm the ancient hippy with ridiculous hair, who can be a bit pompous and suffers no fools.'

Rose can't meet her eye as she thinks of the moniker, Hippy Lady.

'I kind of like it, because some of it is true, but I'm so much more than that. We all are.' She takes a big swig of wine. 'But can we ever truly escape our boxes?'

'Hmm, not sure.' Rose pours more wine for herself and considers this. It's not something she's really thought through. Her first job was to ditch the old box, but won't the new box be just as restrictive? Then she has a brainwave. 'Thing is, if we keep changing what we do, be more impulsive, do things we aren't expected to do, surely our boxes will have to change along with us. So maybe we will have a long string of boxes ... or maybe, just as people are happy with the one they've made for us, we can leap out of it and surprise them.' She does jazz hands. 'Ta da!'

Daisy laughs. 'Well, I think you belong in a crazy box right now. What does it matter what people think of you, anyway?'

'It doesn't really. I'm beginning to realise that at last. I suppose doing different things, and being a different me is my goal right now. I want to feel like I did in the woods that day, as much as I possibly can. This garden is helping so much too. I want to feel that anything is possible – that the world is there for the taking.' All true, but she keeps to herself that she sometimes still wakes at night thinking Glen is beside her, and for a few seconds the shock of losing him is like a punch in the gut.

'Hear, hear,' Flora says quietly, fixing Rose with an intense stare. 'Time to share my story, if you want to listen. No idea why I feel I must, as I said before. I think it has something to do with this magical garden of yours, Rose.' She looks at her *Philadelphus* and takes a breath of the evening air.

'We're all ears,' Daisy says, grabbing a handful of crisps.

'Maybe you're influenced by all the new spring buds and shoots popping up. Leaving the old growth behind. They are encouraging you to push your boundaries,' Rose tells her.

'You might be right.' Flora smiles and takes another deep breath. 'Okay. Here goes.'

Chapter Ten

Now that Daisy and Rose are looking at her expectantly, as if they've come to watch a play at the theatre, what had seemed a good idea a moment ago, seems to Flora like the silliest notion ever. Rose's talk of boxes and rejecting other people's narrow views of oneself, coupled with the view that anything is possible, the magical garden, the warm atmosphere and the wine (let's not forget that), had encouraged Flora to allow them to look through the hole into her past. Allow the plaster to crumble at last and to share what she's never divulged to anyone else. Surely it's time? So here they are waiting, and here she is, saying nothing. The quiet garden feels like it's waiting too, but all she can do is sit there with stage fright, thinking of how to begin. Or if, indeed, she should. Why share now after all this time? Isn't it better to keep the past behind her?

A seagull swoops low overhead, screeching as it wheels towards the ocean, startling them all. They laugh, seemingly relieved that the bird has broken what was becoming an awkward atmosphere. Then before Mother can think of a way to stop her, Flora says:

'I had an extremely domineering mother, my dad died when I was ten, and once he'd gone, she had free rein. Before, Dad would often temper her controlling behaviour where I was concerned, but I'd lost my protector. I felt like a snail ripped from its shell. My soft, plump body waiting to be run through by her sharp beak. I was never allowed to have fun, spread my wings or even speak without being spoken to in public. It felt more like the 1850s, not the 1950s. Then, when I was a young woman, I met a boy at the library, which was the only place I was ever allowed to go to on my own, really. I certainly wasn't permitted to go to the village dance like the other girls.'

Flora pauses and looks at the sky, happy that she's made a start and glad that she wants to continue, but for now, she needs a breather and some inspiration. Daisy sighs and crunches into more crisps, which sounds like an avalanche in the quiet of the garden. Flora notices Rose shoot her a *Be quiet, for God's sake* look. Daisy's eyes flash back a *What's your problem?* and Rose gives a disparaging shake of the head and says:

'Sounds like a tough start, Flora. What happened with the boy?'

The boy. The glorious boy. Suddenly, Flora is holding hands with him again in the scented garden on a summer evening, for a few moments, lost in the past. Then she looks at them both, feeling as if they've woken her from a deep sleep. 'Hmm? Oh, everything. Patrick was my moon, my stars, my sun – the air that I breathed. He was my one true love ... my only true love. But it all came to nothing in the end. Mother made sure of that.'

Daisy and Rose share a look of anguish. Poor Flora. 'That's awful. Why?' Daisy prompts gently. She's stopped crunching her crisps and has her hands clasped around the bowl of her wine glass.

'Because she was an evil old bitch. She wanted me kept at home, fetching, carrying, running errands for her.' Anger at her mother's remembered cruelty builds inside. 'If I had got married to Patrick, she'd have lost all that. Most importantly, she'd have lost her power – her identity as top dog. She was only happy if she was bossing someone around. She had bossed Dad the best she could, and he'd had the audacity to die on her. She couldn't lose me too.'

Once again there's a pause while Flora calms herself and watches past scenes drift before her eyes on the ragged dark clouds stretching across the sky. 'Patrick was so handsome. He worked part time in the library, like me now.' A smile quirks her lips and she nods at Daisy. 'He was a year older than me and he was off to university in Exeter at the end of the summer. The library work was to put a bit of money by before he left. We got talking about books, the classics, all sorts, really. I was captivated by his calm grey-green eyes, like the depths of the ocean on a cloudy day. He had wavy dark hair and an infectious laugh. The librarian in charge used to look over the top of her glasses at him and tut when he laughed too loudly.' Flora takes a drink to stop the choking sensation in her throat. She releases a breath and continues.

'After a few conversations there, he asked me to go to

the local café with him, and I so wanted to, but I knew it would be impossible. If we were seen, it would get back to Mother and she'd lock me away forever. Boys were to be avoided at all costs, didn't I know? They only wanted one thing, and then they'd leave me in the family way. She told me that if I ever got pregnant, she'd throw me on the streets and disown me. I was to wait until I was at least twenty-one before she'd countenance a gentleman caller.'

'Blimey! I was married when I was twenty-one.' Daisy gulps some wine and starts on the crisps again.

'Quite. Mother had unrealistic expectations. But as I said, she couldn't afford to lose me, that's where it all stemmed from.' Flora checks her watch and feels sheepish. Are her friends really interested? Maybe they're just being polite and want her to cut to the chase. 'Sorry, I'm rambling on. Are you sure you want to hear my tale of woe? I decided to do the "sharing" thing without asking. How very like my mother.'

'Pah!' Daisy says. 'You're as much like your mother as my arse ... in fact, my arse is probably a good description of her!'

This has them all laughing and breaks the tense atmosphere a little. 'Of course, we want to hear your story, Flora. I want to know what happened between you and Patrick,' Rose tells her, squeezing her hand.

Flora can tell she's genuine. Rose cares, they both do. They want to know it all, and she's ready to tell them. Nothing could make her stop now, anyway. It's as though there's a weight inside her that's melting away, little by little.

A weight that she's carried for most of her life. She smiles at them and releases another breath. 'Right-ho. Despite the risk of being found out, we met at the café the following week, on Patrick's day off. From then on, I told Mother I was going to the library, and it worked so well for a few months. I fell head over heels in love with him, even though we'd only held hands and he'd sometimes kiss me chastely on the cheek when we walked the woodland path on the way to my house after the café. He didn't come anywhere near my house, of course. I'd confided in him about Mother by then, and he understood, but he felt sad and sorry for me.

'The time was fast approaching when he had to start getting ready to leave for university. We'd agreed to meet on the path in the early morning to avoid being seen, as he said he had something he wanted to ask, and it wouldn't be a good place to ask me in the café.' Flora blinks away tears and downs her second glass. 'I'll never forget the sight of Patrick bouncing along towards me, the sun in his hair, smartly dressed in a suit and tie with this … this…' She takes a moment, and Flora can't look at Daisy, because she can hear her sniffing. 'This beautiful bouquet of hand-picked flowers.' She nods at the *Philadelphus*. 'It had lots of that in it and the scent was heavenly. To my utter astonishment, he stopped in front of me, dropped to one knee and asked me to marry him.' Flora flings her hands up. 'Just like that! I was so shocked, I could only stare open-mouthed for what seemed like hours. Then he pulled a ring box out of his pocket and presented me with a diamond solitaire.'

'Wow. How romantic,' Daisy says and sniffs again. Rose hands her a tissue and finds one for herself.

Flora smiles even as tears trickle down her cheeks. She can see Patrick as clearly as if he is standing there in the garden before her right now. 'It was. Very. I said yes, of course, and we had our first proper kiss. I had no idea if I was doing it right, but it felt right and that was the main thing. We sat in the grass, held hands, kissed and talked of the future. I would wait for him, then once he'd finished his three-year English course, he planned to teach and we'd get married. But as you might have guessed, Mother had other ideas.'

The pain of the memory stops Flora in her tracks and she can't decide whether the cold creeping through her is from the past or the present. It's probably both. She looks at the sky. Night is drawing a curtain across the last few vestiges of light and pulling a chill wind behind it.

Rose scowls and rubs her arms briskly. 'I bet she did. I'm so sorry you had such an awful experience, Flora.' Then she blinks away tears, stands and picks up the empty dishes. 'Okay. I think we'd be warmer listening to the rest inside, don't you, girls?'

Soon they're sitting in the living room, each with a blanket over their knees and a full glass of wine in their hands. Flora suspects her head will suffer tomorrow, but this sad story calls for wine. After a few moments, when she's collected herself, she picks up her thread.

'So, silly old me runs back home, stupidly thinking Mother might be pleased for me, because I was getting married, wasn't I? I'd be a respected married woman, not just going out with any old boy. I was so excited and bursting with joy as I thrust my beautiful engagement ring under her nose, babbling like a brook all about Patrick, how I met him and our plans for the future. My excitement came to an abrupt halt as I watched her face grow stony and her eyes burn in anger. Then … then she pulled her hand back and brought it down hard across my cheek.' Flora's fingers fly trembling momentarily to her left cheek as she relives the scene, and she swallows hard.

Daisy half-stands to give her a hug, but Flora flaps her away. 'I need to get through this, and if you comfort me, I'll be in bits.' She acknowledges Daisy's gesture with a nod and a smile. 'Thanks all the same, you're very kind.'

'Give yourself a minute. Take a deep breath, and release it slowly,' Rose says.

Flora does as she suggests and sets her jaw, determined to get through it. She must. 'I'd never heard language like it. Well, I have now. But in those days people didn't swear much, certainly not women. The names she called me. Told me I was a common trollop, a whore who had the morals of the gutter. Mother went completely out of control. I could do nothing but cry as she pulled two of my new dresses out of my wardrobe and tore them to shreds. Then she told me if I ever saw Patrick again, she'd set fire to my savings that she kept under lock and key. She also said she'd throw me out and tell everyone the reason was that I'd been whoring around.' There's a second's pause as her words sink in.

'Oh my God,' Daisy says. 'That's appalling!'

'Vile,' Rose agrees. 'I can hardly believe my ears. How could a mother be so cruel to her own flesh and blood?'

Flora exhales and slumps in her chair. The effort of parting with these memories is exhausting her. 'Vile is right. Mother made me give her my ring and when Patrick came round the next day to meet Mother, as we'd arranged, she made me stay upstairs. She gave him the ring back and told him never to come there again, or she'd tell everyone that he'd forced himself on me. Patrick was furious and demanded to see me, so she rushed upstairs and told me to tell him I'd made a mistake and I didn't want to marry him – or I would suffer the consequences. She more or less pushed me downstairs and stood there beside me while I obediently parroted her instructions.' Flora shakes her head. 'I hated her so much.'

'Oh no! Couldn't you have found help from someone? An aunt, a friend?' Daisy asks.

'No relatives … and I had no friends, really. Mother's doing, once again. It felt hopeless. It *was* hopeless back then. I would have had nowhere to go, no money, and a sullied reputation. Patrick had no money to speak of either. Maybe we could have eloped, but it would have been impossible to make ends meet. Yes, he could have got a job, so could I, but he was about to start university, had great prospects. I couldn't rob him of that.'

'What about his parents?' Rose asked. 'Could you have stayed with them for a while?'

'It wasn't the done thing. I hadn't even met them because I was worried Mother would somehow find out.

No. I doubt very much that they would have taken me in. And if we'd eloped, they might have resented me putting a stop to Patrick's education.' Flora shakes her head as she realises she's making excuses for herself, even after all this time. *Time to tell it as it was, Flora. All of it.*

'But maybe they wouldn't have. Maybe they would have understood, might have come to our rescue if I'd tried. But I didn't – I was too weak. Too completely cowed by Mother's controlling behaviour. All I felt was the fear of what she'd do to me if I went against her. I let the love of my life walk away, even though he begged me to come with him. He told me he knew I was under duress when I said I didn't want him, and that he'd be back. I insisted I never wanted to see him again. Became quite hysterical. He eventually left. That night, when Mother was asleep, I ran to the back of the shed where I'd hidden the bouquet, hugged it to my chest and sobbed my heart out.'

Flora covers her face with her hands and hangs her head. She can't cry, can't do anything. She just sits still and rigid, like a statue of despair. A moment later she looks up in time to see Daisy and Rose pass a glance of sadness back and forth. Getting to her feet, Rose places a gentle hand on Flora's shoulder. 'Would you like a cup of tea, love?'

Flora lets her hands fall and feels a wobbly smile on her lips. 'The British cure for all ills, eh?'

'It is.'

'Yes, please. I think I've had enough alcohol for one evening.'

'I think we all have.' Daisy drains her glass and gives Flora a sympathetic smile. 'What an awful time for you,

Flora. Did you ever see him again, or find out what had happened to him?'

'Yes. Patrick came back every week for three weeks. I refused to see him and Mother said if he came back a fourth time, she would make good on her threat. He must have got the message. The last time I saw him, he was walking away from our house, shoulders slumped, a totally dejected air clinging to him like a second skin. As I said, Mother had reduced me as a person. Controlled me so much that I felt I had no other option than to let him go. To obey her. Since those times I've met women who have been in controlling relationships, who have been given a lifeline, but haven't taken it. They were too conditioned, too scared to. And so was I. I let my lifeline, my Patrick, walk away.'

Flora looks away from the pity in her friends' eyes. She has to finish this. 'When I was allowed back out into the world, weeks later, I asked after him in the library. As I expected, he'd gone to university. Years later, when I was a teacher, I was in conversation with a friend of a friend, also a teacher. His name came up, as she'd taught with him at some point. He was married and had three children. I'm so glad he found happiness.'

There's a welcome quiet time when they're alone with their thoughts, while Rose makes the tea and brings in a mug for each of them. She asks, 'Did you ever find happiness with anyone else, Flora?'

'No one else. A few dalliances, as Mother would call them, but nobody made me feel the way Patrick did. But yes, I found happiness in my work and after Mother died, I broke out of my box. Retired. Went a bit mad. And so far, I've had seventeen years of total freedom!'

'That's wonderful. What did you do?' Daisy wonders.

'I grew my hair, put dye in it, wore outrageous colours that didn't match, pierced my ears, got a tattoo of a magpie on my arse, because Mother hated them. Said they were harbingers of doom!' Flora laughs and enjoys the new lightness in her chest that now has room to expand. 'I actively tried to be everything that was the opposite of my mother. I travelled, did new things, met new people. Went out of my way to help people and be kind. But mostly, I laughed a lot and had real fun for the first time since Patrick.' She cocks her head at her two friends as a thought comes to her. 'It's so good to laugh, don't you think? To really live in the moment, allow joy to surge through your whole being at the sight of a flower, a rainbow, or the ocean on a stormy day. Not being afraid to openly delight in the fact that you're well, vital and alive.'

Rose makes a choking sound which is a cross between a giggle and a sob. 'Yes! My heart's thumping in my chest and I'm coming over all emotional! Dear Flora. You're such an inspiring woman. To overcome such a plague of adversity after so many long years, and to manage to start afresh with such gusto is incredible.'

Flora's face feels hot, and the weight of the past having been shed, allows the lightness in her chest to spread through her whole body. 'Thank you for saying so, Rose. You wouldn't believe how much better I feel for telling you both about Patrick. It was a big thing to share for me.'

'It certainly was. And I totally agree, Flora. Laughing is

so important, as is enjoying the little things. The little things that are actually the big things, though we don't always realise it at the time. I do realise it just at the minute, for instance. I'm thinking, "Rose, be quiet, before you go over the top." But Glen's twinkly eyes seem to be urging me on from his photo on the shelf over there, so I'll carry on. Flora, you're a real inspiration, and I'm so pleased you're my friend.' Rose laughs and turns pink. 'Goodness. How unlike me to be so open with people I haven't known for a hundred years. It feels great, though, and I'm glad.'

'Me too,' Daisy says, patting Flora's knee.

'Thank you both so much.' Flora is thrilled by Rose's words, and right now feels like she's making a positive impact in her new friends' lives. Maybe she has the makings of a lighthouse. Thinking of which, she holds up a finger. 'Now. I almost forgot. I met a woman called Louise at the library the other day. She's a widow, very lonely, though wouldn't admit it – she's the sort to keep everything bottled up. She confided in me. But she mainly soldiers on and so forth. A bit like us all, I suppose. I'm not a great sharer. Or I wasn't, until I met you both and became a happy little bloom in your magical garden, Rose. Would you mind very much if I brought her up here one time? Her husband used to be a gardener for the National Trust and she reads books on horticulture.'

'Not at all,' Rose says. 'We need all the help we can get, making this garden the best it can be.' She picks up the photo of her husband, Glen, and smiles at him. 'I've a feeling that if we do, it will make us the best we can be, too.'

Flora claps her hands. 'Marvellous! Now, dear Rose. Can

you do one more thing for us before I drag my carcass down the hill to bed?'

'What's that?'

'Sing.'

Daisy winks at Flora. 'What a great idea. I request "Bridge Over Troubled Water".'

Rose looks as though she's going to say that she can't possibly, but instead says, 'Okay. Your wish is my command.'

Chapter Eleven

A few days later, a memory of Glen, proudly revealing a majestic blue agapanthus flower, seeds itself through the remnants of Rose's dream. Still drowsy with sleep, she smiles as she thinks about how much Glen loved agapanthus; he called them Aggies. Or sometimes when he was in a silly mood, Madame Agatha Panthers. He had a particularly grand specimen in a pot, and Rose remembers how exotic and beautiful it was. What on earth happened to that plant? She plumps her pillow and closes her eyes, trying to think. Maybe it died, because she couldn't imagine Glen would have got rid of it. Is it perched on the dip in the back wall along from the little tool shed? It is suddenly very important that she finds out, so she shrugs on her dressing gown and hurries downstairs.

Slippers of morning dew coat her bare feet as she walks across the grass, and the scents of honeysuckle and Flora's *Philadelphus* sweeten the air. A rudimentary search turns up no agapanthus, but an image of a bright-orange-and-black stripy pot rings a faint bell at the back of her mind. Rose hasn't seen that pot for ages, and it's not hard to miss. Behind the tool shed, in a space partially reclaimed by brambles, there's a tumble of old pots, discarded gardening gloves, damp and snail-infested, and at the back of a depleted compost bag there's an orange-and-black stripy pot – broken and mostly empty. Rose picks up the biggest piece and sees that the soil is gone, but the bulb of the agapanthus reclines naked and mushy – slug and snail heaven. How did that happen? Maybe it was last winter when the wind was particularly voracious. It could have whisked the pot from the little stone wall that Glen had built, and there it had lain undiscovered, until now. Rose hasn't ventured out this way since he died. Poor Madame Agatha.

Indoors, a new urgency ignores her thoughts of breakfast and leads her to the laptop to Google information on agapanthus. An involuntary 'Oh...' brings a mix of joy and sadness to the quiet of the kitchen, as Rose discovers that agapanthus means 'flower of love' in Greek. A need to plant a new one in Glen's memory is almost overwhelming, so Rose grabs an apple for breakfast before quickly changing and leaving the house.

A knowledgeable young horticulturalist at the garden centre explains how to tend the fine specimen of bright-blue agapanthus with strappy verdant leaves almost as high as her knee. The blooms are still sleeping, but he assures Rose that in a month or so, the spears will emerge, grow tall and explode in a breathtaking show of splendour, come June or July. Rose thanks him and he lifts it into her trolley. Now for a new plant pot. She wanders down the aisles and into the next section which is full of pots, various tools and bags of compost. Immediately she knows which one to buy. It's olive green with a huge bee on the front. Perfect. Bees are the epitome of nature and the guardians of new life. *Where would we be without the bees?* Rose chuckles at this thought and heaves the pot and some compost into the trolley.

The sense of urgency that found her early that morning is still at her side when she gets back to her garden. Before she does anything else, she will plant the agapanthus and find a safe place for it to grow. They like plenty of sun, apparently, so Rose thinks it might do well by the back wall (though not on it), so it's protected from the wind. She will see it every morning when she opens the kitchen blinds. Everything is ready, apart from the new trowel, which seems to have disappeared. 'Where is the damned thing?' she asks the interior of the shed. 'I only bought it recently when I planted Daisy and Flora's memories.'

Having almost given up the search and now considering using the spade, which would be unwieldy and clumsy, but needs must, Rose notices a rusty little trowel resting in a cobwebby seed tray along the back shelf of the shed. On closer inspection, it turns out to be a child's trowel, a faded image of Danger Mouse on the handle. Bella's trowel. A memory of Bella and Glen planting gooseberries with it thumps into her consciousness with such vibrancy and clarity that she slumps down on a makeshift stool – an upturned bucket. Bella's about six, she's asking her dad if they can make a crumble when the gooseberries are ready, and Glen laughs at her enthusiasm, tells her yes, but it might be a while yet, and they shouldn't make the custard anytime soon.

Rose lets out a long breath as the poignant, but predominantly happy memory fades and she's left staring at dust motes dancing in a shaft of muted sunlight. Strangely, she doesn't feel as bereft and alone as she sometimes has before when she's remembered Glen. Instead, she's surprisingly uplifted. Perhaps it's the garden, the being here in the shed, the smell of damp wood, and compost, the rusty metal of the lawnmower, and if she imagines it really hard, perhaps a faint whiff of Glen's cologne.

Rose looks at the trowel in her hands again and realises she has soil under her fingernails. Her brain makes a tentative connection between creating new life in her garden and her life as a nurse. She tended, nurtured, helped people to thrive and survive, and she's doing that again now with her planting. She's making the connection to Glen too and Bella, on the long-ago gooseberry planting day. The memory was so beautiful and it's left her with a feeling of peace.

Rose realises something else then. It hits her like a train. At last, in this old shed, she can admit to herself she's not really been dealing with her grief. At the beginning, it was too raw, overwhelming, ripping her apart, so she hid from it. Hid it from others in bright smiles and long shifts, in not having time to think beyond work. Now she has plenty of time, she can see it. Rose has blocked it too, just as effectively as a tennis pro returning an ace, smashing it back to where it came from. Game, set and match.

All this new information she's processing isn't really new at all, Rose thinks. It's been there all the time, but she hasn't quite managed to understand what it was. The shape of it kept morphing, changing into something else, just out of reach. Though she didn't try very hard to access it, if she's honest. As a nurse, part of her thinks she should have realised long before now what was happening, as she'd met grief in many guises almost every day of her working life – but this was too close. Too personal. Contentment of sorts comes to sit by her side on the upturned bucket. Grief for her has changed – it's become acceptance. And for that, she's grateful. The little Danger Mouse trowel rests on her knees waiting for action, so she takes it outside to the 'bee pot' and digs it into the rich, dark compost and makes a new home for Madame Agatha.

Sally pulls up outside Rose's cottage and takes a moment to admire the riot of early summer colour in the front garden. She has been only twice before to Rose's, but can't remember such a gorgeous variety of plants, shrubs and flowers. She looks at the little cactus in the carrier bag on the passenger seat, wedged between the cake box and a packet of biscuits, and thinks it might be a bit bland. It might be better off on her own kitchen windowsill alongside the on-its-last-legs spider plant … then she thinks better of it and whisks the bag up and out. As she's walking towards the front door, doubt throws a few arguments into her path, as to why she should have done this before, as she meant to, as it's been a while since Rose left the surgery ... or at the very least, she should have phoned ahead. But Sally had been in the supermarket looking at the cakes, and a now-or-never moment had her buying six of them and zooming up to see Rose.

Thing is, she's kept putting off the visit. Sally knows she tends to put things off, or on the back burner, as she prefers to think of it. Back-burner things aren't forgotten about or rejected. They're just waiting for a more appropriate time. She also knows that she hasn't been in a good place, as they say – appropriate times for things have been shelved in favour of eating cake, drinking wine and watching mindless celebrity this, that or the other on TV. Anything to shut down her gloomy thoughts until it's time for work the next day. The bathroom scales are a testament to her weakness for sugar and sitting on her backside. Pippa told her last week that she needs to get a hold on her binge eating and sort her life out, before 'stuff' spirals out of control. Her daughter didn't elaborate on what 'stuff' might be, but she got the gist. She secretly agreed with Pippa, but as usual, Sally played things down – alluded to the yoga class she'd been to (once, a few months ago), said she would be fine.

Part of her had wanted to retaliate. More than part of her actually, because Pippa had sounded exactly like her dad. It was as if he was there in the kitchen, just like he used to be, pointing out all her bad points – telling her to do this, that or the other. Making her feel small, insignificant. So tiny, so irrelevant, so unworthy that she often felt like she was invisible. Her 'mistakes' were the only thing about her that were ever seen. Sally didn't retaliate, of course, because Pippa had no idea her dad used to be the puppet master. All Paul's snide remarks were reserved just for Sally. Quiet, vicious little weapons dropped into her ears, shredding her heart, scattering shame through her like shrapnel.

Before she can knock at the door, it opens, and Rose is standing there looking ... well, looking quite amazing. She's slimmer, fitter and tanned. Her hair is longer and not as 'done', but it suits her, and there's a 'fizz' popping about her, an energy, that wasn't there before.

'Sally, I thought it was your car pulling up! How lovely to see you!'

This is a relief, as she can tell the greeting is genuine. Sally had wondered if it might be a bit awkward, her just rocking up out of the blue. 'Hi, Rose. My God, you're looking great – whatever you're on, I want some!'

Rose lets out a huge laugh, as if it's the funniest thing she's ever heard and ushers Sally inside. 'I'm high on life, Sally.' She slaps Sally's back. 'Life and new possibilities.'

Soon the kettle's on and Rose is oohing and ahhing at the selection of cakes Sally's putting on a big plate. Then she picks up the little cactus and kisses the pot ... actually kisses it. 'I'd kiss the cactus, but don't want to prickle my lips.' Rose laughs and holds the plant higher to examine every angle. 'It's just delightful. Thank you so much for spoiling me – cakes, biscuits and cactus. What more could a girl ask for?' Her turquoise eyes sparkle with merriment and then she returns to her tea-making.

Sally thinks Rose's 'life and new possibilities' mood is rubbing off on her. There's a bubbly feeling building inside which has been absent for the longest time, and she fights the urge to grin inanely as she looks around the bright, homely kitchen. 'What have you been up to since leaving, then? I've not seen you on social media much.'

'No time for that malarkey. I've been working in the garden mostly. Turns out I've got green fingers – who would have thought it?' Rose wiggles her fingers over her shoulder. 'I go walking and often go down to the beach too. I've booked a horse riding lesson next Tuesday, and then Bella and family are down the day after for a few days. I've not seen them for four months, so I can't wait. I actually painted a picture with her old paints – not sure what she'll make of that. My new friend Flora often pops up and we do a bit of gardening together, or simply sit and look at the flowers. Daisy comes too, when she can. So, I have been quite the busy bee.'

Sally is exhausted just listening to her as she takes a mug of tea with thanks. 'Blimey. You seem busier than when you were nursing.'

'Not quite, but I'm certainly enjoying not being a nurse.' Rose leans forward across the table, fully engaging Sally's attention. 'Do you know, I never thought I'd say those words. When I first left the surgery, I thought my world had been turned upside down. I felt like a boat without a rudder, eggs without bacon, Ant without Dec – you get the picture.'

Sally nods. 'So how come that changed?'

'I went to the woods, found some wild garlic, sang my heart out and made a memory garden.'

'A memory garden?'

'Yep. I was in the loft looking for some old paints of Bella's and found an ancient photo album. There's one of me when I was sixteen, in the woods amongst wild garlic. So off I went to the same woods and relived the experience. It made me feel young again for a while. Made me realise there was still much to take from life...' Rose pauses, looking thoughtful, '...and much to give back. I brought some wild garlic home.' She pulls a sheepish face. 'Okay, I nicked it, and planted it in my garden. It felt ... right, somehow. Anyway, since that day I knew I needed to transform my green space. It had always been Glen's domain before, but I realised I love being amongst growing things. The garden lifts my spirits. It's a well-known fact that being amongst nature is good for you. Flora and Daisy brought plants that have memories attached to them too, and I planted them with mine. I have prim-noses and agapanthus as well as the garlic.'

'Prim*roses*, you mean?' Sally says with a giggle.

'No, I mean prim-noses. Bella called them that when she was little. The agapanthus is to remember Glen. Not that I need a specific plant, as I think about him every day.'

Sally loses the smile. 'Sorry, Rose. It must be hard, still.'

'Don't be sorry. Yes, it's hard sometimes, but thanks to the garden, I'm beginning to accept it. I only really understood that today... Baby steps, as they say. I imagine acceptance isn't a one-size-fits-all. There will be days when I'll need alterations.'

To lighten the mood – hers, not Rose's – Sally says, 'It's a great idea, having plants to remember people by.'

Rose nods her agreement. 'Not just people who have died, though. There are lots of times to remember and treasure, like my wild garlic days, and happy memories too, like Bella's prim-noses.'

Sally notes the bubbly feeling she had earlier is swelling like a balloon. Maybe she needs to be part of this garden if it has such a positive effect on people. Then, without intending to, and out of the blue, she tells Rose about Paul. Rose had an idea she wasn't happy with him and guessed some details, but not all. 'Yes, he was so controlling.' Sally helps herself to another cake ... her third, she realises, and pushes the remaining two in the box away. 'Everything always had to be perfect for him. You know, the house had to be clean and tidy, the food cooked from scratch, the kids looking and behaving like those in a cereal commercial – which they never were, of course – and that was my fault, apparently. I had to look like I'd just stepped out of a salon, and woe betide me if I'd put a pound of weight on.' She sweeps her hand over her midriff and can't meet Rose's sympathetic eyes. 'God knows what he'd say if he could see me now.' Oh shit. She's going to cry now. What a stupid cow she is.

'Hey, who cares what that shithead would say? Seems to me you're well rid of him.' Rose reaches her hand across the table with a tissue in it and Sally takes both, though still daren't look up.

'I tell myself that all the time,' she tells the plate of half-eaten cake. 'Sometimes it works, but not for long. I can't help but think of him with his new, young, slim, attractive woman, while I'm home alone. My daughter has moved in with her girlfriend, and my son is backpacking the world with his friends. Don't get me wrong, I'm happy for them … but oh … I don't know. I made the effort the other night, went out for a drink with a friend, but I felt awkward. Like I didn't belong, and I couldn't find anything nice that would fit me in the wardrobe, which didn't help. Sorry, Rose. I didn't mean to come here and moan. Just ignore me.' Sally lets out a sigh and forces a smile.

'Do not apologise, and I most certainly will not ignore you, young lady.'

Rose has a mock stern tone to her voice. *Young lady* – that's a joke, she'll be fifty next month.

'Come on. Let's go and have a look at the garden. It might cheer you up… Bring your tea.'

Sally's not really thought much about gardens, one way or the other. She can take them or leave them – a bit neutral, she supposes. But this garden is something else. It isn't a show garden like the ones the experts create on TV programmes, or trying to be something it's not. It's just … *uplifting*, is the only word that comes to mind. Actually, no. There are a few others too. Cheerful, inspiring, comforting, welcoming. The afternoon sun throws fat shadows at the fence and back wall, and the honeysuckle cascading down and along like a golden waterfall, pushes a sweet scent before it. A white-flowering shrub stands nearby with a similar perfume, and near the gate, a clump of tall, showy, daisy-like flowers nod in the gentle wind.

Sally doesn't know the names of these flowers and shrubs, but there are pink blousy ones, purple ones at the end of long stems, orange ones that look like the heads of birds with long beaks, and everywhere lush green leaves mingle with tall grasses. Ah, at last there's one she recognises climbing a trellis near the corner of the cottage. 'What a lovely rose you have, Rose.' She strokes her fingers along the velvet yellow petals and inhales the fragrance at the centre of the flower. 'In fact, what an absolutely wonderful garden altogether.' Sally spreads her arms and turns in a circle, a giddy feeling guiding her dance.

Rose snaps a dead flower head, pockets it and joins her. 'Thank you. Yes, this is a Golden Gate rose. Smells divine. We bought it after we'd been to San Francisco on holiday years ago.'

'Ah right, because of the bridge.'

'Yes. I always remember that holiday when I look at it.'

'And is that a veggie patch?' Sally points over at an area that has what looks like feathery carrot fronds waving in the breeze.

'Yes! I thought I'd just try a few things, to see how it went.'

Sally looks at Rose's serene smile and is comforted. Just like when they worked together, the calm and compassion she always carries around with her is working its magic on Sally. The smile reminds her of something too. Or someone. Then it comes to her. Grace Pentewan, who used to live next door to her when she was a kid. She didn't look anything like Rose, but there is a suggestion of her in that smile. Another suggestion comes to Sally too, and before she knows it, she is sharing it.

'I had a neighbour years ago who had a little pond. It had beautiful water lilies, white and pink ones. I loved it. I used to look over the fence at it, and in spring it was full of tadpoles and frogs. She had a couple of fish in it too, if I remember correctly. Grace was the neighbour's name, and she invited me over one time when she saw me peeping over the fence. We became friends. Odd, really – a ten-year-old and an elderly lady. She was wise and kind. She'd been widowed young, but told me she and her husband had been very happy. Told me to never settle for second best in life and go for my dreams. I did settle for second best, though, didn't I? Stupid fool. Stayed with a man who made my life miserable … the best years of my life, too.'

Rose is about to answer, but Sally needs to get the last bit out. 'Anyway, what I was wondering, is … can I make a pond for you? There's plenty of room in the shady bit near the wall. I don't know anything about how to do it, but I could find out… Water lilies would be so pretty.'

Sally had no idea where all that had come from, but she was glad it had. It felt right. For a moment they stood looking at each other. Rose had that serene smile on her lips again and in the air was the perfume of various flowers, the murmur of bees and the faint shush of the ocean.

'I think a pond would be the perfect addition to the rest of this remarkable garden, Sally.'

'Really?'

Rose laughs. 'Yes, really.' She puts her head on one side and with a thoughtful expression, adds, 'You know, your younger years weren't necessarily the best years of your life, sweetheart. You have a fair few to go yet. It's up to you what you make of them.'

A rush of affection for Rose, this garden and Grace Pentewan prompts, 'I've missed you, Rose. It's so nice to spend time with you again ... and thanks so much for agreeing to a pond. I promise I'll try to make it perfect.'

'No. You've done enough of that over the years, Sally. Perfection's overrated. Just do the best you can, that will be enough.'

Sally wants to answer, but she finds she can't. Instead, she links arms with Rose and they wander over to where they think the best place for a pond will be.

Chapter Twelve

B eing Louise's lighthouse is proving to be much harder than Flora had initially thought. Maybe her bulb had dimmed with over-use, starting out as a million-watt at the start of her teaching career, and dwindling to a twenty-watt in her seventy-eighth year. That doesn't sound right when she says it to herself quietly inside her head. Seventy-eight. It sounds even less right when she says it out loud. Not that she does very often, because it's all a bit scary and sinister. Mother would have said she should be grateful she's had a long life so far; some don't have the luxury of getting old. And Flora is grateful, truly. Though it doesn't stop her from being a bit anxious now and then. Flora's also grateful that Mother has been largely quiet over the last while, perhaps because she's feeling more settled here – long may it continue.

Louise has at last deigned to grace Flora's home with her presence. Oh dear. This isn't a very charitable way to think of her new friend, she concedes, and ditches the word 'deigned' to 'felt comfortable enough'. Flora is trying to dismiss unkind thoughts, because she doesn't want to end up like Mother, or encourage her back into conversation. After the first time she and Louise had lunch together, they occasionally chatted on the phone, but every time Flora suggested Louise came over for lunch or dinner, there was an awkward silence and a garbled excuse. The offer of visiting Rose's garden wasn't met with much enthusiasm either.

Flora sweeps the kitchen floor and arrives at the conclusion that Louise has become a bit of a recluse since she retired and lost her husband. Maybe the idea of meeting new people and doing new things is an anathema. Too set in her ways to change. Especially for a person who is so intense about people's feet and shiny shoes. Once again, that thought wasn't the most charitable, but Flora genuinely believes Louise needs to lighten up a little – try to enjoy herself more. Hopefully, after the visit to Flora's home today, Louise can be persuaded to let her hair down (metaphorically, as it is very short), and maybe she will agree to make a date to visit Rose's garden too.

The luxury fish pie Flora's made for lunch is in the oven. It's mouth-watering aroma is floating up the stairs, making her stomach rumble as she combs her hair in front of the dressing-table mirror. A multicoloured blouse is hanging on the wardrobe door alongside a pair of light-blue, boot-cut jeans patched at the knees with embroidered red roses. She glances at them through the mirror and smiles. They always make her smile, as they're so cheerful. As far as she remembers, she bought them in a charity shop at least thirty years ago, and they frayed at the knee after ten. Because Flora liked them so much, she found the rose patches and made the jeans into something spectacular. 'Never throw good things away' was one of Mother's mantras, and on this occasion, she has to agree.

Happy with her appearance, Flora goes downstairs wondering if there is anything in her wardrobe that Louise might like. She's slightly rounder in the middle than Flora, but maybe the beaded green-and-red kaftan would suit her? Taking the fish pie out of the oven, she reminds herself that lighthouses have to guide and lead, not blind people – Louise would probably run a mile if she introduced the kaftan idea so soon. Flora places a vase of stocks at the end of her kitchen table and puts out the cutlery. As she's considering whether to wine, or not to wine, a tap at the front door tells her Louise has arrived.

The first thing Flora notices is Louise's hair. It's plastered to her face and neck in damp tendrils and sweat sheens her pink face. Louise blinks her eyes and shakes her head as if she's disagreeing with an unspoken question while thrusting a yellow gift bag at Flora's chest. 'Here. Hope you like it. I went slightly wrong on the way to your house from town, and got rather hot on the walk here.'

Flora is used to her abrupt way of speaking but notes the navy polo-neck, tweed jacket and matching skirt and thinks it's a miracle Louise hasn't melted away to nothing in the hot May sunshine. And the shoes. Lace-up (very shiny) brown brogues over tan tights. American Tan, Flora thinks, though she's not seen the like for many years.

'Welcome! Come in, come in. And thank you so much for the gift – it honestly wasn't necessary, though.'

'We always bring something when invited round … I mean, I do. Though I haven't been out to anyone's house really, since Matthew.'

That hit Flora with a thump. Poor Louise. Maybe her hunch was right about her reclusive behaviour. 'Oh, that's a shame. I'm glad you're here now, though.'

Louise bobs her head. 'Yes. It's not because people didn't ask me, it's that I felt I couldn't go, now there's only half of me – because that's how it felt at the beginning. Still does, really.' She ruffles her hair and seems surprised to find it damp. Wiping her hand on a tissue, she adds, 'They just stopped asking me in the end.'

Poor love. Flora won't comment further, though, as it's her job to cheer Louise up. In the kitchen Flora gestures to the table and chairs. 'Can I take your jacket?'

'No, I'm okay, thanks.'

Flora belatedly realises there might be a problem with sweat patches on the polo neck. 'Okay. Please take a seat, lunch is ready. Would you like a glass of wine, or a soft drink?'

Louise looks like she's been asked to strip naked and do a cartwheel. 'Wine at this time of day? No, thank you very much. Water is fine. And aren't you going to open the gift? Oh…' She's now staring horrified at Flora's bare feet on the flagstones.

Flora looks at her feet and back at Louise quizzically. 'What's wrong?'

Louise raises her eyebrows. 'Well, I do worry that people

can damage their feet if they go without shoes. You'll only have to catch a little toe on a rough edge of one of these flagstones, or the leg of a chair, and you'll be in agony for days.'

Flora has to bite back laughter as she picks up the gift bag. 'I never wear shoes if I can help it, inside or out. Never had a problem with my little toes.' Ignoring the perplexed glance, Flora opens the gift bag. 'Oh … a shoe horn,' she says, hoping her tone conveys 'What a nice surprise' instead of 'What the fuck?'

'Pretty useless, in the light of what you've said about bare feet,' Louise says through a small mouth.

'Not at all! In autumn and winter it will be especially useful when I've got my heavy boots and shoes to pull on.'

'Good. Though you need to do it gently, or you could damage the shoe … or your heels.'

Before her guest launches into more shoe talk, Flora pulls out a kitchen chair. 'There you go, take a load off and I'll grab the pie.'

Louise sits and points at the vase of flowers. 'Stocks. Matthew loved them, we had hundreds all over the garden.'

'Oh good. Their perfume is wonderful, isn't it, and it's a lovely shade of pink.'

'Yes.' Louise's eyes shine with enthusiasm and she strokes the blooms gently. 'Their Latin name is *Matthiola incana*, they come in lots of different varieties and colours. I like purple, though apricot is nice too. You can use the petals as a garnish for salad – totally edible.'

'Really? I never knew. Maybe we could sprinkle some on the side salad I've made.'

'Possibly. And did you know they were given as tokens of love during the Victorian period?' Flora didn't. 'Sometimes known as Gilly flowers, I believe.' Louise folds her hands on her lap and nods as if satisfied she's covered everything.

'Wow. You know so much about them.'

'I know so much about hundreds of flowers, shrubs and herbs. How could I not, being the wife of a horticulturalist? I read up on things too, in library books – as you know.'

Flora smiles and thinks Louise would really enjoy meeting Rose, if only she would agree to it. It was amazing how her whole demeanour changed when talking about the stocks – much less intense. And enthusiasm lit up her whole face. Shoes, feet and flowers seem to be her specialist subjects... Flora just needs her to talk about the latter more. 'Hope you like fish pie,' she says, placing the dish on the table with a small green salad.

'Yes, thank you. This looks nice ... does it have prawns in it?' A small frown appears between her thick eyebrows, and she pushes her glasses along the bridge of her nose.

Flora bites her lip. She'd not considered that some people don't like shellfish, or maybe have an allergy to it. 'Yes, a few. Is that okay?'

She loses the frown. 'Oh yes. They're one of my favourite foods.'

After lunch, Flora shows Louise into the living room and tells her to make herself comfortable while she makes some coffee. As she carries the tray of coffee and biscuits in, she finds Louise, jacket off (at last), on her hands and knees by the patio doors, moving pebbles from Flora's pebble tray around on the pine floorboards.

'Oh. Sorry!' Louise exclaims and jumps up as if she's had an electric shock. 'What am I like? I was admiring your lovely artwork,' she gestures at the little easel, 'and I just had the urge to make something myself.'

Flora sets the tray down. 'Please don't apologise! I'm thrilled that you like my work and are interested in making something yourself. We'll have our coffee, and then I'll get you a canvas and a frame and—'

'No, I couldn't possibly. It was rude of me to just launch in like that.' She's blushing and hovering by the sofa, as though unsure whether to sit or not.

'It wasn't rude at all.' Flora hands her a mug of coffee. 'Sit down and we'll have a chat about it – plan what you'd like to make. Honestly, you'd be doing me a favour, as I get a bit stuck sometimes when I'm adding colour.' That's a lie, but needs must. 'I'd appreciate your advice.'

Louise looks pleased. 'If you're sure.'

They set to work. Louise makes a vase of flowers with her pebbles, and for a first attempt, Flora has to say, she's very impressed. Louise suggests Flora uses more yellow in her sunset background for her pebble cottage by the sea, and once again, Flora's impressed with Louise's 'eye'.

Setting her canvas on the easel, Flora sits opposite Louise on the sofa. 'You're really good at this, Louise, you know. Why don't you come to pebble-art class with me next time? I'm sure you'll enjoy it.'

A frown. 'Oh … no. I'm not much of a joiner, thanks.'

'Well, it's not as though you have to commit yourself to anything. Try it. If you don't like it the first time, don't come to the next one.'

'Hmm. Can I let you know?'

Flora thinks this means no, but she'll settle for that for now. 'Of course. There is one thing I'd like you to agree to, though.' Louise's frown deepens. 'Coming to visit my friend Rose and see her garden. You'd be very welcome. Rose has a gut instinct for gardening, but she's not as knowledgeable as you are about plants and flowers.' Flora manages a very acceptable chuckle. 'In fact, I doubt many people are.'

The frown skedaddles, leaving pink blossoms in Louise's cheeks. 'I … I will at some point, yes. Thank you.'

Flora goes in for the kill. 'The week after next, Rose's daughter and grandchildren are coming for a few days, but I'll put you in the diary for Wednesday week.' Louise is about to say something, and judging by her expression, it's not, 'Okay, that will be lovely.' 'Rose will be delighted! I've told her so much about you. She's recently widowed – well, two years, I think, so you'll have things in common.' Flora forces a stretchy smile to stay on her face, but it's more like a grimace. Dear God. She can hardly believe what she's just said. *You both have dead husbands, so you'll be sure to get on like a house on fire.* Really?

Unbelievably, Louise finds a relaxed smile. 'Oh, right. Well, if I can be of any assistance in the garden, then I will. Yes, I'll come.'

'Wonderful!'

Louise worries a nail, glances at the patio pots outside and absently mutters *Hydrangea paniculata* to herself. 'Truth be told, I don't go in for new things much ... or meeting new people. It's a miracle I'm here, really.' Her small hand hovers over her mouth as if she's regretting her words, and then wiggles her glasses. Flora holds her breath, hoping her silence will allow Louise to say more. 'Thing is, I don't want to rely on people or get used to having them around. Since Matthew went, I've been pretty much self-sufficient.'

With that, she gets to her feet and picks up her jacket, looking around the room, the mild panic in her eyes suggesting she can't find a way through the awkward silence. Flora's got a lump in her throat, so isn't much use as she follows Louise into the kitchen (she's being a terrible lighthouse), where she'll hopefully find something comforting to say. Poor Louise, not wanting to rely on people because she couldn't cope if they left her, just like Matthew did. Flora's 'Louise is a recluse' conclusion was right, but for different reasons. She's standing by the front door, jacket half on, handbag on the floor at her feet, fully clothed in vulnerability.

They look at each other as Louise shrugs the other half of her jacket on, and just as the silence is getting overwhelming, Flora says, 'I totally get it, you know. You not wanting to rely on people. I've been emotionally on my own my entire life really – well, apart from a short time in my late teens. And yes, absolutely self-sufficient. Even though I lived with my mother, I might as well have been alone... I have some very good friends, though, thank goodness. And I think as long as I never take them or their friendship for granted, I won't be open to being hurt.' Flora drops the lightest touch on Louise's shoulder. 'Don't let the fear of losing people stop you from finding them in the first place.'

Louise does a few slow blinks and bobs her head. 'Thank you, Flora. That makes sense. I'll look forward to meeting Rose … and one day you might tell me about what happened in your late teens.' She opens the door and looks back. 'But only if you want to, of course.'

'I will. And thanks so much for the lovely shoe horn.'

Louise glances at Flora's bare feet, and then with a half-smile on her lips, says, 'Bet you can't wait for autumn.'

Chapter Thirteen

Rose puts the finishing touches to Bella and the children's room – a tall speckled blue vase of Daisy's freshly cut oxeye daisies, and the painting she's done with Bella's old paints. Looking at the painting now on the dresser, Rose wonders if it's worth displaying. A woodland scene with the suggestion of a woman ghosting through a sunny glade. Does the woman look more like a mistake on the canvas that Rose has tried to disguise? Maybe. She is about to take it down, but a resolve to go with her gut and stop worrying about what people think lets her hand fall. When Rose painted it, she felt exhilaration – just as she had when she was in the wood on the wild garlic day. This painting is a nod to that experience, and as such, it should stay where it is.

Bella should be here any time now with Molly and Wesley. Rose has missed them all so much and she's sure she'll see a marked difference in three-year-old Wesley and five-year-old Molly. It's only been four months, but little ones grow so fast, just like the flowers in her garden. The idea that they'd grow stronger and sturdier in Cornish soil rather than Birmingham's can't help pushing its way into her mind, but she pushes it back again. We can't have everything, can we? Nigel got a promotion, and they couldn't turn down a hike in salary like that. She got it. She really did. But getting it and liking it were two different animals.

Rose reminds herself that they have been in Birmingham just over two years and Wesley, especially, won't have any memories of his Cornish roots – but that's where grandmas come in, she supposes. They have enough memories stored up for everyone to share. As she straightens the pillows on the two little 'rollaway' beds for the children, not for the first time recently, Rose wonders if everything is okay between Bella and Nigel. He was supposed to be taking five days off to come down too – but at the last minute, said he was needed at work, as a colleague had come down with some bug or other. Bella often painted quick-brushstroke answers over Rose's questions concerning Nigel, the family and if Bella was happy. Yes, they were all fine; no, Nigel had no problems at work, he was probably working too hard, but that went with the territory; and then she'd change the subject.

A squeal of joyful excitement from Molly heralds their arrival and Rose hurries outside to greet them. Molly's a carbon copy of Bella at her age, so much so that the likeness steals Rose's breath. Wesley is climbing over the luggage, chuckling to himself, in his patchwork dungarees, bottom in the air, light-brown curls ruffling in the wind. Bella locks the car and as she looks up, squinting in the full sun, Rose thinks there are more lines around her eyes than she remembers, and she seems older than her thirty-five years, but the new blonde look suits her.

'Mum! You're looking fantastic.' Bella envelops Rose in a big hug. 'Have you joined a gym or something?'

Rose laughs. 'Yes, it's called doing the garden.' She waves a hand at the blooms, leaves and flowers shooting up from every available space.

'Wow! I've never seen it looking so … so … I don't know. Alive, I guess.'

Rose has to agree. 'What a great description! It's had a reawakening – a rebirth.' Then Wesley stops clambering on the luggage and runs over to his grandmother on his chubby little legs. 'Hello, Granny. Can I have an ice cream?' He holds out his arms to be picked up.

Rose picks him up, noting how heavy he is and how much he's grown. She relishes the touch of his soft skin against her cheek and the lemony smell of his hair. 'Ice cream?' she asks, pecking him on the chin. 'What about lunch first, gorgeous boy?'

Molly slips a warm little hand into hers. 'Wesley has been banging on about ice cream ever since he saw a sign with one.' She rolls her eyes and pulls an expression exactly like her mother's. 'Mummy said Cornwall makes the best in the world.'

Rose puts Wesley down and gives Molly a big hug. 'We

do indeed, my lovely. And after lunch we'll go and get one from the ice cream van at the beach, yes?'

'Yay! I have a new swimming costume, Granny.' Molly turns hopeful eyes to her mum. 'Can I swim after lunch?'

Bella smiles and picks up the luggage. 'Don't see why not. Right, let's get this lot inside, I'm dying for a cuppa.'

Lunch over, Bella's upstairs putting things away in her room while the children are chasing each other around the garden and Rose looks on from the stable door. Chortling children certainly add something to the scene. She thinks the flowers like the sound of laughter too – all the peonies are facing their way and ruffling their petals in pleasure. Or it might just be because of the direction of the wind, but Rose knows which explanation she prefers.

Molly and Wesley are rolling on the grass, play-fighting under the 'bee pot' containing the agapanthus. Wesley jumps up and Rose sees that the agapanthus is taller than him, though the blooms are still encased within their green pods. Molly notices her granny looking on and points at the long green stalks past her shoulder. 'What are these called? They're very tall.'

'Agapanthus.' Rose leaves the kitchen door and goes to stand next to them in the sun.

Molly repeats the word quietly to herself and Wesley watches the movement of her lips and says, 'Panties.'

Rose and Molly giggle at him, which encourages a

madcap whirling dance, punctuated by 'Panties!' on each 360-degree turn.

'They were one of your grandad's favourite flowers,' Rose tells them.

'Grandad had hair like mine and Mum's, didn't he?' She touches her dark curls. 'Well, before Mum made hers yellow.'

Pleased and a little surprised that Molly remembers, as she was only three when he died, Rose says, 'Yes. Can you remember anything else about him?'

Molly screws up her face in concentration. 'I think he used to let me jump up and down on the sofa in my shoes, but Mummy said he shouldn't?'

Rose has to swallow down tears and finds a bright smile. 'That's right! He thought the world of you.' There's a tell-tale wobble in her voice, and Rose hopes Molly won't see beyond the smile. Seems like the acceptance she found in the shed with the Danger Mouse trowel last week has abandoned her today. How Glen would have adored watching these little people grow up.

'It makes you sad talking about Granddad, doesn't it, Granny?' Molly slips a hand into Rose's and sighs.

This kid misses nothing. Rose takes a moment to get her emotions under control and think of the right words. 'Um, kind of, because he's not actually here with us now. But happy too, because he used to be, and he's left lots of good memories behind. Does that make sense?'

A solemn nod. 'Yes. I wish he was here still. He would have liked Wesley's silly dancing.'

Rose nods, because that's all she can manage. And hand

in hand, they both watch Wesley turn in ever tighter circles until he collapses in a heap.

'Who painted this, Mum?' Bella's voice carries from the kitchen door.

Rose turns to see her daughter holding her painting up. 'I did! And guess what I painted it with?'

'Er, paints I'd guess.' Bella angles the canvas and tilts her head. 'Love that ghostly woman.'

'Thanks.' So, it didn't look like a mistake. Good. 'I found your old paint palette in the loft, that you had as a teenager.'

Bella frowns and stares into the distance, then her eyes widen. 'Oh yeah! I remember now. I fancied Mr Proctor the art teacher and he said I had talent. That's what prompted that little foray into the art world.' She giggles and comes outside.

'Mr Proctor, eh? He was the one with the long hair and beard. Hm, I can see the attraction.'

'Ha! Yeah.' She nods at the painting and sets it by the wall. 'I think it's great. What made you do it?'

'You, actually. I was up in the loft, found the paints and had a really vivid memory of you as a teenager. You'd done a lovely picture, but you told me not to look at the canvas, but I looked anyway. It was the sunset over the ocean and it was good – really good. Mr Proctor was right. You had talent and I thought you might have taken it up seriously.'

'Really? I don't remember. Wonder why I didn't want you to see it? I was probably being precious, as usual.' Bella's cheeks turn into roses.

'Precious to me and your dad, that's for sure.'

'Oh, Mum.'

Rose gets another hug and tries to commit the moment to memory, to draw upon during those long months when her 'little girl' is far away. She notices Bella is a bit tearful at the mention of her dad, so steers the conversation back to her antics. 'And guess what else? I went horse riding the other day!'

'Wow! I knew you'd got the voucher thingy, but I never thought you'd go.'

Rose is interested to have her 'box assumptions' confirmed or denied, as they say in court. 'Why not?'

Bella runs her hand gently along the petals of a yellow rose in full bloom. 'Um ... it's not something that I thought you'd do, I suppose.'

'Because I'm too old ... set in my ways? Not something that your mum would do?'

'No. Not at all.' Bella frowns. 'You've just never shown an interest in all the years I've known you, that's all.'

That answer leans towards denial of her box assumptions. Refreshing. 'Ah, but what you don't know is that I've always wanted to go horse riding, but never got round to it.'

'Really? Well, I'm glad you went. Did you enjoy it?'

'No!' Rose laughs and Bella joins in. 'It was bloody scary and there was too much bouncing up and down like a sack of potatoes.'

'Granny said a swearword. Bloody.' Molly's eyes dance with mischief as she looks from one adult to the other.

'Yes, she did.' Bella folds her arms, shakes her head at

Rose in mock disappointment. 'But that doesn't mean you can repeat it, okay, Monkey?'

'But Granny—'

'Never mind what Granny said. Why don't you go inside and get that packet of biscuits on the kitchen table and bring it out here?'

Molly didn't need telling twice. 'Nice diversion tactics,' Rose says with a smile.

'I learned from the best.'

The two women stand admiring the garden a few moments and watch Wesley rolling himself down the incline of the lawn. 'Gorgeous, isn't it?' Rose nods at the yellow bloom climbing up the trellis in front of them, and dips her nose to inhale the heady perfume.

'Ah, the Golden Gate Rose. It's my favourite of all the flowers here, I think.' Bella dips her nose too. 'It reminds me of when I was little, and once the petals fell, you said I could make my "special perfume", as I called it. I crushed the petals, mixed them with water and bottled it. Then every time we went anywhere special, I dabbed a bit on the inside of my wrists like I'd seen you do, sitting at your dressing table. It made me feel very grown up...' Bella glances at Rose and away. 'I always wanted to be just like you.'

Already trying to quell a surge of emotion, the last snippet of information floods Rose's senses. A little 'Oh' is all she says, because her thoughts won't stop whirling around long enough to become full sentences. Bella had wanted to be like her. That's news to Rose. Bella always seemed such a self-sufficient little girl – headstrong, confident, and while not unaffectionate, she hadn't shared many of her innermost thoughts with her mum. Not a heart-to-heart fan. A lot like her dad.

'You sound surprised.' Bella leads the way down the garden under the willow arch, alive with white passion flowers.

'I am a little... I never realised you wanted to be a nurse.' Rose thinks this must be what Bella meant.

'No, not a nurse. I'd be a hopeless one. I meant—'

Rose never gets to hear the rest of it, as Molly runs up to them with a packet of chocolate digestive biscuits, the evidence of a sneaky partaking on her top lip. 'Can I have some milk?' This question sounds distracted and directed to the sky. Something has absorbed her attention. 'Ooh, look – an eagle!'

The two women follow her finger and chuckle at the huge bird of prey hovering over the nearby fields. 'It's a buzzard. Not quite as big as an eagle, but beautiful nonetheless,' Rose says, thinking how fantastic it is to have a child's eye view. Everything is full of wonder and larger than life. A little sad nag sidles in, pointing out that Rose will miss so much of her granddaughter's growing up. She refuses to listen to it further and hoists a rosy-cheeked Wesley up onto her hip, offering him a biscuit.

'They both look so invigorated already, and they've only been here five minutes,' Bella says.

'I thought five minutes wasn't that long, Mummy.' Molly's face is a puzzle. 'We have had lunch and played and done lots of things. Much more than an hour, I think.'

'Sorry to confuse you, it's just a figure of speech.'

Rose notices a little strain in her daughter's voice and can see she's tired. 'How about I tell you about those plants in the big red pot by the door over there, then I'll pop inside and get you some milk, eh?'

'And me?' Wesley pulls himself up onto the wooden bench and Bella sits beside him.

'Of course, my 'ansome.'

'Then we'll go to the beach?' Molly chips in.

'Yes. Okay, those flowers,' Rose points at the red pot, 'are called primroses. When your mummy was little, much littler than you, she called them prim-noses!'

Bella laughs along with Molly. 'Really?'

'Yeah. It was so sweet to hear. Your dad and I were a bit disappointed when you eventually mastered the pronunciation.'

Bella's about to reply, but Molly jumps in. 'I love prim-noses and roses and bees and agapanties! I love this whole garden sooo much. I love, love, love it, so, so much!' She dances around the picnic table singing a nonsense song about the garden, the beach and the flowers. Wesley joins in with the dance, laughing when his sister tickles him.

Rose is about to get the milk when Bella touches her arm lightly. 'Mum, when the kids are in bed, can we have a chat?'

'Of course, sweetheart.' The quiet timbre of her voice tells Rose the chat might be a serious one. A rare heart-to-heart. Rose hopes it isn't anything health-related. She knows that would be the end of her, if anything was seriously wrong with any of her little family.

Rose pours two glasses of red wine and takes them into the living room where Bella's sitting on the sofa, legs outstretched, eyes closed. It's been a lovely day, but the children are full-on, as all children of that age are, and Rose feels as tired as Bella looks after running up and down the beach, swimming, playing in rock pools and building sandcastles with the two of them.

Bella opens her eyes as she feels her mum's presence by her side. 'Oh, just perfect. Thanks.' She takes the glass. 'I could sink a good few of these, I can tell you – even a bottle. But I won't, obviously, not with the munchkins waking at the crack of dawn.'

'I'm here to help. I think you could do with relaxing a bit.'

'If only. I never have a minute to myself. I'm in the supermarket part-time, as you know, then its nursery run, school run, shopping, cooking and being a general dogsbody.' Rose is shocked to hear so much bitterness in her daughter's voice. Then a huge sigh and an even huger gulp of wine are followed by pooling tears.

'Hey, love. Don't get upset. Just take a breath and tell me about it all.'

Bella nods and blows her nose. 'I'm so unhappy, Mum… I don't have time to breathe and Nigel does fuck all.' A hollow laugh. 'Well, not with the kids, me, or the house. He works stupid hours and everything is about the job. No … actually. I'm beginning to realise everything is about him, if

I'm honest. What about me, what about my life? My happiness?'

Rose is unsure whether to say anything at this point. She can tell Bella needs to get everything out, and if she asks lots of questions, Bella might clam up again. Rose shakes her head in sympathy and says, 'Oh love. I'm so sorry – I thought you were happy and settled up there.'

Bella drains her glass and bangs it down on the side table. 'I hate it up there. *Hate* it.' She grabs the glass again, jumps up and returns with a refill. 'I agreed to go because he said it would be the making of us. More money and a stable position and all that crap. I didn't want to go, I was distraught about leaving you, leaving Cornwall. But I couldn't burden you with my woes, as it was only a few months after Dad died that he sprang it on me. You had enough to worry about. He gave me an ultimatum. Either I went, or he'd go alone. He wouldn't allow me to hold him back – to hold our children's future back, as he put it.'

The turmoil inside Rose turned to boiling anger. How could Nigel do that? 'What! That's awful. You could have come to me, love – I would have coped. Please never keep things from me.'

Bella shrugs. 'I'm used to coping with things. Or pretending to, so I told you we'd miss you, but that we were excited to go and it would be a great new life. Anything to put you off the scent.' Bella wipes away tears. 'I mean, if I'd told you the truth, you would have said, "Come and live with me, and we'll work it out." But I couldn't be the one to break up the family – deprive the children of a dad... Turns out they hardly see him anyway. And when they do, he's distracted or half asleep. I always pretend stuff is okay when we chat on the phone, because I want to spare you the misery. And if I started to tell you, everything would come flooding out. Like it has now.' She breathes a sigh of what might be relief.

What a bombshell. Rose doesn't tell her she had begun to wonder if everything was okay between them, as her daughter has obviously tried her best to spare her mum's worries. There's a quiet moment as Rose gathers her thoughts and hopefully the right words. 'Bella, have you told Nigel how miserable you feel ... and what you want out of life?'

'I tried at first, when I realised how much I hated it there. I know it sounds silly, but as well as everything I just told you, I missed the smell of the sea and the salt wind.' A big tear rolls down her cheek and she looks like the child from the prim-nose days. Rose would do anything to make the hurting stop.

'Not silly at all.'

'But he wouldn't listen. Just said it's early days and things would get better. A few weeks ago, I told him I had dreams that I put on hold to allow him to follow his own. I told him that Hannah and I had wanted to try and start our own cake and sandwich business from her converted VW camper – go round the beaches in tourist season. Vegan stuff too. She's stuck in Costa part-time, which she hates. Remember me telling you about that a few years back?'

Rose did remember and thought it would be a great idea. Hannah (who had a catering degree) was Bella's oldest friend and they thought they could work their hours around their children and weekends. If it took off, they would employ extra helpers.

'Nigel just laughed and said we'd no chance. Too many others would be doing it.' Bella stared at the photo of her wedding day on the shelf and shook her head. 'He won't listen. It's all about him. I think he invented this story about a colleague's illness so he didn't have to come with us here. I don't know what to do, Mum.'

Bella looks so lost and vulnerable. Rose wishes she could make it all go away. Kiss it better, put a plaster on it and give her a chocolate milkshake, anything to see her smile again. But the prim-nose days are long gone. It's times like this that she misses Glen. Two heads are better than one and he would know what to say. Then something Sally told her when she came over the other day slips into Rose's mind, and maybe she thinks she has found the right thing to say.

'You have to make him listen, Bella. Make him realise you're serious about it. Make him understand that you won't put your life on hold, your dreams on hold, for him. That you certainly won't put up with ultimatums. A friend of mine told me she'd had to settle for second best because of her husband, and now she very much regrets it. Don't be like her. Act before it's too late. I'll help you in any way I can.'

Bella's tears spill over again, but she smiles. 'That's what I meant when I said I wanted to be like you, earlier. It wasn't to do with nursing. You have this calm strength about you, and when I'm with you, I feel safe. Yes, you were broken for a while after Dad went, but now you have this amazing garden that seems to have given you an extra energy, a lift beyond all expectations. I felt Dad's presence there too – felt calm and at ease when I was amongst the flowers earlier, even though I was tired and stressed. I felt the salt air on my skin, and smelled the scent of honeysuckle and roses on the summer breeze. The children adored it too. And you're the centre of it, Mum. Being with you is like coming home.'

Rose reaches across the space between them and grabs her daughter's hand. They sit together on the sofa, overcome with emotion, lost in their own thoughts, many of which, Rose suspects, will share the same seeds. Tomorrow she'll suggest they take the children to the garden centre to choose some memory flowers of their own. Then they'll all plant them together.

Chapter Fourteen

The light of the early morning sun slides a few fingers through a gap in Rose's bedroom curtains and strokes a muted path across her floorboards. Two days since Bella and the children returned 'home', and she's already keenly feeling their absence. Another fitful sleep, another night of worries growing heavier, and more far-fetched with every passing hour of wakefulness. Rose thinks she drifted off about three o'clock, so that means just over two hours' sleep. She'll be no use to man nor beast today, as her mum would have said. If only Glen were still here. Then she wouldn't feel so worried about what to do for the best. Bella had told her she had an amazing calm about her. Well, right now she feels anything but. Once Bella has phoned and told her that she's spoken to Nigel about how she feels, Rose will be able to relax a bit, uncoil her guts and decide the best way to help her daughter put whatever plans she's made into action. Rose watches the sunlight shift to the dressing table as the breeze lifts and drops the curtains and hopes that Bella *will* actually speak to Nigel and not become another poor Sally.

A low moaning outside has her shooting bolt upright in bed, holding her breath and straining her ears in the silent morning. There it is again … oh, and now there's the unmistakable sound of retching. Rose twitches the curtain to one side, and there in the dawn light is a tall, thin figure in a black hoodie and jeans, evacuating the contents of his stomach over the gate into Daisy's oxeye daisies. Bloody hell! Rose throws on her dressing gown and hurries outside. The vomiting figure is now on his knees, half in and half out of the gate. He's trembling and possibly crying. Rose can't tell, because the hoodie is partially covering his face. The vomit stinks like a brewery. Years of nursing experience snap her into action. 'Okay, boy, let's have you on your feet. Take my hand, that's right, I've got you. Lean against me and we'll sit you down over at that picnic table…'

Now he's on his feet, the hoodie slips back to reveal a very young face – late teens, early twenties, Rose guesses. Ashen-faced, slack-jawed, he tries to push his blond curly hair from his eyes but it flops forward, defying all attempts. 'I… I…'

'No need to say anything. We'll get you sat down and get some water into you. Smells like you've drained a wine cellar.'

'I did and … cider.'

'Nice.'

After three or four attempts, the young man manages to get his leg over the bench and slumps down, head on the wooden picnic table. Rose wonders if she should try and get him inside, but charitable as she is, she doesn't want to be scrubbing vomit from her floors. The distant muted blue horizon, melding ocean and sky, tells her it's not likely to rain, and the sun, despite dodging in and out of low cloud, is gaining strength. 'So ... sorry...' he says, opening his eyes, the colour of moss.

'Don't worry. I'll go and get some water, and a blanket.' Rose did think of adding 'stay there', but she can tell there's little chance of him being fit enough to leave.

Expecting to find him asleep when she returns a few minutes later with a jug of water, a glass and a blanket, she sees him staring at the garden, still slack jawed, but his eyes are lively. The garden is slowly shrugging off the shadows of dawn. The sun comes out again from behind a cloud, and a blackbird sings a cheery song from the willow arch. Rose pours him water and drapes the red-and-yellow checked blanket around his shoulders. He reaches for the water and takes a big gulp.

'Steady. We don't want you being sick again. Just sip it. Little by little, we'll have you rehydrated in no time.'

The young man looks at Rose, his wobbly smile bringing warmth to his eyes and her heart. She wonders what led him to get so drunk and then wander around the streets at dawn being sick in strangers' gardens. 'Thank you for being so kind... I'm not sure I would be, if I were you. Ruining your flowers and all.'

'No real harm done. I'll give the daisies a good watering. What's your name? I'm Rose.'

'I'm Josh.' He breathes a long shuddering sigh and looks a bit woozy. Rose lightly takes his wrist and feels his pulse. A bit fast but not worryingly so. Josh frowns at her. 'You checking my heart rate.'

'Yeah. I used to be a nurse. You're okay. Drink more water.' She smiles as she realises this is the first time she's actually uttered those hitherto dreaded words – 'I used to be a nurse.' Rose is unsurprised that she's absolutely fine with it. 'Retirement' isn't at all the nightmare she thought it could be. She's come a long way in a relatively short time. Though she mustn't get complacent. Complacency tends to get a swift kick in the pants sooner or later, she's found.

'I see. My parents are both GPs.' Josh drinks more water and then his eyes flit round the plants and flowers, settling a few seconds on leaf here and petal there, like curious butterflies.

'So, Josh. How come you ended up here at dawn on this fine Thursday morning?'

Her upbeat tone elicits a quirk of his lips. 'I had to get away from home for a bit to think. I live in Truro with my parents and we used to come here often when I was a kid. I'd swim with my twin sister on the beach down there, build sandcastles and lark about. We spent loads of days here, just having the best time. When you're a kid, summer days seem to go on forever, don't they?'

Rose smiles and refrains from telling him he's actually still a kid. It would come across as patronising, and it's something he'll only realise when he's in middle age.

'I booked a B&B in the village and then spent most of last night in the pub. When they chucked me out, I got a bottle of wine from the supermarket and drank it as I walked up here.'

Rose notes he's not explained why he got so drunk, but doesn't pry. 'Port Gaverne is certainly a lovely spot. I wouldn't want to live anywhere else.'

Josh is concentrating on the garden again and he attempts to get to his feet, but finds himself just as unsteady as before. 'Hell, the world's spinning.' He grabs the edge of the table and sits back down with a bump.

'It will be. Have some more water.'

He does as she asks and points in the general direction of the honeysuckle and Flora's mock orange. 'I was going to go and look at those pink and purple flowers next to those yellow ones. I think I recognise them. Are they sweet peas?'

'They are indeed – well spotted.'

Josh smiles and his complexion warms up a little. He's becoming rehydrated, Rose decides. Maybe she'll make him some scrambled eggs or a bacon sandwich in a while. 'They are the only flowers I know, really. My gran used to grow them. She called me her...' Josh's smile falters, 'her sweet pea, when I was little. Gran. I do miss her. I used to love to play in her garden. Helped her with the gardening too. Simpler times, happy times.'

Rose thinks he might be crying, but he's got his head turned away slightly, resting his cheek on the heel of his hand. Instinctively she knows this young man needs a helping hand. This is not just a one-off drunken binge – something is bothering him, something important. Rose isn't sure if her hands could be the ones he needs, but at least she could give him a listening ear.

'Josh, do you fancy a bacon sandwich?'

He turns a tear-stained face to hers. 'You're so kind... I don't deserve it.'

'It would be my pleasure. You just sit here and look at the garden, feel its healing energy.'

Josh doesn't reply, just nods and looks away.

An hour later, he is looking much healthier and wiping the remnants of ketchup from his mouth. The sun's glinting on his hair, giving him the look of a sleepy cherub.

'I can drive you back to your B&B after you've finished your coffee, so you can rest,' Rose offers.

'I wish I could say I'll manage by myself, to save you coming out, but I'm realistic enough to know that I can't. So yes please, and I can't thank you enough for rescuing me.'

'You looked like you needed it.'

'Yeah. I did ... I do. My life is a pile of shit right now.' Josh presses his lips together and looks away, embarrassed. Rose thinks he might have regretted saying that.

'If you want to tell me about it, I'm a good listener.'

'I've taken up enough of your time already.'

'Not at all.' Rose drinks some coffee and waits. She knows there'll be more.

'Okay. I'll tell you as an explanation as to why I showed up here, legless. It's not an excuse, though, and once again – I'm deeply sorry for my behaviour.'

His demeanour and tone are reminiscent of a public schoolboy's after being hauled up in front of the headmaster. 'Stop apologising, and if I can help, I will.'

Josh gets up and wanders over to the sweet peas, strokes their delicate petals and sits cross-legged by them in the grass. He looks over at Rose and then up to the clouds above.

'My twin sister, I mentioned before, is a lost soul. Lucy's on drugs. No idea where she is. The last I heard she was living on the street in Plymouth. My parents and I tried to find her over the two years since she's been gone and managed it once or twice. She came home, promised to let us help her and then disappeared again a few days later. When she was with us, in her more lucid moments, she confided that she couldn't bear the pressure to be perfect that our parents put on her. Which I completely understood. Lucy felt that no matter what she did, it was never good enough. Her goal was to work with the seals at the Gweek seal sanctuary. She's always loved seals, ever since she was a tiny girl, and what she doesn't know about them isn't worth knowing. Our parents said that was something she could maybe pursue at weekends, but she should maybe tailor her interests into becoming a vet instead.'

Josh sighs and plucks a few blades of grass from the lawn and chews the end of one. Rose walks over to join him and sits down nearby. 'Lucy didn't like that idea?'

'No. She isn't really that academic. Not that she's unintelligent – far from it. But she's never been a hoop jumper. Much to my parents' chagrin. They put us both through private school and they hated the thought of wasting their money.' He tosses the blades of grass in the air. 'Anyway, long story short, she dropped out of school and ran away on her seventeenth birthday. It wasn't that much of a shock to me, as she'd become withdrawn and distant from me ... secretive. Shortly after, we discovered she was an addict and living in a squat. The parents were devastated, of course.' Josh rolls his eyes and affects a plummy accent. 'I mean, imagine the shame, darling.'

The public-school demeanour and tone make a lot of sense now to Rose. 'Poor Lucy... Do you think she might eventually be persuaded, if not to come home, to get professional help?'

'No idea. I hope so. Trouble is, I'm not much help to her at the moment because ever since she left, I've had double the pressure to succeed in my chosen profession.' Josh grimaces. 'That's a laugh. It's *their* chosen profession. As I said, the parents are both doctors and they decided as soon as I emerged from the womb – before I even drew my first breath, I imagine – that I'd follow in their footsteps.'

The despair he's been living with is almost tangible. 'Oh, I'm sorry to hear that, Josh. So you've no interest in a medical degree?'

'No. I've taken a year out, much to the parents' horror. I said I needed a break from studying and time to think. They can't understand that at all.'

'Did you struggle with A-levels?'

'Nah. Sailed through them – got A-stars in all. I've never struggled with anything academic, but I'm really not sure that I want to be a doctor. At first I thought I did, but as I progressed through my teens, I realised it was their dream I was living, not mine. They won't listen, of course. They never do.'

They sit quietly together in the strengthening sun, a sea breeze playing with their hair and keeping a pleasant temperature. Rose picks a sprig of rosemary and inhales the fragrance while she ponders Josh's story. 'From what you've told me, it seems like your parents have put so much pressure on you and Lucy that you've both snapped – she more dramatically than you. I know you just told me that they won't listen. But maybe it's time to *make* them listen – make them really take notice of what you actually want from life.'

'Yeah. It would be nice if I knew the answer to that myself.' Josh follows suit with the rosemary.

'Well, you know what you *don't* want, and that's a start. Besides, you're still young. You should be given time to decide. What are you, nineteen?'

'Yeah, almost twenty.'

'Plenty of time.'

'Not if you're my parents.'

'Have you any ideas at all?'

'Hmm. I like being outside... I like being here amongst nature – growing things.' He gestures to the flowers. 'I like swimming, listening to music. Not much of a job description.' Josh's smile is like the sun coming out from behind clouds.

'It's a start.' Rose smiles back. Then she thinks of the sweet pea comments from earlier. 'You enjoyed helping your gran in the garden. Maybe gardening is something you could consider?'

'Possibly. I've not done anything green-fingered, though, since Gran went. I miss her so.'

Rose nods, knowing only too well how grief can put the brakes on. 'I'm sorry to hear that, Josh. When did she pass?'

A look of surprise gives way to an embarrassed chuckle. 'God, no. Sorry – I can see how you'd get that idea. Gran's not dead … well, I suppose a huge part of her is. She has dementia, and she's in a care home. She used to live with us.'

'Oh, right. Yes, that must be upsetting for you. Does she remember you when you visit?'

He looks away. 'I don't anymore, I'm afraid. I can't face it. She has this vacant stare, then she often becomes anxious and panicky. Sometimes she smiles at me and I think she remembers who I am, but she doesn't. She thinks I'm a carer. I tell her I'm her grandson, but that upsets her, because she only remembers me as a little boy. When she first went into the care home, it was like she was hidden behind curtains, but very occasionally they twitched apart, and I fleetingly glimpsed the old Gran. The curtains are always closed nowadays, though.'

Upon hearing this sad news, an idea bursts open in Rose's head like a new bloom. As well as the memory about the old lady at the end of her life becoming animated when her hospital bed was wheeled out into the garden in the spring sunshine, more recently Rose remembers reading about sensory gardens. Some care homes and hospitals have dedicated green spaces for mental health and dementia patients. They are planted with aromatic plants which appeal to as many of the senses as possible – smell, touch, taste, sound, and, of course, sight. Lavender, rosemary, mint, roses, honeysuckle (hers is now too big for the trellis, so she has encouraged it to grow over the pergola too) and various salad plants, are all favourites, as their scents and textures stimulate the senses and invoke past memories. Bamboo and tall grasses are other favourites, as they are found to have a soothing and calming effect when the wind moves gently through their stems. Sometimes patients do their own gardening, feeling the soil in their hands, weeding and watering plants. Rose was delighted but unsurprised to find that when handled, bacteria in soil trigger the release of serotonin in the human brain. No wonder so many people feel happy when they're gardening.

Rose puts a hand on Josh's arm. 'I have an idea how you might be able to see through that curtain again, Josh.' She tells him all about the sensory gardens and how being close to nature might help his gran.

He listens – a small frown ebbing and flowing across his brow. 'Well, that certainly makes sense, but I'm not sure it would work for my gran. I mean, how would I get her involved? They have a garden there. But it's mostly lawn and a few shrubs.'

'Let me have a think.' Rose stands up and looks down the green sweep of her garden towards the blue of the ocean. There's already an idea taking shape. 'When I've fleshed something out, would you like me to come with you to visit your gran?'

Josh blinks a few times and manages a nod. 'Yes please, Rose.'

'Good. That's settled then. And in the meantime, if you feel in a self-destructive mood, don't go to the pub. Give me a ring instead. Agreed?'

Another nod. Then he reaches out and gives her hand a gentle pat.

'Right, let's get you back to the B&B so you can sleep.'

Josh follows her down the path to her car, but before he gets into the passenger seat, he says, 'Rose?'

'Yep.'

'Thank you for being so kind. For rescuing me.'

'You're welcome. It's been a real pleasure meeting you, Josh.' Rose realises that she means every word, despite her initial worries when he was vomiting on her daisies at the crack of dawn. This young man has a good heart and she knows he will find his way.

Chapter Fifteen

Sally can't remember the last time she really looked forward to something. Okay, she has a happy anticipation when her daughter Pippa comes over and they have a takeaway and movie-night. But they aren't the kinds of 'looking forward to things' that make her a little giddy with excitement if she thinks about them for too long. She knows most people would say, it's only pond building, hardly going on a round-the-world trip type of exciting, but there's a fire in her belly and a determination – a challenge in her gut that hasn't been there since, well, she can't remember when.

With all her equipment loaded into her brother's pick-up truck, she chucks her wellies in the back and slides behind the wheel. As she drives to Rose's, she considers her feelings about the pond. Maybe she's looking forward to it so much because it's something she's thought of by herself. When Paul was still with her, he was always the one who thought of things, decided on how they should be done, and then if the plan involved Sally, he made sure she carried out his instructions to the letter. Even if she did, there would always be something she'd done wrong, or fallen short on. Well, this pond would be *all* hers. She's researched it exhaustively online and spoken to a nice man at the garden centre where she bought the pond liner. He explained about the best plants to get, too, when it was ready, to keep the water oxygenated. Sally also had her eye on some white and pink elegant water lilies, just like the ones that Grace Pentewan had in her garden pond all those years ago.

It's a glorious day for it, and as the green, yellow and blue of the countryside zip past her window, Sally smiles as she thinks about her old neighbour. Such a wise lady, and a shame they'd moved house when she was twelve, because Sally was certain she could have learned so much more from her about wildlife and nature. There had been a real bond between them despite the difference in age, and Sally remembers to her shame, that she'd not even popped round to say goodbye the day they'd left. It wasn't because she was being rude, but because she knew she'd cry. Crying was not encouraged in public by her parents, Dad especially. Neither was being overly emotional in any respect. A sudden flare of anger heats up her insides. It's no wonder she had been so easy to control by her husband. Half the work had already been done, courtesy of her parents.

As she pulls up outside Rose's, she thinks about the question Pippa asked her last week. *Why don't you build a pond in your own garden? You have plenty of room.* At first

Sally didn't know, but she thought about it and eventually answered that she didn't feel her garden needed one. It wasn't the right place for it. She didn't add that her garden had too much of Paul in it, that Rose's garden was special, being there lifted her spirits, it spoke to her, and it had somehow suggested she make a pond, because that would have sounded slightly deranged. Maybe Sally *is* slightly deranged, but who cares? Not her. Well, not as much as she used to. There has been a bit of a shift inside her over the last while, a shift for the better, and she wants it kept that way.

Rose comes out to greet her dressed in green dungarees, her hair a messy golden halo, tendrils twisting in a futile attempt to escape from a multicoloured headband. This new look suits her. Sally tries to match the image of the smart not-a-hair-out-of-place efficient nurse, with this earth mother, and finds they won't fit together.

'Love the transport!' Rose pulls Sally into a quick hug and then strokes a hand along the flank of the red truck. 'You look like a proper handywoman in it.'

'I *am* a proper handywoman. I've got all my tools and pond stuff in the back, these old jeans and a baggy T-shirt and a pair of new green wellies, so I must be.'

'Yup.' Rose smiles and nods at the equipment that Sally's unloading. 'Want me to get the wheelbarrow and help bring stuff in?'

'Yes, please.' Then Sally gets a bit of a prickle at the base of her throat. How does she tell her friend that she wants to do this all by herself, without sounding ungrateful? She tests various scenarios in her head as they shunt everything from the truck to the spot at the back of the garden where the pond will be situated. As Rose takes off her gardening gloves and wipes the back of her hand across her forehead, Sally clears her throat. 'Um, thanks so much for helping ... and for letting me loose on your garden!' Rose laughs, but before she can reply, Sally plunges in: 'I'm really excited about doing this all by myself. It's the first thing I can remember having total responsibility for, and...' Shit, she's run out of the right things to say. She must look like a fish out of water, opening and closing her mouth, gulping for words instead of air.

'Totally get it,' Rose tells her with a slap on the back. 'Over there is my shed, in case you need anything – watering can, pick-axe etcetera, if the ground is too hard to dig. In the meantime, I'll stick the kettle on.'

Grateful for her immediate understanding, Sally watches her go and pulls her gloves on. This is going to be good.

———

Late afternoon slips into the garden almost unseen and presents Sally with a shower of rain and a dilemma. Does she stop work for the rain, or press on, as it's later than she thinks? Her sore fingers give her the answer and reluctantly she downs tools and trudges towards Rose's door. Rose ushers her in after she's taken off her muddy wellies and they sit at the kitchen table, a pot of tea between them and a biscuit barrel to hand.

'How's it coming along?' Rose asks.

'It's hard work, but I'm loving it. Just annoyed that the day has got away from me and my hands, despite the gloves, are developing calluses. I should have worked through lunch. Thanks for providing it, by the way. I'll bring sandwiches next time.'

'You will not! The least I can do is do lunch for you. You're making us a lovely pond and have refused payment.'

'I like the way you said "us" instead of "me". You're very generous, Rose.'

'That's the way I see it.' She shrugs. 'Gardens are for sharing, I reckon. This garden is for all of us to enjoy, and the pond will be a valuable jewel in the crown.'

Sally wonders what the biggest and best jewel is in Rose's personal crown. Indeed, if she owns one. Sally guesses she has two of her own and they have to be Pippa and Angus. Her children have turned out pretty well, considering. Maybe Bella is Rose's. Because there's a lull in the conversation and Sally has never felt comfortable with those, she asks, 'How's Bella and family doing?'

'Hmm. Not too great at the moment, if truth be known.' Rose dips a biscuit in her tea and gobbles it downs in one. 'She's in a similar situation to the one you were in – domineering husband. I'll not say more, because it's her story to tell. Suffice to say, I told her about your regrets about having accepted second best and told her to be careful she didn't end up in the same position. I'm hoping she and Nigel can work things through though, or come to some arrangement or other. I'm hoping for a phone update soon, because not knowing is driving me nuts.'

'Sorry to hear that, and if she ever wants to talk about

anything, just let me know.' Sally's stunned by her own words. She would never have offered advice like that in the past, as though she's an aficionado on domineering husbands. Then again, perhaps she is, after twenty-five years of it. Maybe Rose is growing some confidence plants in her garden and Sally's inhaled a few of their seeds today.

'Thanks, Sally. I'll let her know.'

The rain taps multiple fingertips against the kitchen window, indicating it's too wet for more digging and time for Sally to go home. Climbing into the truck after promising to come back on her next day off, and though she's only managed about a third of the digging, she feels like she's accomplished so much more. Her hands are red and sore, her arms are aching and there's a niggling twinge at the bottom of her spine that feels like it could become a problem if she doesn't watch out. *Not as young as you were, eh, Sal? Listen to your body, plan your movements and take it steady*, she tells herself. Not a bad mantra for life, to be honest.

Sally's only been gone a few minutes when the phone rings.

'Hey, Mum. How are you doing?'

'Bella! I was just thinking about you today when Sally came over. You know Sally from the surgery? She's building us a pond, isn't' that lovely?' Rose is aware she's nattering on. But even though her daughter is miles away, she detects in her ironed-out tone that something's happened, and not in a good way.

'Yeah, really nice of her.' The ironed-out sentence pulls silence after it, adding a sniff as a full stop.

'What's happened?' Rose sits in 'Glen's' ancient but comfy chair by the log pile next to the burner, instantly soothed by the feel of the dip in the cushion under her bottom that her husband's weight had made over the years.

'I talked to Nigel, and at first, he just laughed off my ideas. Said it was too late for all that – we couldn't come back to Cornwall, as we'd chuck away a stable financial future. He expected I'd let it drop, as I usually do if he says no to something, but I kept bringing it up. And last night … last night we had the mother of all rows. I stood my ground and … and…' Bella takes a moment to find her voice. 'I said if he didn't come back to Cornwall, then I'd come home by myself – well, I'd bring the kids, obviously.'

Rose strokes her finger along the impression of Glen's elbow in the leather arm of the chair and wishes for the umpteenth time he was here with her. 'Oh, love. What did he say?'

'He said I was a cold-hearted bitch, and didn't I realise I was breaking up the family on a stupid whim? Ruining the children's happiness? It all got out of hand and I said I couldn't live with him in Birmingham, and the way things were going, I wasn't sure if I could live with him anywhere.' Bella lets out a gasp which twists her mum's stomach. 'Mum, can I come home to you? I've nowhere to go and can't afford rent until I get a job there.'

Rose makes sympathetic noises which Bella can't hear, because she's breaking her heart on the other end of the line. Howls of anguish mix with sobs of despair and Rose wishes she was here with her too. Though this was the last thing she expected she'd be saying when she got out of bed this morning, she replies, 'Of course you can, my darling. You know you always have a home with me.'

'But it's a two-bedroomed cottage, and there'll be four of us living there. It might be a while before I'm on my feet again… Shit, I don't want to put on you like this … but I don't have another way. Oh, Mum, I'm so, so miserable here.'

Rose hadn't a fortune in the bank, but there'd be enough to get by, and everything was fine when they came to visit, with Bella and the kids in her old room. It was a bit cosy, but it wouldn't be forever. In the end, if this was what Rose could do to help her daughter put the next phase of her life into place, she would do it, gladly. 'Listen, love. You just get yourself home and we'll go from there, okay? Stop worrying about everything – we'll manage, and maybe you and Hannah can start that business from the VW camper that you dreamed of, eh?'

There's a huge sigh of relief and a sob. 'Thanks, Mum. Thanks so much. I'll try and be there tomorrow. The sooner I leave the better, because he was in a vile mood when he left for work this morning.'

'You think he'd hurt you?' Rose's stomach is turning over and over.

'No. I don't think so. He's never lifted a finger to me, but then I've never said I'm leaving before and taking his kids.'

'Right. Get your stuff and get out right now. Keep in touch on the way down, yeah? I'll make you something nice for dinner.' *As if a roast will make everything better, Rose. Dear Lord.*

'It might be a bit late for dinner when I get there, but I think you're right about leaving now. Okay. I'll keep in touch. Love you, Mum.'

'Love you too, sweetheart.'

Chapter Sixteen

F lora is putting the finishing touches to a countryside scene and wondering if the pebble cows in the foreground look more like poodles, when her mobile phone does the unexploded bomb thing on her glass-topped coffee table. Damn those things. She's only recently (and reluctantly) purchased one, as she conceded it might be useful, especially now she's getting on a bit. It's a comfort to have one on her person when she's out and about in case she becomes unexpectedly ill. A necessary evil.

It's Rose, how nice. 'Good afternoon, Rose. How—'

'Flora, can you come up? I need an ear.'

If Flora's not mistaken, her needed ear tells her that Rose either has a cold, or she's been crying. Oh dear.

'Yes, I'm not doing anything too pressing. I'll be up in five.' Flora disconnects and thinks she sounded quite 'with it', using that kind of terminology. *Up in five.* She heard an actor say it on TV the other day, and thought it cool. Mother had condemned the use of 'with it' years ago, because what did it actually mean? 'With what, exactly?' she'd questioned, with a turned-up nose, in a voice like Queen Victoria's, even though she was from Redruth. Flora hadn't been sure how to respond, but had said something like 'with modern times'. Nobody ever said 'with it' nowadays. Probably.

Rose's turquoise eyes have red rims, which indicates she's been crying, rather than her having a cold. 'Thanks for coming, Flora. I've had a bit of unsettling news and I needed to run it by someone trustworthy. My news has to go no further, though, as it's personal.' Rose nods at the kitchen table where a pot of tea and a chocolate cake wait for them. 'Sit yourself down.'

Flora does as she's asked, internally glowing from the comment about being trustworthy. Rose has lots of friends, so Flora thinks it's nice to be picked first, like a treasured bloom in Rose's garden. Then the internal glow dims a bit. What if the news is bad? What if Rose is ill? Terminally. What will Flora say to that? She's good at being a lighthouse, but not in a maelstrom. Not in a tsunami. No. She's better at dealing with a gentle swell. At a push, maybe a few brisk choppy waves.

Flora listens with some trepidation, her fingers grasping the handle of her mug so tight, she worries it might snap off. When she realises the problem concerns Bella and her husband and a return to Cornwall, she loosens the grip and blows a sigh of relief disguised as a cooling breath, across the surface of her tea.

'I'm sure she's doing the right thing, Rose. Bullies need standing up to. I should have tried to do that with Mother more than I did, but as you know, things weren't as easy for women back then. I had nowhere to go and no money. But then, when I got a job in teaching, I should have bought the old bag out, or left.' Flora takes too big a swig of tea and grimaces as the scalding liquid makes a fire pit of her gullet. 'I didn't though, did I? because I was conditioned by then. By her, mostly. But she was my mother and I had to look after her – that was what you did.'

Rose nods. 'Yes. It must have been hard for you, and I think Bella's doing the right thing too…'

Flora waits, as Rose stares at the agapanthus blooms in the 'bee pot' slowly climbing out of their pods. Nothing's forthcoming after a moment or two, so she prompts: 'I feel a "but" coming on.'

'Yeah. I went back over the conversation I had with Bella, and I do wonder if I encouraged her to leave too quickly … maybe I shouldn't have. After all, if she comes here, then that little family could be over, effectively.'

'But would you want her to stay and be bullied into living half a life, a mere existence? Her heart and dreams are here, by the sound of it.'

'Yes, they are. But I told her to get out now – today. Come down here as soon as possible. Should I have done that?'

'From what you've said, Bella had already decided she

was going to come here, either with or without your help. Maybe she would have stayed with friends if you'd dissuaded her. Look. You did what any loving mother would do. You gave her a safe place to escape to. A place where she knows she can take a breath and get herself back on her feet.'

Rose grasps Flora's hand across the table and squeezes it. 'Thanks, Flora. I knew I could count on you for sound advice.'

Flora's glow pings back into life and spreads warmth through her tummy like treacle sponge and custard. Which reminds her, she was so engrossed in her work that she missed lunch, and she's not in the mood for cake. 'You're welcome. And I must meet Bella and the children once they're settled. Now, if that's all, I must get back and grab some food, as I missed lunch. My stomach is on the growl.'

Rose looks chastened. 'Sorry, I hadn't realised. You can have some soup and cheese on toast?'

That sounds exactly the kind of thing Flora fancies, but she says, 'No, I couldn't put you out. It's my silly fault for not realising the time.'

Rose rests her elbows on the table and leans in. 'It's homemade with carrots and potatoes grown by my own fair hand.' She raises a comic brow. 'Now, how can a woman resist that?'

Flora can't, and chats with her friend about her pebble art and her library work as Rose prepares a very late lunch or extremely early dinner. Towards the end of a story about an elderly gentleman who asked if Flora could order *The Kama Sutra* as he couldn't find it on the shelf, Louise popped into her head. 'Oh, yes. I've been meaning to ask you about Louise. Remember I told you about her ages ago? Lost her husband, a bit of a loner. Met her at the library.'

Rose nods. 'Yeah, you said her husband had worked for the National Trust as a gardener.'

'That's right. Well, I've eventually got her to agree to come and visit you and your wonderful garden. I think she's slowly letting her guard down a bit.'

'Okay, when?'

Flora shuffles on the chair. 'Um, day after tomorrow. It slipped my mind.' Flora wonders if Bella coming home might mean that Rose will be too preoccupied to have Louise here. Because of her fragility, that might mean Louise could see it as rejection and it could set her back. Flora tells herself she's a silly old fool. Why has she left it so late to mention it to Rose? She carefully studies her friend's expression. She's pensive. Is that a good sign? Flora guesses not. She's in the middle of constructing a white lie to tell Louise, when Rose says:

'I think that will be okay. Bella won't mind. She won't want special treatment – never been one to hog the limelight. I could invite Sally and Daisy too, and we'll have an old-fashioned cream tea. It might do Bella good to have lots of people around her – might stop her thinking about her woes.'

Flora hopes her stretchy smile looks natural and not made from a combination of mild panic and relief. It's mostly mild panic, because she's afraid Louise will be overwhelmed by so many people all at once, and relief that Rose hasn't postponed her visit. Then Mother storms in after a long absence and says: *For god's sake, woman. Where's your gumption? You never used to be such a worrywart.* Then adds nastily, *Maybe you're getting past it!*

Piss off, Mother.

Flora wishes she could say that out loud, but it would take some explaining to Rose. Thankfully, Mother's comment has released a shot of gumption. It will all be okay. She can still be Louise's lighthouse, she just needs to keep her positive head on, that's all. 'Thanks, Rose,' she says. 'That sounds completely lovely.'

———

Flora has been cultivating her gumption reserves over the last few days. Feeding, watering and a bit of deadheading here and there has produced strong, sturdy stems, a mass of verdant leaves and one or two rather grand blooms, if she does say so herself. To complement her newfound energy and vigour, she's dressed herself in a bright yellow kaftan with ruby-edged sleeves and hem. Not real rubies, of course, though extremely pretty, nonetheless. Hopefully, Louise will enjoy her visit and not be thrown by the number of people at the 'impromptu cream tea affair', as Flora's been thinking of it. Though Daisy apparently can't make it, due to grandchildren babysitting commitments. She ties a crimson and gold-threaded chiffon scarf around her head and winks at herself in the mirror. *Not bad for someone who's 'getting past it', eh, Mother?*

On the walk up the hill to Rose's, the gumption wavers a bit when it strikes Flora that maybe she's hiding behind her colourful clothing. An unkind person once suggested that very same thing in the early days of Flora's transformation. The so-called friend had said something like, 'Flamboyant clothes are no substitute for real confidence. Real confidence comes from within and can't be manufactured or window-dressed. Anyone with half a brain will be able to see straight through the pretence.' At the time, Flora had replied that she doubted that the friend had a brain at all and it had all got a bit nasty. Suffice to say, she'd rapidly acquired an ex-friend.

A few years ago, Flora might have looked back and laughed, because none of it was true. But what if it is true now? Sometimes, well, more than sometimes, she does feel more vulnerable than she used to. Perhaps it's come from the huge upheaval she's undergone these past few months. Moving home can be traumatic enough for a much younger person, let alone a seventy-seven-year-old woman, on her own, moving towns after a lifetime in the same place – the same house. No matter how she looks at it, the community Flora built in Truro was now gone. Yes, she could go back and visit, but her roots had been severed. She would be a visitor, not the vital part of the group she once was. And yes, she has made some lovely new friends, but does she really belong? Or is she just seen as some ridiculous old hippy that people feel sorry for, a charity case? 'People' being Rose, Daisy and the others. Is it true that Flora's hiding her vulnerability underneath her outfits?

She stops to get her breath and rests a hand on the stone wall surrounding the garden of a bungalow a few doors down from Rose's. This garden is unremarkable in every way. It's a bit dowdy, uncared for, drab even. There is, however, a gaily painted gate – bright green with some hand-painted white flowers in an arch across the curved top. It can't disguise the garden, though. This isn't lost on her. Is she the gate?

Her low mood allows in more worries. The most prominent one concerns Louise. Louise might not, in fact, turn up. When Flora phoned the other day and offered to pick her up this afternoon, Louise said she wasn't sure what time she'd be there exactly and would either walk or get a taxi. Flora reminded Louise that when she came to hers for dinner, she'd found it a bit of a shlep, to which Louise responded, 'I was unprepared. I won't make that mistake again.' Flora gave the socially acceptable chuckle she's perfected of late, and left it at that.

As it turns out, Louise and Flora turn up at exactly the same time, much to the latter's relief. Louise is climbing out of a taxi, wearing casual blue trousers, a floral shirt and in a departure from the shiny brogue, comfortable deck shoes. The whole ensemble takes years off her, Flora decides, and she hurries forward to give her a hug. Then she thinks better of it as Louise takes a step back and clasps her large red leather handbag to her chest, effectively removing any available hugging space.

'You look nice,' Flora says, leading the way up the path to Rose's front door. When she's met with silence, she turns to find Louise standing by Daisy's daisies, open-mouthed, taking in the entire garden. Flora smiles and tries to see it with new eyes. It's not hard, as there always seems to be something different popping out of the ground every time she comes. Rose says new things appear willy-nilly, even though she's had nothing to do with them.

'This garden is so beautiful,' Louise says, her voice tremulous.

'It's pretty special, alright.' Flora points to her *Philadelphus*. 'That mock orange over there is my contribution. A few of us decided to plant memories here – you know, a plant or flower that reminds us of a lovely memory. It could be happy, sad, funny, inspiring, anything. A memory that means something important to us.'

Louise nods and looks at the shrub. 'You do know its proper name is *Philadelphus*? Mock orange sounds a little vulgar for such a delicate plant, if you ask me.'

Flora wasn't asking. And that wasn't quite the response she imagined she'd receive. Nevertheless, she smooths her ruffled feathers and says, 'Yes, I do know. Do you like the idea of nature invoking memories?' Louise is examining the primroses and says nothing. But Flora's not giving up. 'Primroses are very special to Rose. They remind her of her daughter when she was little. She told me that planting them will be like making sure her memories never fade, as they'll pop back up each year, connecting her to happy times. It's the same with everything here. As long as there's new life growing, there will always be hope and new memories to make.'

Louise eventually turns to her and Flora can see she has tears in her eyes. Oh dear. 'That's so lovely. I wish I'd thought of everything that way, before I sold our old place with all the things my Matthew had planted in the garden.

It hurt too much at the time, so I didn't realise that being amongst them could have helped me eventually.'

Flora kicks herself. Louise wasn't really being rude before, just moved by the garden and her memories of Matthew. The spiky mock orange comment might have been a shield – protecting her emotions from exposure. Flora's no stranger to a shield.

Rose bursts out of the door bringing a welcome distraction and a shift in energy. 'Hello! Great to meet you, Louise.' Rose grins, sticking her hand out, and Louise shakes it, looking a little shell-shocked. 'What do you think of the garden? I'll show you round properly in a bit.'

'It's gorgeous. So many different colours, textures, and perfumes. Many plants I wouldn't have put together just seem to work.' The surprise in Louise's voice isn't lost on Rose.

'Ha! Yes, I'm no expert. I buy things that I like the look of and think about where they'll live later. Other things seem to self-seed. I find things that die back in other parts of the country bloom longer in Cornwall. Might be to do with the micro-climate. All sorts of things surprise me. Look, I have some orange poppies "popping" up over there, pardon the pun!'

Flora laughs. 'Very droll.'

Rose looks at Louise's bemused expression and says, 'I know. Dreadful, right? I won't go on stage anytime soon.' There's an awkward moment where nobody speaks, so she adds, 'Flora tells me you know a bit about plants, as your husband used to be a gardener with the National Trust.'

Louise visibly bristles. 'Actually, he was a

horticulturalist.'

'Ah right, yes. He would have known lots, then.' If Rose is put out by Louise's tone, she doesn't show it.

Louise looks at her feet. 'Yes. He knew everything.'

Just then, a plump woman with dark hair, presumably Sally, comes out of the cottage carrying a tray of scones, followed by a blonde who looks just like Rose – obviously Bella, with a tray of tea and the children carrying plates. Well, the eldest is carrying plates, the youngest is carrying a tub of cream while jumping along the path like a kangaroo and laughing his head off. Flora listens, enchanted, and imagines he's a handful at times, but fun to be around. Rose does the introductions and then they settle down to a cream tea at the picnic table with an extra-small table added at the end for Molly and Wesley.

Louise is quiet, but that's not unusual, and she seems happy enough. Besides, others more than make up for it as they chat about gardens, the weather and life in general. Flora warms to Bella and Sally immediately, particularly Sally. She reminds her of a friend she had at school years ago. Big and bold on the outside, but Flora knows there's a vulnerable interior. Rose had mentioned her personal circumstances briefly, and Flora hopes the pond building and being here in this lovely space will do her the power of good.

The conversation turns to gardening again and Wesley jumps up from his seat, jam and cream all over his face, and says, 'I have a sunflower. It will be big! Molly got one too but mine's better.' Then without warning, he grabs Louise's hand and yanks it. 'Come and see, Weez. Come and see.'

Flora holds her breath, wondering how Louise will react, and can hardly believe it when Louise pushes her glasses up her nose, smiles at him and calmly allows herself to be led up the garden and around the side of the house. Molly wipes cream from her mouth and hurries after them, shouting, 'Oi, Wes, don't you touch my one!'

Rose laughs. 'They insisted on bringing the sunflowers they were growing up in Birmingham. Luckily, they're fairly small at the moment, or they'd have got a bit battered in the car.'

'They seem settled already,' Sally says to Bella, pouring some tea.

Bella gives a shrug and puts cream on her scone. 'I think they are, overall. They adore being here with Granny and they love the garden, of course. But Molly has asked when Daddy's coming, and I've just said he's busy with work. I can't bring myself to tell them the truth.' Flora thinks she's trying not to cry and wishes she could help. 'Not yet anyway. We'll see how things go. I have to get her in school here, but it's July, so I'll send her in September now. A new school on top of everything else would be too much. It's all such a mess, but I can't do everything at once.'

Sally dabs her mouth with a bit of kitchen roll and pats Bella's hand. 'Yeah. Take one day at a time, but stick to your plan. I, for one, know how easy it is to just give in for a quiet life. Trouble is, you forfeit your own happiness in the long term when you do that.'

Bella squeezes Sally's hand. 'Yeah. Don't settle for second best, eh?'

Sally smiles. 'Exactly.'

Louise and the children come back down the path, linked hand in hand in hand like a daisy chain. Flora finds she can't contain a huge smile as she watches the three of them draw near. Louise is in the middle, a child on either side, each carrying a small earthenware pot with a fledgling sunflower in it. Louise has an even bigger smile than Flora's and her cheeks are in bloom. Flora can't remember seeing her look so happy, or even contented. There's an internal glow lighting her face. She looks … radiant. No other word for it.

'Weez said my one is best,' Wesley pronounces, setting his pot on the little table proudly.

'No, she didn't!' Molly huffs and sets her pot down on the big table. 'She said we both had strong healthy plants and they would be big and tall if we took care of them properly. And her name is Loo-eeze, not Weez, you dumbo!'

'Molly,' Bella warns in a stern voice. 'We don't call people unkind names, do we?'

Molly pouts, folds her arms and looks away.

'Weez said she would help us grow our flowers,' Wesley says, looking up at Louise with huge blue eyes.

Louise looks uncomfortable and says to Rose, 'Well, not exactly. I said I'd give them a few tips… I don't want to impose.'

'No, please do come and help! You're not imposing – the more hands we have around here, the better. Especially hands that know gardens.'

Louise looks at Flora and they share a smile. 'Now that's an offer you can't refuse,' Flora says.

'Mummy, can we get the paddling pool out?' Molly asks, fanning her face. 'I'm boiling.'

Bella laughs. 'It's not that hot. Anyway, we don't have a paddling pool.'

'Oh yes we do,' Rose says. 'I saw it in the loft when I went up there looking for your paints. It's your old one. Come and help me get it down.'

'You kept my old paddling pool?' Bella says, incredulous.

'Yep. Your dad always said never throw anything away, because you never know when it might come in handy. I used to moan at him, but in this case, he was right.'

A gentle breeze rustles through the bamboo cane and elephant grass, collecting the scent of honeysuckle and lavender, and as it passes, drops it over the heads of the five women relaxing in deckchairs. Sally adjusts her wide-brimmed straw hat and nods at the children playing nicely together (for once) in the paddling pool. 'What fun a bit of water and a few toys provide, eh? Simple pleasures.'

'I might join them,' Flora says, only half-joking. There is gentle laughter and the splashing of the water as the children fill and tip their buckets over a plastic purple dinosaur and a few farmyard animals. In the dappled sunlight, it looks a most inviting activity.

'God, I can't remember the last time I felt so totally relaxed,' Bella says with a heartfelt sigh.

'It's the garden,' Louise offers. 'The scent of the flowers combined with the sound of the breeze in the elephant grass in this shady spot is most soothing.'

'A sensory garden.' Rose nods. 'This bit of the garden has turned itself into one all by itself without me realising. And when Sally's pond is done, we'll have the sound of water too, trickling down the rocks from a little waterfall. Heaven.'

Louise looks at Rose. 'You mean you didn't design it as such? It just happened in a haphazard manner?'

Rose pauses a moment in thought. 'Yes. Yeah, exactly that.'

Louise nods. 'How amazing. Flora was telling me when we first arrived how much of the garden is connected to memories.' She clears her throat and looks at Flora as though unsure. 'Erm, I was saying I was a bit hasty selling up after my Matthew died. He'd made us a spectacular garden, but it was so painful to be in it without him. The first spring was total agony, as on the one hand I couldn't wait to see which flowers would pop up – he'd planted new bulbs in a little patch. But on the other, it killed me to know he would never plant anything else.' Louise sets her shoulders back and hurries on. 'Turned out to be grape hyacinth. Such cheerful little things.' A heavy sigh. 'After that, I put the place up for sale. Moved to somewhere with just a patch of lawn and a place to put a few pots.'

'And now you wish you hadn't?' Rose asks, gently.

'Yes. Flora told me that you said new life growing means

new hope. I couldn't see it at the time. But now I realise if I'd stayed, each year would be like part of my husband reaching out to me, letting me know how much he loved me. The darling grape hyacinth ... daffodils. Life goes on – perennials show us that.'

Flora's thrilled that Louise has opened up like this. She must be learning to trust again. 'I was also talking about your primroses, and how they remind you of Bella as a child, Rose.'

Rose laughs. 'Yes, prim-noses.'

Bella rolls her eyes as her mum tells the story of her mispronunciation.

Louise looks longingly at the children splashing each other in the pool and says, 'I love primroses. Matthew and I weren't blessed with children. I often wonder what they'd be like now if we'd had them. I like to think they'd be outgoing, cheerful, confident and bold – not like me. Like Matthew. He was my opposite. If our children were flowers, they'd have been primroses.'

Flora knows by looking at the others' faces that they have a lump in their throats just like hers. She washes it down with a sip of tea.

Rose does the same and points in the direction of the agapanthus. 'You can't see them very well from here, but I feel I'm connected to Glen through those. There are lots of other things in the garden that remind me of him, but for some reason those big blue showy blooms speak to me of him.'

Bella leans forward and says to Louise conspiratorially, 'Dad wasn't big and blue by the way.' She gives a theatrical wink to drive away the puzzled look on Louise's face. Flora doesn't think she's ever met anyone who is almost completely devoid of a sense of humour as much as Louise is. It's quite endearing in a way.

'Remembering them when they are no longer here is sometimes very painful, as you said, Louise,' says Rose. 'But the thing is, in the end, we have to be thankful that we had them in our lives. They loved us and we them. And that lasted, long after the exchanging of rings and saying "I do." That love goes on, even now. Not everyone is so lucky.'

Another lump blocks Flora's throat as Rose's words hit home, and she looks at her *Philadelphus* and sees Patrick's handsome face. *We weren't as lucky, were we?* Still, what they had was incredible, despite being short-lived. She had loved and been loved, and for that she is grateful. Then she remembers an appropriate quote and decides to share it.

'There are always flowers for those who want to see them.'

Her friends' expressions reveal varying degrees of understanding. Unsurprisingly, Louise has her little frown firmly back in place.

Flora folds her hands in her lap and says, 'It's a quote by Henri Matisse. I think he meant that when you're in the darkest places and feel you'll never see the light again, really try your hardest to look for the good things, no matter how small. They're the flowers.'

Louise puts her hand over her mouth and does the slow blinking. 'Yes. Yes, I see that now,' she whispers through her fingers.

Rose smiles and gets to her feet. 'Okay, who's for a glass

of wine to celebrate this garden, friendship and looking for flowers?'

Everyone readily agrees, apart from Louise. Then in a quiet voice she says, 'Well, it's a little early for me, but I could make an exception. Thanks, Rose.'

Rose goes off with Bella to get the wine and Louise asks Flora for the memory behind the *Philadelphus*. Flora tells her and is pleasantly surprised to feel Louise's hand slip into her own. They sit there together holding hands, sniffing back tears and allowing the garden to soothe their spirits. Then all of a sudden, Wesley comes running over to Louise on his stout little legs. 'Weez, can I put my sunflower in the paddling pool?'

She laughs. It's a carefree, unfettered laugh which gladdens Flora's heart, and then Louise takes his hand and helps him gently dip the plant pot in the water. 'Okay, that's enough now, Wesley. Sunflowers like to be handled gently. If you drop them, or their soil gets too wet, they won't grow big and tall.'

'You put it back now?'

'I will. Maybe the sunflower would like a little sleep in the peace and quiet.' Louise looks at Molly who's submerging a dinosaur in a bucket of water. 'Shall I take your sunflower for a sleep too, Molly?'

'Yes please, Weez.' Molly laughs at her play on words and amazingly, Louise joins in.

Flora watches Louise carrying the two sunflowers up the path and round the side of the house and thinks what an absolutely perfect afternoon it's been.

Chapter Seventeen

Rose is thinking of reasons why it wouldn't be a good idea to camp in the garden but can't find any. She's never been much of a sleeping outdoors kind of person, preferring the comfort of her own bed. But she has to admit the idea of sleeping under the stars amongst her flowers and shrubs has a new appeal. She'd not be too far from her bed if she was really desperate either. Besides, she reminds herself, she's forging a new path, trying new things, isn't she? Molly is standing next to Madame Aggie Panther, still waiting for an answer. She's looking up at her grandma, her best winning smile firmly in place, her pretty topaz eyes fixed on Rose's.

'Well, providing the tent that Mummy found in the loft hasn't got holes in it, I think it will be okay.'

Molly does a crazy little dance, her excited whoops scaring off a couple of fat seagulls perched on the garden gate. 'Can we camp tonight, Granny?' she asks, pink from her exertions.

'Not tonight, we have to check the tent and sort sleeping bags.'

Molly sighs. 'Tomorrow then?'

'We'll see. Now off you go and have your breakfast. Your mummy's made boiled eggs.'

She does as Rose asks, her brown curls pulled into a high ponytail swinging back and forth as she hopscotches towards the kitchen door, singing. Oh, to be a child again. Finding joy in the smallest things. *The exuberance of youth.* Actually, Rose thinks she wouldn't want to have her life over again. She's happy at the moment and re-learning how to find joy. So far, she's not doing bad at all. A damp breeze kisses the faces of the sweet peas as she passes, wafting a fragrant mix of hyacinth and orange blossom through the air, a gift to Rose. Joyous. There are so many sweet peas now that she's considering picking some for the house, and then a wonderful idea unfurls inside her mind. Josh's grandma might like a little bouquet of these. Rose could add a few other blooms too, and she and Josh could visit her in the care home. How she could help Josh and his gran had been a puzzle until now. Yes, she'd told him they could visit her, but not until now did she realise how flowers, specifically the sweet peas, might give the old lady a lift.

When she and Josh had talked about his gran being involved in a sensory garden, Rose couldn't quite grasp how, apart from bringing her here to see this one. She'd initially thought that would be lovely, but too overwhelming for someone with dementia. But this might be a first step. She pulls her mobile phone from her jeans pocket and calls him.

'Rose, lovely to hear from you. I was only thinking about you the other day and thought I might phone soon for a chat.'

'Are you feeling a bit down still?'

'Yeah, but better since I spoke to you. You talk a lot of sense and don't judge.'

Rose finds herself grinning. 'What a lovely thing to say. Maybe we could kill two proverbial birds. How about we combine our chat with a visit to see your gran? I was thinking about the sensory garden thing, and wondered if just taking her a bunch of sweet peas and a few other blooms might help give her a boost?'

There's a short pause, then Josh says, 'I think that would be a great idea, but I need to prepare myself for it falling flat. She might just sit in her chair by the window and look straight through us. It's definitely worth a try, though.'

'It is. When would you be free to go?'

'This afternoon?' His enthusiasm is palpable.

The exuberance of youth. 'I'll check with my daughter and call you back. Can't see a problem, though.'

If you can't beat 'em, join 'em.

It's a redbrick Victorian house, not quite a mansion, but nearly. Rose thinks it looks almost watchful as it sits at the top of a sweeping drive, its leaded windows looking out over the green expanse of hills rolling to a stop in the shade of a wooded valley. She imagines it was once the home of a rich merchant, as it's not too far from the port of Falmouth.

As care homes go, it's not too shabby, and Rose has seen a few, during a brief stint as a district nurse. As they step through the huge oak doors, Rose can tell that Holywell Heights, both inside and out, is definitely worth the pretty penny Josh's parents must be paying. The staff are all very friendly and welcoming and seem thrilled that Josh has come to visit his gran.

As they walk up the central staircase to her room Rose asks, 'What's your gran's name? I can't call her "Gran". Now, that *would* be confusing.'

Josh laughs. 'It would. It's Lily.'

'Appropriate for a lady who loves flowers.' Rose has a few unexpected butterflies as they walk along the carpeted corridor to Lily's room. She hopes for Josh's sake that the visit goes well. Has she been too optimistic? Though he said he'd prepare for disappointment, Rose knows he's still very fragile. Josh walks ahead of her, carefully carrying the flowers like a nervous pageboy, and then he gives a gentle tap on the door before entering the enormous bedroom.

Lily is dressed in a lilac two-piece, a cream blouse under the jacket and smart brown lace-ups on her feet. She's sitting in a high-backed chair, a cane in her right hand, gazing out through a huge window. Rose thinks she looks a little like the late Queen, ready to have her portrait painted. Lily is certainly not what Rose expected at all, and she can't help thinking that she looks on her guard, ready to leave at a moment's notice rather than relaxing in her room.

Josh hands the bouquet of blue and pink sweet peas, with white alyssum, to Rose, while he draws up two chairs in front of Lily's. Lily has shown little interest in either of them so far, save a first glance as they came into the room. Rose notices her face is subtly made-up, giving warmth to her cheeks and blue eyes.

'Gran, it's Josh. I've brought my friend Rose to see you, and some flowers.' He takes the bouquet and holds it out to her. At first, she ignores him, then her nostrils flare and she takes the bouquet and inhales its subtle fragrance. A hint of a smile wavers on her lips, then as she takes in the delicate petals and colours of the sweet peas, the smile widens. 'Do you remember what these are called, Gran?' Josh touches one of the sweet peas.

Lily looks at him, surprised. 'Of course I do.' Her voice is strong, commanding. Not a voice Rose imagines a lady of Lily's age would possess. 'Sweet peas. I grow them in my garden. My grandson loves them. I even call him Sweet Pea sometimes.'

Josh turns a wobbly smile to Rose and nods at Lily. 'You did. I loved you calling me that.'

Suspicion flits through Lily's eyes. 'You aren't Josh. Josh is just a boy.'

'I was a boy, Gran. I've grown up a bit.'

Rose knows that Josh is just holding it together, so she says, 'Hi, Lily, I'm Rose. I grew those flowers in my garden.'

A benign look pushes suspicion to one side as Lily peers more closely at Rose's face. 'You do my garden? What happened to Graham from next door? He always used to cut the grass.'

'These are from my garden, Lily. We thought you'd like them,' Rose soothes, aware that Lily's getting agitated.

'You're a bit familiar, aren't you, calling me Lily? I don't even know you. Go away.' Lily looks out of the window and taps her cane twice on the floor, very deliberately.

Rose lowers her voice and says to Josh, 'Maybe we should go. We don't want to upset her. I'll go and get a vase for those first … give you a bit longer with her on your own.'

As she stands up, Lily addresses her. 'This garden is a disgrace.' She nods outside. 'Look at it. Walls and bits of grass. Regimented bushes standing to attention like privates on parade. What's the point in that? Gardens and the things growing in them should be allowed to thrive, to develop, to have a mind of their own.'

These sentiments are so much like Rose's philosophy, she's at a loss for words. She goes over to the window and looks out at the wide sweep of lawn and shrubs. Lush, green, but soulless. 'I see exactly what you mean, Mrs, er…' She's suddenly stuck and shoots a pleading look at Josh.

Josh whispers, 'Manville.'

'Mrs Manville. I totally agree that gardens have to be allowed some freedom, to spread their joy, healing and comfort. If growing things are trussed, bound and restricted, they can only give us so much. A bit like we humans.' Rose is unsurprised at what she said or the passion in her voice, but surprised she'd said it out loud.

Lily smiles and the blue of her eyes sparkles like an ocean under a summer sun. The years fall away and Rose can see the girl she once was. 'My thoughts exactly. What's your name again?'

'It's Rose, Mrs Manville.'

'Don't be so formal. Call me Lily.' Josh coughs to

disguise his amusement and she frowns at him. 'How long have you had that cold, Josh? You know you shouldn't run about the house barefoot. I've told you a thousand times. Have some linctus, it's in the bathroom cabinet.'

Josh looks caught between laughter and tears, and Rose pats his shoulder. 'I'll go and get a vase of water for your blooms, Lily. They will look lovely on the windowsill.'

Lily nods, but her smile is fading and she looks through Rose. 'Yes. I grew those myself … I think?' She looks at the flowers in her hands, smells them and the smile grows back. 'Such beautiful colours.'

When Rose comes back with a tall yellow vase, Josh is holding his gran's hand while she tells him all about her twin grandchildren. He keeps wiping a stray tear away and smiling valiantly, but Lily doesn't seem to notice. 'They sound like a lively pair,' he says as Rose puts the flowers in the vase and sets them on the windowsill.

'Oh, they are. Josh is so much like his father at his age. Bright as anything, but often boisterous with it.'

Josh laughs. 'Bet he's a hoot.'

'Yes, he can be. He loves my flowers.' She nods at the yellow vase. 'Sweet peas are his favourite. I grow them in my garden.'

Rose thinks it's time they went, as she isn't sure how much longer Josh can keep smiling. 'Well, we'll be off now. Thanks so much for the chat, it was lovely. Maybe you can come and visit my garden soon? Would you like that?'

'Yes, dear. I'm not sure if I can get out this damned place, though. I've been waiting by the window for the taxi to take me to my son's house for ages today. I've dressed smartly because I know Robert might take me out to lunch too.' She smooths her skirt. 'I don't see Robert much now. He's so busy – a doctor, you know.'

The pride in her voice and the realisation that she's dressed in her best because she's waiting for her son is almost too much to bear. 'Dad comes to see you every week, Gran. You come to lunch at home sometimes too...' Josh says, quietly. 'But you don't remember.'

Lily looks through him vacantly, then at the flowers. Recognition brings a smile. 'Sweet peas. I do love them.'

In the car, Josh wipes away more tears, but he smiles through them. 'Well, that is what I call a result. Though bits of it were heartbreaking, it was mostly uplifting, as she never normally says more than a few words. She recognised me briefly too, when I coughed. That's a first.'

Rose knows they must be cautious, but she's quietly optimistic. 'I think it could be the sweet peas that made the difference. The sight and smell of them obviously unlocked happy memories for her.'

'I'm convinced of it. Can we take her to your garden soon?'

'If the staff think it's a good idea, then yes. It might help that I used to be a nurse and have a little experience with dementia patients.'

'Excellent. Thanks so much again, Rose. Can I run an idea past you?'

'Of course.'

'Could I come and help tend your garden for a while, just to learn a few things, get some experience, you know? This is with a view to maybe working as a gardener.'

'My garden is your garden. A grand idea.'

'Thanks, Rose. When I was in your garden, drunk and disorderly and behaving disgracefully,' He shakes his head. 'Once again, I'm so sorry for that, Rose.' Rose gives him an encouraging smile and pats his hand. 'Anyway, after I'd recovered a bit, I think being there in the garden with the sweet peas and growing things had a really positive effect on me, you know? It linked the me now, back to the me then, when everything was simpler. I get that I can't turn back the clock, but remembering the good times I had with my sister and Gran gave me a boost. Right now, I need all the boosts I can get.' He bowed his head and looked sheepish. 'You helped loads, of course.'

'I'm only too happy to help. Give me a bell when you want to pop over and we'll organise it.'

'This was one of my daughter's better ideas,' Bella says, raising a glass in cheers.

Rose gently clinks her own against it. 'It was. Let's hope we both get some sleep, though.'

The two women are sitting outside the old tent in the garden, the scent of the nearby honeysuckle heavy in the evening air. There's a faint trace of charcoal in it too, as they've spent considerable time grilling sausages for hotdogs, and making s'mores while trying to prevent

Wesley from throwing a whole packet of marshmallows onto the BBQ. Eventually, after numerous bedtime stories and Molly's amateur dramatics, which involved her imagining she could hear wolves in the distance, both children drifted off to sleep in their new sleeping bags. Rose had only managed to find two slightly worse-for-wear adult ones in the loft, hence the dash to the camping stores earlier, and she'd brought out a couple of blankets to ensure they'd all be warm enough. Bella had said she was fussing needlessly, as it was July, but Rose wanted to be comfy.

As she and her daughter relax in their deckchairs outside the tent and watch the pinprick stars flicker on in the lavender sky, she pushes away thoughts of sneaking back up to her big queen-size bed in the dead of night. That wouldn't be a team player kind of thing to do, now would it? Maybe not, but it's tempting, nevertheless. That big snuggly duvet and feather pillows. Bliss.

'What are you smiling at?' Bella asks, offering a bowl of peanuts.

Rose takes a handful. *Oops, caught red-handed.* 'Nothing. Just thinking what a lovely evening it is. The scent of honeysuckle is so strong tonight.'

'It is. The whole garden smells gorgeous. It's got that earthy grassy smell mixed with the day's heat from the sun trapped in the leaves, the lawn, everything.'

This surprises Rose. She's never thought about smells in such detail. 'What does the trapped heat from the sun smell like?'

'Take a deep breath through your nose and hold it a few beats.'

Rose does. 'Yeah?' she replies through a tight mouth as she's still holding her breath.

'Release slowly and then sniff.'

Rose does as she's told. 'Okay.'

'What you have just smelled is trapped heat from the sun. Get it now?'

There's an indefinable earthy warmth running under the evening garden scent. It's as good a description of trapped heat as she can find. 'I think I do, yes.' There's a feeling of warmth running through her too. It's so wonderful to be out here sharing nature with Bella. She's going through so much trauma right now too, but managing to hold fast, battle through and smile while she's doing it. Rose knows she's doing the swan act, serenely gliding through the water while underneath, her legs are paddling furiously, but she's always been a strong swimmer.

'Look at that!' Bella gasps and points south, to where the navy line of ocean kisses the hazy lavender heavens. 'A shooting star.'

Rose isn't quite sure that she saw it, but says, 'Wow. Did you make a wish?'

'Yeah... I've never seen one before,' Bella whispers in amazement.

A gentle breeze soughs through the willow arch and Rose reaches for her daughter's hand. 'How's it all going with Nigel? Heard anything from him today?'

She sighs. 'You know I told you he was texting and ringing every five seconds the day we left and every day after, begging me to go home?' Rose nods. 'There's been nothing for almost twenty-four hours. It's as if he's washed his hands of us… I had hoped he'd come round because I do love him still.'

This makes Rose sad because deep down she thinks Nigel is a decent man. He's just chasing carrots dangled from on high, instead of realising he has many more things to cherish at root level. 'He might still come round. Once he's been without you and those lovely children for a time, he will see how empty his life is and what really matters.'

Bella shrugs. 'We'll see. I'm not giving up, though. When you were out visiting Josh's grandma, I called Hannah and told her what had happened. She's still up for the campervan café idea. She mentioned we could give it a trial run one weekend and see if we get any customers.' Bella's smile falters. 'Thing is, it would mean you looking after the children … and I've asked so much of you already.'

'It would be my pleasure. And if it takes off, I'll help out as much as I can. There's always the brilliant little nursery that Molly went to for Wesley, and of course, Molly will be at school. If you want something badly enough, you can make it happen.'

Bella squeezes Rose's hand and wipes away a tear with the other one. 'I don't know what I'd do without you, Mum.'

'Well, luckily you don't have to find out. Shall we have another cheeky glass before turning in? I'd like to sit outside in this garden paradise awhile and breathe in the trapped sunshine and fresh earthy smells.' Rose laughs. 'I don't have to try too hard to see you pottering around the prim-noses in your vest and nappy.'

'Aw, I bet I was such a cutie.'

'Still are.'

'I'll second that,' comes a voice from behind.

'Nigel?' Bella says, jumping up.

Nigel walks over and gives her a big hug. 'I had to come and see you. I've missed you all so much.'

Rose is in danger of becoming the biggest gooseberry in the garden as her daughter holds him tight and tells him she's missed him too. 'Nice to see you, Nigel. Can I get you a glass of wine?'

'Yes, please, Rose. Sorry for just rocking up, but...' He gets choked up, so Rose pats him on the shoulder and walks past.

Upon her return, the two of them are sitting in the deckchairs deep in conversation, voices low so as not to wake the children. Rose is pleased to hear no angry words or snapping but is unsure what to do next. She wants to leave them to it, but also wants to make sure Bella is okay. 'Anything else I can get you both?' She hands the wine bottle to Bella and a clean glass to Nigel. 'I have some ham and bread rolls, Nigel. You just missed out on the BBQ.'

'I ate on the way down, thanks, Rose.' Nigel pushes his hand through his floppy blond fringe and tries a smile. Rose thinks he looks ten years older, and is it any wonder?

Bella is giving her an 'I'm fine' smile, so Rose says, 'I'll leave you to it. You know where I am if you want anything.'

Ten minutes later as she's making a coffee, Bella comes in and puts her arm through hers. 'Mum, is it okay if Nigel stays in the tent with us tonight? We have lots to talk about and the kids would love it if they woke up to find him there.'

A mixture of relief and worry offer themselves for consideration and Rose acknowledges both. 'As long as you're fine with it, I'm fine with it.'

'Don't worry. I'm still sticking to my guns. Just because he's driven down from Birmingham to say sorry, doesn't mean I'm going to just roll over and give in.'

Bella's always been a bit of a mind reader. 'Well, I'm pleased that you're talking again.'

'Bet you're pleased you will be in your own bed tonight too, eh? Instead of on the hard ground?' Bella's eyes hold a twinkle of mischief.

Heck. She really is a mind reader. Rose laughs. 'As if!' Then she becomes serious. 'I'm here if you need me. Just come and wake me up, yeah?'

'I will. I'm hoping we've turned a corner though, Mum.'

As Rose watches her daughter walk up along the path, her way lit by little solar lights in the shape of daisies, the primroses quiver in the breeze. Rose smiles and takes the memory upstairs with her.

Chapter Eighteen

Sally puts down her spade and flexes her bicep. It might be her imagination, but she thinks there's more definition than there was a while ago. This is the fourth visit to Rose's garden, and the pond dig is almost complete. The bicep definition (if indeed it's there) isn't down to the digging alone, of course. She's joined a gym and for once stuck to her intention to attend twice weekly. Weightlifting was never something she'd even considered before, but while sussing out various bits of equipment, she tried a kettlebell lift or two (under supervision) and found it exhilarating. Physical strength complements mental strength, the instructor informed her, and so far, it seems to be true.

The pond shape is almost perfect, she thinks, as she adjusts the string marking out the two-metre-long by one-metre-deep oval. There needs to be more of a slight curve at the right far end, and then it will be done. The ledges she's created for the plants to sit on have worked well too, and

Sally has to admit she's quietly proud of her efforts. If someone had told her before her husband left, that she'd be enjoying lifting weights and pond building, she'd have thought they needed their bumps read. It gladdens her heart to think of the pleasure everyone will have when they see the finished pond.

It will have a 'natural' waterfall babbling over rocks, which will be so restful and will also help to aerate the water. There will be some swishy medium-height grasses around the edges that will sway in the breeze, and hopefully, lots of wildlife will eventually find a home there. And of course, there will be lilies. Lilies just like the ones she remembers from her childhood. Grace Pentewan would be so pleased if she could see it. Sally tips her face to the cloudless blue sky and smiles. Perhaps she can.

'Coffee's ready!' Rose calls. Sally turns to see her placing a tray of mugs and biscuits on the picnic bench.

'Yay, I'm so ready for that.' Sally joins Rose, noting her muscles don't protest as much as they did a few weeks ago when she climbed out of the 'pond hole'. After a few welcome swallows of coffee she asks, 'How's Bella? Not seen her or the kids since I got here.'

'She's good, thanks. They've popped over to see her old friend Hannah to talk about the idea of running a café from her converted campervan on weekends.'

Sally remembers that Rose mentioned that possibility a while ago. 'It's a great idea, if you ask me. It's true there are quite a few of them around, but not many who provide freshly baked home-made stuff. The vegan and gluten-free options should be popular too.'

'I'm with you. And now she's feeling a bit more settled, she'll have the extra confidence she needs to go for it, with any luck.'

'How's it all going with Nigel? You said he was down here recently, and they were trying to work things out.'

Rose smiles. 'They are. He was here for two days and they talked everything through and he agreed with all Bella's arguments. Nigel realised he'd been blinded to what really mattered and admitted he hated the job anyway. It was the idea they would all be better off financially that drove him, gave him tunnel vision. Bella told me that his family really struggled when he was growing up, and he didn't want that for his own. He's back in Birmingham now but is desperately looking for a job here. Once he finds one, he's out of there.'

Sally's thrilled that Bella hasn't settled for second best, and tells Rose so. 'I must admit I'm a bit surprised that he gave in so quickly, given what Bella told me about him last time we spoke.'

'Yeah. I saw a different side to him while he was here. He was much more like the Nigel I first met years ago.' Rose puts her head on one side and gestures at the garden. 'This green space helped too. I'm convinced of it. He was so relaxed and kept saying how peaceful it was to be out here. Poor man is shut in a windowless office eight hours and more, five days a week.'

Sally can imagine how awful that must be. At least in the surgery, she can see daylight through the double doors from reception, and it's light and airy. 'Everything crossed for them. I do hope it works out.'

'Yes, me too. I'm not naïve enough to expect everything to be plain sailing for them, but at least the intention to work through everything is there. The main thing will be him getting a job here, and at least Bella's stuck to her guns. She's told him there is no way she's going back to Birmingham while he looks for a job here. Nigel seems to have accepted that, so fingers crossed. How's everything with you now? Feeling any better about Paul leaving?'

Sally doesn't have to think too hard about that one. 'Do you know, I am. The hurt's still there, but it's faded loads since I've been going to the gym and coming here. It's still early days, but I'm trying to look to the future more positively. It's a future that I thought I'd be walking towards with my life partner by my side, but that's changed and I've kind of accepted it. I've changed too, and I like the stronger, healthier me I'm becoming.' She stops, suddenly abashed. She always seems to bare her soul without meaning to when she's in this garden.

Rose's eyes catch a sparkle and she slaps the table with the flat of her hand. 'Brilliant! The change in you is obvious. So proud of you, maid.'

Sally laughs. 'Maid? I'll be fifty in two weeks.'

Rose looks shocked. 'Two weeks! Please tell me you've something organised.'

Sally shakes her head. 'Not really. Pippa and her girlfriend Megan are taking me out for a meal, but Angus is in South America, so he can't join in. It feels wrong to have a big shindig without him.'

'Then we must do something, either before or after your birthday. We can have a little shindig instead. Daisy, Flora,

Louise, Bella, the children, and me of course. That'll do. Or you could ask friends from work too, if you like?'

'God, no. I don't want a big fuss.'

'But you'll agree to the little shindig?' Rose indicates the size of the shindig by holding the tips of her forefinger and thumb a few centimetres apart.

Sally ponders a moment and can't find a reason to say no. It just seems a little odd having a 'do' when everything is so very different for her now. It's true, what she told Rose about her feeling stronger, but she's not sure she feels like celebrating just yet. But then again, it could be a good thing. A way of embracing fifty. Despite everything, she's still standing and determined to make the best of life. 'Okay. And thanks for offering, Rose.'

An hour later, Sally is contemplating another break, as the sun has moved the shade round to the other side of the pond, treating her exposed neck to a heat wave. She's had to put her hair up, as it kept falling into her eyes, but that meant she also had to take her hat off, as it wouldn't fit over her top knot. Climbing out of the pond-hole and stepping into the shade, Sally takes a long swallow of water. As she lowers her bottle again, she sees Flora and Louise coming towards her along the path, closely followed by Rose, Bella and the children.

Sally returns their greeting and waves enthusiastically at the children who, upon reaching her, want to immediately get into the hole. Bella admonishes them and explains they will get completely covered in wet earth. Wesley seems to relish this idea and sits on the edge, stretching his little legs to try and reach down to the first ledge. Bella whisks him up and over her shoulder amid his wails and shrieks of annoyance.

'I want some fish!' he declares.

'Fish?' Bella asks, puzzled. 'You don't really like fish. Well, unless it's fish and chips.'

'Not eating fish. Fish in ponds.'

Sally hadn't considered fish. But maybe a couple would be added interest. 'What kind of fish?'

Wesley frowns. 'Ones that swim about.'

Bella smiles. 'We'll wait and see.'

'No. I want them. I don't want to wait and see!'

'Hey, why don't we go and have a look at your sunflowers, children?' Louise soothes, instantly getting silence and a big smile from Wesley. Molly seems less enthusiastic but follows behind as Louise takes Wesley's hand and leads the way down the path and round the side of the house.

Rose raises her eyebrows. 'Wow. That woman is a natural with my petulant little grandson.'

Flora laughs. 'Isn't she just? So wonderful to see.'

Sally looks at Rose. 'You didn't say the gang were coming over.'

'That's because I didn't know. They showed up independently of each other.' Then Rose raises her eyebrows again and stares open-mouthed as a tall youth with blond curly hair and vibrant green eyes comes through the gate, and walks towards them smiling. 'And would you believe it, here comes Josh, too!'

Rose introduces Josh to everyone and goes off to make tea. Sally says, 'It's amazing that you've all shown up at the same time, out of the blue.'

Flora nods and jams her straw hat down on her head as the breeze tries to make off with it. 'It is. Louise was saying, like me, she'd not planned to come here today, just kind of thought it would be a nice idea after she'd had lunch. How about you Josh?'

'Same, really. This place is very soothing.'

Flora nods sagely. 'Heartily agree. I think we all just felt like a garden hit. Maybe we're all drawn here, like the bees.'

Josh peers into the pond-hole and says to Sally, 'You've done all this by yourself?'

The rush of pride she has at his words is maybe misplaced, but she doesn't care. He's hit the nail on the head. It isn't just all about the digging, which took considerable effort. It was her idea, she researched it, planned it, organised it, and followed it all through. Her first small act of complete independence for a very long time. Her reply reflects none of this, of course. People wouldn't get it without lots of meandering explanation, and then the meaning would lose impact. Besides, it's personal to her. She owns it. 'Yep. Totally knackered today, as it's been very warm, but only another half-hour or so, and then the digging bit will be done.'

Josh smiles. 'My hat is off to you.' He looks thoughtful and pushes a hand through his unruly curls. 'How about I finish the last bit – under your supervision, of course. You can have a well-earned rest.'

Sally's immediate response is a gut-twisting no. This is hers. Hers alone. No matter that he looks like an eager puppy, if he does the last bit, hasn't he taken it from her? Aware that the silence where her answer should be is stretching, and that the puppy is looking unsure, she catches sight of the Golden Gate roses nodding in the breeze, and a sense of calm descends. It's her choice, no one else's. Sally is in control. The boy wants to help, so she could let him. 'Let him' is the main point here. She decides. 'If you really want to, you can, Josh. Thanks. I could do with a rest.' Relief floods his face. 'I'm a bit over-protective of this project, though, so you'll follow my instructions, yeah?' Sally's not used to being assertive, but she thinks what she said has struck a middle ground.

'I absolutely get that. You're the boss.' Josh grins and jumps into the hole.

Sally smiles and hands him the spade.

Flora flops down on a deckchair in the shade and fans her face with her hat. Chasing after small children is not something that should be attempted on hot days, certainly not by her, but Louise is in her element. Right now, she's watching Molly and Wesley bounce on a small trampoline that Bella put out in the scant shade of the cherry tree. Louise laughs girlishly and looks closer to their age than her own at the moment in jeans, a T-shirt, and sandals.

Sturdy ones, but sandals nevertheless, and no tights or socks!

The change in her has been miraculous. Flora would never have imagined she'd decide to come here today by herself. Louise had explained that Rose had told her last time to come up whenever she liked to spend time, or help in the garden, and the children would love to see her. So she did. Wonderful. It's the power of this garden. It must certainly be pretty special if it can draw Louise out of her shell. Rose and the others are pretty special as well. They made Louise feel so welcome. Flora tells herself she deserves a little praise too, as she might have had a small hand in preparing the ground. Maybe a big hand. Okay, she concedes, a massive hand. Flora chuckles to herself as she watches Louise climb onto the trampoline and try a few hesitant jumps. Her lighthouse bulb might not be as dull as she'd feared.

Josh has finished with the pond and wanders over clutching a big bottle of water. He flops into the deckchair by her side and gulps down half of the water in one. 'Warm work, eh?' Flora says, unnecessarily, but feels she has to say something to be sociable.

He pulls his T-shirt up and wipes his face with it. 'Yeah, done now, though. It will look stunning once it's complete.'

Flora agrees and wonders if he's in a better place now. Rose told her briefly about his impromptu arrival here recently and the reasons for it – also about visiting the care home. She also wonders if she should mention his gran and the sweet peas. Though he might think Rose had been gossiping to her about his business when it wasn't like that at all. She'd been sharing and discussing the best way to help. Everyone knows that's not the same as gossiping. 'Rose tells me you were thinking of maybe taking gardening up as a career?' Flora is sure this is a safe topic – not gossipy.

He grins. 'Yes. The more I'm here in this space and amongst growing things, the calmer I feel. It's like a kind of therapy, you know? A natural, spiritual therapy that needs no words or radical action. It all started with those sweet peas.' He nods over in their direction and tells Flora all about his depression, Gran, sister, everything.

Flora warms to him straight away. He's thoughtful and sensitive and she's honoured that he is confiding in her, so encourages him further. 'Will you bring Lily here soon?'

'We plan to. We'll see how it goes, take it slow. If she likes it, we could make it a regular thing.' Josh looks searchingly at Flora. 'I think she could warm to you, as she used to be a teacher too. Maybe you could come up one time and talk about that?'

'Maybe we could. A nice idea, Josh.' Flora watches Louise struggle off the trampoline, still laughing, much to Wesley's disappointment.

'Weez! Come back on. It's fun.'

'In a little while, once I've had a rest!' She flaps a hand at him and makes for Flora, Josh and the shade.

'Sit here,' Josh says, quickly vacating his seat. 'I'll grab another chair.'

Louise protests, but gladly flops down as Josh insists. Both women watch him walk down the path to get another deckchair from the shed and Flora says, 'He's such a lovely young man. He has his troubles, but that's his story to tell.'

'Yes. He certainly seems to be. Doesn't mind getting his hands dirty either.'

Inside Flora's head, there's a 'two birds with one stone' idea. It has a lighthouse in its beak, hovering and ready to drop. 'Funny you should say that. He's considering a career in gardening. He doesn't know much about it at all but feels an affinity with growing things. He was just telling me how it lifts his spirits.' Flora looks sidelong at Louise and does some theatrical stroking of her chin. 'Hmm. Now, if only we knew someone who could help him. Someone who knows almost everything about horticulture.'

Louise's trademark frown starts to make headway between her eyes, and then she gets it. 'Well, you can't mean me.' She folds her arms, lifts her foot and examines a scuff mark on the side of her red sandal.

Flora wonders if she's been too presumptuous and hurt Louise's feelings. 'Er, well, I did mean you, actually,' she ventures tentatively.

A snort. 'Well, I think you'll find I know everything. Not just *almost* everything.' The sentence is tempered by a sly smile.

And there it is. Louise's first quip. An obvious, and very dry attempt at humour. Wonders will never bloody cease! 'Ha! Oh, you had me worried there.' Flora gives her a gentle nudge.

Louise grins and nods as Josh comes back up the path with the chair. 'Should I offer to talk him through a few plants, do you think?'

'I think that would be a splendid idea.' Flora is surprised that she used the word 'splendid'. Nobody says that now. Mother used to use it on occasion and thought herself grand when she did. Mother has been quiet for a while, so Flora will let it go. Splendid can stay, as long as it doesn't have a habit of popping out unasked for.

Josh is thrilled by the suggestion and Louise takes him first to a towering group of blue-and-white spear-like flowers rustling in the soft breeze. 'Now, what are these?' Louise runs her hand gently along one sturdy stem.

'Erm. Not sure. My gran used to have them in her garden, I think.' He folds his hands behind his back and Flora has the impression of a schoolboy been tested on homework. Louise waits. 'Um, lilac?'

'Not a bad guess. But no. They're lupins, or *Lupinus*, to give their scientific name. They are perennials, which means they come back year after year. They first flower around May but can continue through August if deadheaded properly.' She frowns and parts a clump which have half gone to seed. 'These need a deadhead or two. I'll do it with some snippers later. They're doing well in this spot as they love sun and hate wet feet. Rose might have chosen this area more by accident than design, though. She tells me things often thrive by fluke and there's little planning.'

'Right, yes, I remember the name now. They have a delicate scent, really subtle.' Josh inhales a bloom and smiles at Louise as she does the same. He looks like a kid in a sweetshop. Flora can easily see him making horticulture his career. Pointing further down the lawn to where the path bends, he says, 'Those purply ones sticking out over the path. Lavender, right?'

Louise smiles like a proud mother. 'You are correct. That type is *Lavandula angustifolia* – Munstead, if I'm not mistaken. Lavender is generally fairly easy to grow here, despite its Mediterranean origins. Like the lupin, they like sun on their faces and hate soil that's too wet and heavy round their roots.'

They walk over and Josh rubs the head of a flower very gently between his fingers and smells the scent. He closes his eyes and smiles. 'This takes me back to Gran's garden too. She said it was part of the mint family … I think?'

Louise's eyes nearly pop out of her head. 'Yes, that's right. You have good recall, which will help if you decide to take the gardening path.'

He gives a little smile. 'Thanks, I'm a fast learner, hence the glowing exam results. But it will take years to be as good as you.'

'Luckily, you have years. My late husband Matthew was about your age when he got his job with the National Trust as a junior gardener. He learned on the job, and what he didn't know about horticulture wasn't worth knowing. The Eden Project even consulted him on one or two growing matters.' At each side of a big smile, Louise's cheeks are in full bloom and the pride in her voice is unmistakable.

'How wonderful.' Then Josh points to a white hydrangea a little way off and their voices fade as they walk towards it. Flora sighs contentedly. Louise is thriving, Josh is getting there, Rose is full of energy and adventure, Bella and the children are being nurtured, Sally is growing well,

Daisy when she's here is as light as a dandelion spore, and is a great companion in the library, and Flora? Flora has put down roots. Strong roots. Her petals are open and she's taking in light. By the honeysuckle, her beloved *Philadelphus* waves its delicate branches at her and she waves back, not feeling silly in the slightest.

Josh comes back to sit with her a little while later as Louise has been commandeered by Wesley. 'What a nice lady Louise is, and so knowledgeable. I should have brought my notebook.'

'I'm sure you'll see her again when you pop over. In the meantime, will you enrol on a course, or try to get a post and learn on the job like Louise's Matthew did?'

A few dark clouds sail across Josh's sunny expression. 'I'm not sure. It will depend on the parents' willingness to help out financially. I don't have the money to wash my hands of them and support myself, much as I'd like to. And yes, I could get a student loan, but that will need paying back.' He rubs his chin. 'Maybe learning on the job would be the right thing. The pay wouldn't be great I'm guessing, but it would be money. Perhaps I could get a bedsit or something with help from the social.'

The injustice of such a lovely generous boy, being held back by the selfish wishes of his parents, lights a forge in Flora's belly. He wouldn't be held back if she had anything to do with it. He could come and stay with her, if need be, but that would be a last resort. Josh needs to be independent, learn, grow and thrive in his own soil. 'Josh, I know I don't know you very well … but can I offer some advice?'

'Of course. I need as much of that as I can get.'

His sunny smile is back so she takes a deep breath. 'I let my mother rule and ruin my early life. I won't bore you with the detail, but suffice to say I could have been so much happier if I'd stood up to her when she threw down the metaphorical ultimatum – it was her way or the highway. I should have chosen the highway. It would have been better than staying in her thrall, but I didn't have the guts. My confidence was always at rock bottom, thanks to her. Please stand up to your parents. Tell them you're serious and you'll leave if needs be.'

Josh gives a sad smile. 'Your story sounds familiar. My sister left because of their domineering ways and she lives on the streets now – I'm not that brave.'

There are so many expletives on her tongue waiting for release and if his parents were here, she'd let them have them all, but Flora knows that calm is needed. 'Please try. Tell them about your newfound passion, about growing things, about how being in nature makes you feel. You told me earlier without a problem, so just pretend you're talking to me, not them. And if they are still hell-bent on sending you to medical school, there's a spare room at mine.' That hadn't meant to slip out, but bugger it. 'Mind you, you might prefer the street.' Flora lets out her socially acceptable chuckle.

Josh looks caught between laughter and tears, and he shakes his head. 'Wow, Flora. That's incredibly generous of you. I don't know what to say.'

'Say you'll talk to them as soon as you can.'

Josh is about to answer, when his mobile phone does the

unexploded bomb thing in his pocket. As he answers it, Flora watches his face drain of colour and he jumps to his feet. 'Yeah. I'm on my way.'

Dear God, what's happened? 'Bad news?'

'My sister Lucy is in hospital … an overdose.'

'Josh, I'm so sorry!'

He nods. 'Please tell Rose and the others I said goodbye. I'll keep you posted.' Then he sets off at a run down the path, blindly crushing a few heads of lavender beneath his feet as he passes. Their scent drifts back to Flora as if to give comfort, but she's too sad to take it.

Chapter Nineteen

The wet sand dune is the colour and texture of cinder toffee as Rose and the children run down it to join Bella on the beach. Crumbling underfoot, the sand slides away as Wesley takes great 'moon landing' jumps and goes into a forward roll. Laughing, Rose tells him to be careful, but it's too late as he surfaces, at last the right way up, with a mouthful of sand.

'Mummy!' His wail has a nearby family whipping their heads round in surprise. 'Mummy! It tastes nasty!'

Bella leaves setting up the beach tent and runs to his aid with a wet wipe, which doesn't help, because that apparently tastes like shampoo and sets off more wails and tears. She looks at her mum in despair as she struggles with her son and mouths, *Help!*

'Hey, come on. You'll be perfectly fine. Keep spitting and then have a drink,' Rose says, in her best calming yet authoritative tone. The one she perfected in the days of 'I used to be a nurse'.

Molly thinks the whole thing is hilarious, then sneakily grabs a biscuit from the picnic bag when she thinks everyone is preoccupied with her bother, and nobody has noticed. Rose has noticed but says nothing.

Eventually, Wesley is quiet, save a few shuddering sobs as he sits on his mum's knee. 'How about a biscuit to cheer you up and take the nasty taste away?' Rose suggests. She looks at her granddaughter. 'Can you pass one please, Molly?'

'Yeah, I'll have one too.'

'You've already had one just now.' Rose tries to keep her face straight as Molly gawps, incredulous.

'I ... I—' Molly stops and shrugs, as she knows by her grandma's face she's not getting anywhere. 'Okay, fair cop.'

This deadpan response from a six-year-old sets Rose off laughing, and it's some time before she can get her breath back. She sits quietly, taking in the golden sand, the shush of the waves rolling to shore, the laughter in the eyes of Bella and the giggling children and wishes she could capture this moment forever. Joyous. Times like this – plain, simple. Pure joy.

'That one should be on the stage when she grows up.' Bella finishes setting up the tent and hands Rose a sandwich.

'She should be on the stage right now, if you ask me.'

'What stage?' Molly asks, her mouth full of ham and cheese.

'In the theatre or on TV, because you're so funny,' her mum replies.

'Yes! I'd love to be on TV.'

'And me!' Wesley punches the air and his sandwich falls from his fist into the sand. His face falls. 'Mummy!'

'Never mind, here's another,' Rose laughs.

After lunch, the children dig holes in the sand while Rose and Bella sit on beach chairs sipping a well-earned coffee. She can't remember the last time she came to Crantock beach, but it has always been one of her favourites. A wide expanse of golden sand and sheltered by sand dunes. 'Peace at last.' Bella sighs and pats her mum's arm. 'Thanks for helping out, Mum. You're worth your weight in gold, and such a calming influence on the kids.'

Is she? She hadn't really noticed, but she's glad Bella thinks so. 'You're welcome. I'm just loving spending time with you all. And even though everything isn't sorted yet with a home and the job situation, it's brilliant to have you back. It'll all work out, I'm sure of it.' Rose isn't given to adding platitudes to conversation for the sake of it. She really does think it will work out.

'Me too. Call it a gut feeling.'

Rose smiles. If both of them think it will work out, then the chances are they're right. She wishes she had a similar feeling about Josh's sister, Lucy. It's been four days and the poor girl is still on life support. He's kept her posted and she's talked him through some tough times, once in the early hours. Again, her nursing experience helped, but she wishes she could do more.

'You heard any more about Lucy?'

221

'I think we are psychically connected today!' Rose laughs. 'I was just thinking that I had the same gut feeling about things working out for you, immediately before you said it. Then I went on to think of Lucy.'

Bella looks pensive. 'Wish we were psychic. Then we'd know exactly what was coming and how to plan the next steps.'

'Hmm. Not sure I'd like that. Anyway, no. I haven't heard anything, which is unusual. I normally get a text from Josh early – even if it's to say no change.'

'What's your thinking? You know, from a professional angle?'

'I haven't a clue, really. I don't know enough. All I know is that she took cocaine, various amphetamines and booze. Nobody knows if it was deliberate or accidental, because she was found alone in the park. Either way, they've said it's a waiting game, but being young and strong is in her favour.'

'Her shitty parents have a lot to answer for. I will never be like them, no matter what. My kids can do whatever the hell they want, as long as they're happy,' Bella says passionately.

'You'll never be like them.'

'No. Because I've had a good teacher, teachers plural, counting Dad of course.'

Rose acknowledges the sharp stab of resentment that Glen's absence brings. Not at him, but at life. Why wasn't he here sitting on the beach beside them, eating ham and cheese sandwiches, watching his grandchildren play – watching them grow? Why did people like Josh and Lucy's parents get to live while he didn't? She knows she should feel grateful for what she has, and she is. She really is. And she's improved, changed and developed as a person so much, since feeling at sixes and sevens in the early days of not being a nurse.

She's burnt her box/boxes. Her garden is her saviour – her sanctuary. She has her family and friends – her comfort blanket. But – because there is always a but, isn't there? – she would be even happier with her husband by her side. Glen, her wonderful, Glen. To stop being swept along by this unexpected downward spiral, she gives herself a kick in the pants. *Life is unfair, Rose – get over it.* There will be days when she has to ride the downward spiral and hold on tight. Life after nursing is so much better than she expected, but it's not all sweetness and light, is it? How could it be without Glen? The gap that nursing left is slowly being filled, however. Apart from Bella, she's helping Josh, Lily, and all her other friends in lots of different ways. The garden is her medical bag nowadays, as well as the forty years of 'people person' experience.

Bella says, 'You okay, Mum? I haven't upset you by mentioning Dad, have I?'

'Course not. I just miss him, that's all.' Rose watches a gull dip its wings as it wheels overhead and then out across the wide blue ocean. Maybe it's Glen telling her he's watching over her. A fanciful notion, but it comforts her.

'So do I. I'm sad that he never got to see these two grow up, amongst other things.'

Rose gives her a squeeze and thinks if not psychic, they really do have a strong connection today, and that comforts her too. She knows Bella is in danger of getting entangled in her own downward spiral, so she changes the subject. 'I was chatting to Daisy the other day about Sally. They know each other a little, as Daisy sometimes would come to the surgery to collect me when we were meeting up. Anyway, Daisy reckons that even though Sally says she doesn't want a fuss for her birthday, she'd be up for organising a surprise party. After all, Sally organised one for me when I left the surgery, so maybe she would secretly like to be surprised. Daisy's convinced the perfect venue would be my garden. I'm not sure if she'd like a surprise one. What do you think?'

Bella considers this, a little frown very much like Louise's deepening between her eyes. 'It could work because, as you say, she organised a surprise leaving do for you. But maybe don't invite loads of people. She might feel sad that her ex won't be there. And how will you make it a surprise? '

'Daisy suggested we did an "unveiling of the finished pond" evening. Which we will, but unbeknownst to Sal, we'll combine it with a party.'

Bella likes that idea, which settles the matter for Rose. There's already a wiggle of excitement forming as she thinks of Sally's face when they spring it on her.

Idyllic as the rainless month may seem for everyone else, Rose finds the opposite to be true as she lugs the watering can up the garden for the eighth time that evening. The water butts are all dry and the hosepipe ban is still in force. Not that she likes to use the hose, because it's such a waste of water. So, the outside tap by the kitchen window is all that's left to her, and like it or lump it, the watering can is (slowly) getting the job done.

The lupins shiver as if in pleasure in the evening zephyr as she waters them thoroughly. The blue and green stand out against the stone wall and they're looking so healthy. Rose sets the watering can down and peers between the stems. She was sure there were dead flowers in the middle of the clump the other day, and she'd been going to deadhead them but never got round to it. But no, they seem to be gone. Then a memory of Louise with the secateurs in one hand and spent lupins in the other comes to her. Ah yes, Louise did it. Louise is a welcome addition to her circle of friends, and Wesley adores her. She shyly asked Rose if she might plant a memory of Matthew soon, as she felt such a connection with the garden. Of course, Rose readily agreed, and she can't wait to see what kind of plant it will be.

Bella calls from the stable door that dinner is ready, and Rose's stomach growls in anticipation, reminding her she's not eaten since the early bite on the beach. She's been too busy with the garden and the grandchildren. Briefly she contemplates how she could have imagined, upon retirement, that there would be long periods of nothing to do. Time stretching like endless empty corridors, leading nowhere apart from mindless TV and the wine bottle. How fortunate she is to have found an all-consuming passion in something that has always been there – just waiting. Her garden. Hidden in plain sight.

As she's about to walk through the kitchen door, her phone rings. *Josh. Please let it be good news.*

'Rose, Lucy's okay. She's awake and talking!'

Lightheaded for a few seconds, she leans her hand against the wall of the house, its sun-warmed stone immediately grounding her. 'Josh, at last! I left a few messages but when you didn't get back, I feared the worst!'

'Sorry, yeah. It's been full-on here. We were all so overjoyed and in the moment. My phone ran out of juice, too, this morning.'

'Don't worry. I'm so overjoyed for you too, love.'

'Thanks, I can hardly believe it. I felt sure we'd lose her and had a huge fucking rant at my parents in the car last night. Sorry for swearing, by the way.'

'Ha! Fuck that!' she responds, with a burst of laughter.

'Mrs L, I'm shocked.' She can tell his echoing laughter is a physical release, with relief and exhaustion riding tandem. 'Yeah, anyway, I told them what I thought of them. That they were responsible for Lucy's mess, that they were like some fucking puppet masters, getting off on their control freakery. Their holier-than-though, condescending attitude because they were GPs and thought they knew everything. Thought they could buy happiness and order other people's futures. I told them I wouldn't go back to med school and that I was going to work in horticulture, and if they didn't like it, then they'd never see me again. Then they would have lost both children.'

Josh is laughing manically now, but Rose can hear tears

behind it. 'Wow. Well done, Josh. So—' She's about to ask more details about Lucy, but he cuts her off.

'Yeah, I shot an adapted quote from Oscar Wilde at them. *To lose one child may be regarded as misfortune; to lose both looks like carelessness.* God knows where it came from, but bloody hilarious, in a dry kind of way.'

Josh is giggling uncontrollably and Rose wishes she could be there to comfort him. 'Where are you, love? Do you want to come over?'

'In my bedroom at home, absolutely wired, but exhausted.' He sniffs and Rose can hear tissue rustling. 'I'll try to go to sleep after this call, but thanks for offering. I'll come and see you soon. But guess what? After my rant at them, they went completely silent. Then Mum cried like a baby and Dad wasn't far behind. He said I might have a point and we'd discuss it all when things were a bit calmer. Then today, Lucy woke up, and once the doctors said she was going to be okay, Mum and Dad hugged the life out of me and told me I could do whatever the hell I wanted – they'd back me a hundred per cent! That was *not* what I was expecting.'

'Really? Thank goodness! I'm so pleased, Josh. I think nearly losing your sister gave them pause for thought. Perhaps they realised what was really important in life.' The parallels between them and Nigel aren't lost on her. 'In my book, it's happiness. Having your children happy and being happy yourself is the main thing.'

'I think you have the same book as me, Rose.' Josh yawns long and loud.

'Now, time for sleep, young Josh. Call me tomorrow and take care.'

'I will, Rose. Speak soon.'

Bella comes to the door with a tea towel over her shoulder. 'This gourmet meal of sausage and chips is getting cold, Mum. Who've you been gabbing to?'

'Josh. It's good news about Lucy – she's awake and they think she'll be fine.' Rose looks at Bella, hair escaping from her top knot, a smudge of ketchup on her cheek, and sees her as a child back in the prim-nose days. She wants to scoop her u p, love and protect her, never let her go.

'Wow! That's brilliant!' Bella says with a grin.

'Come here, you.' Rose pulls her daughter into her arms and gives her the biggest squeeze.

'What's that for?'

'Just because you're you, my little prim-nose.' Rose kisses her cheek and then pretends to elbow her out of the way. 'Right, where's me sausage and chips? I'm starvin'.'

Chapter Twenty

James Morgan might be slowly moving from the 'almost friend' camp to the friend one. Flora considers this while he's talking about her latest artwork, pointing to her 'unusual' use of colour, and 'inspired' composition. It's not because he's praising her work (though that helps), it's because he's started to smile and laugh a bit more of late. He was only put in the 'almost friend' camp, because he was a bit too serious for her liking, plus the fact that he runs the art class, which could prove tricky if she decided she'd had enough of attending. If they were friends, she'd feel bad about letting him down.

'So, what do you think?' James is looking at her, head on one side like an oystercatcher at the shoreline.

Flora had been too busy inside her own head to listen to everything he was saying. 'About what?'

'Having a go at painting outside. Forgetting the pebble art for a bit – trying something new.'

How had she missed this? Painting outside sounds just the kind of thing she'd enjoy. 'Okay. What kind of thing?'

'Something you love. A landscape, the ocean, trees…' James raises his bushy grey brows over soft brown eyes and spreads his hands. 'Anything at all.'

'My garden?'

'Absolutely.'

Flora wonders what the others in the class think of the idea, but when she glances around, she finds they're alone. 'Right. When would you like me to bring it in?'

James gives a hesitant smile and then tightens the band on his ponytail. 'Um … I thought I'd come and paint with you … be there to lend a hand. Not that you'll need one, I expect,' he adds hastily.

Flora puzzles a moment as she watches his cheeks grow pink above his beard line. Why is he bashful all of a sudden? She's not sure she's ever seen a seventy-four-year-old look bashful before, especially not this one. James always seems a bit aloof – pleasant enough, but distant. Though as she reminds herself, he had begun to slowly thaw, hence the promotion from the 'almost friend' camp. Maybe he's not used to making new friends and feels a bit awkward, hence the blushing. Mother's trying to whisper something into her subconscious, which is wholly inappropriate and extremely unlikely, so with an effort, she shoves the old crone back into her cage.

'That sounds lovely,' Flora says, turning her head to look at her work in progress, mainly to break the intense stare he's giving her.

'Tomorrow's supposed to be a nice day. Shall we meet up at yours after lunch, or before?'

'Mine?' Flora thinks she might have missed something again.

'Yes. To paint your garden.' James looks as puzzled as she feels.

Now it makes sense. 'Ah, well, you see, the garden is at my friend Rose's home. Well, I kind of think of it as mine too, as do our other friends. Rose tells us it belongs to us all. Like a community garden, really. It's such a special place – it brought us all together. We planted our memories there.'

James had begun to look less puzzled, but now the frown's back. 'Planted memories?'

Flora laughs. 'I'll explain tomorrow when we're there. It'll make more sense. Now, why don't you come for lunch, about 12.30? I'll quickly jot down the address here.' Flora tears a scrap of paper off an A3 sketch pad and babbles on about how much she loves flowers and all kinds of plants, while all the time she feels she's standing apart from her physical body, looking on and listening to herself with growing panic.

What the hell is she playing at? Rose might not like her turning up unannounced for lunch, and with James. What if Rose isn't even in? How embarrassing would that be? Why does she not think before acting? Mother always said she was too rash. Impetuous, spontaneous, radical even. Radical! The most radical thing she ever did when Mother was alive was paint her toenails green. If only she could see her now, inviting people to lunch out of the blue, dressed in orange harem pants hemmed with purple sequins, a lilac vest top, long dangly turquoise earrings and a scarlet bow in her hair. A giggle is trying to erupt, as she hands him Rose's address, but she clamps her lips tight together.

James takes the scrap of paper and gives her his biggest smile to date. 'Thanks. I'll see you tomorrow, then.'

Flora nods. 'Yes, see you then.' She waits, but he doesn't appear to be leaving. Then she realises it's because they're in the community centre at the class he runs, and it's her who should be leaving. Dear God. 'Bye, now,' she flings over her shoulder in a squeakily high voice as she hurries for the exit.

All the way home, Flora wonders what on earth has got into her. She was like a woman possessed in there, laughing and wittering on like a ninny, inviting James to Rose's like that. Trouble was, she'd gone so far, it was hard to double back, even though she knew she should. Mother had escaped her cage and was champing at the bit, poking fun, so she ploughed on, maybe to prove a point. The old hag had the audacity to suggest that James had a romantic interest in Flora. At their age. Really? That was preposterous! Flora was determined to ignore her nasty comments and to accept his friendly invitation – because it *was* just him being friendly, but she'd got carried away. How impetuous of her. The only thing for it is to call Rose and tell her what she's done. Hopefully everything will be okay.

A strong cup of tea and a whisky chaser sit on the coffee table next to Flora's bare feet. Ending her call, she replaces the phone in its cradle, which reminds her that Mother used to call it a holster, indicating her dislike of cordless telephones. What would she make of mobiles? With a sigh, she's torn between relief and anxiety. Relief for three reasons. One is that Rose just told her that Lucy's on the mend. Hallelujah! Two, she said it wasn't a problem if James comes over. She's off out to Daisy's anyway with Bella and the kids – their grandchildren will be playing together. There will be a spare key left under Madame Agatha's bee pot. Three, she won't have to think of a humiliating excuse to tell James why he can't come. But she's anxious because she might be awkward around James, now they've moved their relationship on a stage. By 'relationship', she means friendship, obviously. Nevertheless, they'll be alone in the garden, having lunch and painting like … well, like… *Like what, Flora? Friends do that kind of thing all the bloody time!*

Once more, worries that she's being tolerated, a charity case, surface. These worries are never far away these days, even though the smiles and laughter of her new friendship circle banish them for a while. Maybe Rose feels obligated to allow Flora the run of her garden. Being the lovely person that she is, she hadn't wanted to say no. More unhelpful! thoughts crowd in now. What if she never actually had been the vital part of her community in Truro that she'd always prided herself on? What if she'd been hiding her drab, uninspiring garden behind a brightly painted gate all those years? Maybe Mother is right. She's actually just a waste of space.

Anger builds. Mother is winning. Even though she's

been dead for years, she's still jerking Flora's chain. She grabs the whisky glass and downs it in one, gasping as the liquid turns to fire in her throat. That's better. Mother can 'do one', as the youngsters say. Imagining her mother 'doing one' is hysterically funny, for some reason, and it's a while before she's calm enough to drink her tea. Tomorrow will be lovely, she decides. In the morning she'll pop into town to get something nice for lunch. Some freshly made sausage rolls or pasties, and maybe even a couple of her very favourite chocolate eclairs from the bakery. James is sure to love them. Her image of James enjoying the lunch suddenly screeches to a halt. What if he's vegetarian or vegan? Should she give him a call and ask? Flora watches her hand hover over the phone like an indecisive butterfly. *No. Stop it. This won't do at all.* She flicks on the TV and there's a programme about novice climbers. It's snowing and they're struggling at the foothills of a forbidding mountain. Flora's right there with them.

James was right about the weather. The heat of the last few weeks is tempered by a fresh breeze, but not so fresh that it could become a nuisance for those who might like to paint outside. Those, being Flora and James. The anxiety from last night hasn't followed her into this morning, thankfully, and she gives her old picnic basket one last check-through, before making her way up the road towards Rose's cottage. Thoughts which try and make her second guess about

James's food preferences, and question her decision to pop a couple of bottles of local cyder into the basket, are banished.

Today she has her positive head on, as well as one of her best multicoloured kaftans, complete with silver bells on the cuffs. And no, it isn't to hide her drabness. It's because that's who she is. A vibrant shrub, with sometimes prickly leaves – so watch out, Mother! Flora decides to do her hair in two plaits tied with bee-patterned ribbons, because of the breeze. The last thing she wants is her hair joining in with the painting.

Letting herself in to Rose's, she puts the cyder in the fridge and flicks the kettle on in case James prefers tea. It feels a bit odd, being in the cottage without Rose, but she feels welcome, nevertheless. The worries of yesterday try to creep back in, but she's having none of it. At exactly 12.30, James knocks on the stable door, the top half of which is open to let in the gorgeous, scented air.

'Hello!' James's broad smile immediately puts Flora at ease. 'What a lovely place this is.'

'It really is.' Flora steps through the door and nods to the canvases and painting equipment under his arm and in bags. 'Put that lot inside and I'll give you the tour. Then we'll have lunch, yes?'

James does as she asks and then pulls a bottle of wine from one of the bags. 'I'm not sure if you like wine, or if you drink at all, but I got a light white, as it's lunchtime.' It's clear by his tone he's nervous, and the skin above his beard starts up a competition with the poppies on his patterned shirt.

'Ha! Yes, I do drink. I got us some little bottles of cyder too. So, we're spoiled for choice.'

'Good job my son dropped me off, then!' James laughs and tightens his already tight band on his ponytail.

Flora notes he did that yesterday. Must be a nervous habit. And he has a son? That's news. But then, what does she actually know about James? He used to be an art teacher and he runs a pebble-art class once a week – that's it.

'Yes, we don't want you done for drink driving.' Flora chuckles, but it sounds like a stuttering cough. His nervousness must be catching.

While Flora puts the wine in the fridge and gets the plates out for later, James chats more about the cottage and how pleasant it is. Then he compliments her on the kaftan. 'We are both quite colourful in our choice of clothing today.' He grins and points at his poppy shirt and green jeans.

He's not normally so colourful, Flora thinks. He usually wears denim jeans, flip-flops and some sort of a nondescript T-shirt. 'Yes, we are. Though I do wear plenty of colour most days,' she says pointedly.

He folds his arms and leans against the table. 'Yes. I've noticed. You really stand out in a crowd, and being so colourful gives you a cheerful aura, somehow. So today, I decided to take a leaf out of your book.' He lifts a finger and waggles it. 'And seeing as we're going to paint a garden, I thought that a *leaf* would be very appropriate.'

Flora laughs, though it wasn't that funny a joke. Good job she's not Louise. And she must admit, in view of her worries, the 'standing out in a crowd' comment is welcome.

Setting her shoulders back, she draws on her confidence and reminds herself of why she changed in the first place. It's what she wants to be. It fits in with her philosophy, with her 'rebellion' after Mother died and retirement. The wanting to be different, the free spirit, the colourful hair and clothes, the magpie tattoo on her arse. She wonders what James would make of that! Flora leads the way out of the cottage and up the garden path before her own blush becomes obvious.

He follows in her wake, oohing and ahhing at the bounty of nature – large and small, colourful, scented, tall, showy, shy and timid, all thriving together in this wonderful space. 'My word, Flora.' He stops at the highest point under the rampant honeysuckle, yellow trumpets dancing in the breeze, and turns in a circle. 'This place is...' He frowns and strokes his beard. 'Well, I can only describe it as joyful.' Then he takes a delicate trumpet between his forefinger and thumb and inhales deeply. 'What a sweet, heady fragrance.' Lifting his arms up and out, he says in wonder, 'This entire garden is absolutely delightful ... so uplifting.' Then he spies the almost finished pond, lets out a whoop of excitement and hurries down to get a closer look.

Flora follows on, laughing. It's like having an oversized Wesley on the loose.

As she joins him, he gets on his hands and knees by the pile of flat stones Sally has left to one side. 'What will these be?' he asks, twinkly-eyed.

'Sally, the lady who's building it, is constructing a waterfall with them. The really tall grasses in pots over there by the shed will go around the edge at the back, and various plants and grasses will be dotted in and around. There's talk of a couple of fish too. But she's most looking forward to putting her water lilies in. They're her memory plants.'

James nods. 'Yeah, what does that mean, exactly? You mentioned planting memories last evening.'

Flora tells him she'll explain over lunch, and together they bring everything out to the picnic table.

'Okay, cyder or wine?' Flora didn't bother asking if he wanted tea, she could guess the answer.

'Let's try that local cyder first. It certainly looks good. And so do these pasties. Are they from Nicki B's?'

'They are indeed. I hope you eat meat – I wasn't sure if I should get a vegan one as well…'

'No, I eat everything.' He frowns. 'Well, almost. I don't eat oysters.'

'Me neither. I can't stand the look of them when you get them up to your mouth, wobbling like mucus in the shell.'

James holds his palm up and shudders. While they eat, they talk about the garden and how Flora knows so much about plants. Without intending to, she finds herself opening up to him like a daisy at dawn. Everything comes out. Her mother's dominance, her job, her rebellion (apart from the location of the magpie tattoo), the move from Truro, her newfound friends, the power of this amazing garden, the healing nature of growing things and the significance of planting memories … everything apart from her recent misgivings, her own memory plant and the reason behind it.

Flora's sure that will be best kept to herself. She's talked too much already. The poor man has barely said two words because of her yap, yap, yapping. She's only had a glass of cyder, so she can't blame it on the booze. Maybe it's the garden's influence. She recalls Sally telling her that being here is cathartic. *It coaxes what you keep locked away inside, up into the outside. A bit scary, but you feel better for it.*

'Which is your memory plant, Flora?' James pours her a glass of wine and studies her face, expectantly.

Now what does she say? Maybe she can skirt around it somehow. She can see the *Philadelphus* behind his left shoulder in a beam of full sunlight. It looks like a rising star in the spotlight on opening night, but before she can find an understudy, out it all comes. Her darling Patrick, the dawn bouquet, their brief engagement, her mother's sabotage. All. Of. It.

The feel of his big warm hand enveloping her own brings her out of a shocked trance. To her surprise, she finds her cheeks damp. 'Oh… Sorry, I've completely taken over the whole conversation. We've not even started painting yet!'

James notices her awkward glance at their entwined hands and releases hers. 'Please don't apologise. I'm honoured that you shared your story with me. It's so very poignant and all too familiar, I'm afraid.'

Flora notes that his eyes look a bit glassy, and she doesn't think it's because of the bright sunshine. 'You know someone with a similar story?'

'Yes. Me.'

This is not what she's expecting at all. 'You never married? But you have a son.' Flora stops, embarrassed. People have children out of wedlock all the time, for goodness' sake. She must sound about two hundred years old.

'Yes, I married. I have a son and a daughter. My experience is very similar to yours, though. You were prevented from marrying by your mother, while I was pushed into it by my father. It felt like an arranged marriage … well, kind of. I never loved her.' He laughs, though it ends up being more like a snort, actually.

Maybe he's laughing to lift the mood, but while he might make light of his situation, she can never see missing out on a life with Patrick as anything more than a tragedy. 'How very hilarious,' she says, dryly.

James's face falls. 'Sorry. I know it's not funny at all – but if I don't laugh, I might cry. Your story has brought everything back for me. The sadness, the frustration, the sheer hopelessness of being twenty-one, with your heart set on another girl, while your parents browbeat you into marrying the daughter of their close friends. Janet and I were inseparable growing up. We went to the same school, shared the same interests, we had a laugh, and we really got each other. She was pretty, she was good company – but friends is all we were. At least on my part.'

Flora forgives him his laughter, as she watches the shadow of painful memories grow and diminish across his face. 'Janet was in love with you?'

'Yes. She'd told her parents as much too. Her dad was in

partnership with mine – they were solicitors. Senior partner at that. When we were in our late teens, there was so much pressure on me from Dad to take her on a date. Apparently, she told her own dad that I was the only man for her, but she daren't ask me out. It wasn't really done for women to make the first move back then, as you know. Dad said it would be awkward for him at work if I turned her down. He said if we went on a few dates, it might pacify her, and besides, who knew where it might lead, if I let it?'

James takes a big swallow of wine. 'We went on a few dates and had a nice time, but then she got really serious. Said she loved me; said she couldn't live without me. I was clueless. I knew I didn't feel the same, but I had been her friend since we were tiny. I didn't want to hurt her. Time went on and both sides put pressure on me to marry her. Mine especially, as I said.'

He stares wistfully at the sky. 'And if I'm honest, I was flattered, to an extent, that Janet was so besotted – I was stupid, and naïve too. As I said, I thought I loved another girl at the time, but she wasn't interested. But I didn't try very hard to win her over. I gave in to my dad's wishes in the end. Got married. Got divorced after twelve years.' James finishes his wine. 'Janet was devastated. I'd broken up the family. I hated myself, hated my parents. But most of all, I hated myself for being weak in the first place and later causing so much misery to my wife and children.'

Flora knows she should be finding platitudes, words to make him feel better. But she has none. Though in truth, maybe she doesn't need them. His story is so incredibly sad and should be acknowledged as such. Silence, save for the distant call of gulls and the whisper of the breeze through the tall grasses, are words enough. The telling of the story needs time to sit between them, to settle in the calm of this glorious Eden, to allow the sweet scent of the gathered summer blooms to act as a salve to his wounds. To hers too. Because Flora knows he's right. Their stories are so similar in some respects, yet completely opposite in others. The end result is the same. Lost love, lost time, self-loathing, and Flora expects on occasion, both of them have a barrowload of 'what ifs' trundling through their minds as they lie awake in the small hours staring at the bedroom ceiling.

James doesn't seem in the least thrown by the silence, and Flora knows that's because he gets it. He's a kindred spirit, and he's so firmly in her friend camp now, she knows she will find it hard, should he ever decide to leave it. But that's enough of that now. Time to look forward.

'Thanks for telling me your story, James.' She gives his hand a quick squeeze and opens the bottles of cyder. 'I agree, we share similar experiences, and trauma leaves scars. The self-loathing took some time to get through, on my part. The rebellion I told you about when the old bat died helped with that. I became a butterfly, a free spirit. I'd broken the shackles. Years of put-downs, negativity, thou-shalt-nots.' She takes a swig from the bottle and blocks Mother's derisory comment. 'Thing is, from time to time I hear her in my head.' Oh dear. She'd not meant to say that. A puzzled look crosses James's face, as well it might. Then he smiles.

'Yeah. Me too.' He laughs. 'Not your mother, of course – my dad.'

This tickles her, and is such a relief. It's not just her then; other people hear voices of long-dead relatives. 'Right, that's cheered me up a bit. I sometimes worry that I'm going ga-ga. Though I don't hear her as much as I used to in the early days.' *Though she has made an unwelcome comeback very recently. Since I moved, actually.* These words remain unspoken, because James doesn't need to know. If she tells him, she'll have to talk about her insecurities, and she's had enough of thinking about those lately. 'It's obviously because she had so much of a grip on me, that her negativity still has an influence. Makes me question the little things that I do, like drinking out of this bottle instead of a glass, for example.'

James clinks his bottle against hers and the sun winks off the glass. 'Yep. How uncouth of us. So, after the divorce, Dad more or less washed his hands of me. Told me I was a coward and needed to grow a backbone. I explained I'd grown one, hence the divorce. Mum and Dad adored my kids, though, which meant he couldn't disown me completely as he was worried he wouldn't get to see them, but he was distant and cold with me until the day he died. I'd brought shame on the family, you see. I wish I'd told him exactly what I thought of him, but my backbone didn't extend to that. As a consequence, I heard his disapproval about certain aspects of my life on a regular basis, the choices I made. I still do, even now. I've had one or two brief relationships since Janet, but they didn't last. Because of me, really – the way I became. I've struggled with depression over the years, found it hard to be light-hearted, to laugh.'

This explains a lot to Flora. 'I did note that you were a very serious kind of guy when we first met. Don't get me wrong,' Flora adds as his face falls, 'you were always pleasant and informative, sometimes animated, especially when you were talking about art. But yes, serious overall.'

James looks at her. 'Yes. I've found it easier to laugh just recently, though.'

'Yes, I've noticed. Why's that, if you don't mind me asking?'

'Not at all. It's because of you.'

'Me?' Flora squeaks, completely taken aback.

'Yes. You're such a colourful, vibrant character. Some people have more light about them than others, don't you find?'

Flora's too dumbstruck to reply.

'It emits from their manner: caring, warmth, sense of fun – others gravitate towards it.' He stops and Flora can tell he's feeling awkward because he tightens the band of his ponytail. 'You're one of those people.' He gives a simple shrug. 'I like being around you.'

It takes three swigs of cyder and a false start or two before Flora can say, 'Thank you, James. That's one of the nicest things anyone has ever told me. You might laugh, but in my teaching years I thought of myself as a lighthouse. I loved being someone who people could depend on – learn from, find guidance in. And even after I retired, I have often been someone's point of reference, in various guises. It makes me feel a useful part of my community. Recently, I have doubted the wattage of my lightbulb from time to time, maybe because of my advancing years and the mutterings of Mother. So once again, thank you, James. Thank you.' Flora shuts up, because she's aware she's yapping again, but mainly because she doesn't want to cry.

James folds his arms and puts his head on one side. 'Never doubt the strength of your lightbulb, Flora. It's certainly helped guide me to sunny shores these last few months.'

Flora's smile feels wobbly, so she dabs the corner of her mouth with a bit of kitchen roll and in her best no-nonsense teacher's voice says, 'Well, how very lovely. Now, shall we attempt to put brush to canvas before nightfall?'

Chapter Twenty-One

S ally can't decide who is more excited about the trial switching on of the waterfall, herself or Molly and Wesley. On balance, she thinks it's her. She's now on holiday from work and it's taken three solid days of building, arranging the waterfall stones (and then re-arranging), filling the pond with water, letting it settle, and then planting her beloved pink and white water lilies. Then there was the 'surprise' fish for Wesley to sort; she hopes he'll be thrilled with them. But now it's ready. At last. Bella, Rose and the children are poised ready for her signal, while she adopts a strong-woman pose, bicep pumped, right foot braced on a rock, a big triumphant smile on her face.

'Okay, tilt your chin to me a bit,' Bella says, adjusting her phone camera. 'Perfect.'

Sally looks at the children who are jointly holding the remote control for the waterfall pump. 'Ready?' They nod, and Wesley lets out an ear-splitting shriek. 'Okay. Five, four, three, two, one. Go!'

They press the button and everyone waits. There's a hiss and a faint trickle of water cuts through the still afternoon air, then it gets stronger as they all watch the waterfall come to life. The children whoop, Rose cheers, and Bella's camera phone clicks away as Sally throws back her head with joyful laughter. 'It worked! It really worked!' she yells and joins the children in a crazy little dance.

'Of course it worked,' Rose says. 'Because *you* built it!'

Sally acknowledges a rush of pride, which is quickly overtaken by unease as she notices the water lilies rocking gently on the surface of the pond. Hurrying over, she says to Rose, 'Are they far enough from the waterfall, as they prefer calm water.' Sally would be devastated if she had to choose between lilies or waterfall. Though lilies would have to win, as the memory of them is what gave her the idea to do it all in the first place.

'Yes, turn down the force of the water now, Molly – just let it trickle.'

Molly does as she's asked, and immediately the lilies stop rocking and Sally is reassured. 'Perfect.' Then she takes Wesley's hand and makes him crouch beside her. 'Wes, can you see something moving under the lily pad over there?'

Wesley screws up his face in concentration. Then he leaps into the air. 'Fish! I can see fish!'

'Yes! Make sure you don't scare them, though,' Bella says, crouching down next to him. She looks at Sally. 'Thanks so much, for making this little man so happy, Sal. It's really wonderful.'

'It will be wonderful next week when we have our pond unveiling party,' Rose says, slipping an arm around

Sally's shoulder. 'Your hard work has created a thing of beauty and calm. The perfect addition to our memory garden.'

'Thanks, Rose. I can't wait. Are you sure I can't contribute some food or wine?'

'I'm sure. The evening will be a little thank you to you, as well as a celebration. Talking of which, would you like to stay for dinner? We could have a pre-celebration celebration?'

Sally politely declines and takes her leave. A small part of her would have liked to stay, but most of her wants to go home for a long hot bath and bask in the knowledge that she's done what she set out to do, all by herself. A challenge she wouldn't have dreamed of while she was married to Paul. Even if by some miracle she'd come up with the idea, he would have ridiculed it. Ridiculed her.

Sally looks at her naked form in the bathroom mirror and doesn't turn away ashamed like she did a few months ago. Paul's poisonous voice whispering in her ears hasn't disappeared completely, but it's fading. The *Too fat, too flabby, too wrinkly. Always too something* is mostly buried under the mounds of earth she's removed for the pond. Now, although she's not perfect, but then who is? (And what exactly *is* perfect anyway?) Sally's at last comfortable with her appearance. More than comfortable. It's not just because of the new weight loss and muscle tone, it's because of a new inner strength that can't be seen on the outside. Being in that wonderful garden and making the pond has been the making of her too. She's stronger, confident, happier and open to more challenges. Sally doesn't know what they are yet, but she knows they're there – just waiting.

———————

After her bath, she dresses in shorts and a vest top, has a light meal and plans to put her feet up with a glass of wine. Before the pond build, right about now, she would have felt lonely and wished Paul had been home to keep her company. Now she realises she's happy that she can do whatever she goddam likes, without him dictating their viewing, or tutting if she has wine on a weeknight. She smiles to herself as she gets the bottle out of the fridge and pours a good measure.

One challenge is already making itself known to her as she settles on the sofa. Paul's been gone almost five months and for most of that time (though actually, she's not heard from him for a week or so) he's pestered her to put the house on the market and asked for a divorce. She's always put him off, until recently, to her shame, secretly hoping against hope that he'd come to his senses and move back home. But it's time to do as he asks. It can't be put off any longer. The house has increased ridiculously in value and the mortgage is almost paid. She should be able to afford a decent house and start again anew, without the memory of how happy she and her husband had once been (at least in the first few years) haunting every room.

Idly flicking through the channels, Sally's surprised to hear the doorbell – it's nearly 9.30pm. Odd! She opens the front door and her stomach rolls.

'Sal, wow! Look at you!' Paul steps back so he can get a better view, a lascivious smile curving his lips. 'You've lost so much weight, and your hair's gorgeous in that style. It's shorter, but shiny and bouncy. You've got bigger muscles than me, too.'

He laughs like they're old friends and this is normal behaviour. Sally wishes she'd put a dressing gown on, because he's looking at her breasts, which thanks to the chill evening air, are obviously braless under the vest top. She folds her arms over them. 'What do you want, Paul?'

'That's not a very nice welcome. No invite in?' He turns his bottom lip down like a child. 'I could have just used my key, but I wanted to be polite.'

'Oh, how very decent. How can I ever thank you? It's gone 9.30pm. What's so important?' Sally stands her ground and is surprised to see his eyes fill with tears.

'Please let me in, Sal. I need to talk to you. I *have* to talk to you.'

Because she can count on one hand the number of times she's seen him cry, she realises it must be something big and stands to one side. 'Come in, but you aren't staying long, okay?'

'Okay, promise.'

As they walk past the coat hooks in the hall, Sally grabs a hoodie and slips it on. That's better. In the living room she takes the armchair, he takes the sofa. 'What's up?'

Again, to her surprise, Paul wipes a tear and then completely breaks down. Big, snotty, ugly-type crying ensues, with a few wails thrown in for good measure. But this isn't an act. She knows he's genuinely broken.

Eventually, he blows his nose and says, 'I've made such a mess of everything, Sal. Such a monumental fucking mess! I made a massive mistake going off with Naomi. I realised a little while back that I don't love her. Not like I love you. I think it only happened because I couldn't face the fact that I was coming up to fifty. And so, when a twenty-nine-year-old showed interest, my head was turned. Stupid, I know.' He looks straight at her and gives a watery smile. 'Thank God you didn't agree to the divorce and sell this place when I asked. You knew deep down that I'd come back with my tail between my legs, didn't you? You always were the wise one.'

Sally stares at him, incredulous. She can hardly process his words. He's actually saying he wants to come home, after everything he put her through. The heartache, the trauma, the excruciating, almost physical pain. And for what? Because he made a mistake? His poor little head was turned because he was getting older. She should take him back, just like that? She feels like she wants to laugh, but she wants to punch him more. How dare he? How *dare* he do this to her? How dare he treat her like she was something on his shoe for all those years too, and make her believe somehow that was what love looked like?

It dawns on her that not long ago she would have been overjoyed, would have pulled him into her embrace, thanked God that he was home. It's then that she realises how far she's come. How much she's grown, how far behind her she's left the downtrodden, pathetic mess she used to be. The woman *he* turned her into. Sally wipes away tears and stares at him, her heart thumping, contempt building in her chest.

'I can see you're shocked, sweetheart. I was too when I realised I wanted you back, and that I'd made this gigantic...' He gesticulates wildly, apparently searching for the word.

'Mistake. Yeah, you said.' Her voice sounds as cold as the chill running through her blood.

Paul pushes his floppy dark hair, now strangely free of grey, from his forehead and fixes her with apologetic green eyes. 'I can tell you're angry. And you've a right to be.'

'Don't tell me what I have a right to be. You don't get to tell me how to think, or feel, or look, anymore, Paul. Ever.' She says this quietly, but the anger in her tone is abundantly clear.

He holds his hands up in surrender and looks sheepish. 'I'm sorry. Truly ... but I have just three words for you: "I love you."' Paul's serene smile makes her want to spit in his face. Then she looks at him some more and her anger abates. She decides she won't even waste negative energy on him now. He doesn't deserve it. He deserves nothing from her.

Sally stands up and turns to face him at the door. 'And I have three words for you. Pin back your ears and listen carefully, because they're *very* important. Fuck off, Paul.'

Chapter Twenty-Two

R ose is still chuckling half an hour after ending the call with Sally. How she wishes she could have been a fly on the wall to see Paul's reaction when Sally told him those three important little words. Rose is so proud of the way her old friend stood up to her ex after all those years of being his proverbial doormat. She's even prouder of the way Sally has changed and grown stronger in the last few months too. Sally is convinced it's because of the inspirational garden she's spent so much time in, and Rose tends to agree. After all, she's had a similar experience. She might have set out to transform the garden, but she has to admit, it's probably the other way around. Although she's happy she's lent a hand, the garden is a law unto itself, really, springing up new flowers, shrubs and grasses here, there and everywhere.

Rose leans her arms against the half-open stable door and gazes out at the multitude of colours bursting from the green, inhaling deeply the competing scent of garden flowers, and sea air. The passion flowers threaded through the willow arch shiver in the breeze and Rose realises it's not just new life springing up. Over the last few months, older, forgotten-about plantings have been brought to Rose's attention, like the willow. Under the nurturing guidance of the garden, she's tended and nourished, watered and fed, eventually seeing the renaissance of things originally planted years ago, mostly by Glen. She likes to think they are a sign he's always with her. She also knows he'd be proud of what she's done. Not only for the garden, but for herself and for those dear to her.

A warmth spreads from the pit of her stomach into her chest as she realises something else. The garden has created a renaissance in her too, and in Flora, Sally, Josh and Louise. Bella has drawn sustenance from its calm sanctuary, while the children are young shoots, full of spring sap, energising all those around them. Rose remembers yesterday when Wesley wanted to show 'Weez' his sunflower, which he said was bigger than Molly's now. And it is. Rose thinks Weez might have given it some plant food last time she was here, but she'll keep that knowledge to herself.

Daisy, though she's not here as often as the others, calls the garden her little piece of paradise, and talks to her daisies (and her dad) as she comes through the gate, and is so excited about the surprise party for Sally. She told Rose she's organised some music too, and it would be wonderful if she would give them a song or two. Apart from family and friends in the wild garlic days, Rose has never sung in front of an audience, but she reluctantly agreed. The last few months have taught her that new things should be welcomed. New friendships, new hobbies, new ways of being, new growth. Life does have a tendency to be too short – something she witnessed on a regular basis in her years as a nurse.

Thinking of which, Louise will be here soon to plant her memory of Matthew. Louise told Rose the other day that when she sees his memory plant blooming year after year, it'll be like part of him living on. The bees will be nourished by him, and in turn they will help to pollinate and distribute new growth in an ever-turning cycle of life. Rose thinks that's a lovely idea. Louise also said that before she met Flora, Rose and the gang and visited the garden, the thought of planting a memory for Matthew would have brought her terrible sadness. Her main thought would have been that he was gone and she was alone. Now she's looking forward to it with hope and acceptance. Rose takes a deep breath and hugs herself. Nature works in mysterious ways, her wonders to perform. She knows that isn't quite right, and might be seen by some as sacrilegious, but for Rose, it's perfect.

Louise trundles a little trolley behind her up the path and waves at Rose, who's deadheading the *Convolvulus*. 'I'm here! Are you ready to see what my memory is?'

Rose lays her secateurs on the wall. 'Yes. I can't wait!' Rose has an orange tiger lily in mind for some reason, but she finds she couldn't have been more wrong when she hurries over and looks in the trolley. It's a leafy shrub with an abundance of delicate white star-shaped flowers. 'Oh wow. It's so gorgeous … is it a jasmine?'

'It is. I won't tell you its Latin name, as it's hard to pronounce, even for me.' Louise shoves her tortoiseshell glasses up the bridge of her nose. 'But it's an evergreen star jasmine. It likes to grow up a warm wall, so I thought it would be ideal along from the roses, and its delicate scent will be the perfect complement to theirs.'

Rose touches her nose to the petals and inhales the sweet perfume. 'Stunning.' Straightening up, she notices Louise looks a bit tearful and wonders about the memory behind the jasmine.

Louise fiddles with the hem of her navy smock top and gestures towards the shrub. 'It was Matthew's favourite flower. I once asked him which one he liked best and he said he couldn't possibly say, as he loved so many of them. But eventually, he said it was this one. Mainly because…' She stops and Rose can see she's struggling.

'You don't have to tell me, it's fine.'

'No. I want to. It's a happy memory, and as I said the other day, watching it grow will be like ensuring part of Matthew lives on. So, he said it was mainly because the jasmine reminded him of me. On the surface, I present as delicate and understated, but he knew my depths, my beauty and strength. This jasmine remains evergreen through the coldest winters and thrives again in the spring. It's constant and steadfast … like our love.' Louise smiles as she blinks back tears.

Rose squeezes her arm and a look passes between them

which says all that's needed. 'I'll get the spade,' she says, and makes her way to the shed.

On the day of the party, Rose's kitchen has been a hive of activity from early morning as she and Bella have been busier than the bees in the garden, baking, cooking and making sure all the party food is ready to go. She checks her list again and finds it's all present and correct and everything has fallen into place very well. Cooked chicken (two kinds), glazed ham, sausage rolls, scotch eggs, tiny pasties, a variety of nuts, crisps, sandwiches and salads, new potatoes and savoury rice. Flora's bringing some homemade quiche too (and James, a new friend from art class) and Louise is contributing salmon. Josh is bringing himself, as he agreed to come last minute. He wasn't sure if he should, with Lucy still being in hospital, but his sister insisted he came and let his hair down.

Everyone is bringing a bottle too, so in addition to the drinks Rose has, everyone should be catered for. Although, there are three old workmates and their partners coming too, as Rose accidentally let it slip to one of them in the post office. Then she felt obliged to invite them and the others. Never mind, it will all be grand. It's now 6pm, everyone will be here in half an hour and the surprise party can begin. Just time to change, and then when they arrive, make sure everyone acts normally until Sally goes to check the pond for the unveiling. Then at Rose's signal, the cake will be carried in by Angus, Sally's son, who miraculously came back from his travels yesterday.

Rose checks the positioning of the number 50 candle on the cake again, and thinks how lucky it was that Angus came back in time. Rose got in touch with Sally's daughter Pippa, to tell her about the surprise party and invite her and her partner Megan. Pippa told her that she knew that Angus was aiming to surprise his mum, coming home a few days before her birthday, but he was staying at his friends in Exeter last night, as their flight got in late. She'd pass the details on to him. He was travelling down to Cornwall this afternoon and agreed to come to the surprise party. It will be the extra icing on Sally's cake when he appears.

'You should go and get changed, Mum. Stop faffing and double-checking everything,' Bella says, coming into the kitchen. She puts some of the party food on two paper plates for the children as it's getting a bit late for them to eat, and Wesley's gearing up for a rebellion.

'Yeah, I will. I'm excited, but I just want it to be perfect for her. She's had such a shit time this year with all the upset over Paul, she deserves some fuss.'

'It will be grand. You excited about singing too? Daisy's just arrived with her husband and a few musicians, they're setting up in the garden.'

This is news to Rose and she's not sure she likes the sound of it at all. 'I thought it was a karaoke machine thingy. Where the hell has she found musicians?' There's an unsettled feeling in the pit of her stomach. She didn't agree to sing with a proper band, for God's sake.

Rose makes for the door, but Bella stops her. 'Mum, go

and get changed. It will be fine. You don't want people to see you with food stains all over your top.' Bella points at the stairs. 'Go!'

The unsettled feeling grows as Rose imagines her voice drying up mid-note, or forgetting the words, and she wishes she'd said no to Daisy. Her singing was for the people she knew and was comfortable with. Her voice came from the heart, lifted her spirits and hopefully those of her audience. But how can she sing with people she's never met? This is not something Rose has planned for at all, and thoughts of singing and being the centre of attention, perhaps scrutiny, are in danger of ruining the wonderful evening she's organised for Sally.

Applying scarlet lipstick to match her red dress and strappy sandals, Rose wills herself to be happy and forget about Daisy's silly band. The main thing is that she needs to relax and enjoy the party. Rose decides she has no obligation to her oldest friend, because she moved the goalposts without warning her, didn't she? New challenges might be one thing, unwelcome hurdles are quite another. Rose needs to be true to herself and do what she feels comfortable with, and if telling Daisy she's not singing helps her do that, then so be it.

———

The garden is alive with laughter, the buzz of conversation and quiet anticipation. Rose and Bella enlist the help of Louise and Josh to carry all the food out to three trestle tables which have been set up next to the picnic table, and

Flora and James take out glasses and drinks. Rose likes James straight away and thinks he and Flora look like they've just returned from Woodstock, fifty-odd years on. Both are tall, with grey hair in ponytails, she in boot-cut jeans and a yellow fringed top, he in similar jeans and a purple T-shirt. They seem to embody the spirit of the hippiedom and the summer of '69. They are laughing a lot together, Rose notices as she ventures out into the garden. It's a joyful sound which helps to put her in a better mood. Daisy and her 'band' have their backs to her at the far end of the garden under the pergola, and the evening shadow and rampant honeysuckle prevent Rose getting a clear view of them.

The children try to help with putting out the food but just get under everyone's feet, so Louise takes Wesley off to measure his sunflower. There's also a worry that the little boy might give the game away to Sally about Angus. When he arrived a little while ago, before they'd squirrelled him away in one of the bedrooms, Wesley had asked if Angus was Jesus. They had all fought to keep a straight face, because the tall, blue-eyed, dark-haired, bearded youth was indeed a dead ringer.

Sally comes up the path towards Rose, a half-smile on her face. 'I can't believe all these people are here for the unveiling of the pond. I hope they're not disappointed.' She looks towards the pond, where a tarpaulin suspended from poles obscures the whole area.

'Of course they won't be disappointed. It's marvellous.'

'Do you think the fairy lights in the shrubs and grasses

behind is going a little over the top?' Sally fiddles with her beaded necklace and starts to worry a nail.

Rose has the fleeting impression that Sally wants to be anywhere else but here, but that she's rising to the challenge. Strength and resilience learned during the break-up and creating this pond are making her stay, and Rose wants to give her a big hug. This might not be the best idea, though, as it could set her off, and then she'll be in a complete state for her surprise before it happens. The right time for that will be when she sees the cake and Angus..

'I think the whole thing is absolutely perfect, Sally. Now stop worrying. I'll quieten everyone down in a few minutes and then we'll charge our glasses. Josh and Bella are standing by to drop the tarpaulin when I give the signal.'

A few minutes later, Rose takes Sally by the hand and leads her to the tarpaulin. Flora gives them both a glass of fizz and then Rose takes a deep breath and taps a spoon against her glass. Everyone gathers round in quiet expectation, even the children are silent for once, and she takes a moment to appreciate the gathering of friends in her little Eden. To Rose, it seems like even the flowers are taking part, charging the air with their scented energy.

'Ladies, gentlemen, and children,' she winks at Molly and Wesley. 'Tonight, we've come together to see the end result of this lovely lady's efforts over the past month or so.' Rose slips her arm through Sally's and is unsurprised to feel it shaking. 'Sally had an idea, or should I say a vision, of how to make this wonderful garden that means so much to us all, even more special. Her contribution will add to the sensory nature of this space, and provide a calm and contemplative area for us. And those beautiful lilies floating on the surface there will be in remembrance of Sally's dear friend and neighbour, Grace. Thank you, Sally.'

Rose nods to Josh and Bella, who unhook the tarp from the poles, and Louise helps Wesley and Molly to operate the remote for the waterfall. Bella flicks on the fairy lights and as the waterfall trickles into life, there's a round of applause and a whoop or two. Sally's chin trembles, but she's holding it together. Just.

'Thanks so much, everyone. I have adored working on this, and it's given me the confidence to try other projects I never dreamed I could have attempted a few months back.' She looks at Rose. 'And of course, I couldn't have done it without the encouragement and generosity of this lovely woman, who agreed to let me loose in this fabulous garden in the first place.'

Rose gives her a quick hug and looks to the stable door to see Angus give her the thumbs up. 'There is a little surprise that Sally doesn't know about, though.' The little knot of people share knowing looks, and a few chuckles, while Sally slides Rose an apprehensive glance. 'This wonderful lady will soon be turning fifty, and so we thought we'd celebrate that too. Happy birthday, Sal!'

Everyone echoes the sentiment with raised glasses, and Rose nods to Angus, who steps down from the doorway carrying the cake. Sally's hands fly to her mouth and she says through her fingers, 'Angus! I can't believe it…'

As Angus reaches them, he hands the cake to Rose and envelops Sally in a big hug. 'Happy birthday, Mum.'

Everyone sings happy birthday as Rose lights the

candle, and when Sally's calmed down a little and wiped her tears, she manages to blow it out. 'Did you make a wish, Mum?' Angus asks.

She smiles. 'I was going to, but then I didn't, because everything I could wish for is right here in this moment.'

The party starts in earnest as everyone migrates to the food tables, and Rose thinks she couldn't be more satisfied with the way everything has turned out. She discovers she's suddenly ravenous and then remembers she's not eaten since breakfast, as she's been so busy. Grabbing a plate, she's about to help herself when she sees Daisy making a beeline towards her. While Rose was saying those few words for Sally, she noticed Daisy hovering at the back, unwilling to meet Rose's eyes. Rose suspects that she knows she's gone too far and is apprehensive about broaching the singing subject.

'Rose. Can I have a moment?' Daisy's grin looks a bit set, as though it's masking apprehension, and Rose thinks her assessment is correct.

'Hi, Daisy. Yeah, but I'm starving – we can chat while I stuff my face.'

'Grub looks fab.' Daisy grabs a plate and follows suit.

Rose wonders when her old friend is going to tackle the live band issue, because the space between them is full of the sound of their munching, but nothing else. It feels awkward, but there's no chance Rose is going to make it easy for her.

Daisy swallows a mouthful of quiche and then the set smile is back. 'Let's take our drinks over there.' She nods towards the pergola where the sound of a guitar tuning up winds sinuous notes through the evening air. 'Come and meet the band.'

Rose sighs. She knows Daisy is unsure about her response, and so she should be. 'Look, Daisy, I know your heart's in the right place, but I'm disappointed that you didn't ask me first about singing tonight. It was scary enough when I thought it was going to be karaoke, but this...' Rose gestures towards the band. 'I'm not happy about this at all.'

Daisy looks genuinely shocked. 'Oh? I thought it would be a lovely surprise for you.'

'Really? Then why have you been acting so weirdly tonight?'

Pink-cheeked, she replies, 'Well, there *is* one part of the surprise that I'm not sure you'll be totally okay with.' Rose is beginning to get frustrated now and it must show on her face, because Daisy adds with a sigh, 'Come on. It'll be easier to show you.'

As Rose approaches the pergola, she can see three men. One is Daisy's husband Steve, he's on drums; one is vaguely familiar, maybe an old friend of Steve's, on keyboards; but the one on guitar, she has no idea about, because he has his back to her. Daisy goes over and whispers something in his ear and he turns to face Rose, a big smile on his face. It takes a few moments to register the steel-grey hair, bright-blue eyes, assured smile. It can't be. Tristan Carthew. No way.

What the fuck, Daisy? For a second Rose thinks she's spoken those words out loud because Tristan's smile is erased by a puzzled frown. It's probably because she's staring at him daggers. Then he steps forward, looks like he's going to hug her, but instead, lightly touches her arm for a second. 'Rose, it's so good to see you.' He tries the smile again. 'You look like you've seen a ghost.' He nudges Daisy, who's anxiously scanning Rose's face. *And so you fucking should be anxious,* Rose wants to say. 'Told you that you should have warned her, Daze.'

'Yeah, *Daze*, it might have been nice to get a heads-up,' Rose says quietly, with a glare cold enough to wither the entire honeysuckle.

Daisy lets out a self-conscious laugh. 'I thought it would be a nice surprise. Tris came down for the school reunion last week and he's having a bit of a holiday at ours. Steve, Tris and Ron have been jamming in our garage, they're even considering a few gigs...' She's talking so fast, the words keep bumping into each other. 'Tris has his own band back in Wales and they play pubs on weekends, don't you, Tris?' He gives a small nod and looks at the floor.

Maybe it will swallow him up with any luck, Rose thinks.

Daisy glances at the floor too. 'And I suddenly thought, what a nice idea it would be to have you on vocals, like the old days.'

She stops abruptly when there's no response from Rose. Not even the hint of a smile. Rose watches Daisy swallow hard and fiddle with her earring, something she's done since they were kids, when she knows she's messed up. The awkward silence grows between them until it feels like a physical wall. They're both staring at Rose, and with an effort she remembers her manners. It's not Tristan's fault, after all.

'Well, I must say it's nice to see you, Tristan. I'm not sure my vocals will be up to it, though – you know, singing with a live band. We've had no time to rehearse and I've no clue of what you're going to be playing.'

Tristan looks like he's been thrown a bone. 'Hey. No problem.' When he smiles, it's so genuine and warm that she can see echoes of the young man she knew and finds herself thawing a bit. 'We thought we'd play all the ones we used to sing together, and just in case you're hazy on the lyrics, I got them printed out.'

'Oh, I don't know … it's all a bit sudden and as Daisy knows,' she says pointedly, 'I haven't sung in public before.'

He shrugs. 'Have a think, no rush … just let us know.'

Rose isn't sure what to think. What she does know is that the little challenge of doing a bit of karaoke has morphed into a formidable shit show on a grandiose scale. This was supposed to be a cosy evening to celebrate Sally's pond and her birthday. Now it feels like everything is ruined because of Daisy's misguided attempt to give her a 'nice surprise'.

She gives him a tight smile. 'Yeah, I'll have a think.' Without looking at Daisy, she turns and hurries off.

She's not sure where she's headed, until she finds herself tucked away around the side of the house, far from everyone else. The evening sun angles in between the shed and the cottage, floodlighting Madame Aggie Panther as she dances with the breeze in her beautiful bee pot. Glen. She wants Glen, and she always feels closer to him when she's next to Aggie. Rose runs her hands along the four tall stems, strokes the petals the colour of Glen's eyes and thinks about him. What would he say she should do, if he were here? Probably that she should stop worrying, go for it and knock everyone's socks off. Then it occurs to her that this situation wouldn't have arisen if Glen had still been here. Daisy had manufactured the whole thing because she had some stupid romantic notion about Rose and Tristan. Rose hadn't gone to the school reunion exactly because she wanted to avoid all that silliness, but no, Daisy wouldn't take no for an answer, would she?

'I'm sorry for upsetting you, Rose.' Daisy's standing behind her looking like a chastised child. Rose is calmer now, but not up for forgiving her just yet.

'Then why did you? You told me you were unsure about my reaction to the Tristan part of my "nice surprise". That should have been enough for you not to have done it. I already said no to the stupid reunion, for god's sake.'

Daisy claps her hands together as if in prayer and then stares past Rose at the Aggie blooms. 'I just thought it would be lovely for you to sing again. You were so happy when you had your wild garlic experience, as you call it. You remembered how you felt when you were sixteen – said singing out loud made you feel young again, made you realise there are still new things to do – new challenges to take. You ripped up your box.' She flits her eyes to Rose's and away, as though she's unsure the connection will be welcome. 'I know I never let on, but I remembered that

Tristan was a big part of that day too. I took the photo, after all ... so...' She uses folded arms as a full stop.

The breeze jostles the huge head of one of the Aggies into Rose's arm – a nudge to respond. Anger, resentment and disappointment subside as she looks at her old friend's downcast face. Daisy's actions came from a good place. Rose needs to take apart why she was so angry, but at the moment she finds she can't coordinate some of her thoughts properly. A few of them gain clarity and she says, 'Look, Daisy, I get that you were trying to do something nice ... I really do. But the Cardinham Woods days have gone. We can't recreate them, nor should we want to. I loved the way I felt amongst the bluebells and garlic in the spring of this year in the woods. The memory of that day in the past helped me come to terms with no longer being a nurse and to sort out my future, as you've just said. But I wanted to remember those times as they were.' Then Rose's thoughts get so tangled, she has to leave them inside her head.

'I'm so sorry, Rose. I've ruined your night...'

Rose touches her arm. 'You haven't. Look, I'll be okay in a while. Go back to the others, I'll get a glass of something and have a think.' Then she walks away before Daisy can say anything else.

Chapter Twenty-Three

F lora thinks the evening is turning out to be one of the best she can remember. Sally has had her well-deserved celebration, the food is superb, and James has got on famously with her friends. He has, she thinks, become a little obsessed with the idea of painting the jasmine, however, declaring it to be the prettiest flower he's ever seen. Flora acknowledges he's had a few glasses of wine, but nevertheless, she can tell he won't be happy until he's accomplished his goal.

The other day, when they came here with the express intention of painting, they found they'd talked for so long that they only managed a rough sketch each before it was time to go. She doesn't regret it, though, because the time was used to learn so much about each other. Flora smiles to herself as she remembers how afterwards, she boosted James from the friend camp into the kindred spirit camp, members of which total precisely one – James. This is purely because, in their youth, they were both dealt a similar bum hand, but managed to make a royal flush of them in the end. A long, rough road, but well travelled.

Flora decides to find Rose and ask what might be a convenient time for James to come and paint the jasmine. She imagines Rose would say whenever he likes, but she will do the polite thing and ask. Rounding a corner, Flora spots a gloomy Rose hurrying away from Daisy, who, if she's not mistaken, looks a bit dejected. This strikes her as very odd. Flora knows the two women are each other's oldest friends, so she wonders what's happened. Rose is pouring herself a drink by the trestle table as Flora approaches. She looks like she's having a good time as she's laughing with Sally and Angus, but Flora knows Rose well enough now to see through the pretence.

'Hello, all!' Flora does her now-perfected chuckle while she scrutinises Rose's face. 'What a wonderful evening it is.'

'It really is!' Sally says, hugging Flora, which is a surprise but appreciated. 'Thanks to this one.' She elbows Rose. 'And thank you for coming, Flora. It's so wonderful to see so many friends here for me.'

Flora can see that Sally is on the way to being legless, which accounts for the hug. 'It's a pleasure.' Then to Rose she says, 'Can I have a quick word?'

When they are away from the main party, Rose frowns and takes Flora's arm. 'What's up with you? You look a bit glum.'

'It's not me who's glum.' Flora indicates they sit on the grass next to the lavender. 'I saw you and Daisy looking like you'd had an argument and thought I'd check on you.' While Rose is thinking about that, she adds, to lighten the mood, 'Oh, and I wondered if you could let me know when James could come up and paint the jasmine.'

'Oh, whenever he likes. He's a very lovely man, Flora.'

'Yes, he is, isn't he.' She doesn't like the knowing look that's found a home on Rose's face. She glances away, as her own face feels too hot all of a sudden. Most puzzling. 'Anyway, what's going on with you and Daisy?'

Rose frowns and Flora isn't sure if she's going to tell her anything, as she shuffles on her bottom as if she's ready to get up and go. Then she sighs and tells Flora all about Tristan, an old boyfriend, how he relates to the wild garlic day, and that he's here right now in the little band that Daisy's organised. She also tells her that she's worried Daisy is trying to match-make and that if she agrees to sing in the band, she'll be going along with it.

'Are you likely to have any romantic feelings towards this man?'

'Of course not!'

'So I don't see the problem.'

'Okay. But that's not the worst of it.' Rose frowns and takes a mouthful of wine. 'There's also the fact that I'm completely terrified that if I do sing, I'll dry up, forget the words, or both.'

Flora takes a sip of her wine and thinks that Rose needs a push. She's a strong woman who has coped admirably with some huge changes recently. She's still coming to terms with the loss of her husband and her career, but she's risen to the challenge and made new inroads into the rest of her life. A life that she imagined after retirement would be dull, lonely and boring. For the past forty-odd years, Rose has given of herself to the community, her family and friends, willingly and unselfishly. Her next steps going forward are supported by a belief in the power of nature, the tranquillity and healing ability of this growing space, and enabling it to help herself and others. The memory of the wild garlic day had set her on this new path ... and singing was a big part of that, so why is she putting up barriers against it?

'I think I have the answer,' Flora says slowly a few moments later. 'It's because you're afraid of sharing your experience with those who don't fully understand it. It's personal to you. You once said that you thought people shared too much these days – social media and so forth – and you preferred to keep some things private. I was exactly the same, remember? I was brought up to keep everything in, Mother preferred it that way. And is there any wonder? God knows what would have happened if I'd opened up to people about how I felt about the old witch. But, as a rule of thumb, people did keep their thoughts under lock and key back then. When I did open them up to you and Daisy that evening, I said it was the influence of this place, remember?'

Rose nods. 'Yes, and I felt compelled to do the same – but you and Daisy are my friends – you get me. You're so wise, Flora. And absolutely right. If I sing with Tristan again, I think I'm worried that I'll get too emotional, I'll forget the words, dry up, or all three. Then the old days will be trashed by a stupid attempt to recreate them. The special memory of my long-ago sixteenth birthday will be tarnished, forever changed by it.'

Flora is thrilled that Rose thinks her wise and counts her as a friend. She can tell it's genuine, it came from the heart. So why is she always worried that she's not really part of this new community? Concentrating on Rose's dilemma now, she asks, 'Is that what you think you'll be trying to do? Recreate those days?'

'It feels like that's what's expected.'

Flora laughs. 'And you always do what's expected of you?'

'Well, no.'

'Exactly.' Flora knows she's making sense and perhaps getting somewhere. 'I love your voice. It makes me feel uplifted, I can feel the positive energy coming from you in waves. Why not share it? And having been around a bit longer than you, I think you'll be creating new memories actually, not reliving old ones. The old ones are safe in the past. This is the Rose now, not the Rose then. You'll bring everything you have become, all your life experience, to the songs tonight … but you'll always carry that sixteen-year-old with you. Don't worry about that.'

Rose blots under her eyes with a napkin and pulls Flora into a tight hug. 'Are you trying to turn me into a blubbering mess, for god's sake?'

'Yes. It's my speciality.' Flora laughs and finds she might benefit from a napkin too.

Daisy looks like she's won the lottery when Rose agrees to sing. 'Really? I'm so thrilled!' She gives her a big hug. 'I couldn't bear to think I'd caused all this upset – I was just going to suggest we packed up and headed off.'

'Yes, I was going to suggest you did too, until Flora had a word with me. Look, it will all be fine. Just me having a wobble.' Rose doesn't want to go into the ins and outs of it all again. She's had enough emotional soul-searching for one day – it's bloody exhausting and this is supposed to be a fun evening.

'Right. I'm sure you'll love it. Just first-night nerves.' Daisy leads her up to the pergola where the three men are sitting on a bench looking a bit deflated. They all look up at her like meerkats when she walks over.

'Hi, Rose. Okay?' Tristan asks with an uncertain smile.

'Yes, all good. If you let me know the songs, I'll give the vocals a go.'

A little while later, it's Daisy's turn to tap a spoon against her glass. 'Ladies and gentlemen, I—'

'And children!' Molly shouts. Rose has to laugh. Her granddaughter is high on party atmosphere and too much sugar.

Daisy smiles. 'And children, I do beg your pardon. Can we put our hands together for our fantastic band this evening – Phoenix! And on guest vocals, our very own Rose!'

Phoenix, really? Rose inwardly cringes as she taps the microphone, but gives a bright smile as the little gathering whoop and clap.

Tristan steps up to his mic and introduces himself and the others, counts down the drummer and then launches into 'Dreams' by Fleetwood Mac. As the first few guitar chords soar up into the pink-and-lilac sky over the ocean, Rose is glad she has to concentrate on her cue, or she'd be a blubbering mess for the second time tonight. She closes her eyes, releases a deep breath and lets her voice free, sending it soaring up to join the music.

She opens her eyes and sees the joyful expressions on her friends' faces as they wave their arms in the air. Just like the day earlier in the year, when she sang in the woods, almost independent of her control, Rose's arms rise and stretch, and she's lost in the music. All her nerves subside and she's lost in the moment too, and the memory, twirling and dancing through the bluebells and garlic, her head tilting from side to side, hair falling across her face. This time, though, she's in her own haven, her own Eden, her lungs filled with the perfume of honeysuckle and jasmine, and the overwhelming positive energy of this space and of those gathered.

Glancing to her left, she shares a wide smile with Tristan. She can tell he's similarly overwhelmed too, and yet again, she catches a glimpse of the young man he once was. Flora, as usual, is absolutely right. Rose is bringing everything she has become, all her life experience to these songs tonight ... but she's also acutely aware of the sixteen-year-old she carries within her.

Chapter Twenty-Four

A month on from the party Rose is still incredibly energised and uplifted. She sings every day, mostly to herself in the garden, where she's convinced the notes are purer, but sometimes to Bella and the children in the evenings. Wesley is a very demanding audience, and at the end of every song, always says, 'Again, Granny. Again!' Bella keeps insisting her voice is getting better all the time, which isn't likely, given her age. Rose is sure the singing voice diminishes like everything else as time progresses. Though she's happy to believe it, if Bella says it's true.

Daisy and she are all good again, and Rose apologised for her 'drama queen' outburst. She was genuine about the apology, but there was only so much of her that went along with the drama-queen description. Rose had real concerns about ruining her early memory in the woods that day, and she's so thankful that didn't happen. She's found that the two experiences are able to co-exist side by side without arguing with each other.

Today she's putting the finishing touches to a chocolate cake. Baking is something she never had much time for as a busy nurse, but lately she's remembering the therapeutic benefits of weighing, mixing, sprinkling, and melting to create something so deliciously comforting for all to enjoy. Rose lets the children lick the mixing spoon, just as she used to with Bella, and just as Rose's own mum did with her. Making a cake, she decides, is more to do with providing love than food, and the added bonus is the delicious aroma of a cake baking in the oven.

Wesley runs in as she's spreading the last of the chocolate icing on top. 'Wesley have some now, Granny?'

'Not yet. We have visitors coming later, so we'll save it for then. You can have a big bit, of course.'

Wesley pouts but doesn't make a fuss and runs off. He's growing up so fast, Rose notices. Four years old next month, then he'll be at school before she knows it. Goodness. It doesn't seem that long ago that Bella was starting school. When she thinks about it sometimes, it's almost impossible to imagine that her daughter is a mother herself. Where have all those years gone? Rose runs water into the sink and reminds herself it's pointless to wish time would slow down. Actually, on second thought, she doesn't want it to. Instead, she's thankful she has them all here. Something she thought had gone forever when they moved up country. She mentally crosses her fingers that Nigel gets the job he's going for at the end of the week too. If he does, then Bella can start looking for a place to live for them all nearby. Rose will be thrilled for them, of course she will, but the cottage might feel a bit empty after all that explosive energy, otherwise known as her grandchildren, has gone.

As she puts the scones she made earlier on a cooling rack, she realises that these days her cottage is rarely empty for long. There's always someone popping up, and this afternoon she's really looking forward to welcoming Josh and his gran, Lily. There's a little apprehension at the back of her mind, because being in a new place could be disorienting for Lily and this could make her dementia worse, but at least they're prepared for that eventuality. Rose is delighted that Josh's sister Lucy is coming too, as she's making a wonderful recovery, and Josh told her she'd love the garden.

A few weeks ago, James and Flora were here for a couple of days, sketching and painting the jasmine. James is such a brilliant artist – in fact, Rose was surprised just how good. Flora, as she's fond of telling people, has a good eye for composition and colour, and while she's not as talented, the two finished paintings complemented each other perfectly. Rose thinks the artists themselves do the same – but she instinctively knows Flora wouldn't like that mentioned. At first, Rose was thinking of joining them with Bella's old paint box, but something told her they'd be best left to their own devices.

———

Josh draws his car up outside and Rose looks through the stable door, arms folded, worry suddenly at her side. Lots of 'what ifs' chase each other around her head as she watches Josh and Lucy – his female double – help their grandma from the front seat. What if Lily can't cope outside the home, and as a consequence, what if she has a meltdown? What if she becomes unmanageable – throws herself to the floor? What if she becomes violent? Rose tells herself she used to be a nurse and would be able to handle the situation, but just 'what if'? Rose thinks Lily looks even more like the late queen today, as she has on a tweed skirt, paired with a blue twinset and pearls. Lily takes a few steps towards the sweet peas and her vacant expression is blown away over the sea on the breeze, along with Rose's what ifs.

A sunshine smile puffs up her cheeks and she waves at Rose as she approaches. 'Look at my sweet pea flowers,' she says, cheerily. 'Aren't they splendid? I grew them from seed, you know.'

'They are indeed splendid, Lily. You must have green fingers.' Rose takes her hand briefly and Lily looks at Rose as though she can't quite place her. 'I'm Rose. Remember, I visited you a few weeks ago?'

'Of course I do.' Lily snorts and taps her cane twice on the path, but looks unsure.

Lucy smiles and shakes Rose's hand. 'Hi, pleased to meet you. It's an old cliché, but Josh has told me so much about you.'

Even though they're twins, Rose can't get over how alike they are. The same tumbling curls of gold, the same moss-green eyes, earnest expression and half smile. She laughs and replies, 'Now in answer to your cliché, I respond – all good, I hope?'

'All good.' Lucy takes a breath and turns in a circle.

'And he told me so much about this place too. It's simply stunning. I can feel the good vibes already and the scent in the air is extraordinary.'

'And all the colours of the rainbow,' Lily says, nodding sagely.

Josh takes her arm and they do a slow tour of the garden, much to Lily's obvious enjoyment. 'Look at the beautiful pond, Gran,' Lucy says, pointing. 'Gorgeous lilies.'

Lily laughs. 'Like me! I'm a gorgeous lily too.' Then she walks over to the Golden Gate rose. 'You lot – come and smell this. It would give Chanel No. 5 a run for its money! Nothing like the smell of a natural rose, I always say.'

Josh whispers to Rose that he can't remember his gran being so animated for years. 'This place is certainly bringing her out of herself.'

'Oh look, sage, rosemary and mint! I do love some mint on my new potatoes.' She turns to Rose. 'Have we had lunch yet? I could eat some potatoes... I grow them in my garden.' Lily's smile droops as she looks one way and the next. 'Where's my vegetable patch? It seems to be missing.' Then more urgently. 'I can't see my vegetable patch!'

Rose takes her elbow. 'Don't worry. We'll look at it later. How about we have some tea and homemade chocolate cake, Lily? I've made scones too.'

Rose's firm but encouraging tone calms Lily instantly and a smile lights her face. 'Cake. Yes, I do like cake. Homemade cake, especially.'

Rose leaves Josh and Lucy to settle Lily on a chair by the picnic table, as she isn't sure Lily would manage cocking her leg over the attached bench. She's in two minds whether to allow her to meet Bella and the children, because she's already shown signs of distress over the 'missing' vegetable patch. Bella suggests they could easily come back inside if Lily can't cope, and Rose agrees. Molly and Wesley were briefed that the elderly lady visiting them this afternoon might not like lots of yelling or running about, and they should be on their best behaviour. Wesley said he always behaves bestest when he has cake, which sent his mum and grandma into fits of laughter.

Rose takes out the cake and scones on a tray, while Molly carries the plates and Bella and Wesley follow behind with the tea and butter. As they approach, Lily looks up from sniffing a sprig of lavender Josh picked for her and smiles broadly when she sees the children. 'Hello. What lovely faces you have. You aren't twins, though.' Lily winks at Molly. 'You are definitely the bigger one, young lady.'

Wesley just stares, but Molly says, 'Yes. I'm the eldest.'

'I have twin grandchildren. They have lovely faces too.' The twins share a smile. 'Josh is boisterous and Lucy is very pretty. Funny too. She has an infectious laugh. Do you laugh?' Lily leans forward and scrutinises Wesley's face.

'Yes.' He looks at his mum. 'But Mummy says I have to be quiet today 'cos the old lady won't like noise.'

'What old lady?'

He gives her an incredulous stare. 'You.'

Rose feels the adults hold a collective breath, but Lily's

raucous laughter, braying through the summer afternoon, puts them at ease, and they laugh along too.

'I do like you, young man,' Lily says when she's got her breath back. 'Who are you and what's your name?'

'I'm Wesley and my sister is called Molly.'

Molly huffs. 'I can say my own name, thank you very much.' To make up for being upstaged, she smiles at Lily. 'Here's a plate for you. My granny made the cake. Rose is my granny,' she jabs a finger into Wesley's arm, 'and she's his granny too.'

Lily takes the plate, but her smile is a little vague and she glances at Bella. 'You can't be Rose then, you're too young to be a granny.'

Molly screws up her face in disbelief, and is about to jump in, but her mum heads her off at the pass, explaining who she is, and points to Rose. 'Rose is my mum and she made the cake.' Bella takes the cake slice and slips it onto Lily's plate. 'Do try some.'

Lily takes a forkful, makes appreciative noises, and thankfully there the matter rests. Rose gives her daughter a grateful smile. 'After we've had tea, maybe we could sit in the shade on those deckchairs under the pergola.'

'I'd like that very much,' Lily says. 'The honeysuckle is beautiful, wild and free as it should be. Too much unnecessary pruning goes on these days. That garden I can see from my window in that...' Rose can tell by her irritated expression that she's searching for the words, '...that other place I stay in ... is regimented, sterile.' Lily twists her nose to the side as though there's an unpleasant smell under it.

'That's right, Gran,' Josh says. 'You always say the garden should be allowed to have a mind of its own.'

'I do,' Lily says, with a proud smile. Then scrutinises his face. 'You're my Josh. My sweet pea, aren't you?'

Josh has a mouthful of cake and looks as though he's about to choke, so Lucy jumps in, 'That's right, Gran. And I'm Lucy, remember?'

'Lucy ... but you're a young woman, she's little.' Then she shrugs and dabs her mouth. 'I suppose you must be, because you have her eyes.' To Rose she says, 'That cake was delicious, by the way. Can we go and sit with the honeysuckle now? The perfume is so enticing.'

Josh was ecstatic that she remembered who he was and was utterly convinced it was because she was here in the garden amongst the familiar smells, colours and sounds that she remembered from her own cottage garden many years ago. He's now sitting with his gran, who's nodding off in a deckchair under the pergola beneath the honeysuckle. Bella and the children are at the park, and Rose and Lucy are sitting on the grass next to the pond. Rose says how therapeutic it's been for Lily to spend time in the garden, and maybe they could pick her some sweet peas, to take back to her room in the care home.

Lucy tries, but can't hide her sadness. Rose guesses it's about Lily not recognising her as she does her brother. Her guess is confirmed when Lucy says, 'I know I must sound like a whining kid, but I think Josh must be her favourite.'

She holds her hands up as Rose is about to speak. 'Yeah, I know it's rare for her to remember anyone at all now, and I shouldn't let it get to me. But he's always been her favourite. Her little sweet pea.'

'I doubt very much that she has favourites.' Rose has no clue if this is true, but Lucy needs a lifeline. 'Lily told Wesley that you were pretty, clever and had an infectious laugh, remember?'

Lucy nods. 'Yeah, but Josh was the one she'd take round the garden when we were little, pointing out this flower and that plant. Telling him all about them.'

'But Josh told me he always loved being in the garden – that he was interested in growing things from an early age. Maybe you weren't as bothered?'

Lucy considers this and then gives a nod and a shrug, which Rose expects is a concession to her argument. 'Hm. Anyway, I'm glad she remembers him. And I'm glad he's going to work in horticulture. Josh told me the other day he'd applied for three posts, as he prefers to learn on the job, rather than get academic qualifications. I think he's had academia up to his eyebrows.'

'Yes. He's a natural. And I'd argue doctoring is vocational. I've known a few over the years who were pushed into it, like your parents aimed to do with your brother, but their heart wasn't in it. I could tell.'

At the mention of her parents, Lucy's already serious expression turns gloomy. 'They have a lot to answer for, the two of them, that's for damn sure.'

Rose wants to ask Lucy about her life on the streets and how she's feeling about everything now, but feels it is too soon, on the one hand, and that she hardly knows the girl, on the other. Something noncommittal yet sympathetic might be best. 'Yes, Josh told me much of his background. You both had it tough.'

Lucy gives her a quick glance and then she leans back on her elbows, turns her face to the sky, allows the sun to find it, and closes her eyes. They sit in companionable silence together, listening to the waterfall and letting the whisper of the perfumed breeze through the grasses soothe them. 'This place is heavenly. So relaxing. I adore being next to water. The sea especially, but this waterfall is a balm for the soul too.'

The calming effect of this space is exactly what Rose hoped would happen when visitors came to it with troubled minds. 'I'm so pleased you like it. I know I'd be lost without it now. It's a place where memories grow, and so much more. I love to share them with my friends.' Lucy's puzzled, so Rose explains.

'Ah yes, Josh said you told him something along those lines about this garden,' says Lucy. 'I have a few memories I'd like to plant here to remind me that life is worth living and worth the effort. I'm not a big flower person, though. Maybe I could plant seaweed?' Lucy laughs, but Rose notes the sadness behind it.

Even though she's unsure of overstepping her boundaries, she finds herself saying, 'You can talk to me about how you ended up in hospital, or anything else that might be bothering you. I'm a good listener, and it goes without saying, I'll keep anything you say to myself. Only if you want to share it, obviously.'

Lucy looks thoughtful. 'You used to be a nurse, yeah?'

'Yeah.'

'Okay. I think I'd like to tell you … you might get it more than some people – being a caring type – and you made this garden, so you have to be pretty special. Josh says you are anyway, so I trust you.' Lucy rolls her eyes. 'I'm burbling on. Okay, I've not told anyone apart from my counsellor, but the overdose wasn't an accident.'

Rose takes her hand but says nothing.

'I'd had enough of being weak, having no direction, disgusted with myself for needing the drugs, but powerless to stop. I felt worthless. I *was* worthless. The things I did to get a fix … you wouldn't believe.' Lucy's shame and self-loathing contort her face.

Sadly, Rose would believe it. She's seen and heard the stories of so many Lucys turning up at A&E far too many times. Though this doesn't stop her heart aching afresh. 'I'm so sorry.'

Lucy squeezes her hand. 'Thanks. So am I. One night, I just thought, *Fuck it. I've had enough.* You know? What's the point in life?' She gestures at the growing things all around her. 'Now I'm on the mend, I'm seeing the answer to that question everywhere here. Can you imagine what would happen if a sweet pea or rose thought "fuck it" and gave up every time a storm kicked its arse? Or the bees? They have a tough enough time as it is, struggling against loss of habitat and all sorts of toxic shit in the atmosphere and on crops. But do they give up? No. They keep coming back time after time, no matter how tough it is. That's nature for you.'

Rose is finding it hard to keep her emotions under

control. Lucy looks so impossibly young right now. She's been through so much, but she has such an expression of determination in her eyes. 'We can learn a lot from nature, that's true.'

'One good thing came out of all that, though.' Lucy plucks a blade of grass and chews it. 'My parents have now realised what a monumental shit show they've made of everything. Josh helped too, of course. He told me he'd threatened to leave if they didn't change. Anyway, I've agreed to stay living at home for a while, just to see how it goes. They know that if they return to their old ways, both of us are gone.' She looks at Rose, head on one side. 'But you know, I think they've learned their lesson. Shame it had to be at my expense – Josh's too, to a lesser extent. They fucked us both up.'

'But you're putting that right already. And soon, with counselling, you'll feel well enough to go for your dreams.'

'Hope so. I'm getting help with my drug addiction too – that won't be an easy fix.' She winks at Rose. 'Ged it? But yes, working with marine life is my dream. Always has been.'

'Yeah, Josh told me you'd like to work at the seal sanctuary at Gweek, if possible.'

'I would. That's a long way down the line – but I'll get there.'

'I know you will. And if you'd like me to come with you to the sanctuary to help get the ball rolling, I will.'

'Thanks, Rose. But that's the kind of thing I need to do for myself.' Lucy smiles and hugs her knees. 'Though I'd like to come back here from time to time, if that's okay? I'm going to try to do what makes me happy from now on, and being here does.'

'I'm glad. And it's more than okay. I'd like that very much.' An idea comes to Rose and she says, 'I think it might be nice for you to come and plant that memory you mentioned. Something that has to do with the sea. Obviously not seaweed, as you said.' She chuckles. 'I'll have a think. Maybe ask my friend Louise. She knows everything about plants.'

'Thank you. I'd love that. Then every time I see it, I'll remember how far I've come.',

----

Later, just before they leave, Lucy presents a bunch of sweet peas to her gran. 'These will look nice by your bed in the cream-and-lemon vase, Gran.'

'Yes. Thank you very much. I love sweet peas.' Then Lily puts her nose to a bloom and smiles. 'You have the look of my granddaughter Lucy. She's a bright one.'

Rose shares a warm smile with Lucy and then she gives Lily a quick hug. 'It's been so nice to have you over, Lily. You must come again.'

'I will, Rose. Thank you, and the cake was delicious. Goodbye.' Lily taps her stick on the path and sets off for the gate.

Josh laughs. 'I'd better catch up with her before she disappears down to the beach. Thanks again, Rose. This place has done her the power of good.'

Lucy gives Rose a big hug and nods at Josh as he helps

their gran into the car. 'Josh is right. She's more like the old Gran than she's been for years. Thanks, Rose. And for the chat.'

'I've loved having you all. And you're so welcome. See you soon, I hope.'

Rose watches the road long after the car disappears over the brow of the hill, lost in thought. Just before Lily came, she'd had a text from Daisy asking if she'd agree to sing with the band again at the weekend. They'd arranged a little pub gig in Port Isaac and the band would love it if she'd join them. Immediately she'd dismissed the idea. It was great fun last time, but she didn't want to make it a regular thing. But something Lucy mentioned earlier made her think. She said she was going to try and do what made her happy from now on. Singing in general makes Rose happy. Singing with the band last time definitely made her happy, so maybe she should reconsider. She'll ponder on it. She imagines Glen rolling his eyes at that, and smiles.

Chapter Twenty-Five

F lora and Louise are standing outside the nursery door in the village, pondering. Well, Louise is pondering, Flora has already pondered and reached a decision. She taps the glass window of the case containing a noticeboard. 'Just go in and ask, Weez. What could it hurt?'

Louise pushes her spectacles up the bridge of her nose and frowns. 'I don't want to look stupid. And stop calling me Weez.'

Flora chuckles. 'Spoilsport, I like calling you Weez. And why would you look stupid?'

'I'm nearly sixty-six and have no experience of working with children, so they'll most probably feel embarrassed for me if I enquire.' She turns from the noticeboard and looks at Flora. 'Heck, *I'll* feel embarrassed for me if I enquire.'

Flora is hopeful that all Louise needs is a little push. 'Look, you've been talking about this since you saw the advert last week.' She taps the glass again and reads, '*Part-time help needed for the play group, two half days per week. Please ask inside for more details.* Where does it say you have to be young, or that you need experience?'

Louise shifts her eyes to the advert again, though Flora imagines she knows it word for word. 'It doesn't, but—'

'Never mind "but". And anyway, you have the Wesley experience to draw on – that's up there with snake-charming as a very dangerous occupation. Lion taming, even. But you make it look easy.' There's a flicker of amusement dancing at one corner of Louise's mouth but nothing else is forthcoming. 'Right. Go and ask, I'll wait for you.' As there's still no response or movement from her friend, Flora makes as if to go inside. 'I'll ask for you then, shall I?'

'No! Gosh, you're such a nag.' Louise straightens her already straight pale-blue cotton jacket cuffs and checks her navy canvas shoes for dust – Flora's pleased to note the highly polished lace-up-type ones seem to have completely disappeared. 'Right, cover me. I'm going in.'

Flora laughs out loud as she watches her friend march straight-backed through the door of the nursery. Weez has certainly blossomed, relaxed and grown a good number of new shoots since she started to visit the garden of memories. And though Flora was joking about Wesley, he really was putty in Louise's hands. His sunflower was at least five feet high now, a good head and shoulders above Molly's. Wesley would show his sunflower to anybody and everybody who visited, proudly standing by while (at his insistence) they took a photo of him by its side, looking up in wonderment.

As she waits, her phone goes off in her pocket. Two

messages. She opens Rose's first.

Great news! Josh has a job learning on the job with the National Trust! I know you're with Weez today, can you let her know? I sent her a message but she's not seen it and I sent it ages ago. She'll be so proud he's following in Matthew's footsteps. Xx

Flora sends back: *That's the best news! I'm so thrilled! Xx*

Weez will be thrilled as well. She can't wait to pass the news on. She smiles to herself. Though she's not sure her friend will be similarly thrilled to know that Rose is now using 'Weez' too.

The second message is from James.

Hi there, if you have no plans this weekend, would you like to go out for a drink on Saturday? Possibly a meal? J x

Flora feels more than a few butterflies mass together in her chest. This is unexpected – both the butterflies and the invite. Hitherto, she and James have gone to Rose's to paint, and once or twice out for coffee – normally on the way to, or on the way back from the garden, or last week, to an exhibition of local artists. But this sounds more like ... the word 'date' hovers in her mind, tries to settle, make itself comfortable, but Flora pulls the rug from under it. Yes, she sees James as a kindred spirit, yes, he makes her laugh, yes, they share many interests, but that's as far as it can go. The whole romantic thing is preposterous. At their age, for goodness' sake? The very idea of it. It would be an unmitigated disaster – two old crocks trying to be Romeo and Juliet? Besides, if it went wrong, it might very possibly ruin their lovely friendship.

How should she respond without seeming rude, though? She knows that James will have seen that she has seen his message, because of the two little blue ticks. So he might be wondering why she's taking so long to answer. Then Louise comes through the door and provides the perfect excuse.

Out with Louise. Will check my diary and get back to you.
F x

She hesitates over leaving the *x*, but he sent one, and it'd be churlish not to return it. Everyone leaves a kiss nowadays anyway. It doesn't mean anything. It's like additional bloody punctuation. She sends her reply and looks up at Louise with a big smile that feels a bit guilty, for some reason. Mother whispers something, but she's instantly slapped down.

'Guess what!' Flora waves her phone at Louise. 'Josh has got a job with the National Trust!'

Louise clasps her hands to her chest in delight. 'How wonderful!'

'It is. Rose messaged you, but I expect you've left your phone at home, as usual.'

'Yes, like you, I'm not fond of them.' Louse's hazel eyes shine with happiness. 'It's so incredible that Josh will be following in Matthew's footsteps. I know without a doubt he'll do so well! Such a lovely young man.'

Flora couldn't agree more. They chat about Josh for a few minutes, and then she remembers why they're standing in the street outside the nursery. 'So, what did they say?'

Louise pushes her glasses along her nose and says through a big smile, 'They said they would like to give me a trial day to see how I get on with the children, and if I think it's for me.'

'What a brilliant day this is turning into!' Flora says, then remembers the message from James. *Well, apart from that.*

'It is. They weren't concerned that I had no formal training. I mean, it's not as if it's many hours, and it's voluntary too. But I did tell them about Molly and Wesley. Wesley especially. In fact, I did go on a bit, which as you know, isn't me.'

'It didn't used to be, but you're more outgoing and upbeat lately. It's nice to see.' Flora hopes this doesn't sound too patronising.

'I think so too.' She squeezes Flora's arm. 'It's got a lot to do with you. You pulled me out of myself, got me to trust people again.' Louise's face is bright red now and Flora knows sharing like this isn't easy for her.

'Well, thank you. It has a lot to do with Rose's garden and a certain bundle of energy called Wesley, too.'

Louise laughs. 'You're right there.' She slips her arm through Flora's and points along the street. 'Okay, let's go and have some cake and coffee to celebrate. My treat.'

Flora is thrilled her lighthouse quest has been successful.

The old lamp just needed a bit of a polish, after all. Job done. Was she at last overcoming her recent worries about hiding behind clothes of many colours? Was she actually much more than a drab garden fronted by a pretty gate? She thinks so. Although, as they walk towards the café, Flora thinks about James's message again and wishes she had someone to guide her to safe waters too.

Rose knows she has to get this right. Flora has that beady-eyed 'miss nothing' stare as they sit opposite each other on the picnic bench. Flora's hair is twisted into a messy top knot, strands of which have escaped and keep blowing across her eyes, but she still stares at Rose unflinchingly. 'More wine?' she asks, tilting the bottle of red over Flora's glass.

'Not until you answer my question, Rose. You're doing my head in, as the youngsters say.'

'Okay. Do I think that James has romantic intentions towards you, and is this a date you'd be going on? I have to say yes, and yes, I think it would be.' Rose holds her breath and hopes Flora doesn't go off like a firework. She's already told Rose that she'd hate to lose James as a friend, but that she's afraid that's exactly what would happen if she agreed to go for this drink or meal on Saturday.

Flora puts her head in her hands and says to the table-top, 'Gawd. I feared as much. I knew I wasn't imagining it.'

Rose thinks she might as well come clean. 'Yes. I'm not surprised, to be honest. There is a lovely energy between you two. You are very alike and ... I don't know ... kind of fit together really well.'

Flora's head jerks up as if someone has pulled an attached string. 'Eh? You think I like him too ... in that way?'

Come on, Rose, no time to chicken out now. 'Erm ... yeah, I think you do.'

'But we're in our late seventies, for God's sake! Well, I am,' Flora says, aghast.

'I don't see why that matters.'

Flora opens and closes her mouth a few times, then resorts to sighing and shaking her head. 'The whole thing is preposterous. How ... I mean ... I don't think I could ... you know ... at my age.'

Rose watches a crimson tide rise up her entire face. Does she mean what Rose thinks she means? Luckily, her 'used to be a nurse' experience comes to her rescue. Flora needs no-nonsense advice. 'If you're talking about sex, there's no reason why you can't, Flora. But intercourse isn't the only way to express intimacy. Maybe a nice cuddle in each other's arms as you're falling asleep will be just as fulfilling.'

Flora's complexion is slowly returning to normal, as is her sense of humour. 'Thank God. I can't be doing with bedroom aerobics at my age. I've only indulged a handful of times, as it is!' Her braying laughter puts them both at ease and she accepts more wine.

'So, you admit to having romantic feelings for him?' Rose presses gently.

An exaggerated lift and shrug of the shoulders. 'I'm not

sure. Who knows? Yeah, okay, I might. But what if it goes wrong? What if it's awkward? What if it ruins what we have?'

'What if it doesn't? You need to stop worrying about what ifs.' *That's rich coming from you, Rose.* 'Just go along on Saturday and see where it takes you.'

Flora stares at the *Philadelphus*, her expression unreadable. 'Hmm. Maybe James has no romantic feelings for me anyway. Maybe I'm reading too much into it.'

'Maybe you're not. If I had to bet, I'd say he does. But don't overthink things. Enjoy the evening, relax and have fun.'

'Where do you think we should go? Nowhere too quiet or obviously romantic. It would feel really awkward then.'

Rose considers this as she spots another agapanthus, much smaller than the one in the bee pot, but an aggie nevertheless, shooting out from behind a patch of heather. Nature never ceases to amaze her. 'You could always come and watch me sing with the band in the local pub?' *Eh?? Where the fuck did that come from?* Rose feels her own crimson tide start up and she turns her face to the sea breeze.

'Oh, I didn't realise you were doing that!'

'Neither did I, until this second, apparently. I've been pondering on it and it appears I've made a decision.'

'How lovely. And yes, I think that would be ideal. We could have a meal earlier and then wait for your performance. Perfect! I'll message him back now.'

Rose takes a deep breath of salt air and holds it, and then allows its slow release. What on earth made her come out with that? She'd almost decided she wouldn't do the gig after all, just before Flora rang and asked if she could pop over this evening. It all seemed a bit too much, if she was honest. Singing in front of friends and family was one thing, singing in front of complete strangers who may or may not be receptive to her, was another. Then from nowhere she's decided the complete bloody opposite. The little agapanthus catches her eye again, and she wonders if the decision actually came from nowhere after all.

'Well, I messaged him. I feel all schoolgirly and wiggly inside.' Flora's eyes are bright with excitement and Rose is glad.

'What's schoolgirly?' Rose laughs.

'It's how I feel inside. Do pay attention.' Flora laughs in return. 'What a day of surprises it's been. Josh gets his dream job, Weez is maybe going to work at the nursery, I'm going on a date.' She throws her arms up and a row of metal bangles clash together as they slip down her arm. 'A date, I tell you! And you're going to be gigging with a band. Amazing!'

That's one word for it. 'Yes. It's certainly that.'

'Mum! Mum!' Bella comes running up the path from the house, a huge smile on her face, eyes sparkling with excitement. 'Nigel's just phoned. You know I told you he'd got through to the last two on the panel at his interview, and that they'd let him know this evening or tomorrow?'

'Ye-s.' Rose's heart is doing loops and she hopes she knows what's coming.

'They just called him. He's got it! He's got the job and he's moving back here just as soon as he's worked out his notice!'

Rose leaps up, arms outstretched, and is caught in a half-hug, coupled with a crazy circular jumping dance. Flora joins in and they all whoop and yell at the tops of their voices. Rose laughs and feels the tension and apprehension about Saturday drain into the grass underfoot.

'What a bloody momentous day this has been,' Flora gasps, leaning a hand on the table to get her breath back and steady herself.

'It certainly has,' Rose agrees, just as Molly and Wesley poke their heads out of their bedroom window.

'What's all the yelling about? We're trying to sleep here!' Molly shouts.

The three women look at each other and burst out laughing, which makes Molly even more disgruntled. She huffs and bangs the window closed. 'We should pull ourselves together,' Bella giggles.

'No. I like being *not* together. It's a freeing experience,' Flora guffaws.

'Yes, I'm all for being *not* together too!' Rose punches the air, which sets them all off again.

Later that evening as she gets into bed, Rose watches the full moon ride high above her garden and is happy to find no trace of apprehension or worry in her mind about the gig. Like the moon, this is her time to shine, and she's really looking forward to it.

By the time Saturday arrives, Rose is feeling a little differently. It's one thing lying in bed imagining how lovely it will all be, performing in front of strangers, sharing her love of singing, wrapped up in the excitement of it all, but it's another thing waiting backstage (the ladies' cloakroom) ten minutes before curtain up, with her stomach churning like an old washing machine. Running the tap, she holds both wrists under the cold water to cool herself down and calm her nerves. Rose's mum told her that trick years ago and it normally works, but her hands are shaking so much, she suspects it will fail her this evening.

Through the mirror she sees the door open and in bursts Flora, resplendent in black and gold. The black trousers are smart and tailored, while the sequinned top is reminiscent of something a game-show host might have worn in the 1980s. Nevertheless, with her hair piled up in a messy bun, sparkly earrings, winged eyeliner and bright-pink lipstick, Flora somehow manages to pull off the entire ensemble, in the way that only Flora can.

Rose turns off the tap and musters a smile, though it isn't returned. Flora looks rattled, harassed, out of sorts – a manifestation of Rose's own feelings. Despite her outfit, Rose thinks Flora appears somehow diminished ... but why? Then she spots it. The air of confidence that is normally worn as one of her accessories is missing this evening. 'You okay, Flora?'

Flora shrugs slightly and considers her pink nail varnish as if she's surprised to see it. 'I really don't know. I was so looking forward to this evening. I was fine when I left the house, fine when I walked into this pub, and fine when I bought myself a drink. But as soon as James came through the door, I had this overwhelming need to use the toilet. Except I didn't. I made it up so I could escape.' She looks at Rose, sad and bewildered. 'What if I've made a mistake agreeing to this date, or whatever you want to call it? What if it's awkward?' She presses her lips together as if to stop any more what ifs coming out, and stares at her reflection in the mirror.

Rose can sympathise, totally. She feels exactly the same about agreeing to sing. Nevertheless, her friend needs her. 'Hey, we've been through this. It will all be fine once you relax and have a few drinks. I'm nervous too. Here, do what I do.' Rose runs the cold tap and explains to Flora about the calming effect. Flora frowns but does it anyway, and then a flicker of a smile hovers at the corner of her mouth.

'Hmm, it does seem to help a little.' She pulls a paper towel from the dispenser and dries her hands. 'And you have absolutely nothing to be nervous about, Rose.' She sweeps a hand over the length of her. 'You look absolutely stunning in midnight blue. Is that dress new?' Before Rose can reply, she continues, 'And your voice is extraordinary. Everyone will love you, believe me.'

Rose looks at the sparkle in Flora's eye and her big smile, and does believe her. A quiet calm and confidence is making a few inroads, and with her friend's hand in hers, she thinks she can do this. 'Thanks, Flora. And I might say the same thing. You look stunning and James will love you, believe me.'

Flora makes a squawking sound and flaps a hand. 'Eh? Love? Too soon for all that malarkey. Come on. Let's get out there before we both change our minds!'

Arm in arm, they walk through the door laughing. James raises a hand and Rose gives Flora a little push. 'Go and knock his socks off,' she whispers in her ear. Before Flora can respond, she hurries over to where the band are warming up on the little stage.

Tristan looks up from his guitar, smiles at her, and suddenly the nerves come rushing back in. The other band members start chatting to her and she answers questions, nods and smiles in all the right places, while all the time her heart is thrashing about against her ribs. Then across the room she sees Flora give her the thumbs up and James raises his glass to her. She realises she isn't alone; she has friends here. Rose takes a breath and lets Flora's pep talk fill her mind. It will all be fine, everyone will love it…

Tristan comes over and says quietly, 'You okay? You seem a bit nervous.'

Rose sighs. She's not such a good actress after all, then. 'I am. This is the first time I've sung in front of people I don't know.'

'You'll be great. Just sing like you did at Sally's do, let yourself go and lose yourself in the music.' Rose smiles and he tilts his head towards hers. 'I'll be next to you if you need a prompt. I'll mime the lines.'

This makes her laugh. He always used to make her laugh and she immediately feels more relaxed. Dear Tristan, he was always in her corner when they were young, and she realises he's there for her now, too. They all are. 'Thanks, Tristan. I think I'm ready now.'

Steve takes the mike and introduces the band to the packed room. There's a ripple of applause and everyone waits expectantly. There are loads of people here … many more than she imagined. *Okay, Rose. Time to shine.* Rose blows a kiss to Flora as the introduction to 'Dreams' starts up, and after the first line, her nerves vanish. Her voice sounds strong and confident, as though she's been doing this kind of thing all her life. The crowd are swaying with the music, waving their arms to and fro in time with the beat, and they are smiling. Rose is too, inside. An incredible surge of joy rushes through her and she abandons herself to the moment. Unspoken questions that filled her mind as she ran water onto her wrists, and just now before she began to sing find answers. This is why she does it. This is what it's all for. Making herself and others happy. She's so proud of herself, and Glen would have been too.

'Wow, they're absolutely fantastic!' James yells in Flora's ear, after the band launch into their fourth song. 'Even better than last time in Rose's garden!'

Flora realises he has to shout above the music, but her poor ear is begging for mercy. 'Yes,' she yells back. 'Absolutely incredible!' And they are. She can hardly believe that's her lovely friend Rose up there, looking like … well, like a famous popstar. It's as if a light has come on within her and it's shining on all of them. Flora is thrilled that Rose went ahead with it, and when she looks up at James swaying next to her, his eyes dancing in the spotlights, she's thrilled that she went ahead with him too.

James catches her gazing at him and takes her in his arms. 'Dance with me, Flora,' he whispers in her ear, which she has to admit is so much nicer than his yelling. There's a little tingle developing as his breath and lips brush her neck. Goodness, she feels quite giddy.

'I haven't danced in years,' she laughs up at him. *Certainly not with a partner.*

'Nor I. But it feels like we should.' James's smile is both encouraging and something else. Something else that she's not altogether comfortable with. It's … it's sexy. There. She's admitted it. What on earth is happening to her?

As if she has no choice in the matter, her feet start to move in time with the music, following James's lead, and soon he pulls her closer. So close that there's nothing between them at all, apart from the thudding of her heart against his. Here she is, Flora Granger, a spinster in her seventy-eighth year, dancing with a man. A handsome, sexy man. Stealing a glance up, their eyes meet, and an overwhelming feeling of belonging finds a home in her heart. Belonging and joy. Hell, she feels lifted, intoxicated, like a young girl again as they turn in a slow circle.

James smiles again, his eyes holding hers in an intense gaze, and without thinking too much about whether it's a good idea, she says, 'This is lovely. I'm so happy right now, James.'

He drops a soft kiss on her cheek and whispers in her ear again, 'So am I, Flora. And it's all because of you.'

Chapter Twenty-Six

R ose's policy of 'just sing and go' has stood her in good stead these past three weekends. Last night was the final gig they'd been scheduled for, and now, a Saturday alone tending her garden and relaxing in the sunshine, lies ahead of her like a gift. She stretches and slips out of bed, the songs of last night still playing in her head, the applause of the pub audience loud in her ears. Exhilarated, is how she'd describe the experience. Joyous. A little like being in her garden. But not as calming, nor grounding. Periods of intense excitement, she's decided, have their place and are the perfect complement to her calm, happy, nurturing spirit which she's lucky enough to have living inside her every day. She adores making the audience happy as well. Too much of it could become unmanageable, however. Hence the 'just sing and go' approach.

Daisy always asks her to stay on after the gig for a drink and a chat, but Rose doesn't want to get drawn into all that. She doesn't want it to become the norm – a thing that is expected of her. She arrives in time for a sound check and leaves more or less after the last guitar notes wind up to the rafters. Rose catches sight of herself in the bathroom mirror and honesty kicks the thoughts she's just manufactured into touch. Who is she trying to fool? 'Just sing and go' is her plan, mainly because she doesn't want to get too friendly with Tristan. He always gives her that old smile, the one she could never resist when they were together, and often puts a friendly arm around her shoulders. Daisy told her that he's divorced too, which also flew a red flag in her mind. Rose is happy with her life and wants to avoid any kind of tricky situation, thank you very much. Getting happy with her life has taken time and effort, and there's no way a few unwise decisions are going to ruin it.

The garden is changing colour every day, shrugging off its summer blooms, and there's an underlying feeling of lethargy, of a hunkering down, of preparing to sleep. Rose loves September and has learned to appreciate every season, a little like appreciating every stage of her life. The latter is something she's learned recently. Contemplating, pondering, being thankful for the time she had with Glen and Bella, especially in the prim-nose days, but also accepting she can't hang onto it forever. Then the fear of retiring, of losing her identity as a nurse, of stepping into the future, alone, directionless. She couldn't have been more wrong; thanks to this glorious Eden she shares with her friends and family.

Of course, there are still times when she lies awake, wrapped in the past, staring at the ceiling and wondering what she'd be doing now if Glen were still here. Would they go off on the cruise he always said they'd do when she retired? Would they be docking into far-flung harbours, filled with the excitement of embarking on new adventures? Probably. And yes, she'd absolutely love this, but what's the point in torturing herself? It can never happen. She's learned to face these memories head on. Face them, cry, shout her anger at the ceiling, and then put them away. Sometimes they refuse to leave until the dawn creeps under the curtains; other times they leave immediately. One thing Rose knows for sure is that they're unlikely to leave completely. But because of who she is now, she has the tools and the strength to face them.

Rose is able to manage her feelings much more now too. She doesn't mourn the passing of summer, the dying of the sweet peas, agapanthus, honeysuckle, roses and the rest. She will always have the memory of them to keep, and of the people they gave happiness to. Flora, Lily, Weez, Sally and Josh, to name a few. Autumn will soon be here and then, after a period of winter inactivity, the miracle of spring will see nature rousing again and bursting with green shoots. Full circle. New life. New hope.

It's so therapeutic being here alone in the garden, Rose thinks. The wind is light and the only sounds she can hear as she goes about her deadheading, are the snip of the secateurs, the drone of a few sleepy bees on the lavender, and the quiet shush of the ocean in the distance. The children are at Daisy's, playing with her grandchildren, and Bella and Hannah are out down the coast in the VW for the second weekend in a row, selling their gorgeous sandwiches and pastries to the last remaining tourists.

Bella was ecstatic last week when she came back. All the food had been sold, and lots of people had asked if they would be back again in the future. Rose is overjoyed to see her fulfilling her dreams at last. And next week, the little family will be moving into their own place, just a mile away. They're renting for now, but once Nigel had settled into his job, they plan to buy. Bella told her yesterday that she and Nigel are getting on better now than they have for years. He's totally on board with her new venture and gets that he was too controlling in the past. Best of all, if they do have a disagreement, they talk it through.

Flora and James seem to be getting on well too, though she can be a little cagey if Rose pushes for more detail about their relationship. Flora tells her not to be nosy and her cheeks turn into apples. Rose says she's not being nosy, just showing an interest. Actually, she has to acknowledge that she probably *is* being nosy, but she's dying to know how it's all going. What she does know is that the first 'date' they had at the gig ended in a chaste kiss on Flora's doorstep. After divulging this, Flora came over all unnecessary and Rose could get no more out of her.

A little while later, a grumble in her stomach reminds her she's not had lunch yet, and a freshly baked quiche is waiting on the kitchen counter. Maybe she'll have some salad with it too. The smile on her face at the thought of her tasty lunch shrivels and dies on her lips, like the petals on the rose bush, when she sees Tristan walking up the path towards her. His long easy stride and confident manner, complete with 'that' smile, irritate the hell out of her. How dare he just rock up unannounced?

'Tristan?' she says a little stiffly. 'I thought you'd gone back to Wales this morning.'

'I'm all packed and ready.' He nods at his car parked outside the gate. 'I just thought we could have a chat before I went. We've not had two minutes to catch up, have we?'

That's because I planned it that way. Now what? 'Erm, well, I was just about to have lunch.' As soon as the words are out, Rose wishes them back in again. That could be interpreted as an invitation.

'Sounds like a plan ... unless you don't have enough for me?' The smile disappears as he clocks her stony face. 'Sorry, if I misunderstood.'

Oh, for goodness' sake, he's an old friend. Get over yourself. 'No, course not. Yeah, there's enough. Only quiche, though.' She turns and leads the way inside, cursing under her breath.

As she gets lunch, Tristan looks around the kitchen and pops his head round the living-room door. 'A fabulous place you have here. And that garden, wow!' He gestures out the window. 'It's amazing. Flora was telling me the other night how hard you've worked on it and how much your friends love to visit. Planting memories … that's so special.'

Rose bristles with annoyance and she's glad she has her back to him. Bloody Flora, sharing all Rose's business like that. 'Right, yeah. I didn't see Flora at the gig last night?'

'No, it was the first gig we did at the pub. You left early, like always, and I had a chat with her and James.'

How very cosy for you all. Rose gives a non-committal grunt and wonders why she's getting so grumpy. Flora was just being her usual gregarious self, she imagines. And Tristan is a very friendly guy. He'd have told her all about how he knew Rose too, she expects. 'Do you want tea, coffee, or a cold drink?'

'Whatever you're having, Rose.'

I'm having a fit of pique, Tristan, and I need to calm myself. 'Okay, take your plate out to the old picnic bench near the pergola, and I'll bring the drinks.'

Tristan is in rapture over the cheese and onion quiche and the home-grown tomatoes, lettuce and cucumber on the side. 'I once had a go at growing stuff years back, but I don't have your green fingers. The slugs ate all the tomatoes, so I didn't bother again.'

'Now, where would nature be with that attitude, eh? What if the bees and flowers just gave up after they'd been battered by a storm?' Rose paraphrases Lucy, but it doesn't sound as impactful.

'Hm, yep. I'm not the best at weathering storms.' He dabs his mouth with a bit of kitchen roll. 'Used to be, but I lost my daughter when she was six. Had a full-blown breakdown and yeah … well.' He blows down his nostrils and looks away. 'Sorry, Rose. That came from nowhere and I've no idea why. I'm such a fucking loser for dropping it on you like this'

To say Rose is dumfounded would be an understatement. It seems she can find no appropriate response in her 'used to be a nurse' bag either. They sit looking at each other and she's not sure who seems most upset by his revelation. She finds she wants to cry, but takes a sip of tea and says gently, 'Sally, the lady who made the pond, remember? She reckons sometimes this garden has a cathartic effect. It's been known to draw deep thoughts out into the open. Stuff you thought was safely locked away. She said it was scary, but she felt all the better for it in the end.'

Tristan shrugs. 'Perhaps. I had no idea I was going to tell you about Gemma, but then out it came.'

'You can tell me all about it … only if you want to, of course.'

Rose listens as he explains that twenty-six years ago, Gemma, his youngest daughter, was round at a friend's house. They were playing ball in the front garden and the ball bounced into the street. Gemma ran out to retrieve it, didn't look where she was going, and was hit by a car.

'It was quick, so we have to be thankful for that. My

little one didn't suffer. But my god, it was tough for my wife and Gemma's sister and brother. As I said, I had a breakdown and was no good to anyone for nearly a year. My poor wife, Diana, had to do everything alone.' He shakes his head and picks at the dry skin around his thumbnail.

To Rose, Tristan Carthew had seemed confident, outgoing, self-assured – just as he'd always been. Who would have guessed that behind it all, he would be carrying the weight of such unimaginable grief? 'Is that what led to the divorce?' she asks, instinctively knowing he needs to get it all out.

'No.' Tristan puts his head on one side and looks at the honeysuckle, lost in thought for a few seconds. 'Well, maybe it *was* the beginning of the end. But we've only been divorced three years.' He drinks some tea. 'No, it was a Paul Simon song that did it.' He laughs at her surprise. 'I was listening to "Slip Slidin' Away" on the radio as I was driving home from work one day. The meaning of the lyrics suddenly jumped out and hit me like a ton of bricks. It was incredible. Almost like an epiphany. I can't remember them exactly right now word for word, but he says something like – we go to work, collect our pay, believe we're gliding down the highway, but instead we're slip slidin' away. We only have so long on this earth, and I realised I had to be honest with myself. I wasn't happy. Hadn't been for a long time. I'd been married to Diana for over thirty years, but we never had what you call a knock-your-socks-off passionate relationship. Don't get me wrong, I loved her, but not in the way I ought to. Not in the way…'

He tails off and picks at the dry skin round his nail again. Rose has the uncomfortable feeling that he was about to say, *Not in the way I loved you*. He shouldn't say it. He mustn't say it. To make sure he's side-tracked, she asks, 'Why did you marry, if that was the case?'

'Diana fell pregnant. Simple as that. We got married. That's what you did then, I guess. Many still do now. And like I say, I loved her in my own way. But those lyrics made me realise I needed to make a radical change before I went slip slidin' away. I've got more years behind me than in front, and I want to feel like I'm actually living them to the best of my ability, you know?'

Rose does. 'Of course. At our age we need to live for every day. At any age, really. Bet it was a big shock for your wife, though.'

'At first yes, but in the end, after many discussions, she admitted she wasn't that surprised. She'd had similar feelings and we were very honest with each other. She told me that when I fell apart after Gemma died, she resented me. She felt abandoned, unsupported. She knew I couldn't help it, but she said something that was tethering her to me loosened, and later on, somewhere down the line, she guessed it just snapped. Diana realised that she'd been going through the motions, same as I had, for years. We agreed it was over, had an amicable divorce and now she's met someone else. I'm very happy for her.'

Rose watches Tristan's Adam's apple bob as he swallows his emotions. The poor guy has had such a different life to the one she imagined. The box she made up for him. 'Well, at least you have a good few years ahead now. I'm sure you'll make the most of them.'

'I'm trying my best.' He gives her a big smile. 'Flora told me you had a very happy marriage and that your family are here with you now. Must be a comfort after losing your husband.'

'Is there anything that woman didn't bloody tell you, for god's sake?' A bit snotty, but she can't help it. Seems like her whole life story had been poured out to Tristan down the pub, along with a few pints.

'Sorry. I don't think Flora was being indiscreet.' Tristan pushes his hand through his hair. 'It's obvious how much you mean to her.'

The truth of this hits home and Rose thinks about apologising, but she changes the subject instead. 'Yeah, I guess. So, when your parents dragged you kicking and screaming to Wales the summer we both turned sixteen, what did you do with yourself? I'm guessing you didn't form a band and get more famous than Fleetwood Mac, or I would have seen you on TV.'

He laughs, and she remembers the boy from the wild garlic day. Feels a rush of warmth towards him.

'No. I worked in the same engineering plant as my dad. Then I met Diana and you know the rest. I did play in a band at weekends, though it kind of fizzled out when the three children came along, and life makes other plans for you, doesn't it? Now I'm retired, I'm overjoyed to be back into that scene. Especially now we have you on vocals.' He smiles at Rose. 'Overjoyed to be back home too. I never saw Wales as home.' He holds up a finger. 'Don't get me wrong,

I made lots of lovely friends, but Cornwall will always be where I belong.'

Rose gets that. She couldn't call anywhere else home either. She's glad that he's so happy singing again, but she can see a problem. 'Won't it be difficult to maintain, though – playing with a Cornwall-based band? I know you've been staying at Daisy and Steve's for a bit of a holiday, but long-term? Wales isn't exactly round the corner from Cornwall.'

Tristan nods and gives her that engaging smile of his. 'Yeah, it wouldn't work long-term. Thing is, I'm thinking of moving back. It's a tough decision, because my children and grandchildren are in Cardiff, but it's only three hours or so away – not that bad. And in the end, they have their own lives. As I said, I want to make sure that I get the best of what's left of mine.'

Rose is only half listening as he goes on to tell her all about his eldest son, Mark, and his middle daughter, Jade. The idea of him moving back here makes her feel unsettled and she doesn't like it. Tristan belongs to her past, and though she's enjoyed singing with him and the band, she imagined that when his holiday here was over, he'd slot back neatly into the past where he belonged. Now there could be a messy overlap between past and present, and she doesn't want there to be. He's looking at her with a question in his eyes.

'Sorry, what did you say?'

'I was wondering if, when I visit again soon, I could plant a memory here for my Gemma? I thought a rose. I looked it up and there's one named Gemma – a pink one, very cheerful – like she always was.'

Rose watches his Adam's apple bob again, which pushes her unwelcome thoughts of 'past and present overlap' to the back of her mind. 'Of course you can. That's a lovely idea.' They do the smiley staring thing across the table, while Rose thinks of a polite way to bring things to a close. 'Okay, I must get on with this gardening before Bella and the kids get back. No rest for the wicked, eh?'

She thinks she notices a flicker of disappointment in his eyes, but he hides it with a chuckle and stands up. 'No rest for me either. I best get home and start the ball rolling on the house hunt.'

That was fast. 'Thinking about moving' has morphed into 'looking for houses' within a few minutes? 'Yes, good luck with it.' Rose leads the way back to his car and stands to one side as he goes through the gate.

'Thanks for the lovely lunch, and the catch-up. It was ace.'

'Ace?' She laughs. 'We always used to say that years back, didn't we? Great word, but nobody uses it now.'

He grins. 'Well, they should. We should make a point of using it, and then it will come back into fashion.'

'Perhaps.' Rose thinks he should go now, because there's a big cloud of awkwardness rolling in over the sea. Her grin is too stretchy and it's starting to make her face ache. Tristan takes a step forward. *Oh no. He's actually going to…*

'Thanks again, Rose. See you soon.' His hug is firm and heartfelt, and then he quickly brushes her cheek with his lips.

Rose steps back, face like a furnace, and says, 'Yes, maybe at the next gig. I know Daisy was saying there might be one this month.' Once again (like the lunch 'invite') she's said something that could be seen as encouragement. Out of the blue, uncalled for, and very irritating.

'Yeah. And let's keep in touch. Flora gave me your number, so I'll message you. Bye, Rose!' Tristan raises his hand, gets in the car and drives away.

Bloody Flora! Rose stomps back up the path to collect the lunch things from the picnic table, all the while cursing under her breath. Flora needs to butt out, and she'll tell her exactly that, next time she sees her.

Chapter Twenty-Seven

Flora is sitting in the bath hugging herself because she's cold. She's cold because the bath water has gone decidedly tepid, but she doesn't want to get out of it. If she gets out, she'll have to see James, because he's coming over just before noon. Flora is always punctual, and it's just gone 11.40, so there's no time to top up with hot water, relax and pretend everything's okay. Because it's not okay. Everything is far from okay. Last night she lay awake worrying herself stupid about her and James. The very thought of a 'her and James' makes her giddy. There's never been a 'her and anyone' since Patrick, and she never thought there would ever be again. Who in their right mind would? She's an old woman. James is an old man – admittedly, not quite as old as Flora – but old in anyone's book.

Why do people say that – in anyone's book? Or in my book? Where are these imaginary books that we mark things down in, opinions that we adhere to, come hell or high water? Flora looks at the wrinkly skin on her fingers (wrinkly because she's old, but even wrinklier because she's been too long in the bath) and tells herself to stop avoiding important issues by letting her thoughts scamper off down surreal paths. Paths that lead her away from making tough decisions. Sometimes she thinks the inside of her mind is like a Pollock painting. A mess of drips and splashes – big blobs of colour, one thought on top of another, building in texture and form, until she can't make out which way is up anymore.

The cold eventually drives her out of the bath and into a fluffy towel. As she passes the bedroom, she longs to curl up under the duvet and sleep. Hide from the day, until night comes rolling by again, covering her with darkness. But she can't. She needs to see James – needs to tell him how she feels. Mother was the cause of her sleepless night. She'd poked her awake in the early hours and wouldn't leave her mind, no matter how much Flora tried to shut her up.

Mother laughed at the idea of her and James. Then out came a tirade of questions. Why is he interested in her? Nobody else has been, since that foppish youth Patrick all those years ago. Nobody has had so much as a passing interest in her for fifty-odd years – well, apart from those few men who probably saw her as an easy lay. So why does James want her now? Why would *anyone* want her now?

Flora found no answers to these questions, so Mother did the honours.

James seems an intelligent man, a talented artist, so she must be just his passing fancy. Maybe lost causes like her appeal to his artistic temperament. He could be bored – at a loose end. He's stringing her along as a stopgap – just until he meets someone else, or finds a new hobby to pursue. And another thing. Isn't she too set in her ways to compromise – to accommodate another's needs and wishes? Hasn't she preferred being free to make her own choices without having to consider another's?

Once more, she had no reply, so Mother summed up. Flora is one of life's loners, and should remain so. She hasn't experienced proper love, not really. Patrick was a crush, a silly teenage crush. She's not worthy of James – not worthy of love, if truth be known. Flora should end this embarrassing charade before it goes any further. It will be best all round.

———————

The yellow-and-white cheesecloth blouse she put out earlier looks too cheerful for the task at hand, but she can't be bothered to sort through her wardrobe again. Jeans and the top will do, James won't be at her house long, so she can take the blouse off again once he's gone, and get under the duvet. Shut out the world.

Without her make-up, and wild hair escaping from the clip she shoved it into while taking a bath, Flora thinks she looks every one of her seventy-seven years and more. A sleepless night and a heavy heart haven't helped, but as her fingers hover over her eye pencil, she wonders if she should make the effort. A darker place in her mind sends a chaser after that – what's the point in actually making the effort with anything anymore?

James perches on the edge of the armchair and looks like he can't make his mind up whether to go or stay. Flora's not surprised, because the mood she's in must be blatantly obvious from her mumbled greeting when he walked through the door, and the way she deftly side-stepped his embrace.

'I won't offer you tea, James, because I have something to say, and it won't take long. It's not a very pleasant thing, but it has to be said, nevertheless.'

James's frown already knitting his brow deepens and apprehension grows in his eyes. 'Sounds serious.'

'It is.' Flora bobs her head and reaches for the words which have abandoned her. They have scarpered into a safe room and locked the door. She has to find the key. She must. It's not helping that James is twisting the band in his ponytail as if he wants to pull it off. The poor man is looking anywhere but at her, and repeatedly clearing his throat. Time to get this over with. 'James ... I don't think we should see each other anymore.'

He looks at the ceiling and shakes his head. 'I was afraid that was your "something serious".' When he looks across at her, tears are swimming in his soft brown eyes. 'Why, Flora? I thought we were getting along great together, enjoying each other's company. We have so much in common, we chat all the time, laugh together and ... I'm very fond of you, Flora. Very.'

This nearly crushes her resolve, but she can't go back now. 'We were, we are, and I'm very fond of you too. But is this…' She falters. 'Are *we* a good idea? I mean, I have one foot in the grave, almost two, and here I am, getting romantically involved. It's ludicrous. What on earth were we thinking?' Flora throws her hands up and chokes back tears.

James leans forward, elbows on knees. 'Where's all this coming from? You seemed happy enough before.'

'I was … well, kind of. But I've always had misgivings. Thoughts about being too old and set in my ways have always been there, skulking about in the recesses of my mind. Thoughts of why on earth you would want to take up with me…?' Flora can't continue and covers her mouth with a shaking hand.

James comes over and sits beside her on the settee. He gently takes her hand away from her mouth and holds it tight. 'Because you're a lovely, kind, generous, funny and very attractive woman.'

A bark of laughter escapes her. 'Attractive! Me?'

'You.'

'That's crazy.'

'Do you find me attractive?' His intense and steady gaze wakes up a few butterflies in her chest.

'Yes…'

'Well, there we are then. We must both be crazy, if you're to be listened to.'

The only way to break this powerful connection is to look at the floor. 'It's all too late, James. Far too late.' With an effort, she pushes away the image of her dancing in his arms on their first date and buries the remembered feeling of joy.

He sits back a little, his thoughtful expression eventually giving rise to, 'Are you afraid of death, Flora?'

Her head jerks back up. Is she? Not exactly, as it's as inevitable as the sun rising, but death is often in her mind. Probably because she's much closer to it than she used to be. She has been known to wake in the night and wonder how many years she's got left, and will she be spared a long lingering departure, or will she be in some hospital ward, in terrible pain, slowly being ripped apart by some vile disease or other? And at the end of it all ... will there be anyone there to hold her hand?

'Yes and no. But I do think of it quite often.' Before he has time to answer, the words that she needed are at last ready to come out of the safe room, and they pour forth in a torrent. 'I often feel like a fraud, hiding behind my colourful clothes – maybe I'm not the interesting, outgoing woman I like to portray. I worry that people will see through me. I worry I'm not good enough to be welcomed into the little community I've insinuated myself into. I worry I'm not good enough for you too. Then I tell myself that's all nonsense and I'm worrying for no reason.' Flora stands and throws her arms up. 'For god's sake, I don't even know who I am! I'm still finding myself. At my age? Really? I never used to feel like this. It's preposterous.' She folds her arms and walks over to the window, stares at a flurry of dry autumn leaves blowing round the empty plant pots.

'It's not preposterous,' James says, quietly. 'And in a way it makes perfect sense that you're questioning everything right now. Because you're growing older, maybe your confidence isn't as strong as it was. I know mine isn't.'

She turns to face him. 'It isn't?'

'No. I think in part, the world we live in puts us in different categories or camps. We're the older ones, the ones who might need more help, the ones who are more vulnerable than we used to be because of illness, or because we're not as able in lots of ways as we once were, for example. But it's made worse because even if we don't feel that things have changed much – well, apart from being a bit slower to do things, and maybe having the odd ache and pain – we're encouraged to think they have. So the fact that we are starting out on a new relationship might seem like a really crazy thing to do. Love is for younger people. Younger people aren't in our category. We lose our confidence, start to accept the concept of what it is to be old, and act accordingly.'

Flora thinks that James is making lots of sense. It would certainly explain why Mother's got such a strong hold on her now. And he said 'love' … did he actually mean…? Dismissing that thought, she says, 'Seems plausible. It's a bit like having a box.' James looks puzzled. 'Never mind, Rose will tell you all about those.' She smiles at him and isn't sure where to go next.

James continues, 'And I don't think anyone can say they have truly found themselves. Because we change all the time, don't we? I'm still finding new bits of myself.' He laughs. 'I don't mean an arm, or a leg, that would be bizarre.'

Flora laughs too, relieving a corkscrew of tension that has twisted itself into her belly.

'No, what I mean is, it feels that each new situation or

challenge, and how I deal with it, teaches me something about me. We're all diamonds in the rough, and every hurdle we manage to overcome gives that diamond a bit of a polish. Hopefully, by the time we cark it, we'll be twenty-four carats.'

His warm smile encourages her to return one. 'That's a lovely way to look at things... Maybe my move from my childhood home in Truro to here has been more traumatic than I realised – hence the constant worry and the re-emergence of Mother.'

James pats the seat next to him. 'Exactly. Now, come and sit down next to me.' She does as he asks. 'So is the influence of your nagging mother behind you wanting to break things off between us?'

Flora nods. 'Yes ... sometimes I think I will never be free of her disapproval, no matter how long I live. She did so much damage ... so much.' Then Flora allows herself to be pulled into his arms, rests her head on his chest and is helpless to do anything but sob her heart out.

―――――――――

Later they sit side by side sipping tea, the rain lashing the windows, the flames of the log burner dancing shadows up and down the walls. Flora feels safe, comfortable and relieved that James is still by her side.

'So do you still want us to break up?' James slips his hand into hers.

Flora doesn't have to think twice. 'No. Not if you still want me. I'm sorry for saying I did.'

'Don't be sorry. It was all perfectly understandable, given everything we just talked about. And of course I still want you. I will *always* want you.'

Flora glances up at him, noting the affection in his eyes dancing with the reflection of the flames. 'I hope so.'

James lifts the back of her hand to his lips and gently brushes his lips across it. 'I love you, Flora. Plain and simple ... and please don't feel under pressure to reply in kind. I'm just happy that we're back on track.'

Even if Flora wanted to reply in kind, which she knows she does, she can't, because her heart is too full. Instead, she snuggles into the warmth of him and closes her eyes.

After lunch, they're sitting cosily together on the sofa with their feet up, sharing a glass of wine, but Flora thinks James seems a bit quiet. He keeps looking at her and away, clearing his throat, shuffling in his seat and fiddling with the band on his ponytail. In the end she can stand it no longer. 'James, is everything okay? You seem unsettled.'

James lets out a heavy sigh. 'I *am* unsettled. I have something to say, but I'm not sure how you'll react. We've just got back on track, and I know I said there's no pressure to tell me how you feel about me ... but...' He takes her hand and searches her face. 'I keep trying to ignore it, but I have this overwhelming desire to...' James clams up again and sighs.

Flora's mind is in a spin. What the hell is it? Has he suddenly changed his mind about her after all? Because if he has, she's not sure if she could cope with it. In fact, she *knows* she couldn't. 'Just spit it out James, you're driving me nuts.'

James gets to his feet and then with the aid of the sofa arm, lowers himself to one knee. 'Flora. My lovely, lovely Flora. Will you do me the honour of being my wife?'

Chapter Twenty-Eight

Rose is undecided about the 'celebration for everything' day, which is a bit of a bugger, because it's today. It was Bella's idea. She said so many wonderful things have happened recently and they should celebrate them. The wonderful things are, in no particular order: Bella and family moving to their new home last week; Josh's job; Nigel's job; Flora and James getting together; Louise's work at the nursery; Bella and Hannah's mobile café taking off; Wesley's birthday tomorrow; and Sally's had an offer on her house. It's not that Rose disagrees that these things are wonderful, it's just that she has agreed to a gig here again in the garden later, and it all feels a bit full-on.

Still, there will be many hands to the pump, and Flora has something to tell Rose, apparently. Something that can't be told over the phone, because she wants to see Rose's expression. It was a good job that Flora couldn't see Rose's expression a while ago when Tristan told her that Flora had given him Rose's number, and generally divulged all of her business without so much as a 'by your leave'.

Rose butters bread rolls and thinks about her resolve to tell Flora to butt out. When the opportunity arose, she couldn't bring herself to. Flora wouldn't have done any of it maliciously, and she guessed that Tristan probably asked for the number, rather than Flora offering it. Rose acknowledges she was upset at the time, because things to do with Tristan seem to be happening outside her control. That past and present are blurred, smudged, unclear.

Tristan has been making good use of her phone number too, messaging her regularly about this and that. The weather, the gig, the house-hunt. Nothing deep and meaningful, though, and she's been delighted to see photos of his family. But what if? What if Tristan has feelings for her? Then she rationalises it. *Let other people have their own thoughts and feelings. You can't do anything about those. Just make sure you are in charge of your own.*

Two wonderful memory plantings will be done today, which makes her very happy. Louise came up with the perfect plant for Lucy. Sea campion – a white flower that grows happily along the coast and would be best grown along the stone wall, as it prefers sandy soil. The flowers are edible too. And Tristan's bringing the rose for Gemma. He sent a photo of her. A beautiful little girl with big blue eyes and dark curls. She was at the beach, laughing at the camera, an ice lolly in her hand. Just heartbreaking that she never got to grow up, to live her life. The rose with her name will hopefully bring some comfort, and Tristan will be able to see his precious memories reflected in its beauty.

Flora walks up the road to Rose's with a bag of goodies for the celebration day. James is meeting her there and she's looking forward to seeing everyone again. She's also looking forward to seeing someone she hasn't met yet – Lily, Josh's grandma. Flora is not looking forward to one aspect, however, even though the aspect is of her own making. It's something she needs to run past Rose, but she's not sure what she'll make of it all. Flora herself isn't sure what she makes of it all, so how does she expect anyone else to? All she is sure of at the moment is that she needs a lighthouse. Rose has done a good job of guiding her to safe harbour in the past, and Flora hopes she's polished her lamp today.

As she walks through the gate and up the path, she sees Rose putting some nibbles in bowls on the picnic and trestle tables. She seems to be alone, which is what Flora planned, as she's arrived an hour before everyone else. Rose looks up, a little surprised to see an early first guest, but smiles and waves nevertheless. 'Hi, Flora, come to lend a hand?'

'I have indeed. But I wondered if we could have a little chat before your other helpers arrive, and everyone else, of course.'

'Yeah, you said you had something to run by me. Let's sit down for a few minutes.'

As soon as Flora sits opposite Rose at the picnic table, her stomach ties itself in a big knot and her tongue follows suit. She looks away from her friend's searching eyes and finds a safe focus on the *Philadelphus*. Patrick's smiling face looks back at her through the years and she climbs inside the memory of the dawn bouquet once more. That memory was full of hope, love and the giddiness of youth. Now she's heading towards seventy-eight and incredibly, she feels something akin to that again. It hasn't hit her like a lightning bolt the way it did when she was a girl, but instead, it's grown strong and steady like a grapevine in a Mediterranean climate. Clearing her throat, she says:

'Rose... I hardly know where to begin. What I have to share sounds crazy to my own ears, so I'm guessing it will to yours. It's about James. You know he and I have become very fond of each other, and are now a little more than friends?' Rose nods an encouraging smile. 'Well, he ... well, we ... the thing is, he...' Flora can't say it. She's hot and bothered and the words she wants to get out keep sliding back down her throat.

'He's asked you to marry him,' Rose states.

Flora is astonished, not just because Rose has guessed, but because she sounds as if this is a perfectly okay question for a seventy-four-year-old man to ask a seventy-seven-year-old woman. She nods, mutely.

'How absolutely wonderful!' Rose says, clapping her hands together, an excited gleam in her eyes.

'It is?'

'It is!'

'I'm not so sure.'

'Have you not accepted?' Rose's smile falters.

'I've said I'll think about it.'

Rose laughs. 'What's there to think about?'

'Everything! Our age, for one.' She's still a bit worried about this aspect, despite the talk she's had with James recently. 'Where we'd live for another, because I don't want to leave my cottage. Would he get on my nerves, for another? I have never lived with anyone apart from Mother, and that was less than perfect, as you know. For another…'

'Mother doesn't count, as she was an old witch. The only thing that matters is that you love each other. You can work all the rest out.' Rose fixes her with a no-nonsense stare. 'Do you love him, Flora?'

That knocks all the wind out of her sails and she starts to drift towards the rocks. 'I… I…' She looks at the table top, the *Philadelphus* and back at her friend. After a few agonising seconds, Rose's glare won't let her stall any longer, and she turns her ship towards the lighthouse, pushing before it a heartfelt and honest response. 'Yes. I know it's madness, but I do. More than I ever thought possible.'

'Then tell him so. Put the poor man out of his misery!' Rose rushes round the table and gives Flora a big hug. 'I can't tell you how delighted I am for you both. You're made for each other and you'll be very happy together, I'm sure of it.'

If Flora looks past all the silly worries and excuses she's dredged up since James proposed three days ago, she knows Rose is right. Rose is always right. Being with her here in this garden is right. She's lifted, grounded, at peace with her decision. Maybe it's one she always knew she'd make, but it would have taken her much longer and many sleepless nights to arrive where she is now in a matter of minutes. 'Thanks for helping me to see the light, Rose.'

'If I have, then it's my pleasure.' Rose pops a crisp into her mouth and pokes Flora in the arm. 'Right. When's the wedding?'

'Well, I suppose if we're going to do this crazy act, it will have to be sooner rather than later. We haven't got time on our side, after all!'

'Excellent, because I'm going to announce it later when everyone's here.' Flora's about to protest until she gets a pointy finger and a cheeky wink. 'Got you there.'

Rose tells her it goes without saying that she'll keep this under her hat until she gets further news from Flora, though it will be hard to do so, as she's bursting with joy about it.

As Flora takes pizzas out of the oven a little later, she finds that she's in a similar state of bursting too. She hopes James comes soon. because she wants to give him her answer. Flora knows exactly where she wants to do it, too. The *Philadelphus* has helped her remember the happiest time of her past, and now it will be part of another happy time today. Flora also knows she and James will have many more to come, and she needs to remove all her obstacles, real or imagined, from her overthinking brain.

James arrives with the wrapped gift they've agreed to give to Weez under his arm, and he sets it carefully in Rose's hallway. Then Flora gives him what she hopes is an enigmatic smile, takes him by the hand and leads him down the garden, past one or two others who have arrived, and are at the trestle tables helping themselves to food and a glass of wine. James is slightly disgruntled, as she's ignoring his questions about where they're going, and can't he have a drink first?

Sally is under the pergola with Daisy, chatting about Sally's house sale and where she's planning on moving. Flora's planning on moving both of them, because what she has to say to James is for his ears only. 'Would you be so kind as to step out for a moment, ladies, and please keep anyone else away from this little area? I need to speak to James alone.' Daisy gives Flora a questioning eyebrow, but slips her arm through Sally's and they move off towards the picnic table. They have their heads together deep in conversation, and occasionally look back over their shoulders, but Flora's satisfied they won't be disturbed.

By the *Philadelphus*, Flora takes his hand and gives him an intense look. This is a momentous day and she wants to remember every second of it. The scent of the last remaining blooms gifted to them by the salt air, the warm sun on her back, the subtle fragrance of James's cologne, the conker brown of his eyes. Those eyes which are now flitting to the other guests, the plants, her pink beaded top, anywhere but at her. When he does look at her face, she can tell he's a little anxious, concerned even, so she decides to put him out of his misery.

'James, you asked me a question three days ago and I have my answer.'

He tightens his grip on her hand and looks away, shakes his head. 'You're letting me down gently. I get it. But can we still carry on as we were? I couldn't bear it if you ended things between…' He tails off as she throws back her head and laughs. 'Flora?'

'You wonderful, gorgeous, fantastic man. I'm not letting you down. Gently or otherwise. I…' Flora finds her voice has given up on her and she hopes the soppy smile and tears rolling down her face will tell him what she can't.

James wipes his eyes too and whispers, 'Are you saying yes? Yes, you'll marry me?'

She hopes her voice has come back as she opens her mouth and yells, 'Yes! Yes, I will!'

As they embrace, she hears a babble of voices behind and they turn to find Daisy, Sally, Rose and Weez staring at them with their hands over their mouths, their eyes alight with excitement. Rose gives her a tentative thumbs up and Flora chucks a vigorous nod back. Looking up at James, she says, 'I know it's all still new to us, but I'm bursting to tell people. What do you think?'

'Yes! I want to tell the world.' He digs an old red box out of his pocket and says, 'But before we do, I'd like to give you this. My grandmother gave it to me – said I should give it to the love of my life. I didn't give it to the woman I married, because as you know, she wasn't… But you, my dear Flora, are.' He pulls a wry expression. 'Not sure how long I've got left of my life, but I know I want to spend all of it with you.'

Flora opens the box and there's something shiny in it, but it's a bit blurry – okay, it's a lot blurry. Finding a tissue, her vision clears enough to reveal a sapphire and diamond ring, in the shape of a flower. 'How absolutely perfect,' she hears herself say.

James slips it on her finger, and amazingly it fits. 'A flower for my beautiful Flora.' He nods over her head at her dear friends beyond. 'Shall we tell them now? Looks like they will collapse with curiosity if we don't.'

As they walk hand in hand towards them, Flora feels as though she's floating. For the first time in her life, she knows she is enough. She is a good person. She *is* worthy of love. *I'm getting married, Mother. Yes, me, at my age. And no, it's not absolutely preposterous, it's absolutely bloody beautiful. Stick that where the sun don't shine!* And in that moment, Flora knows that's the last she'll hear of Mother. Ever.

Rose hands the trowel to Lucy. 'Okay, you can do the honours, make sure the root is covered, but try not to disturb it too much.' Lucy puts the little sea campion into the shallow sandy hole that Rose has made in the top of the stone wall and sprinkles gritty, sandy soil around it.

'This is such a lovely delicate little plant, but I have a feeling it's going to survive,' Lucy says with a smile at Rose.

Josh places a hand on her shoulder. 'A bit like you then, sis.'

Lucy looks up at him, and Rose can see she's overcome with emotion.

'Yes, it's a survivor alright, as are you,' Rose says. 'Josh is right. I can't believe how much stronger you seem, even after just a few weeks.'

'Thanks. I think I am. I'm even going to the seal

sanctuary next week to ask if I can volunteer at weekends, just to see how it goes.'

'That's wonderful.' Rose smiles and points down the garden to where Flora is chatting to Lily at the picnic table. 'They seem to be getting on well.'

Josh smiles. 'The change in Gran is remarkable. She recognised me a few times last week and adores the flowers for her room that I take in fresh from the garden.'

'She even recognised me the other day!' Lucy says with a giggle. 'I took her round the garden at the home and she's loving what Josh is doing with it.'

'Oh?' Rose wonders.

'I'm making a sensory garden. I've already put grasses and bamboo in, and I've started a pond. I had a word with the care home owners about how sound, smell and touch could help memory and bring feelings of calm and peace, and they were delighted. My parents are paying for it too, so they had no objection to anything I came up with. I'm going to plant lots of scented flowers soon – colourful ones, leave them to do their own thing, as Gran says.'

'How absolutely wonderful,' Rose says. 'I bet I know which seeds you'll be sowing come October?'

'Sweet peas.' Josh nods and pulls Rose into a brief hug. 'Thanks for everything, Rose.'

She's about to say she's done nothing really, but they both know it's not true and so she just smiles. Lucy hugs her too. 'Thanks from me as well. Both for the sea campion memory and the wise words last time we spoke. I know I don't know you that well, but I feel like I do, if you get me?'

'I get you. Now off you both go and get some food, before it's all disappeared.'

After they've gone, Rose makes sure the sea campion is secure in its new home and looks around for Tristan. There's his Gemma to plant in a warm place not too far from Madame Agatha. She will look after Gemma and help her grow. At one time, Rose would have questioned such a thought, but not now. Now it seems perfectly reasonable to believe that some plants and flowers would help each other. She knows it's a fact that planting flowers close together is a good idea, as they preserve their collective moisture better. So maybe Rose is right to stick to her beliefs.

She hasn't found Tristan, but Weez has found her. Rose marvels at the difference in her as she hurries up the path towards her, a canvas under her arm. She's wearing what look suspiciously like trainers on her feet, jeans and a casual green T-shirt. Weez is allowing her once short salt-and-pepper curls to achieve some length, and the longer hair softens her face. 'Look what James gave me!' she says, holding up the canvas for Rose to see, her eyes alive with excitement.

Rose looks at the fantastic painting of the jasmine that she's admired so much. 'Wow! That's lovely of him.'

'Yes. He said that now the flowers on the memory jasmine have died back, it would be nice for me to have this in my house to remember my Matthew by over the winter.' She pushes her glasses up the bridge of her nose. 'Not that I need a reminder, but I know what he meant. It's one of the nicest things anyone has ever given me.'

They walk along to sit on the grass next to the pond and

listen to the bubbling of the waterfall and the sigh of the breeze through the grasses. 'Tell me about your nursery work. Are you enjoying it?'

'I adore it,' Louise says, as though bewildered. 'I would never have thought that I'd be working with the littlies. Me, who's never had anything much to do with them before now.'

'You have had the experience of our little one.' Rose nods over to where Wesley is being a human wheelbarrow, yelling as his big sister grabs his legs and he runs forward on his hands.

'Ah, yes. The darling Wesley.' Then Weez's hazel eyes catch Rose's, the large glasses intensifying her gaze. 'Flora, you, this garden, many of the others here today, and that sweet little ball of energy otherwise known as your grandson, brought me out of myself. You all made me realise I could trust people again – let them into my heart without the fear that they'd leave me alone once more. Apart from when my dear Matthew and I were together, this is the happiest I've been in a very long time.'

'I'm so pleased, Weez.' Rose realises she's said 'Weez' out loud instead of in her head, and she grimaces. 'Oops, sorry. Wesley started it and Flora and I carried it on.'

Weez laughs. 'It's grown on me, actually.'

'Good. And I've decided to gracefully accept people thanking me for being a friend, or helping them, instead of saying the British thing, *please don't mention it*. Or, *I didn't do anything, really*. But it goes two ways. Thank you for being so great with my Wesley and helping Josh. You taught him about plants, made him realise that he could go for his gardening dream.'

'I think you had a bigger hand in that than I did.' Weez is obviously struggling against ignoring British politeness. 'But I'm glad I helped him, thank you for saying so.'

Flora gives her a quick hug. 'Time for Wesley's birthday cake soon. Would you mind taking orders for tea and coffee?'

'It would be my pleasure.'

Right, where the devil was Tristan? At last, she spots him laughing by the gate with James and Flora, and Rose waves as he scans around and then up the incline towards her. He does the thumbs-up and comes over. 'There you are! I was late coming down from Wales – traffic was horrendous. Then I got talking to Sally and Daisy, and after that, I stopped to have a few words with Flora and James.' He pushes his hair back and gives her his sparkly blue-eyed smile. 'Isn't it brilliant news about their engagement?'

'It really is. I couldn't be more thrilled.' She nods at the little pink rose shrub in his hands. 'This is Gemma?'

He nods and becomes serious. 'Thanks again for letting me plant this memory. Where do you think she should be?'

'I've prepared a bed next to Madame Agatha Panther. She's dropped almost all her petals, but she's strong and will be back next year. Follow me.'

As they walk around the side of the house towards the area between the shed and the back wall, she answers his question about why she calls the agapanthus Madame Agatha. When they arrive at the spot, Tristan turns to her and says, 'Does it sometimes make you sad when you look out of the kitchen window and see a reminder of Glen?'

Rose thinks about this for a moment. 'Yes, sometimes. But mostly it brings me comfort. With the help of my family and friends and my newfound love of nature and tending this garden, I've learned to accept lots of things this spring and summer. Though I suppose some things I will never completely accept, like the loss of my Glen, who I miss every day. But I've definitely made peace with my retirement, and I've realised that the rest of my life can still be full of so many wonderful possibilities, if I want them. I just have to believe, and make them happen.'

Tristan smiles and hands her Gemma. 'Thank you. I think she'll be very happy here, Rose.'

Rose slips her gardening gloves on, removes the rose from the pot, and settles her into the hole she prepared earlier. 'I know she will. And Aggie and my Glen will watch over her, help her grow.'

Tristan looks as if he's about to say something, but instead watches in silence as she finishes planting. Then he gives her the lightest kiss on the cheek and walks away.

Rose is putting away her trowel and gardening gloves when Bella, Nigel and the children pop up behind her. 'Hi, Mum. It's nearly time for the cake. You ready?'

'I am indeed. Are you ready, my little monkey?' She bends down and showers Wesley with tickles and kisses.

He giggles, then becomes suddenly solemn. 'You can't say I'm little after tomorrow, Granny, 'cos I'll be four. And four is a big boy.'

Molly huffs and shakes her head. 'Wait until you're nearly six, then you'll be a big boy.'

Wesley sticks his tongue out at her and runs away. The three of them watch, laughing as she gives chase. Nigel slips his arm around his wife's shoulders and heaves a sigh of contentment. 'It's so good to be back home in Cornwall. Thanks for being there for us all, Rose. And for raising such a strong, sensible woman who made me realise what's important in life.'

Rose slips her arm through his. 'My pleasure. Me and her dad are so proud of the woman she's become.' Bella's eyes fill with tears and she flaps a hand at her mum. 'I know you are all going to be very happy.'

'Stop it, Mum. I'll look like a panda if you carry on.'

'Good job we have some bamboo over there, then, in case you get peckish.'

After the singing of happy birthday to Wesley and he's blown out his candles, people start to gather around the pergola where the band is tuning up. Rose wishes she could drift off to her sofa, put her feet up, and stay there for the evening. She's tired and in a can't-be-bothered mood, as she guessed she would be after such a long day of preparing food, then non-stop socialising. She also knows it's too late to pull out now, though, as she'd let everyone down. Just before she reaches the pergola, Flora grabs Rose's arm and pulls her over to one side.

'Before you sing, I wanted to say what a lovely time we've had. It's been made even more special because of this.' Flora wiggles her ring finger under Rose's nose and looks about seventeen, rather than seventy-seven right now.

'It's been a lovely day. And I can't tell you how thrilled I am for you.' Rose gives her a huge hug and feels a powerful rush of emotion. Her life is so much richer with this extraordinary (sometimes annoying) woman in it.

Flora steps back, a wobbly smile on her lips. 'I'm convinced it's because of meeting you, this place, and all the right stuff in the universe aligning at the right time.' She pulls an incredulous expression, as though surprised at her words. 'Whatever I just said – can you explain it back to me?'

Rose chuckles. 'Not entirely. But you're right about this garden. Special things happen in it.'

Flora gives a vigorous nod. 'Exactly. I mean, look at Weez.' She gestures over to where Louise is laughing with Bella, Nigel and the children. 'She's hardly recognisable as the serious, shiny-shoed mouse I first met.'

'She's changed, that's for sure. Bloomed.'

Flora grasps the air as if picking an imaginary flower. 'Bloomed! That's the word. People are like flowers. If you give them the right environment in which to grow, they bloom. And why? Because people need similar things to flowers. A bit of sunshine, a safe sheltered spot, water, food

… and love. Most of all, that.' She squeezes Rose's hand. Then she nods towards the remaining few people up by the pergola. 'And if I'm not mistaken, I know who would be happy to give you lots of the latter.'

Rose frowns at that and scans who's there. Daisy, Steve, Tristan and Sally. Tristan catches them staring and gives them a cheery wave.

Rose gets the message and turns her frown back to Flora, but she's already hurrying away before Rose can tell her to buzz off.

Considering Rose didn't want to do the gig, she has to admit it was one of the best nights ever. Once she'd started singing, her tiredness evaporated and she let her voice carry her through. Now completely energised, she's toying with maybe singing one more song, after she's had a little rest. She shrugs a warm jacket on, walks along the garden path lit with solar lights and sits down on a bench near the pond with a much-needed glass of wine. After a few minutes, she has to admit that now she's stopped, the adrenaline rush has suddenly decided to exit stage left.

Closing her eyes, she absorbs the sounds and smells of the garden. The drone of conversation and laughter, the clatter of plates, the clink of glasses and the whiff of perfume from a late rose, drifting on the ever-present salt breeze. Rose realises she finds comfort and pleasure in the smallest of things nowadays. And in the big things. It's a big thing for her to dress up and go out on a regular basis to sing for strangers, but she's used to singing in front of friends and family now. It's become second nature. Though she acknowledges, a lot of it is to do with singing for herself. It lifts her spirits, makes her heart dance.

'Falling asleep already?'

Tristan's voice next to her ear jumps her out of her reverie. 'No. Just thinking.'

'Great gig, yeah?'

'One of the best.'

'I've been doing a lot of thinking, lately.'

Daisy comes over with another glass of wine for Rose and then leaves with a wink. *What the hell? First Flora, now Daisy.* She takes a big gulp of it and replies, 'Really? What about?'

'About what makes me happy. Like I said when we chatted over lunch at yours that day, I want to make the most of the time I have left. So I'm definitely going to move home here – I put my house on the market and there's already interest. It makes me happy to be here, I feel like I'm back where I belong. I love playing with this fantastic band, to be back with my old mate Steve, Daisy too ... and you, Rose. I love being with you too.'

Rose can see the joy in his face and she's thrilled for him. She thinks she can see something else too, though. Something that gives her that unsettled feeling, the one that makes her stomach churn and her pulse race. 'That's great, Tristan.' She raises her glass to him and then knocks it back. 'Truly happy for you. Right, that's me done. People look like they're drifting off home now, which is good, as I'm truly shattered.'

She notes his crestfallen expression as she pats his shoulder, zips up her jacket and rushes past.

Outside her gate she waves the stragglers off and looks up. The moon's high in the velvet-dark sky, shining them a path home along the street. Rose takes a deep breath and thinks how unusual it is that Tristan seems to have gone without saying goodbye. He was never one to go off in a huff. About to go indoors, she feels a hand on her arm.

'Rose, can I have a minute?'

Not gone then, after all. She expected this. 'Only a minute, Tris. I really am knackered.'

'I feel like you're pushing me away... Have I done something wrong?'

Has he? No. No, he's just brought himself out of the past and muddied her future without so much as a by-your-leave. Her future that she's only just tried on for size and found it's the best fit she could have ever dreamed of. But then he's not done it on purpose, has he? Tristan has no idea what she's feeling. 'No, not really.' *Come on Rose, be honest with him.* 'But I do feel you could be mixing up the old us with the new.'

'Would that be so bad? We were so good together, so in love. I never forgot you... I never—'

'Yes, but we were kids.' Tristan looks so dejected, she almost stops, but he needs to hear this. 'Don't get me wrong. I'm not saying what we had wasn't special.' She smiles at him. 'This year I remembered that day in the woods on my sixteenth birthday, when we sang our hearts out amid the bluebells and wild garlic. Yes, we were in love and we had all our lives in front of us. It was exhilarating, exciting. When that memory came back to me, I was exhilarated all over again. I even went back to the wood and ate some wild garlic and brought some home to plant in the garden. But I went for *me*, Tris. To remember the girl I was. Not for *us*. What you're feeling for me is the memory of us then. It's not the reality of us now. It can't be. Too much has changed, too many years have passed – we're different people now.'

Tristan leans his hip against the gate and looks at his shoes. 'So, you're saying I shouldn't come back?'

Is she? 'No. No, I'm saying come back if it makes you happy. Because I *do* want you to be happy, Tris. But come back for you. Don't come back for me.'

He heaves a heavy sigh. 'Okay … but are you saying there will be absolutely no chance for us someday?'

Rose wants to go to him and give him a big hug, because he's never looked more like that boy she first fell in love with in the wild garlic days. But she can't, because that would undo everything. And would there ever be a chance? They look at each other for a long moment and then she says, 'Never say never, but it's a definite no right now.'

Tristan takes her hand, kisses the back of it. 'Never say never? That's enough for me. See you, Rose.' And then with a half-smile, he turns and walks through the gate and down the road.

Rose finds her cheeks are wet and part of her wants to follow him, to tell him she's made a mistake, but it's a small part. Too small a part. She's happy with her life, her family and friends, and of course her garden. She told him to do what makes him happy, and she will continue to do the same.

Rose raises a hand in a fond farewell, even though he can't see her, and walks back up the path. She has her memories to grow and a future to tend.

Acknowledgments

Firstly, a huge thanks as always must go to my wonderful editor Charlotte (Legend) Ledger. Her expert advice and guidance has made this book the very best it can be. Her belief in me as an author means such a lot too! Thanks also to the entire One More Chapter team for their hard work and dedication to each and every book.

To my wonderful family and friends who always support me on my writing journey and put up with my worries and woes during the writing process. You know who you are. I have included some wonderful quotes from some of them about how being in gardens and nature makes them feel. The first two are from my grandchildren. Thanks for doing that, everyone!

As you will see from the quotes, being close to nature is so important for our mental and physical well-being. Like the main character in this book, Rose, when I'm tending my garden, I always feel uplifted, and have a renewed sense of hope.

To my great writing buddy who always lends and ear, an eye and is ready with words of encouragement, thank you. It means such a lot to have you in my corner, Linda Huber.

A massive thanks to more writer and blogger friends

too, for reading early copies of this book and saying such lovely things about it! Celia Anderson, Anita Waller, Caroline James and Lamorna Ireland, if you haven't read their books, please rush out now and do so. All talented writers and lovely people. Now for the brilliant reviewers and bloggers, Anne Williams, (beinganne.com) Yvonne Bastian (Me and my Books Vonnibee.com) and Linda Hill (lindasbookbag.com).

A huge thanks to the wonderful Emma, who always stocks my books and hosts a signing every year at Hurley Books, Mevagissey. And to the lovely Alice who always stocks my books in the St Ives Bookseller. Independent booksellers are vital in the success of local authors. Fantastic support both, much appreciated!

Last but not least, thanks to you, dear reader for choosing my story. I sincerely hope you enjoyed it. If you did, a little review would make my day!

Quotes

'The birds and wildlife make you feel free.' – Esmé

'A garden feels like your own world, where it's just you and nature.' – Ronan

'Rather than an escape from reality, a garden encapsulates reality in all its fullness.' – Martin and Carrie.

'Trees make me feel connected to nature.' – Tanya

'The colours of nature brighten my day – it's therapeutic.' – Carol

'When I'm in nature I feel grateful and at peace. – Emma

'The beauty of a garden is that it works positively on all the senses. From the scent of sweet peas or roses, to the sight of water lilies opening amid the soft waters on a pond.' – Roger

'Relaxing amongst the sights, sounds and smells of the garden helps to keep me calm in an anxious world.' – Brian

'Being in nature gives me a sense of peace, of being part of a bigger picture.' – Linda

ONE MORE CHAPTER

YOUR NUMBER ONE STOP
FOR PAGETURNING BOOKS

The author and One More Chapter would like to thank everyone
who contributed to the publication of this story...

Analytics
Abigail Fryer
Maria Osa

Audio
Fionnuala Barrett
Ciara Briggs

Contracts
Sasha Duszynska
Lewis
Florence Shepherd

Design
Lucy Bennett
Fiona Greenway
Holly Macdonald
Liane Payne
Dean Russell

Digital Sales
Lydia Grainge
Emily Scorer
Georgina Ugen

Editorial
Kate Elton
Simon Fox
Arsalan Isa
Charlotte Ledger
Bonnie Macleod
Jennie Rothwell
Caroline Scott-
Bowden

International Sales
Bethan Moore

Marketing & Publicity
Chloe Cummings
Emma Petfield

Operations
Melissa Okusanya
Hannah Stamp

Production
Emily Chan
Denis Manson
Francesca Tuzzeo

Rights
Lana Beckwith
Rachel McCarron
Agnes Rigou
Hany Sheikh
Mohamed
Zoe Shine
Aisling Smyth

**The HarperCollins
Distribution Team**

**The HarperCollins
Finance & Royalties
Team**

**The HarperCollins
Legal Team**

**The HarperCollins
Technology Team**

Trade Marketing
Ben Hurd
Eleanor Slater

UK Sales
Laura Carpenter
Isabel Coburn
Jay Cochrane
Tom Dunstan
Sabina Lewis
Holly Martin
Erin White
Harriet Williams
Leah Woods

**And every other
essential link in the
chain from delivery
drivers to booksellers
to librarians and
beyond!**

Three years ago, Joy Pentire lost her firefighter husband and she still hasn't returned to the woman she once was. But then she meets Hope, one of the residents at the nursing home where she's a carer.

Hope has a secret gift that she wants to pass on.
And Joy's life is forever changed.

Surrounded by the community in her Cornish hometown, Joy's unexpected inheritance soon leads to new opportunities, new friends, new love, and the part of herself she'd thought forever lost … her joy.

Available in paperback and ebook!

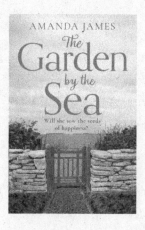

A precious heirloom passed down from mother to daughter…

Lowena Rowe's beloved mum always claimed her family seed box was special. Said to contain soil from Tintagel, the mysterious seat of the legendary King Arthur, whomever made a wish upon the box would have 'a beautiful garden, bountiful crops and love of their fellow man'. Lowena isn't inclined to believe the myth but can't part with the box, knowing how much it meant to her mum.

Starting over with a new home and a new job in the Cornish village of St Merryn, Lowena can't help feeling lost and alone… but she isn't the only one. Now, as a community of misfits finds solace and friendship in the shade of her growing garden, she realises there might have been truth to the mythical box after all, and she may just be growing the life and love she's always wanted…

Available in paperback and ebook!

When journalist Rosa Fernley's ailing gran, Jocelyn, passes on a long-held secret of her past in her dying days, Rosa embarks on a quest to Cornwall to find answers and resolution to free her grandmother from guilt and pain as she leaves this earth.

But in the wild, beautiful landscape of Tintagel, Rosa encounters something she could never imagine as the past comes to life and walks the beaches once more. Unravelling the truth of what happened to the man her grandmother once loved and left leads Rosa on an unexpected journey, one which unlocks not only her gran's secrets, but the secrets of who – and what – Rosa truly is…

Available in paperback and ebook!

1938
One midnight in June, 15-year-old Lamorna Williams
throws a message in a bottle into the Atlantic at Magic
Cove, hoping to meet her one true love – and someone
writes back.

1997
On the other side of the world, Lamorna tells her story to
her 16-year-old great nephew Ethan inspiring him to do the
same. But this time, his message isn't found for over twenty
years…

Present day
Single mum, Merrin Pascoe, is told of the legend of Magic
Cove. In a moment of madness, Merrin wishes on the moon,
and next day she finds a bottle in the sea. Will the cove cast
its spell once again…

Available in paperback and ebook!

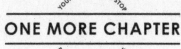

ONE MORE CHAPTER

One More Chapter is an
award-winning global
division of HarperCollins.

Sign up to our newsletter to get our
latest eBook deals and stay up to date
with our weekly Book Club!
<u>Subscribe here.</u>

Meet the team at
<u>www.onemorechapter.com</u>

Follow us!

 @OneMoreChapter_

 @0neMoreChapter

 @onemorechapterhc

Do you write unputdownable fiction?
We love to hear from new voices.
Find out how to submit your novel at
<u>www.onemorechapter.com/submissions</u>